BEAUTIFUL
Liar

BEAUTIFUL
Liar

ZARA COX

FOREVER

New York   Boston

Forever
Hachette Book Group
1290 Avenue of the Americas
New York, NY 10104
hachettebookgroup.com
twitter.com/foreverromance

Previously published as the ebook *Porn Star* in 2016.
First trade paperback edition: April 2017

Forever is an imprint of Grand Central Publishing.
The Forever name and logo are trademarks of Hachette Book Group, Inc.

The Hachette Speakers Bureau provides a wide range of authors for speaking events. To find out more, go to www.hachettespeakersbureau.com or call (866) 376-6591.

The publisher is not responsible for websites (or their content) that are not owned by the publisher.

Library of Congress Cataloguing-in-Publication Data is available upon request.

ISBN 978-1-4789-4538-3 (trade paperback edition)
ISBN 978-1-4789-7018-7 (ebook edition)

Printed in the United States of America

LSC-C

10 9 8 7 6 5 4 3 2 1

BEAUTIFUL
Liar

PART ONE

1

CASTING

April 2015

There's no reason for me to be here. I don't need to do it.

Not another one.

I have more than enough to work with. I should end it now.

It's what I've been telling myself for months now.

Shit, who am I kidding?

Enough will *never* be enough. He has to pay for what he's done with absolutely everything I can take away from him.

Besides, I have big enough balls to admit it's become a rush. The delayed gratification is part of the game. It's an addiction. In my jaded world where everything comes to me with a snap of my fingers, risky highs like these are to be treasured.

They'll be gone in a blink of an eye. Just like every other pleasure in my life.

I peer at my watch.

5:58 p.m.

I rise from my sofa, walk down the wide hallway, and enter the empty room. It's not completely empty, but it might as well be. I haven't bothered to decorate since acquiring it six months ago when my time in Boston was done and I moved back to New York. It's as if my subconscious knew I'd need it just for this purpose.

In the middle of the room, I grab the remote on the table and hit the power button. Three screens flicker to life. I sit down in the leather chair I'd placed in here earlier. Three faces stare back at me. The darkness and mirrored glass mean they won't see me as clearly. Even if they do, my mask is in place. My black clothing and leather gloves take care of the rest of my disguise.

Anonymity is key. I'm too well-known for anything else to be acceptable. Or acceptable for now, at least. Who knows what'll happen a month, two months from now? Every day I fight my impulse. I might wake up tomorrow and decide the time has come to give in, unveil my plan.

I'm not ashamed of taking this route to achieve what I want. Far from it. In fact destroying myself in the process is exactly what I'm aiming for. I want there to be absolutely nothing left to be sustained or redeemed by the time I'm done.

For now, though, my public role is integral to my grand plan. And since my sins are already numerous, I don't have any qualms about adding vanity to them and admitting I love my other life. Keeping my identity secret adds to the thrill.

It's all about the thrill for me. Without it, I risk prematurely succumbing to the dark abyss. The abyss my shrink keeps warning me I'm rimming.

She thinks it's a revelation, that morsel of news she dropped in my lap three years ago. Little does she know I've been staring into that abyss since I was fifteen years old. I've stared into it for so long, it's fused with me. We are one. We haven't done our final dance yet, but it's only a matter of time.

I'm twenty-eight years old.

I won't live to see thirty.

It's an immutable inevitability, so I take my pleasures where I can.

"You each have scripts in front of you. When I tell you to, read them out loud. You go first, Pandora." I use a voice distorter because my natural voice contains a distinctive rasp that could give me away.

Because of who I am, I've had cameras shoved in my face more times than I've had sex. And that's saying something.

Pandora—fucking idiotic name—giggles, and her golden curls bounce in an eager nod. I suppress a growl of irritation and relegate her to the *possibly maybe* list.

"*May I feel, said he.*" She giggles again.

Ten seconds later, I place her firmly in the *hell no* list and press the intercom. She's escorted out, and I switch my gaze to the next girl.

The redhead is staring into the camera, her full mouth tilted in an *I-was-born-to-blow-you* curve. I admit the lighting is better on her, but her eyes are a little too wide. Too green.

I adjust the camera and scrutinize her closer. "What color are your eyes? And don't tell me they're green. I can see the edges of your contacts."

She flushes. "Umm…they're gray."

I check the notes on my tablet. "Missy, is that your real name too?"

She nods eagerly.

"Did you read the brief?"

"Umm…yeah," she answers, her voice trailing off in a semi-question. This one is clearly dim.

"What did it say about lying?"

The *blow-you* expression drops. "They're just contacts." She leans forward, nearly knocking out the camera with her double Ds. "Here, I can take them out—"

"No, don't bother. Your interview is over. Leave now, please," I command in my best non-psycho voice, and press the intercom again.

I may be slightly unhinged, according to some spectrum my shrink keeps harping on about, but Mama, God rest her pure soul, taught me to be a gentleman. Mama's worm food now, but that's no reason for me not to honor her with a touch of politeness.

Missy's lips purse, then part, as if she's about to plead her case. The burly guard who enters the room and taps her on the shoulder convinces her words have lost their meaning at this point.

I turn to the last screen.

Her eyes are downcast. Her lashes are long enough to make me wonder if I have another fake on my hands. I sigh, then take in the rest of her face. No makeup, or barely any if she made the effort. Her lips are plump, lightly glossed. I use the controls on the remote to zoom in. There's a tiny mole on the left side of her face, right above her upper lip. Not fake.

I zoom out, examine the rest of her that I can see. Her gray T-shirt is worn to the point of threadbare, and her collarbones are a little too pronounced. Malnourishment wouldn't be a crowd-pleaser, but that problem can be easily taken care of.

Unlike the previous stock from which I plucked my prior subjects, she doesn't seem like the BDSM club-going type. For a second, I wonder where my carefully placed adverts unearthed this one.

Beneath the T-shirt, her chest rises and falls in steady breathing, although the pulse hammering at her throat gives her away. I zoom in on the pulse. The skin overlaying it is smooth, almost silky, with the faintest wisps of caramel blond hair feathering it.

Something about her draws me forward to the edge of my seat. I like her pretended composure. Most people fidget under the glare of a camera.

My gaze flicks to her skeleton bio. "Lucky."

Slowly, she raises her head. Her eyelids flick up. Her eyes are a cross between green and hazel with a natural dark rim that pronounces its vividness. I can't pinpoint it exactly, but something about the look in her eye sparks my interest.

Hell, if I had a heart, I'd swear it just missed a beat.

"Is that your real name?"

She shrugs. "It might as well be," she murmurs.

Fuck, I have another liar on my hands. "Cryptic may be sexy if you're auditioning to be the next Bond Girl. It's not going to work here. Tell me your real name. Or leave."

"No." Her voice is a sexy husk, enough to distract me for a second before her answer sinks in.

"No?"

"With respect, you're tucked away behind a camera issuing orders. I get that you hold the cards in this little shindig. But I'm not going to show you all of mine right from the start. My name, for the purposes of this interview, is Lucky. It may not officially be on my birth certificate, but I've responded to it since I was fifteen years old. That's all you need to know."

Well…fuck. I note with detached surprise that I'm almost within a whisker of cracking a smile.

I rub my gloved finger over my mouth, torn between letting her get away with mouthing off to me this way, and sending her packing.

Sure, she intrigues me. And whatever relevant truth I need would be dug out before she signs on the dotted line, should it come to that. But for this to work, she needs to obey my commands, no questions asked.

"Stand up. Move away from the camera until you reach the wall."

She rises without question, restoring a little goodwill in her favor. Moving the chair out of her way, she backs up slowly. The hem of her loose T-shirt rests on top of faded jeans. Even before she's fully exposed to the camera, I catch my first glimpse of the hourglass figure wrapped around the petite frame. She's a fifties pinup girl dressed in cheap clothes. Her breasts are full but not quite double Ds, her thighs and calves shapely enough to stop traffic, with a naturally golden skin tone denoting a possible Midwest upbringing.

She's knockout potential—subject to several nourishing meals. But I've seen enough and done enough in this twisted life of mine to know her body isn't what would draw attention. It's the look in her eyes. The secrets and shadows she is trying hard to batten down. They're almost eating her alive.

I don't really give a shit what those secrets are. But the chance to fuck them…to fuck *with* them, expose them to my cameras, sparks a sinister flame inside me.

"Turn around, let your hair down."

Her fingers twitch at her sides for a second before she faces the wall. One hand reaches up and pulls the band securing the loose knot on top of her head.

Caramel and gold tresses cascade down her back. Thick enough to swallow my hands, her wavy hair reaches past her waist, the tapered ends brushing the top of her perfectly rounded ass.

I watch her for a few minutes, then speak into the mic distorting my voice. "Do you have any distinguishing birthmarks I should know about, Lucky?"

The question sinks in. Her back goes rigid for a second before she forces herself to relax. "Yes."

"Where?"

"At the top of my thigh," she responds.

"Show me," I reply, although I don't really need to see it. My carefully selected stylists can disguise any unseemly marks.

Slowly, she turns around. I expect her gaze to drop or a touch of embarrassment to show, but she stares straight into the camera as her fingers tackle the buttons of her jeans. The zipper comes down and she shimmies the denim over her hips. Her white cotton panties are plain and the last word in unsexy. All the same, my eyes are drawn to the snug material framing her pussy lips.

I also see the hint of bush pressed behind the cotton.

I shift in my seat, but don't reach for the hardness springing to life behind my fly. Hand jobs are a waste of my time. I either fuck or I don't. It's that simple.

She lowers the jeans to knee-level and twists her right leg outward. The round red disk just on the inside of her thigh is distinctive enough to need covering up. I make a mental note.

"Thank you, Lucky. You may put your clothes back on."

A hint of surprise crosses her face, but she quickly adjusts her clothing. When she's done, her hands return to her sides.

"It's time for your screen test. Sweep your hair to one side and come closer. Place your hands flat on the desk, bend forward, but don't sit down."

She follows my instructions to the letter. I adjust the camera so it's angled up to capture her face.

"Are you ready?"

She gives a small nod.

"You've just walked into a bar. You don't know me. But you see me, the guy in the corner, nursing a bourbon. And I see you. All of you. Every fantasy you've ever had. I want to give it to you. You've found me, Lucky, the guy who wants to fuck you more than he wants his next breath. Do you see me?"

Her nostrils quiver slightly. "Yes."

"Good. Look into the camera. Don't blink. Show me what I want to see. Convince me that you're worth fucking. Convince me you're worth *dying* for."

Her lids lower, her face contemplative, but she doesn't blink or lose focus. Slowly, her expression drifts from disinterested to captivated. Her lids lift and she's a green-eyed siren. Her attention is rapt, unwavering. Her bruised-rose lips part, but she doesn't swirl her tongue over her lips as I expect. She just…breathes. In. Out.

She swallows, a slow movement that draws attention to her neck, then lower to her breasts. Mesmerized against my will, I watch her nipples harden against the thin material of her top. Her fingers gradually curl into the hard wood and every inhalation and exhalation becomes a silent demand.

In…fuck…out…me…

In. *Fuck.*

Out. *Me.*

I remain still, even though my fingers itch to twitch and my muscles burn with a restlessness I haven't felt in a long time.

I watch her command the camera, her body rigid with lustful tension. Her eyes widen with the need to blink, but she doesn't.

She stays still, hands curl into fists, and she just breathes sex. Her eyes water and a tear slips down one cheek. The sight of it is curiously cathartic, a tiny climax.

I subside into my seat. "That was convincing enough. You may sit down, Lucky."

She blinks rapidly before she sinks into the chair. A quick swipe and the tear never existed. Neither does the promise of the fuck of a lifetime that was on her face a moment ago.

Her acting skills are remarkable. For a second, I'm not sure if that's a good thing or a bad thing. I don't want her to be too polished. I dismiss the notion and glance down at her notes.

"You list your address as a motel?"

The address in Queens is unfamiliar to me, but the motel chain is notorious for being exceptionally bad. I hide my distaste and wait for her answer.

"I arrived in town recently. I don't have a permanent address yet."

The secrets in her eyes, the threadbare clothes, the unkempt hair and unshaven pussy begin to tell their own story. She may be brave enough to sass me when she risks losing a job that promises a once-in-a-lifetime payday, but she's also desperate.

How desperate is the question.

"Are you currently working?"

She nods. "I work on and off for a catering service. But it's nothing I can't work around, if needed."

"So you'll be free to do this if I want you?"

The desperation escalates, then a hint of anger flashes through her eyes. "*If?* You mean I did all of this for nothing?"

I give a low laugh at her gumption. "You didn't seriously think you'd waltz your way into a million dollars on a simple three-minute screen test, did you?"

The anger flees from her eyes, although her mouth tightens for a moment before she speaks. "So it's true? It's not a con? This job really pays a million dollars? For...sex?" she rasps.

"You think I'd admit it if it was a con? What did the ad say?"

Her delicate jaw flexes for a second.

"*One million uninhibited reasons to take a leap.*

One million chances to earn a keep

One million to give in to the carnal

Are you brave enough to surrender,

For a payday to remember?"

It speaks even more to her desperate state of mind that she remembers the ad *verbatim*.

I remain silent and wait for her to speak.

"So...assuming it's *not* a con, how will this work, then?"

"If you pass the next few tests, and I decide you're a good fit, you get the gig. You'll receive one hundred thousand dollars with each performance."

"So…ten performances…over how long a period?"

"Depending on how many takes are needed, anywhere between three weeks and a month. But I should warn you, it's hard work, Lucky. If you think you're just going to lie back and recite the Star-Spangled Banner in your head, think again."

Her fingers drum on the table, the first sign of nerves she's exhibited. "I…I won't be doing anything…skanky, will I?"

"Define skanky."

"This is going to be straight-up sex. No other…bodily stuff? Because that would be a firm no for me."

My mouth attempts another twitch. "No waterworks, waste matter, or bestiality will be involved in the performances."

Her fingers stop drumming. "Okay." She waits a beat, stares straight into the camera. "So when will I know?"

I hear the barely disguised urgency and I rub my finger over my lip again. "Soon. I'll be in touch within the week." I'm not sure exactly why I want to toy with her. But I sense that having her on edge would add another layer of excitement I badly need.

When she opens her mouth, I interrupt. "Goodbye, Lucky."

A passing thought about the origin of her name is crushed into oblivion. I press the remote to summon the bodyguard to escort her out, and I leave the room.

In my study a few minutes later, I bring up the screen on my desk and activate the encrypted service I need. I open the application and within minutes, the members of my exclusive gentlemen's club are logging in.

My e-mail is short and succinct.

The next Q Production is scheduled for release on May 20, 2015.

Limited to ten members.

Bidding starts in fifteen minutes.

I start the countdown and rise to pour myself a neat bourbon. I swallow the first mouthful with two prescribed tablets, which are meant to keep me from going over the edge, apparently, and stroll to the floor-to-ceiling window. I look down at Midtown's bumper-to-bumper traffic. This midlevel penthouse is one of many I own in this building and around New York City.

Technically, I don't live here. I only use it when volatile pressures demand that I put some distance between the Upper West Side family mansion and myself. I would never stray far for long. For one thing, I've accepted that my family would never leave me alone.

I know what I know. So they've made it their business to keep me on a short leash. But with over three hundred properties in my personal portfolio, and a few thousand more under the family firm's control, there are many places to disappear to when the demons howl.

Today, the Midtown penthouse is my temporary haven.

I turn when the timer beeps a one-minute warning.

I return to my desk and adjust the voice distorter. When the clock reaches zero, I click the mouse. "Gentlemen, start your bids."

My words barely trail off before the first five bids appear on the screen. Sixty seconds later, the total bid is at a quarter of a million dollars. I steeple my fingers and wish I were more excited. The money means nothing. It never has. It's the end game that excites me.

My mind drifts back to Lucky. I turn the gem of her elusiveness this way and that and admit to myself she has potential.

I want to take a scalpel to all her secrets, bleed them and soil my hands with the viscera. I also want to fuck her until her body gives out. Right in this moment, I'm not sure what I want more.

So I concentrate on the numbers racing higher on the screen.

Half a million. One million. One point five.

My phone beeps twice. I pick it up and read the two appointment reminders on the screen.

7pm – Dr. Nathanson. My shrink.

9pm – Dinner with Maxwell.

I reconfirm the first and delete the second.

Canceling dinner with Maxwell will bring a world of irritation to my doorstep. No one cancels dinner with Maxwell Blackwood. For a start he's one of the most powerful men in the country.

He's also my father.

Yeah, my name is Quinn Blackwood, heir to the Blackwood Estate, only child of Maxwell Blackwood and Adele Blackwood (deceased). My family owns a staggering amount of property across the eastern seaboard of the United States and a few in the west. According to the bean counters, I'm personally worth twenty-six billion dollars.

But tangling with my father in hell is what I live for. Have done since I was fifteen. So I ignore his summons and watch the stragglers fall away until I'm left with the top ten bidders. The bids wind down, and within the space of half an hour, I'm just under two million dollars richer.

I spot the familiar name of the top bidder and I sneer. Taking his money on top of everything else is darkly satisfying.

Once the bidding ends, I shut down the application and call up another list. Dozens of charity websites showing pictures of starving children flood my screen. Within minutes, fifty charities are the grateful recipients of two million dollars.

I may be Quinn Blackwood, occasional user of prescribed meds to keep the demons in check, who moonlights as Q, porn star to an exclusive few who pay millions for my work.

And I may be an unhinged asshole with serious daddy issues.

But no one said I wasn't a giver.

2

PRE-PRODUCTION

"How are you feeling today, Quinn?"

I sigh. "I'll pay you a hundred thousand dollars, if you promise to drop that question from our sessions."

Adriana Nathanson regards me silently for a full minute from the top of her rectangular glasses. She looks good for a woman in her mid-forties, would even pass for a decent blonde-and-blue-eyed MILF, although I glimpse signs of a burgeoning Botox habit. "Why do you want me to drop it?"

"Because we both know whatever answer I give would be a lie."

"Here's an idea. Why don't you try the truth for once?"

"Here's an idea. Fuck off, Dr. Nathanson." My pulse barely rises, but there's more than a hint of venom in my response, which surprises even me.

Her thin lips purse. "I thought we were past the hostility stage, Quinn. Making progress."

"Did you?" I query with zero interest. "And why would you think that?"

"Because you haven't shown signs of it in over a year." She scribbles in her notes.

I remain silent.

Eventually she looks up. "Quinn?"

"*Doctor?*"

"Did something happen since our last session? You appear… agitated."

I crack my knuckles loudly. "No. I am not."

We stare at each other. We've played this game a thousand times.

"How are the nightmares?"

The space between my shoulder blades twitches. Have to hand it to her. She has her moments. They're not many or I wouldn't have been coming here for ten years. Although, technically there's no cure for what I have.

I lean back, rub the twitch against the leather chair. "They're still three shades above garden variety."

"There's nothing garden variety about them, Quinn. Tell me about the last one."

The twitch intensifies. I shrug it off. "It was no different from the one before that. And the one before that." No matter what I do, how loud I scream, she still dies in the end.

Her lips purse again. "It'll help to talk through it."

"I'm absolutely sure it won't."

She sighs, lays her Montblanc pen on top of her notes, and removes her glasses. I'm hit with a set of determined baby blues. "Your father is back in town. Have you seen him yet?"

I freeze. The twitches abruptly cease. Before it manifests, I sense it. The abyss. It's like a deadly virus, worming its way through me. It starts in my left wrist. Feeds through my veins and takes root in my brain. It's not easy to control it, but I give it a shot. "No, I haven't."

"And your stepmother?"

I crack a sinister smile. "That's a stupid question, Dr. Nathanson."

She has the grace to look ashamed. We both know my stepmother has been banned from seeing me without my father present. Ergo…

"How do you feel about his return?"

"Half a million."

"You can't bribe me not to ask you questions, Quinn."

"Then ask me different ones."

Her head tilts. As if I genuinely puzzle her. I know I don't. She knows exactly what I am. What lies beneath this mockery of civility.

"Don't you want to get better?"

Another idiotic question. We resume the staring match. She uncrosses and re-crosses her legs.

"I called your office earlier today. Your EA said you left early."

"Is there a question in there?"

She shrugs. "It's not like you to leave the office until at least ten o'clock."

"Again, I'm not hearing a question."

"I was in the area. I thought I might join you for lunch."

"Why?"

She gives a nervous laugh, the first sign she's about to crack. I almost laugh. She's so predictable it's boring. "Why does anyone eat lunch?"

"No. What makes you think I'd want to eat lunch with you?"

"Because it's what normal people do." She immediately realizes her slip and grimaces.

"But I'm not normal, am I, Dr. Nathanson? Isn't that why I've been seeing you every week for the last ten years? Isn't that why you've been letting me come in your mouth since I turned eighteen?"

"Quinn—"

"Are we done, Doctor?"

"I need you to start opening up a bit more—"

"*Are. We. Done?*"

"For today, yes."

"Thank fuck. Do me a favor? Please stop pretending you know everything about me. You only know what I share with you in this room." I crack my knuckles again, a disgusting habit I've never been able to quit. I wait for her to close her leather-bound notebook and set it down on the table next to her. When her blue eyes return to me, I sit back and eye her. "Stand up." She does as instructed. "Turn around, face the door. Is it locked?"

She shakes her head. "No." Her professionalism is gone and her voice shakes with excitement. For a second, I yearn for a slice of that excitement, but what the hell. I'm about to pass a decent ten minutes.

"Good. Take off your clothes."

The prim black suit comes off, followed by her cream silk blouse. She folds the clothes away and straightens. I take in her tightly knotted hair, the gold clasp of the pearls resting at her nape, the dove-gray lace underwear, the garters, the heels.

My ennui intensifies.

"Turn around."

She obeys. Her front is marginally improved by a decent rack. I stare objectively. She's beautiful, if a little on the too-thin side. Her legs are shapely, hips and thighs lean and toned. My gaze rises to her face and I read the myriad of emotions flitting over her features. None of them touch me. The black poison seeping through me deadens me from the inside. I lay my head against the chair and shut my eyes.

"Take the rest off and come here," I say.

Her approach halts two feet from me.

I smell her pungent arousal. She's as wet as fuck, and I wish I were in the mood to fuck her. My hands drop palms down beside my thighs on the sofa.

It's the tacit permission she needs to drop to her knees. She tugs at my belt and unbuttons my pants. Cool hands reach into my briefs and she pulls me out. I hear her excited gasp a second before her greedy mouth closes over my flaccid head. Saliva lands on my dick and eager hands rub me up and down. Muscle memory kicks in.

The spark is there, but it's pathetically negligible.

I open my eyes and stare at the white ceiling. In my periphery, I see her head bob up and down, faster and faster to keep me interested. I count the sconces, then drop my gaze lower to examine the genuine masterpieces and numerous accolades draping the walls. Absently, I count them. Twelve impressive citations.

Adriana Nathanson is accomplished.

But clearly she's getting progressively worse at sucking cock.

I sigh loudly. She bobs faster. One hand creeps over my abs and up my chest.

"No."

She returns it to my cock.

I sigh again.

I'm being blown by my thousand-dollars-an-hour shrink, one of the most acclaimed in New York City. She's bare-assed naked and on her knees with her office door unlocked. Depending on who walks in, she could lose her license. I should be excited.

Instead, I'm losing my barely-awakened wood.

Just as I'm about to push her off me, a face slides into my mind.

Lucky.

My cock twitches back to life. Adriana moans and gags with happiness as I thicken in her mouth. My eyes drift shut and the image sharpens. Tumbling caramel hair replaces ice blond. Worn T-shirt replaces pearls. A full, soft pink mouth wraps around my cock, tongue swirling. A teasing graze of teeth along my thick vein. I roll my hips. She takes more of me into her mouth. I hit the back of her throat. She growls low and long, her membrane vibrating against my cock head.

Air expels in a half gasp. The veil shrouding my ennui ripples, attempts to lift. Sea-green eyes rest on me as she devours me.

Her hand creeps over my abs and up my chest.

My eyes blink open.

Adriana.

"No," I snarl again. Disappointment blackens my mood.

Her hand returns to my cock and she attempts to deep-throat me. I'm too big for her. Her gag sickens me.

"Stop."

Shock hits her eyes. My deflating dick pops out of her mouth, wet and heavy.

"Quinn? Is something w—?"

"Get the fuck off me."

She has the nerve to appear hurt. Rapid blinks designed to imitate held-back tears make my mouth twist. To her credit, she retreats without protest.

I tuck myself back in and zip up. She's hurrying into her clothes as I stand and buckle my belt.

"Next week, same time?" I say sarcastically.

She pauses mid-dress. "I can fit you in later this week, if you want?"

I know why she's offering. My father is back in town. And perhaps the rare chance that I might fuck her. "I don't want."

Concern attempts to shift her Botoxed forehead. "Quinn, I'm really worried about you," she murmurs.

I laugh. A genuine, hearty-as-apple-pie laugh that splits my face. Sadly, it doesn't last. It too is sucked into the empty void. "You're worried about me?" There's only a thin veneer of reason left. I need to leave this place. Now. Her nod stops me.

"Yes," she replies. Her hands tremble as she resumes dressing.

"You really are delusional, aren't you?"

She finishes buttoning her blouse and zips up her skirt. "I don't know why you're being this way."

I laugh again. "Don't you, Adriana? What does your shrink say about our little *arrangement*?"

She pales and her mouth drops open. "How do you know about that?"

I scoff at her expression. "What, you think it's some big secret that you have a shrink too? I guess I should be comforted to know you're not too far gone to recognize that you need help. So, tell me, is there a diagnosis for *your* condition?"

The breath shakes out of her. "I...I'm not prepared to discuss it with you. Like our sessions, mine is also confidential. You get what that means, right?" She's regaining her composure. Her voice holds a touch of warning. I want to laugh again, but the whole fucked-up situation suddenly weighs me down.

"Cut the confidential crap, Adriana. I started coming to you when I was seventeen. You've been sucking my cock since my eighteenth birthday—I'm guessing crossing the line into pedophilia was a step too far for you?"

Her bravado vanishes. She holds out a hand. "You're not...You can't tell anyone about us, Quinn."

"There is no *us!*" I hiss. "And don't deny a part of you wants to be discovered. You blow me most of the time with your door unlocked, after all. The idea of someone walking in on us gives you a cheap thrill, doesn't it?"

Her pale face turns guilty. But her gaze rushes over me with sickeningly carnal hunger.

I stride to the door and wrench it open.

"Same time next week," she says behind me.

I leave without responding.

* * *

Two hours later, I'm in the VIP lounge of XYNYC, the Soho club I co-own with a West Point buddy. It's one of several business ventures in which I'm a silent partner because all that obscene Blackwood money needs to go *somewhere*, right?

I nurse another whiskey and watch scantily clad girls dance below my roped-off lounge. Several cast suggestive glances my way. I clinically assess and discard, my gaze searching but not finding what I'm looking for. I wonder why I even bother. Maybe I don't want to give in to the inevitability of the expanding blackness just yet?

In spite of knowing and accepting my fate, does a part of me want things to be different?

My phone buzzes in my pocket, the fourth time since I got here. I abandon my useless thoughts but ignore the phone. I'm not in the mood to deal with Maxwell Blackwood. He can wait.

I settle on a skinny brunette in a silver backless dress and crook a finger at her.

The swiftness with which she abandons her friends and hops up the steps to me is almost comical. I nod at the bouncer to let her in and take her back to the velvet couches grouped in the back. My private waiter delivers a glass of vintage champagne to her. I sit back in the seat and don't protest when she settles her long-legged figure next to me. Over a thumping *The Weekend* number, she babbles about fuck knows what. I don't speak. With her third glass of champagne, she grows bolder. She leans closer and her fingers tease my shirt button. Sultry words whisper in my ear.

I allow my hand to play in her hair as I slip deeper into my personal void. I note absently that the blackness is increasing since I gave up my attempts to hold it back.

My phone buzzes again as her hand creeps over my crotch.

I lay my head back and unlock the vault where my darkest plans reside.

In eighteen months, I'll be thirty.

I'll inherit fifteen billion dollars.

I'll be one of the richest men on earth.

I'll also, if my plans succeed, be a murderer.

3

TABLE READ

LUCKY

One million dollars.

The three words echo in my head as I pull the baseball cap low over my brow and huddle into the battered leather jacket I found discarded near a thrift store yesterday morning. It's three sizes too big, but at least the scent of cheap perfume and spunk has faded a little after the quick wash I gave it in my motel room.

I hurry along the sidewalk, careful to avoid the morning rush-hour crowd. I bumped into someone by accident two days ago. The abuse hurled at me by the guy in the snazzy suit was eye-watering. Had I not been reluctant to draw attention to myself, I would've responded with a few choice words of my own. But keeping my head down was more essential than losing my shit on him. The worst that happened to him was a few drops of ten-dollar, fancy-assed coffee spilled on his suit.

What could happen to me should I be discovered is an outcome I wouldn't wish on my worst enemy. So I keep my head down, the soiled tips of my worn boots guiding my feet on the wet sidewalk as I speed walk.

The train ride from my ratty, roach-infested Queens motel to Wall Street is thankfully uneventful, but I'm even more nervous when I exit the subway station. In the sea of suited stock-market traders and high-fliers, my cheap clothes and poor disguise stand out. Not enough to attract notice unless you were really paying attention.

Problem is, someone is paying attention.

Clayton Getty is looking for me. So is the man I grew up thinking was my father. Between the two of them, they have endless resources with which to find me, regardless of where I am.

Right now, the problem isn't *if* they find me, but *when*. It's the time between now and when that I'm desperate to prolong. It's the *when* that drove me to the pay phone on the street corner near my motel, where I risked precious money to make a frankly absurd phone call and send my picture to an unknown social media account. It drove me to risk leaving my cell number on a stranger's voice mail in the hope that I'd land a job that promises a ridiculous payday.

Even as I told myself I was old enough to know better than to fall for a scam, the fear and desperation that gnawed like acid in my stomach spurred me on. It led me to a sterile room that reeked of money and sinister intentions in a Midtown penthouse, and a mechanical voice that still echoes in my head and sends shivers down my spine.

The semi-cryptic ad I tore from the real estate magazine I found in the rec room of my new workplace is real enough. It's a solid presence in my back pocket. But it could all be for nothing. It could be some bored asshole's idea of a cruel rhyming joke to pass the time. Besides, ads like that belong in appropriately sleazy tabloid rags, not expensive glossy magazines. So the voice that has haunted my dreams the last three days could be the perfect *fuck you* to the cosmic fuckup that is the sum total of my life. But I can't get *it*, and the possibilities, out of my mind.

That cryptic article in a discarded newspaper started a chain of events that I know deep down could be my undoing.

It's given me *hope*.

And right now, hope is all I have left.

One million dollars.

For sex. For my life.

It's unthinkable to me that anyone would pay that much for sex. Back where I'm from, lap dances cost sixty dollars, blow jobs are ninety-five. Sex attracts the princely sum of a hundred seventy-five, often negotiated down to a flat one-fifty if your belly's full. If you were caught in the gleeful talons of starvation and you were stupid enough to let your desperation show, you'd be lucky to walk away with eighty.

Unless you were fortunate enough to be promoted to a job at The Villa. The special wing at The Villa is where every girl aspires to be. The Villa is where Clayton Getty rules his kingdom with titanium fists, aided and abetted by my father, his second-in-command.

It was where I was born and where I lived until I was five, when my mother was unceremoniously tossed out, and I was introduced to Trailer Trash Central.

I didn't know how thankful I should've been with my lot until Ma died and my absentee father reappeared and dragged me back to The Villa.

Initially, I thought that karma decided to stop shitting on me. The food was great, the showers hot, and the bed gloriously lump-free. Little did I know that karma was merely taking a short nap while the clock, and Clayton, counted down to my seventeenth birthday; that the six months between Ma succumbing to her fucked-up liver and my seventeenth birthday was just a pit stop between Armageddon and Hell. A mere dress rehearsal for the patrons of The Villa.

And what a show it was. I was dressed up like a doll every night. Paraded before hungry assholes while closely guarded by Ridge, Clayton's top dog. The months-long *look but don't touch* threat sent them into a frenzy by the end, and on the morning of my seventeenth, Clayton was all but salivating. His disappointment that I wasn't a virgin was obscenely palpable. Still, he had every sleazy patron eating out of his hand.

The night the man I thought was my father delivered the news that I was elevated to Clayton's Top Whore, I vomited all over his shoes. That earned me a backhand, the sting of which I can still taste. The ones that came after have faded with time, but, as the song goes, you never forget your first...

I round the corner onto Wall Street and get hit in the face by a cannonball of chilly wind. A shiver rattles my teeth. I'm not used to freezing conditions. The town outside Fresno, California, where I grew up may have been a shit hole, but at least it was a *warm* shit hole. Going from perpetual sunshine to interchangeable weather has been a body shock. But the weather is the least of my worries.

There are even more street cameras here and fewer people dressed like me.

I raise my head a fraction and see the building I'm headed for two blocks away.

Blackwood Tower.

More specifically, the basement.

I have no clue what goes on above street level. I haven't gone anywhere near the Internet since I hightailed it from Fresno. The one and only time I attempted to use my phone, Clayton found me within the hour. I ditched that phone at a rest stop in Iowa, stuck to hitchhikes all the way to New York, and bullshitted my way to a burner phone.

Whatever high-flying business happens up in the glass-and-steel tower is none of my concern. All I care about is that this job pays in cash, and that, as long as I keep my head down, no one notices me.

I hurry past the entrance of the building to the side street door that leads down into the cavernous basement. I enter the security code, walk through a large industrial kitchen, then down another set of stairs to the sub-sub-basement level. I shove the heavy double doors open, and a wall of steam and the sound of clanging plates greet me. A smaller side door leads me to the rec and locker room, where I quickly change out of my jeans and T-shirt into my work gear.

The white shirt and matching pants hang loose on me, the result of one too many missed meals. I secure the pants with the cheap rope belt I brought and make sure my hair is tucked under the black hairnet before I head back out.

"Hey, sweet thing. You're early," a voice greets me over the rattle and shake of rows of machines churning out glasses and plates.

I slow my stride and nod at Miguel, but I don't stop as I pass his station. I've noticed his eyes on my boobs and ass more times than I'm comfortable with. So far my mild fuck-off vibe is working. I'm not sure how long it'll last, though. Experience has taught me that a half-decent set of tits and ass blinds most men to just about everything else.

"Yeah," I respond. "I lucked out with the subway." I reach my station and activate the machine. Seconds later, the first stack of clean, steaming plates arrives in front of me.

"That's great. So...uh, where is it you said you commute from again?" He raises his voice to be heard above the sound of the plates I'm stacking on the tallboy trolley.

I turn and spear him with a cold look. "I *didn't* say."

He looks taken aback for an instant. Then he grins. "Come on, *muchacha*. I'm just trying to get to know you. No need to be so prickly."

I turn away without answering. He gets the hint because he doesn't engage me again for the rest of the morning.

An hour before the lunchtime rush is when hundreds of dirty plates are sent down. I found out through a talkative Miguel that not only are Blackwood Tower employees given three squares daily free of charge, the top executives are also given brunch, hence the late-morning madness. The only sliver of a lull comes after lunch, but we're allowed to take fifteen-minute breaks twice a day besides our lunch break.

During the first break, I pour myself a cup of cheap, but free, coffee from the rec room, grab the burner phone from my locker, and head upstairs. Outside, I head deeper into the side street and make sure I'm alone before I turn on the phone.

My heart hammers and my palms grow clammy as I wait for the

blue wheel to stop spinning. My rational brain tells me it's a burner and Clayton will have no way to trace it unless I do something stupid, like call someone back at The Villa. I don't intend to. For one thing, nothing and no one back there triggers anything near nostalgia, although every now and then I suffer a twinge of guilt for what I did.

All the same I'm nearly dizzy with fear as I check for missed calls. Nothing.

My heart drops, thankfully along with a large dose of terror once the phone is powered down. But in its place, anxiety rises.

It's Thursday. The stranger with the mechanical voice said he'd be in touch within the week. Did that mean in the next seven days or within this week, i.e., before Friday? I stare into the middle distance and mull the words over. The longer I think about what happened in that room, the more surreal it feels.

The stunning, but starkly minimalist apartment. The light gray walls with the uncomfortable, artsy chair. The mirror. The futuristic-looking camera.

His robotic, hypnotic voice.

Had that all really happened?

"Elly."

My mind frees itself from the lingering fear. I conclude that I must have fallen into some Kubrick-style, hunger-induced delirium and fantasized the whole thing after reading that stupid ad.

"Elly?"

Which means, my life is still set on a countdown clock, which spans days, possibly a week or two, tops. Because Clayton *will* find me. And when he does, he'll kill me. It might be slow or it might be fast. But death will be the ultimate penalty.

"Hey, *Elly!*"

It takes a nanosecond for the name to register as mine. Snapping fingers emphasize the call and I turn to find Miguel hovering five feet from me. A cigarette dangles from his fingers as he stares at me funny.

My skin prickles with thoughts of discovery, thoughts of flight. I force myself to remain calm, not give away the fact that the name he's calling me by is as familiar as it is alien to me. "Yes?"

He laughs. "You didn't hear me? You spaced out there for a sec, huh?"

I slowly slide the phone into my pocket. "Did you want something, Miguel?"

"Not me, no. But the boss wants you."

My heart skips several beats. "Why?"

He shrugs. "Hell if I know. But he wants to see you, pronto."

I manage a nod and keep a sensible distance between us as I leave the alley.

"Uh...Elly?"

My back stiffens, the name a reminder of why I'm here in this cold, noisy city awaiting a gruesome fate that looks exactly *like* death. I look over my shoulder.

"Is everything okay with you?" Miguel asks.

"We don't know each other well enough for you to ask me that."

He shrugs. "Maybe not. But I'm asking all the same."

I think of all the answers I can give. Then settle on the only option available. "I'm fine." I dispose of my Styrofoam cup and hurry inside before he can stick his nose further into my business.

The man I work for, Sully Manning, overheard me inquiring about a short-term job in the shop where I bought my phone in Queens. His shrewd, pale-gray eyes assessed me throughout my conversation with the shop owner. He followed me outside, scaring the shit out of me before he said he might be able to help. It took two tries before I conquered my fear long enough to call the number he gave me.

Now, as I approach his office, I wonder if that fear wasn't justified. Have I been too trusting? Hunger and terror have a way of messing with your mind. By letting one overrule the other, have I walked into a trap?

My feet falter. Fight or flight spikes adrenaline into my veins.

Sully sees me through his window and beckons me with a beefy hand. I look behind me. Should I make a run for it? How far will I get?

"Elly! I haven't got all day."

I press clammy palms against my pants and present myself in his office doorway.

"Umm, you wanted to see me?"

"Yes," he snaps. He's Irish-Italian with a brusque manner that keeps everyone in the catering support team in line. He moves a few papers around on his desk before his head snaps up. "You wanna earn some extra money?"

"I...yes?"

He head-tilts. "You don't sound sure."

I swallow hard, wonder if this is another acid-trip offer without the actual acid high. "I'm sure."

He nods a gray head. "Good. Good. Two of my servers have called in sick. Some bullshit stomach bug or other. I need you to step in."

My alarm escalates. I push it down and manage to nod. "Okay. What...what do you need?"

"Go see Meg in the uniform department. She'll find one of the girl's outfits for you. You need to be upstairs in fifteen minutes."

I'm glad I don't have to answer because sheer terror has overtaken my vocal cords. I belong in the basement, in the bowels of the earth where no one can see me. I don't belong upstairs doing...whatever Sully wants me to do. But I need this job or starvation will claim me long before Clayton does. Ninety-nine percent of my cash goes into paying for my shitty, but extortionate, motel room. The owner chose to overlook my *no-name-or-address* status in return for a thirty-dollar-a-week hike-up on normal prices. Right now, I have twenty-two dollars to my name.

So I force my feet to move.

"Oh, and Elly?"

I stop. Sully stares back at me.

"Remember how you got here. We all have pasts we don't want held up to the light. I'm not going to peek at yours. Return the favor by not letting me down. Deal?"

I nod. "Deal."

He waves me away.

As I leave to go in search of Meg, relief punches through me.

I've been rightly wary about Sully's motives. He knows I'm hiding something. But unlike Miguel, he's chosen to leave well enough alone. For that, I'm glad. Because tossing my particular closet open will reveal putrefying skeletons.

The first of which would explain why I don't respond well to Elly. Before arriving in New York no one called me by that name.

My real name is Elyse Gilbert, nicknamed "Lucky" by the waste of space who briefly labeled himself my father, because according to him, I'm the unluckiest person alive, and I'll die the same way I came into the world: naked, screaming, and dirt poor.

So far, he's been right about the unlucky part. Also dead right about the dirt-poor part.

But what he didn't predict was that at twenty-two, I'd be on the run for arson and murder. Or that one of my hunters would possess the single goal of trying to pry my secret from me before he puts me in the ground.

4

SCENE 1

LUCKY

I arrive at the service elevator in my new server's uniform of black button-down dress and a white apron. I've swapped my hairnet for a white mini-cap and my boots for nude tights and flats courtesy of Meg. If my heart wasn't slamming so hard against my ribs, I'd grimace at how ridiculous I look.

The service elevator has two buttons—*B. Restaurant* and *B. Executive*. My shaky finger hits the second button. I swipe at the sheen of sweat dimpling my forehead, suck in a deep breath, and reassure myself of the unlikelihood of Clayton finding me here. The assurance rings hollow.

He once tracked a girl who stole two thousand dollars from him, all the way to the ends of Clusterfuck, Alaska. It took four months, but his patience was inexhaustible. He found her, dragged her back to Fresno, and chained her to a wall in his *special* room, reserved for clients with the sickest proclivities. When he let her go a year later, Abby left The Villa, and walked straight into oncoming traffic.

I chose New York because I hoped the sheer density of the

population would buy me some time. That doesn't mean I'm comfortable hiding in plain sight. I'd give my pinkie to be back in the basement, handling piles of dirty plates and enduring Miguel's ever-increasing cocky advances.

The elevator pings open and my heart threatens to give out altogether. I step out into a skylit atrium decorated with stunning water features, horticultural masterpieces, and stylish furniture I've only ever seen in glossy magazines. Contrary to my fear, the room isn't crowded, but again, I know I stand out like a nun in a whorehouse.

Already I'm attracting stares by standing in the middle of the sun-drenched space. I avert my gaze and head toward the sound of a hissing coffee machine. Two waiters, a young guy and woman about my age, are standing in front of a glass-and-chrome counter that looks like something out of a sci-fi movie. Behind the counter, a stocky chef fires off instructions to a team of four about specific dietary requirements and the temperature of foie gras before he spears me with a hard stare.

"Are you the extra I requested?" he snaps.

I clear my throat. "Yes, my name is Elly. Sully sent me up."

His mouth compresses, and he points to the far side of the counter. "Stand there, don't move. You'll get your brief in five minutes."

My brief? To serve food?

He returns to barking instructions at the two servers, who nod briskly and whisk away silver trays to opposite sides of the executive restaurant.

I wait, making sure to stay alert so I don't repeat the spaced-out-in-the-alley incident Miguel witnessed. But my gaze wanders and lands on a magazine rack three tables away. On the front cover is an aerial picture of Blackwood Tower and on either side two men—one older and one younger—facing each other. The caption reads: *Dynamic Duo or Dynamite Duel?* Even in profile, both men are eye-catching enough to snag my interest. I'm just about to lean closer to scrutinize the cover when a throat clears next to me.

The chef looks even more annoyed than before. "You'll be serving Mr. Blackwood today. He takes his lunch at exactly one o'clock."

I nod. "Okay." He starts to walk away. "Umm, I'm sorry, which one is Mr. Blackwood?"

The servers pause to stare with open shock at me.

The chef swears in a language I don't understand and shakes his head. "How long have you worked here?"

"Two weeks."

"And you don't know what the man whose company you work for looks like?"

I shrug. "I wash plates and glasses in the basement," I murmur.

He stares me up and down, his mouth twitching with disdain. "Figures," he mutters under his breath.

I swallow the anger that rises and force my fists not to ball. "If you wouldn't mind pointing him out to me, I'd appreciate it."

His gaze doesn't move from mine. "*Mr. Quinn Blackwood* is sitting in his usual seat by the north window. He doesn't like being spoken to, so don't try to be clever and engage him in any form of chitchat. He takes his coffee with a dash of cream and two sprinkles of cardamom, in that order. Stir without touching the sides or bottom of the cup and leave it in front of him along with his meal. Think you can manage that?"

"Of course," I respond briskly, while frantically memorizing the list.

I know firsthand what craziness power and wealth induces in people, but what the chef's describing borders on the ridiculous. But I'm in no position to complain. Sully has promised more money for working up here today. Pandering to some rich dude's peculiar lunch ritual will go a little way to increasing my chances of survival for a few more days.

When the chef returns to hover over the poor minion who is preparing the tray, I look around again, trying to find my bearings. Where the hell is north? Geography wasn't a strong subject in school. In fact, the only thing I excelled in was math and English, both of which account for zero when all you're required to do is suck cock or lie on your back and zone out until whatever asshole on top of you is done.

My gaze frantically swings back and forth, trying to work out the exact position of the sun. On the third pass, I freeze.

He's sitting beneath a window, sure, but then so are three other stylishly dressed guys. But while the other men are talking into cell phones or tapping away on tablets, this man is staring straight at the view.

I can only see the back of his head, but even that grips my attention. The slant of sunlight hits dark, glossy hair and lights up the silky, wavy strands that caress the collar of his gray suit. Whoever he is, he could easily be a top contender for a shampoo ad with that hair. My gaze drops to broad, well-muscled shoulders and thick arms. It's clear even from across the room that this man takes care of his physique. His seated position means I can't see the rest of him, but as I watch him, I realize what has absorbed my attention.

He's deathly still.

Despite the hum of activity around him, he hasn't moved a muscle. It's disarming enough to send a shiver down my spine. And I know, even without bruising my brain by further trying to work out which way is north, that he is Quinn Blackwood.

"Remember my instructions, Plate Girl?"

I jerk around, and stare down at the tray. Everything is laid out in pristine condition. China and silver that I'm sure cost more than Clayton's prized hot rod sit at exact angles from each other. "Yes."

"Lay it out precisely as it is on the tray. And come back here. You'll wait until he's done, then clear his table. Understood?"

I nod. He hands the tray to me. I take a step forward and realize my legs are shaking. I pause, take a deep breath.

It's just food. It's just a goddamn tray of food.

I make my way to where he's sitting. The table next to his is unoccupied. I set the tray down on it and take the time to work out the angles and distances.

I pick up the gold-rimmed porcelain plate with the distinctive Tiffany blue pattern, and turn.

My breath dissolves to nothing.

Holy heaven above.

He's…*beautiful.* Easily, the most hauntingly captivating man I've ever seen.

Quinn Blackwood doesn't acknowledge me. He's staring at the view, although his gaze is narrowed and lowered, stopping me from seeing the exact color of his eyes. But the square jaw, the dimple in his chin, the sculptured curvature of his cheekbones, all align into a face that is so visually and powerfully stunning, my limbs slack in shock, before blood pumps full-bore through my veins.

He blinks, still without looking at or acknowledging me, but the tiny movement draws my attention to his lashes. Long, curved. Perfect.

And his mouth…

Jesus.

For a second, I wonder if I'm back in my alternate universe, where my life isn't in danger and a million dollars is truly within touching distance. Is this another hallucination? If so, I never want to wake up this time.

My gaze drops to his hands. They're big, a little out of proportion with the rest of him, but they in no way detract from the magnificent package.

As I stand there, caught in a web of what I can truthfully term as my very first genuine sexual arousal, his eyelids flutter. His chest continues to rise and fall in even, unhurried exhalations, but a spark of awareness lances through the air.

Perhaps it's another dimension of this weird hallucination. But whatever it is, it takes hold of me, fires through my body to the very soles of my feet and back up again. My mouth dries and I firmly refuse my body's urge to blink. I don't want him to disappear. I don't want him to be a figment of my imagination. Just for a little while, I desperately want this feeling to replace the constant fear that blankets me.

I'm not sure how long I stand there.

His forefinger taps once. Twice.

The movement jump-starts my spatial awareness. My fingers tighten on the plate when I feel it slip in my clammy grip. I take a hurried step forward and set it down before him. I instinctively know not to step into his light, so I arrange the place setting from the side of his table, his profile a constant threat to my equilibrium. Somehow, I manage to finish laying the table.

I recall and follow the instructions about his coffee and when I'm done, I step back reluctantly.

"Thank you," he murmurs. His voice is low, coarse, as if he hasn't used it in a while.

The sexy tenor of it shivers over my skin and I'm stuck in a vivid loop of imagining how it would sound were he to murmur extremely hot and incredibly inappropriate somethings in my ear.

From the corner of my eye, I see the chef and servers looking my way. It's clear I'm at risk of crossing some sacred server-employer line. Fighting everything inside me to avoid another torrid glance at Quinn Blackwood, I grab the tray, clutch it to my chest. "You're welcome," I reply before I remember that I'm not supposed to address him.

I risk a glance at him, gauging to see if I've earned a black mark.

His gaze doesn't stray from the view, but he reaches for the pristine napkin, unfolds it with a viciously sexy snap, and drapes it over his lap. There's an animal grace in that move that almost halts the step I'm about to take.

But the chef is rounding the counter, heading my way. I unfreeze myself and hurry away from the table.

He intercepts me halfway across the room. "Serve him and return to the kitchen. That was your brief!" he hisses at me.

"And that's what I did," I clip out.

"No, it was most certainly not what you did. You were just standing there, gaping at him like a decapitated fish," he snarls.

The heat that rises up my face is unavoidable. "I just…" I pause, because what can I say? That the man is a visually arresting masterpiece? That he's the first ever member of the opposite sex to make my panties damp just by *existing*? That even now, the urge to turn around, feast my eyes on him again, is proving almost impossible to resist? I clear my throat. "It won't happen again."

"No, it won't. That is not how we do things here, Miss Plate Washer. Now, are you able to follow simple instructions or would you like to return to more familiar subterranean surroundings?" he sneers.

The money, Lucky. Think of the money. "I want to stay and work."

He stares at me, thin-lipped, for a handful of seconds, then thumbs the opposite side of the restaurant from where Quinn Blackwood is sitting. "Tables need clearing over there. Try not to break anything. Each plate costs more than you'll earn washing plates in a year."

I lower my head and walk away, reminding myself why I can't let anger take over. It burns like a bitch, but I've learned the hard way that in a fight for survival, there is no place for pride. I have to let some things go.

I stack used plates from three tables in quick succession and take them to the kitchen. As I return from retrieving the remaining dishes, my gaze swings to Quinn Blackwood's table. His gaze is still glued to the view, but he lifts his coffee to drain the cup.

I can't help myself. I stop and stare.

There are men who command attention for varied reasons.

From the way everyone around him gives him a wide berth, I get the feeling this man commands visceral awe and respect without lifting a finger.

He sets the cup down and rises. Sunlight bathes him from head to toe.

He's tall, over six feet, and my initial assessment that he's a man who takes his physical well-being seriously is evidenced by his streamlined physique. Every inch of Quinn Blackwood demands attention. I realize I'm staring again and rouse myself as he fastens the single button on his business jacket and turns away from the table.

The moment I start to cross the room with my heaped tray of dirty glasses, I know our paths will collide.

I should stop. Turn away. Lower my head.

But I keep moving, my feet gripped with unbreakable compulsion. My gaze drops to adjust the tray, but I sense the moment his lands on me.

The sensation is electrifying enough to snap my head back up.

He's smooth, I'll give him that. But I witness the tiny stumble when our shadows merge. Glimpse the ephemeral hesitation that tenses his body before he regains absolute control of himself.

It is worth absolutely nothing to me in my life's ultimately fucked-up dynamic, but a tiny part of me frees itself from debilitating terror long enough to perform the smallest of cartwheels.

That is until our eyes meet.

Eyes of piercing silver blue surrounded by a jagged ring of black stare at me. My cartwheel disintegrates and I wonder if this is why everyone avoids this man.

Quinn Blackwood's eyes are soulless pools.

Staring into them is like staring into a bottomless abyss in the middle of a post-apocalyptic nightmare.

Something inside me wants to recoil, but I can't look away. The power of his stare is extremely hypnotic. I stand, frozen, as he remains in front of me.

"Your name." It's not a question. It bristles with ultimate power, and demands an answer.

"L…umm, Elly."

"You served me."

"Yes."

He stares for a fistful of heartbeats. "Thank you, Elly."

"Yeah…sure."

He walks way without a backward glance, leaving me with a strong notion of what it feels like to be a victim of mind control.

Because Quinn Blackwood, in those thirty seconds he pinned me with his eyes, could've talked me into doing anything for him.

I return the tray to the kitchen in a daze. Although I do my job, I remain in a mild fugue state until Chef Fancy Pants dismisses me from his lofty kingdom.

Sully calls me into his office when I return downstairs and hands me an envelope. Inside I find two hundred dollars, enough to secure a roof over my head and food for a week if I'm careful. I form the appropriate words of thanks, but when he dismisses me, I hardly recall changing my clothes and leaving Blackwood Tower.

The incident upstairs still has me in its grip.

I regain my common sense long enough to mind my surroundings as I take the subway back to Queens. I devour half of the leftover sandwiches I took from the rec room and wash them down with a can of soda, then shower with tepid water from a barely functioning showerhead.

There was no time to pack personal items when I fled The Villa, save for a couple of precious keepsakes, one of which is a picture of my mother and me, taken on my sixth birthday. I fish it out of my backpack and stare at it beneath the harsh motel room light.

She was stunning. According to some of the girls at The Villa who knew her back in the day, she used to be Clayton's prized whore until she messed around behind his back. Knowing Clayton Getty, I'm not exactly sure how she managed to talk him into letting her stay at The Villa after I was born.

I lie back on the bed that stinks of urine and other unthinkable fluids, clutching the picture. Out of the meager possessions I grew up with, I know why I'm hanging on to the photo.

Amid the telltale signs of her losing battle with alcohol abuse, there's hope in Renee Gilbert's face. She didn't give up hope despite Clayton Getty's single-minded mission to turn her life into a living hell. It was that hope with which she clung to my hand.

Despite the futility of my situation, a part of me desperately channels that hope.

Eventually, my body and mind let go of the perpetual fear long enough for me to fall asleep.

I jerk awake somewhere around two a.m., heart hammering. The glaring lightbulb blinds me for a few seconds before my eyesight adjusts. I raise the picture from my chest and stare at my mother's face, wondering if my fate will echo hers and we'll both perish at the hands of Clayton Getty.

As my fingers glide over the glass, another face slides into my mind. Quinn Blackwood.

There's no room in my life to ponder other people's shit, but I find myself intrigued all the same.

His body.

His deathly stillness.

His mouth.

His unwavering focus on the view.

His soulless eyes...

My breath catches. Mild shock engulfs me as I set the picture aside to watch my nipples peak beneath the T-shirt I wore to bed. I'm semi-fascinated by my body's reaction. Enough to jerk upright in bed seconds later when I feel a distinct tingle between my thighs.

What the fuck is wrong with you, Lucky?

He's hot, granted. But he's clearly fucked-up in that special way only rich, powerful people can be, despite having the world at their feet. Fantasizing about Quinn Blackwood will bring me nowhere near finding a way to get Clayton off my back.

In a last-ditch act of desperation, I grab my phone, take a deep breath, and turn it on.

My heart leaps into my throat when the mail sign pops onto the screen. Fingers shaking, I press it.

Monday. 6 pm. Midtown. Be punctual.

5

THE SCOUT

She walks in at 6 p.m. on Monday.

I watch her through the monitors, and finally admit to myself what I've shrugged off all weekend. The unexpected twist of her turning out to be a Blackwood Tower employee has shifted the tide in her favor. When I gave instructions for the ad to be placed in Blackwood Quarterly, my company's magazine, the best I hoped for was minuscule but twisted private satisfaction in the interim; knowing I was toying with Maxwell, with the larger pleasure to be reaped when the unvarnished truth came to light. I didn't anticipate this turn of events.

Lucky. Elly. And whatever the hell other names she has tucked beneath that cheap uniform and velvety skin, has managed to achieve the impossible; she's piqued my interest for a second time.

There's a deliciousness in knowing she could be serving me by day without knowing I'd be fucking her by night. That unanticipated morsel has elevated my mood from deadly lethargy to mere languor since Friday.

Well, that and keeping Maxwell twisting in the wind.

Avoiding Maxwell won't last, of course. He won't let it. He's never been great with being ignored. And after almost a week of unanswered summonses, it's only a matter of time before that particular bough breaks. Languor fades, and I imagine I can feel something.

The intercom next to my elbow buzzes from the team I have waiting next door. "She's here. Shall I take her in and explain the procedure to her?" Fionnella Smith, the team leader, asks.

"Not yet. I want to talk to her for a minute. I'll send her out when I'm done."

"Okay."

I slide my voice distorter into place and wait.

She's shown into the room five minutes later. She pauses at the door. Her eyes warily assess the room, her body poised with more than a hint of self-protection. Intrigue heightens.

She's scared of something. Or *someone*.

The urge to bloody myself with her secrets escalates.

I cross my legs and wait for her to enter. When she doesn't, I speak, "It's good to see you again. Come in, Lucky. No one's going to bite you today."

The provocative words achieve the desired results. She steps in and shuts the door behind her, while one eyebrow spikes. "No one's going to bite me any day."

"Is that your definitive view on the subject of biting?"

She drops her tiny backpack and pulls out the chair in front of the camera, a frown crawling over her exquisite features. "Do I get docked points if I say no?"

"This isn't a game show, Lucky. I merely want to assess your boundaries. I bite sometimes when I fuck. Will that be a problem?"

Heat engulfs her face, and her fingers drum on the table before rising to curl around the ends of her ponytail. One shoulder lifts. "I'm okay with it, I guess, as long as you don't draw blood."

"Noted."

Her gaze flickers for a second, then she does what I've wanted her to do since she walked in. She stares straight into the camera. She's better composed now than she was in my executive restaurant on Friday. She's had time to prepare for this meeting whereas then, her reaction to me was raw and unfettered.

I muse over the possibilities as I stare back at her.

Eventually, the question spills out, "So, I've got the gig?"

I pause for a long minute. "Yes, Lucky, you have the gig."

The sharp breath she takes is curious. Her expression isn't one of happiness or the ecstasy of gluttony satisfied. It's overwhelming relief that stems from abated terror, like a person snatched back from the jaws of certain death.

Her whole body trembles with the release of the paralyzing feeling. Her lower lip quivers, but she kills the telltale action by catching it between her teeth and gnawing on it.

"Thank you."

"Don't thank me just yet, Lucky. There's a reason I'm paying you a million dollars for your time. You will be fucked with, and not always in ways you'll find...pleasant."

Her fingers find her hair again. "But, you won't hurt me, physically?"

"Not intentionally, no."

She clears her throat. Decision made. "You chose me, and I don't intend to fail." Determination born of self-preservation.

Against my will, pique digs in a little deeper.

"No. You won't. I won't allow it."

Her lashes sweep down for a moment as she gathers herself. "What happens next?"

"Next you get prepped."

"Prepped?"

"A minor ground rule, Lucky. Don't make me repeat myself. Don't ask for explanations for things that are out of your control. A million dollars buys me unlimited access to your body and a button on your lip, barring further ground rules to be hammered out. Is that clear?"

"Yes."

"Good. That said, you have questions. I'll allow a few. Make them count."

I sit back and sip the whiskey at my elbow. She doesn't instantly launch into questions. She takes her time, considers. I approve of that.

"Am I going to meet you before we start?"

"No."

"But aren't you worried we might not be compatible?"

I recall the flicker I felt when she served me on Friday. She almost succeeded in piercing the outer layer of the seething blackness with her unexpected presence. At her initial interview, I overestimated what a wall of bricks and glass could achieve. Sensing her close in the restaurant, looking into her eyes afterward, I'm almost certain the flicker turned into a daring little spark. "I'm not worried."

Cynicism twists over her face. "You sound very sure about that."

"I have a cock, you have a cunt. We're compatible."

Her nostrils flutter at the uncouth words, which surprises me in light of the hardened look I've glimpsed in her eyes.

"Does my language offend you?"

She shakes her head. "I've heard worse."

I slot the info away, for what purpose, I don't know. "Glad to hear it. Do you have any other questions?"

Green eyes probe the camera lens. "What…umm, do you have a name?"

"I do."

She waits a beat, then I get the cocky eyebrow again. "Are you going to tell me?"

"No."

She frowns. "Then what should I call you?"

"What would you like to call me?"

Her head tilts. "Mechanical Man?"

"That won't suit."

"I'm not great with terms of endearment."

"I don't require one."

Exasperation filters through. "So you want me to call you nothing?"

"If you could pick a name or an initial for me, what would it be?"

She stares into the camera for a few seconds, then her gaze drops. The corner of her lower lip twitches, as if she's worrying her flesh from the inside. Her fingers still in her hair, her breathing alters and a light flush drifts over her skin.

"What are you thinking about, Lucky?" I murmur.

"Nothing."

"*Who* are you thinking about, Lucky?"

Focus returns to her eyes. She blinks rapidly and shakes her head. "Nobody. I don't feel comfortable just slapping a name on you when we haven't even met."

"A number then. Or a letter." I derive detached amusement in herding her where I want her to go.

Predictably, her nose wrinkles. "It'll be weird for me to call you by a number."

I remain silent.

She sends the camera another direct stare. "*J?*"

"I'm not a bird," I drawl.

Her sumptuous lips purse. "*M.*"

"Too British spy movie. Tell me who you were thinking about a minute ago."

She shakes her head again. "I'd rather not."

"If you insist. Do you have any more questions?"

"The...umm, money. How will you pay it to me?"

"However you want. When the time comes you can furnish me with your wiring details."

Her brow creases. "Can I be paid in cash?"

"Of course." I press the intercom on the table next to me.

The knock sounds on her door a minute later. She jumps up immediately, her stance firmly in fight-or-flight mode. "That is Fionnella. She works for me. Let her in."

The fight drains out of her, but her approach remains wary.

Fionnella enters and smiles at her. "Hello. I'm head of the team hired to prep you. May I call you Lucky?"

She eyes the woman cautiously, then nods.

"Great. Would you like to come with me?"

"Umm, I'm not sure if we're finished here." She clears her throat and glances over her shoulder at the camera. "Are you still there?"

"Yes."

"I have some more questions."

"They can wait."

She hesitates, flicks a glance at Fionnella. "Where are you taking me?"

Fionnella smiles. "To another room, to answer a few questions to start off with."

Lucky tenses. "What sorts of questions?"

Fionnella indicates the clipboard in her hand. "Routine questions about your health, your diet, boring stuff like that. Then we get to the exciting part." Her smile isn't reciprocated.

Lucky slides her hands into her pockets in a feigned gesture of calm. But still she hesitates.

"Go with her if you want the job, Lucky. Or leave."

She won't leave. I already know that. Fear and desperation hang over her like dark clouds. She casts one last glance over her shoulder before she nods. "Okay."

I watch her leave, track her via the monitors until she reaches the studio set up to begin her transition. I find myself wondering how far I can push her. How fast her resistance will hold. Whether I can exploit her fear, take this game to another level, or satisfy myself with finding out what her secrets are.

It's clear she'll do just about anything for the money, despite her feeble attempt to set boundaries. I also get the feeling her boundaries have already been tested.

But I can't imagine they've been stretched as far as I intend to stretch them.

And fuck if that doesn't make my black soul twitch.

6

LIGHTS, CAMERA...

LUCKY

I follow the plump lady with the clipboard and giddy smile down a dark gray hallway. The rooms we pass are all empty, but just from the expensive wallpaper and light fixtures alone, I can tell a lot of money has been spent on this apartment.

Clayton blew a ton of money on a major revamp of The Villa a few years ago in a bid to attract clients from as far as LA and Frisco, but it was nowhere near this classy. This is solid gold compared to Clay's nickel-plated efforts. The hardwood floors gleam beneath my feet, and inside the rooms the curtains I catch glimpses of are heavy and expensive looking.

"Would you like something to eat while we complete the forms?"

Fionnella's question jerks me back to the present. Her hand rests on the handle of a wide door at the far end of the hallway, and she stares up at me from a diminutive height.

For a second, I wonder what a woman who seems to vibrate motherliness is doing in a place like this. Then I catch myself. I'm pretty certain she's not here out of the goodness of her heart. She's being paid, same as I hope to be. And money can pretty much buy you anything. Even temporary absolution from death. I should know. It's what I'm attempting to do.

"I have a menu if you'd like to see it?" she presses. "It's not very extensive but there's a good selection to choose from."

The timely gnawing in my stomach reminds me I haven't eaten since a rushed half burrito at lunchtime. "If it's no trouble, thanks."

Her smile widens as she throws the door open. "It's no trouble, honey. Besides, putting a little more meat on your bones is part of my brief."

Brief. I swear I've heard that word more times in the last week than any other time in my entire life. True, I've also thought about it, specifically the part where it involves my brief interaction with Quinn Blackwood.

I haven't been able to get him out of my head, although the actual reliving of our meeting has been kept to a minimum, simply because it messes with my head and body in a way that scares the shit out of me.

Even more alarming was the gutting disappointment not to have been summoned into Sully's office today and sent to help upstairs. A lingering look from a cop on the way here reminded me why risking exposure in any way could shatter the thin layer of protection I've managed to buy myself.

I enter the room and stumble to a halt. I hadn't quite understood that a team would mean more than Fionnella. Three more people from sectioned-off corners of the room turn to stare at me, and I can't help the visceral chill of fear that rises.

"Let me introduce you. This is Wendy, my assistant," Fionnella says, pointing to the woman seated at a table draped with lingerie. Beside her are three racks of clothes. Wendy nods, and returns to her sorting.

Obviously not as bubbly as her boss.

"The camera-wielding fiend over there is Todd." She smiles at a tall, skinny guy with dirty-blond hair at the far side of the room. He sends me a two-fingered wave, but his attention returns to the expensive-looking camera in his hand. Scattered around his workspace are all types of lighting equipment, back lights and three large floor lamps. "He's just setting up. You won't work with him or Wendy until your grooming gets under way."

I drag my gaze from Todd to a woman in a skirt suit who approaches with a serious face and an outstretched hand. "And this is Dr. Allen. She'll be in charge of your blood work, and a couple of other things. I'll let her explain, after we get you something to eat." I shake hands with the woman, who then disappears behind a screen. Fionnella smiles encouragingly. "Do you have the menu, Wendy?"

Wendy rises without responding and presents me with a heavy folded menu, the kind you find in posh restaurants, only in miniature. She retreats just as silently, but not before I catch a look I've been familiar with for most of my life.

Contempt.

I choose to let her keep the stick up her ass. One less person who takes an interest in me is one less person to worry about exposing myself to.

Fionnella indicates a desk with two chairs on her side of the room. As I walk to it, I wonder again about the man behind the camera.

The man without a name.

I look around what was probably a great room or a small ballroom in the original design. The walls, like the rest of the apartment, are beautifully lined and there are elaborate ceiling designs that I'm sure didn't come from some mass production line in Taiwan.

On the far side nearest Todd, a set of French doors looks out onto a softly lit terrace. I don't have to be money savvy to know that terraced penthouses in Manhattan cost millions of dollars.

Right now, the room is divided into four spaces. The last space is unoccupied, but I see what looks like a portable massage table and several baskets of grooming products. There's also a makeup table and chair set up. "You'll meet Angela later. She'll go through makeup with you."

I nod and take a seat in front of Fionnella's desk. When she gestures encouragingly at the menu, I open it. My mouth waters immediately, and I want to point to the first thing I see, which happens to be a triple cheeseburger and fries. I swallow the surge of saliva and force my gaze down the list.

Pasta and prosciutto in white wine sauce.

Beef and spinach stuffed ravioli.

Rib-eye steak with Cobb salad.

My stomach rolls in painful anticipation. "I'll have the burger and fries, please."

Fionnella smiles. "Anything else?"

"Soda?"

Her gaze drops over my body. "How about we make it a milkshake? Unless you don't like milkshakes?"

I barely stop myself from telling her I'd give both pinkies for a banana milkshake. "Okay. Banana. Thanks."

She gives me a happy nod and picks up a sleek phone on her desk. My order is relayed in crisp tones. "It'll be here in ten minutes. Now, let's get started." She places the clipboard in front of her and spears me with a slightly less maternal look. "Fair warning, it's in your best interest to be as truthful as possible. Everything you say here will be held in the strictest of confidence, but the boss doesn't take well to liars. Okay?"

I want to cough out the fear knotted in my throat. But that would give me away. So I nod. It satisfies her and she's back to being kind and gentle Mother Superior.

She clicks her pen. "I have your contact details but you don't have a permanent address?"

"No, not yet."

"Okay. For the purposes of this job, this will be your address. Is that okay with you?"

I want to ask why she's asking. It's not like I'm going to file taxes or cite this gig on my resume anytime soon. But the look in her eyes says she wants an answer, so I nod again.

"Great!" She looks me over again for a second. "If you don't mind my asking, are you normally this weight?"

"No."

"Can you tell me how much weight you've lost recently?"

"Umm, about twenty pounds."

She nods thoughtfully. "And is the reason a medical one? You're not on drugs or anything, are you?"

"I'm not on drugs, no."

She pauses. "Let me be specific. We're going to put you on a healthy meal schedule. Will there be anything stopping your weight from coming back to normal if you eat right?"

"No."

She smiles and scribbles on her clipboard. "Do you exercise regularly?"

I curb a hysterical laugh. Sure, I exercise regularly if you take a cross-country run for my life as exercise. "I keep fit," I prevaricate.

"Perfect. You'll be assigned a fitness instructor as of tomorrow."

I frown and remember a work schedule was one of the questions I meant to ask Mechanical Man. "I have to work tomorrow."

Fionnella's brow creases. "I'll check with the boss. I'm sure we can rearrange a few things." She scribbles some more and ticks a couple of boxes, then turns over the page.

"You're sexually active?"

"Yes."

"When was the last time you had sex? Weeks or months?"

Ridge's sweaty face swims before my eyes and I suppress a shudder. "Umm, weeks," I say. My voice doesn't emerge as firm as I wish, and I earn a peculiar look from Fionnella.

"Dr. Allen will go through this more thoroughly with you, but are you on birth control?"

"No."

I'm not sure if this pleases her or not because her expression neutralizes. She ticks a box.

"Have you ever had a colon cleanse?"

"A *what*?"

"I'll take that as a no. You have to have one once a week."

"Why?"

"For the anal scenes," she states without blinking.

I stare at her, unable to form words. She stares back. A throat clears beside me.

I jump and snap my head to see a man in chef's attire holding a tray of food.

"Ah, great, thank you, Georg."

Georg nods and sets the tray down in front of me. The burger's aroma hits me in the face and I almost drool. Fionnella's smile widens.

"Go on, eat."

I'm not sure I want to eat while having a discussion about my colon and anal sex, but hunger takes no prisoners. I grab the burger and take a huge bite. Fionnella grins as if she's personally responsible for curing world hunger. She waits for me to swallow before she looks back down at her notes.

"So you're okay with that, right?"

I pick up a fry. "Does it hurt?"

She shrugs. "I'm told there's a small degree of discomfort, but I expect it won't be anything to worry about."

"Okay." I take another bite of food. The first pull of the divine shake makes me almost moan in pleasure.

"It's good, right?" Fionnella grins at my plate.

"Incredible," I mumble around another bite.

"Okay. Almost done. Do you have any piercings, inside or out?"

I shake my head.

"Do you have a toy preference?"

"Toys?"

"Sexual toys. The boss has his own selection, of course, but you're allowed one or two of your own."

"Ah...no, I don't have a preference."

"Are you good at deep-throating or do you think you need instruction?"

I nearly gag and my stomach attempts to twist in on itself. I'm not sure if it's because of the conversation or because I ate a little too fast. I suspect it's a mixture of both. "I...uhh..."

Fionnella drops her pen. "The boss doesn't like gagging. You'll need to know how to swallow him properly. You can be taught how to relax your throat to avoid gagging. Are you good with that?"

"Can I...say no to performing the act?"

"No," she replies firmly, then makes up her mind one way or the other and scribbles on her notes.

The sensation of living a weird fantasy returns. I quickly polish off the burger and fries. If I'm about to wake up from a hallucination, I'd much rather do it having enjoyed the best meal I've had in my life.

I look up from an empty plate to see Fionnella going over her notes. "That's about it from me. I'll go and have a word with the boss as to when to start your grooming and exercise regime while you talk to Dr. Allen."

She escorts me to Dr. Allen's side of the room and leaves.

The doctor waves me to a chair. "Sit down. I'll try not to keep you too long," she says briskly.

I get the feeling she's trying to be as professional as possible without letting her true feelings show. On the sliding scale of friendliness, I put her third after Fionnella and Todd. Except I'm yet to experience the camera guy so maybe I should reserve judgment—

"Fionnella went through a few sexual questions with you, but mine will probe deeper." No apologies. No niceties. Just straight to the point.

The whole operation is smooth enough to make me wonder how often the man with the mechanical voice organizes one-million-dollar sex gigs.

I don't care. The money is all I'm after. Selling my body to buy my life is an exchange I can live with.

"Have you ever had an STD or suspect you might have one now?"

I jerk back to myself and shake my head. "No. Never." Use of condoms was a number one rule at The Villa. One of the very few things Clayton got right. Although I suspect buying rubber was cheaper than forking out for medical bills, or worse, having a prized girl off work.

"Do you suspect you might be pregnant?"

"No."

"You have to go on birth control. The boss prefers Depo-Provera. It's quick. It's noninvasive—you get a shot in your arm, and the side-effects are minimal." She passes me a leaflet on birth control. "Read up tonight. You get the shot tomorrow unless there are reasons you can't get it."

I stuff the leaflet in my pocket.

"Do you bruise easily?"

My heart lurches and my precious burger and fries threaten to re-gurgitate. "Why would you ask me that?"

Dr. Allen doesn't blink. "The camera will pick up blemishes, even with makeup. I need to know whether to provide you with a fast-healing cream should you be bruised."

A perfectly reasonable explanation. In a very fucked-up world. "I guess I'm normal on the bruise scale."

She makes a note. The rest of her questions are as mundane as a thorough scrutiny of my sexual history can be. When she asks me to, I undress and hop onto a bed behind the screen for an internal ex-amination.

Fionnella returns after my blood has been drawn and we leave Dr. Allen's area to return to hers. She hands me a brand-new phone. It's sleek and expensive looking.

"The boss wants you to keep this on at all times." Her gaze catches and holds mine. "It's untraceable and it's got my number pro-grammed in there. From now on, you call me when you have work-specific questions."

I look down at the phone. "Does that mean I won't be talking to the…boss again until…"

"Yes."

Something inside me tightens a touch. "And when will that be?"

"Depending on how your diet and exercise go, a week to ten days."

The knot tightens harder. I mentally frown at it. "Right. Okay."

"I need to know your work schedule, then you're free to go."

I tell her and she frowns. "I was told your time would be more flexible than this. We have a lot of ground to cover."

In the grand scheme of my fucked-up existence, I choose not to take offense. "I have to work." I don't elaborate.

She meets my gaze again and nods after a minute. "Okay." She does the let-me-escort-you-out gesture.

Just before we reach the front door of the apartment, I remember my backpack.

"I need to get my stuff from the camera room."

She nods and returns to the large, empty living room. Having been here twice, I know where the interview room is without direction. I enter, grab my bag from the floor and straighten. The camera has a red light on, as if it's still active.

I hesitate, then walk closer.

I'm not sure what compels me, but something inside wants to hear that voice one more time. I bend forward, stare into the lens. I open my mouth but can't think of any words to say that won't make me feel like a complete idiot talking into a camera.

After a minute, I straighten. But I still can't leave the room.

"Lucky."

I jump out of my skin at the voice I've been recalling in my head. "You're still there?"

He doesn't respond. Irritation and embarrassment duel inside me. Of course he's there. When my fingers protest in pain, I look down and realize I have a death grip on my brand-new phone.

I wave it at the camera. "Thanks for this."

"You're welcome."

I should leave. My business here is done for now. Time to return to my hellhole.

"Did you want me, Lucky?" he asks, that robotic voice weirdly spellbinding.

I rack my brain, dig out what I wanted to say to him before.

"Yes, I've thought about it…a name for you."

"Yes?"

How could a mechanical voice be so smooth, so sexy?

"Q. I'd like to call you Q."

He doesn't answer immediately. I begin to feel like an ass.

"Q. Are you sure?"

I shrug. "Not really, but it's the only one I can think of that's not pretentious or absurd. If you're not okay with it—"

I may be imagining it, but I hear faint amusement in his voice as he replies, "Say it again."

Yes, definitely ass territory. A knot of embarrassment forms in my throat. "Q."

"Thank you, Lucky. Q works very well for me. Bravo."

Bravo? I'm not sure exactly what that means, but I can't ignore the tiny pulse of something heady that moves inside me. "Okay."

"Goodbye, Lucky."

The finality of it is a command I heed. The light on the camera blinks off.

I leave.

7

ACTION

I put my tweaked plans into motion first thing on Tuesday morning. Axel, my business partner, and the guy who strays within a whisker of what I term a friend, doesn't blink when I make the request. This is why our dynamic works. We've made such requests of each other in the past. He will need this favor reciprocated in the near future, and I'll step up, no questions asked.

We make sure to keep our sheets balanced. Imbalance doesn't suit either of us.

Once I'm sure the obstacles I need removed are on their way to being dismantled, I e-mail my executive assistant with my second request. I watch her through the glass partition of my corner office.

She looks up, nods, and picks up her phone.

Satisfied, I frost the glass and stare at the e-mail sitting in my inbox.

Maxwell.

I click on it without disabling the notification button. The summons is pretty much the same as it's been all week. Dinner at the Upper West Side mansion I grew up in.

I reply with my agreement. He opens it immediately and I can almost see the smug look on his face as he reads it.

It takes me a minute to work through the need to succumb to the void inside me. That is what he does to me. For as long as I've known him, my father has had this effect on me. Even long before Mama died. Even before I knew where and when my end would be, I knew he was partly responsible for the blackness of my soul.

The passage of time has merely confirmed and cemented that belief. Sure, I could've stopped myself from feeding it. The head shrinking and pills would've possibly stood a chance if I'd allowed it. If I hadn't let Adriana Nathanson offer me her version of extra-credit therapy by getting on her knees and sucking my cock when she should've been tending my mental health.

But I am Quinn Blackwood. Rich. Entitled. Unapologetic asshole with a death wish. I accepted that a long time ago. I don't intend to change. For myself. For anyone.

I exhale and pick up the first file on my desk—a condominium deal on a revamped Miami beachfront that's almost at completion. Once it's done, it's going to sell for at least three and a half mil apiece. More money to add to the overflowing Blackwood pile.

I pick up the phone and hit ten on my speed dial.

"Quinn, I was just about to head up."

"I need to cancel lunch, Ash," I say to the head of my contracts and planning team.

"Oh, okay. But we need to get the Denver deal done. The consortium is getting antsy that we keep postponing."

"Blackwood is backing the project seventy-thirty. Let them wait."

He sighs. "You pay me to give you advice so here it is: if there's no legitimate reason for stalling on this deal, let's just get it done. Fostering bad blood just for the hell of it may give you a momentary high, but it's not worth the aggravation we'll garner down the line. If your father were here, he'd say the same thing."

I hit the speaker button and set the phone back in its cradle. I don't answer until I hear him fidget. "Ash?"

"Yeah?"

"You're fired." I kill the connection.

The knock comes ten minutes later. Five minutes later than anticipated. Perhaps he made a detour to the bathroom to change his soiled pants.

"Come in," I say without raising my voice.

A pale-looking Ash Langston enters, palms already outstretched. "Look, Quinn, I know you don't make idle threats or"—he takes a deep breath—"or fire people just for laughs. I was just trying to smooth things along, do what you hired me to do."

"And you think I'm being irrational for stalling on the Denver deal." I eye him as he paces the front of my desk.

"Not irrational, no. Just…look, I'm sorry. You want to wait, we wait. You're the boss."

I don't reply. My gaze drifts to the silver antique clock on my desk, silently willing the time away.

I want to see her again. I want to confirm if that spark is real.

Before me, Ash tries to keep his composure, but the man is unraveling. I bet he can see his quarter-of-a-million gambling debt rushing at full speed toward him. Or perhaps it's the potential loss of the Soho loft where he stashes his mistress that's making him sweat.

"Do you know that two of the consortium members indulge in underage sex? Or that the head has quashed four counts of domestic abuse brought by his wife in the past two years?"

He stops pacing and his mouth drops open. "No! Jesus, I had no idea, Quinn, I swear to you. We did all our due diligence, used the investigation firm we always use."

I shrug. "They were good at covering their tracks, but I'm better."

Ash nods. "I…of course. I'll stall for as long as you want me to. Or we can tear up the contract. I'm sure we can find a loophole that'll protect us. Failing that, we'll tie them up in court for years."

"No. I'll handle the consortium."

His face turns chartreuse as if he's about to hurl. Sweat drips down his temple. "Quinn, I'm begging. My twins are about to go to Yale. I've remortgaged the roof over their heads just to pay for tuition. I can't lose this job. Give me another chance."

He's lying, of course. He remortgaged his house to pay for his mistress. His wife is paying for his kids' tuition with her inheritance.

I stand and round the table to perch against my desk. "You want to save your job?"

"*Yes!*"

"Tell me, what are the top five properties my father still keeps his eyes on? His pet projects."

Ash looks uneasy. "But...you've taken over his portfolio."

I deliver a ghost of a smile. "I know he calls you once a week to check on some of the deals we're working on. Top five. I need the names." I harden my voice.

His Adam's apple bobs. "I, uh, there are two in Boston— Blackwood One and Blackwood Two, the condo project in Miami, the stud farm in Montana your stepmother insisted he buy last year, and a building that houses the junior philharmonic orchestra in Philly."

I wasn't aware of the stud farm, but the rest are as I guessed. I hitch my thigh over the side of the desk and cross my arms. "How much did we give away to charity last year, Ash?"

"I don't have the numbers at hand but I can check for you."

"Ballpark it."

"Uh...possibly in the region of a quarter of a billion."

"How much of that was recouped in tax breaks?"

Another dribble of sweat makes its way down the side of his face. "All of it."

I nod. "Here's how you get to keep your job, Ash. By five p.m. today, I want an ironclad contract ready for me to sign, together with a press release."

"I...sure, just give me the details."

I stand. "It'll be in your inbox by the time you get back. Don't fail me, Ash."

"I won't. Thank you, sir."

He scurries out and I return to my desk. My gaze immediately zeroes in on the time. Quarter to one.

The faintest of tremors shakes through me. I hit send on the e-mail I prepared for Ash before I rang him. I take care of a few more business items, until my intercom buzzes. I lay my pen down.

"Send her in."

The first thing that comes through is the solid silver executive trolley given to each Blackwood Estate board member two Christmases ago. I look past it as the door widens.

She enters with a touch of hesitancy, which she covers with a brisk intake of her surroundings.

Her green eyes meet mine and she swallows. The clench in my abs tells me I haven't imagined the effect she has on me. Or I on her. She stares at me for charged seconds before she heads for the twelve-seater dining table set on the far side of my office.

I track her, take in her coiled hair, her fragile nape, her curvy form. The petiteness of her frame rams home as she passes my desk pushing the trolley. Her unremarkable dress affords me an impression of her lightly bouncing tits and a first glimpse of her smooth legs. They're shapely, firmly muscled with delicate ankles I can't wait to wrap my fingers around. My senses tweak to the decadent morsel she'll make once I get my hands on her.

Observing her this way on Friday would've given me away, but here in the privacy of my office, I indulge myself.

Without speaking, she reaches the table and starts to lay out my lunch in precise movements. I scrutinize her body again as my cock wakes. Despite being on the thin side, her proportions are flawless.

Put simply, she's perfection wrapped in drab work clothes.

Hell, even her hands are delicate.

I rise and return to the front of my desk as she leans forward to place the last of the domed dishes on the table.

"It's customary to acknowledge the occupant of a room when you enter," I murmur.

She stiffens, turns, and grabs hold of the trolley handle. Our eyes meet for a charged second before she looks away. "I'm not normally that rude."

"But?"

Her face pinches in a quick grimace. "The chef...he *briefed* me on how you like things."

"I sincerely doubt he has the first idea of how I like things. But please, enlighten me."

Her gaze meets mine, again for a furtive second, then darts away. I want to be irritated by that. But I know what she sees when she looks in my eyes. I know what everyone sees. So I let her get away with it.

"You don't like being engaged in conversation. You don't like the noise of cutlery. And you like your dishes to be laid out in precise angles."

"Lord," I murmur. "You must think I'm a freak...?" I raise an eyebrow.

"Elly," she supplies, her voice a touch on the husky side.

"Tell me, Elly, do I look like a freak to you?"

Her breath catches. The sound is faint, strangled at the last moment, but her gaze returns to my face. I've given her permission, and she takes her time to drink me in. The tinge to her cheeks is evidence that she likes what she sees.

My cock thickens. I cross my legs at the ankles, which draws her gaze lower. Her eyes widen on my crotch and she blinks before averting her gaze once more.

"Umm, no, you're not a freak."

"Thank you." I straighten and approach the dining table. Her fingers tighten on the trolley, but she doesn't move away. I reach her and slowly inhale.

No perfume. No expensive shampoo or cosmetics. Just cheap soap. And yet, I want to rip the uniform from her body, lay her bare on my dining table, and devour her instead of the food.

Perhaps she senses my forming intentions. She takes a few steps to the side, dragging the trolley behind her. When she continues her retreat, I pause in the act of pulling out a chair.

"Where are you going?"

This time when her eyes meet mine, they stay for more than a second. "Back to the restaurant."

"No. You'll wait until I've finished. Then you'll clear up. I can't abide the lingering smell once I'm done eating."

She seems caught between mutiny and surrender.

"Is there a problem, Elly?"

She shakes her head. "No. But I don't want the chef thinking I'm slacking."

"Are you in the habit of doing that?"

An affronted frown unleashes before she visibly reels it back. "Of course not. But he's a bit…temperamental."

"Is he?"

She grimaces. "Please don't tell him I said that."

"I won't. It'll be our little secret. Let go of the trolley and come here, Elly."

I walk to the opposite end of the table and wait. Her movements are slow but she obeys. When she reaches me, I pull out the chair.

"Sit."

Her head tilts back, and I catch the hint of the rebellion I've seen in Lucky's eyes. But too soon, secrets and trepidation overcome rebellious fire. She lowers her head and slides into the seat.

"Have you eaten?"

I know the answer to that, but I wait for her to tell me.

"Yes."

"Would you like something more?"

She shakes her head. "No, thanks."

I take my place and unveil the first dish. And then in silence, I polish off an excellent *chateaubriand*.

8

TRANSITION

"Are you out of your goddamned mind?"

I calmly hand my coat to Felix, my father's gray-haired, unflappable butler, brush the specks of rain from my hair, and straighten my cuffed sleeves. "Good evening, Dad. How was your trip to Albany?"

"Answer me, boy!"

"Am I out of my mind? We both know the likelihood of that answer leaning toward yes is high. Sadly, ten years of therapy later, Dr. Nathanson hasn't found her way to a clear diagnosis. Perhaps we should invite her over, discuss the matter over cheese and wine?"

He rushes toward me, six foot one of thoroughbred Blackwood stock. I keep a loose-limbed stance, but my blood spikes in anticipation.

He stops a dozen feet away. I'm disappointed.

"Is everything a joke to you, son?"

My bark of laughter strangles off within a nanosecond. "I never joke about wine. Or cheese."

At fifty-one, Maxwell Blackwood is in prime, Blackwood condition. He's fourth generation in a long line of power-wielding Blackwoods, built from the ground up in pure New York royalty. His brief but illustrious stint in the army has also added a touch of grit to his innate charisma. What Maxwell Blackwood couldn't obtain with a smile he claims with an iron fist. It's what makes him one of the most respected and feared men in the country.

We face off in the wide hallway of the mansion. Felix hovers at a discreet distance, his decades-long service to my family having anesthetized him to confrontations such as these. I stare at my father. His snowy-white tuxedo shirt indicates he's just returned from one of the many functions that demand his time these days.

Hands planted on lean hips, narrowed eyes two shades darker than mine, he glares in white-hot anger. "Did you or did you not give away my Miami condo project to a fucking homeless charity?"

Maxwell seldom swears. So twice in two sentences is an achievement.

"Oh…that. The quarterly charity drive is weeks away. I thought I'd get a jump on it."

A vein pops in his temple. "That project is worth eighty million dollars. You didn't think to discuss it with me first, before you issued a goddamn press release announcing the donation?"

I slide my hands into my pockets before he can see them bunch. "Frankly, no."

He looks furiously incredulous. He starts to whirl away, but checks back almost instantly, points a finger at me. "You will cancel the contract tomorrow, Quinn. Take out another press release stating you made a mistake. Give them something else if you must, but you will not give them the Miami project."

"I could, but then how would you look, Dad? The donation was made in your name, from a company that bears your name. Think of the *embarrassment* factor."

"*Jesus Fucking Christ*, you're the goddamn embarrassment!" He reaches up and yanks loose the first stud securing the tuxedo.

I roll on the balls of my feet. "Thanks. Now, are we going to get to the real reason I'm here, or shall I leave and go back to ignoring your phone calls?"

"What the hell is wrong with you?"

I'm almost tempted to tell him. Surely, he can't be that dense? But then I remember that hubris is a giant flaw of the Blackwoods.

So I shrug.

"I need an answer, dammit. A shrug isn't going to cut it, son."

I grit my back teeth against the tug of satanic rage that engulfs me every time he calls me *son*. "If you say so."

We go back to facing off again.

Felix clears his throat. "Mister Quinn, can I get you something to drink?"

"That would be excellent," I reply without taking my gaze off my father. "You have any of that Macallan '46 still tucked safely away, old man?"

"Of course. Coming right up, sir. Same for you, Mr. Blackwood?"

My father breaks my stare long enough to glare at Felix before he turns and stalks off. "No," he snaps. "Quinn, we'll finish this in my study."

I nod at Felix before I follow at a much more leisurely pace. I'm halfway to my destination when I hear the click of heels behind me. I don't turn around. The faint cloud of Coco Mademoiselle is enough to announce her.

Warm hands slide over my shoulder to rest at my nape. Somewhere along the line, she's gotten it into her head that she owns me, or at least enough of me to touch me when no one's watching. "I thought that was you, Quinn," she murmurs in my ear. "Nothing else fires Max up quite like you do."

"You sure about that?" I drawl.

The husky laugh is exaggerated. "Well, I won't lie. I have my moments of inciting Max-related fires too."

"You'll be good enough to spare me the details, of course."

Another laugh as she steps around me to block my view of the portraits of generations of Blackwoods lining the walls. She does so without letting go of my nape, filling my vision completely. My gaze rakes her from neck to toe.

She's wearing a kimono-style leisure gown in black with bold gold swirls. The V-shaped neckline and the cinched-in waist empha-size her many considerable assets.

A tall and statuesque ex-stockbroker, Delilah Blackwood dragged herself from dirt poor to powerful adversary in a little over a decade. She's stunningly beautiful, with straight, jet-black hair that falls to her waist. Combined with the razor-sharp fringe nearly touching her lashes, and perpetually scarlet-painted lips, she is difficult to look away from when she walks into a room.

I give her her due, let my scrutiny linger complimentarily before I greet her gaze with a guarded, less hostile one while she continues to play with the ends of my hair.

"Of course. I know how you hate the details." She offers a dazzling smile I don't reciprocate.

Eventually, all attempts at playing the unflappable mistress of the house leave her face. Behind her we both hear my father pacing his study. He lets loose another curse and his footsteps grow louder.

Delilah leans in close and under the pretext of kissing me hello, whispers in my ear, "I've missed you, darling. Albany was hell with-out you."

"But isn't hell where you thrive best, Stepmother Dearest? I bet you had the staff running around in circles to make hell more inter-esting for you?"

For a naked moment her gray eyes blaze with a sinister light, un-cloaking the real Delilah Frost. When you strip away the gloss and polish, she's an alley cat in the basest form, ready to claw and gouge with gold-digging talons to keep what is hers. Her unvarnished thirst for power saw her land the biggest fish in New York at twenty-five. But she has a thirst for other things, namely rough, dangerous sex. The rougher, the better. The kind she made clear from the beginning she was not getting from Blackwood senior.

"I haven't got all night, Quinn. For the love of God, can you show me some respect—? Oh, Lilah, I thought you were already in bed?"

Delilah swivels on stiletto slippers, her face rearranged in an adoring and accommodating *wifely* smile. "I was just about to head there, when I heard the heated discussion. Then I remembered you said Quinn would be stopping by. I thought it would be rude not to say hello."

Maxwell's tension eases a fraction as his arm slides around his wife's waist. At thirty-five, she's the right age not to attract veiled sniggers of cradle-snatching attached to such powerful and high-profile relationships. She's also very quickly made a name for herself where it counts to the extent that those who don't know her can almost be forgiven for thinking she's my father's equal.

She's not.

And it's that last rung of elusive acceptance that makes her watch me with blatant hunger that would've been almost amusing had it not been for a simple, hard truth.

She's Mrs. Maxwell Blackwood. But the title doesn't belong to her. She took it by unforgivable force.

"At least someone around here appreciates the basic concept of good manners," Maxwell snipes, narrowed eyes leaving his wife's to clash with mine.

A noise swirls in my head, rising in volume with each heartbeat. "You'll have to take me as I am, Dad. I'm far too big for you to put me over your knee."

The growl from his chest fades away beneath the soothing hand his wife places on his chest.

Delilah sighs. "You two wear me out with your constant wrangling. Darling, I think you should go pour yourself a drink; let me speak to Quinn for a minute?"

Maxwell starts to shake his head. Delilah steps in front of him, demands his attention. "Max. Go."

Fury aimed at me is tamped, and he stalks back into his study and slams the door.

Delilah whirls to face me, her eyes fierce and determined. "I want to see you again. This week."

"No. Tell me why he wants to see me."

"Agree to see me first."

I turn around and head back down the hallway. "Fuck off, Delilah."

She rushes after me. "Don't speak to me like that!" she hisses.

"I'll speak to you any way I damn well please."

She reaches my side and lays a hand on my arm. I'm about to shake her off when I see Felix heading my way, a sterling silver tray with a single glass on it. Delilah's hand falls away without an ounce of guilt.

I snag the glass from the tray and knock back ten thousand dollars' worth of prime whiskey in one swallow. I swear I catch a wince from Felix as I set the glass back on the tray. "Thanks, old man."

"Always a pleasure, sir."

"Tell my father something came up, would you?"

Felix opens his mouth. Delilah beats him to the punch. "Really, Quinn. Do you have to be so difficult? You bothered to come all the way here. And you're just going to turn around and leave again?" There's a frisky little fire in her eyes that I want to stoke, but being in this house, with so many reminders, risks setting me off.

"Tell him to send me an e-mail or you tell me what this is about." Delilah transfers her attention to Felix. "That will be all, thank you." The old man retreats with a stiff nod.

"I mean it, Quinn," she whispers fiercely. "I *need* to see you. It's been months."

"And the last time you asked me nicely, I accommodated you. I believe the you-owe-me-one box is ticked in my favor?"

She swallows. "That...it wasn't the same." Her hand finds my arm, her grip firmer. "Please, baby. I can't function."

I ignore her plea and jerk a thumb toward the study. "What the hell does he want? I won't ask you again."

She waves an impatient hand at the question. "It's something to do with schedules and the campaign."

My brain ticks over for a minute. "What about the campaign? Is he thinking of not running?"

She frowns. "No, quite the opposite. Since you played an integral part last time, he wants to go over a few things with you. He just wants to get the ball rolling asap, that's all. But I don't want to talk about that. I want to talk about us..."

I exhale slowly, let her words drift over me. My plans would remain the same regardless of which course Maxwell takes, but this is a better outcome.

I thought he intended to discuss Blackwood Estate business even though he no longer plays a day-to-day role in the company. Now I know what the summons is about, the cogs in my plans resume spinning.

"Quinn?" Delilah presses harder.

I step away from the clinical analysis of my plans and stare down into her face. She swipes a tongue over her lower lip, leaving it glistening in the hallway light.

I cover the hand on my arm with mine. "Fine. I'll be in touch in a few days. Are you able to bear waiting that long?"

Relief and triumph swirl over her face and she gives a sultry laugh. "I'll manage. Just about." I start to walk away, to head back to the study. Her grip tightens. "Will it... I want it to be just you and me this time."

I tap the tip of her nose. "You know better than to make demands, Delilah. You get it the way I give it to you. Or you don't get it at all. Is that going to be a problem?"

Her face drops along with her hand. "I don't know why I tolerate this from you, Quinn."

My finger traces the side of her pursing mouth. "Spare me the affronted routine, hmm? We both know it's fake. Now run along back to bed. I'll be in touch." I walk away without a backward glance. I know she's still watching me because I don't hear her footsteps retreating.

I enter my father's study without knocking. He's standing at the window, his gaze on the square of darkness and light that forms Central Park at night. When he turns, he's holding a crystal cut glass similar to the one I just used.

The fury in his eyes hasn't abated, but I can tell he's fighting to get a handle on it. Use it to his advantage. "Can we discuss the reason I asked you here, like two adults?"

I shut the door behind me, shove my hands back in my pockets and stroll to the center of the room. "By all means, *Dad*. But perhaps I should save you the trouble of a discussion and offer my congratulations?"

He looks taken aback.

I allow myself a smile, but I don't go to him or offer a handshake. There's a reason my hands are in my pockets. Touching my father is one step too far for me. "Delilah gave me the good news. She also mentioned you wanted to talk schedules?"

"Yes, I do."

I give a carefree, accommodating shrug. "No problem. Just get your campaign manager to liaise with my EA. I'll make sure we work something out."

His mouth goes slack for a second. Then he gives a brisk nod. "I appreciate it, son. I thought this would be yet another battle with you. Although I'm still far from thrilled about the Miami thing—"

"The Miami thing is done. There's no going back. Unless you want to look weak?" I taunt.

Fury washes over his face but the seductive allure of power dilutes it. "Fine. But I want your undivided attention on this campaign when I need it."

My gaze skates over his shoulder to fix on a skyscraper in the distance. "Of course. This is important to you. I get that," I lie.

He pauses for a moment. Then, "Thank you, son."

I look into his eyes and the words trip smoothly off my tongue. "Not at all. Your second term as governor of New York will be a memorable one for the Blackwood name. I'll make sure of it."

His sigh of relief echoes in my ear as I walk out and pass the generations of Blackwood portraits decorating the hallway.

The first one dates back to the Mayflower. My steps slow and I look up at the painting of Ichabod Blackwood. He wears the same arrogant pride I see on my father's face. I smile at the portrait, revel in the stern admonishment in Ichabod's gaze.

"Take a good look, old man. This train is never going to make it back to the station. Your line is going to end with me."

I salute the portrait and walk out of my father's house.

9

RECALL

LUCKY

When I round the corner of the block where my motel is located, my practiced stance of head-down-body-hunched is fully in place, so I don't see the brewing commotion until I almost trip over it.

"What the hell do you mean, I gotta leave?" A half-dressed guest is shouting at the manager.

"I don't know how else to explain it to you, mister. Department of Health says I have to shut down immediately, so yeah, you and every guest here need to pack up your shit and leave. The inspector is coming back in an hour. With new locks."

An icy rock drops into my gut. My feet freeze on the uneven parking lot asphalt as I absorb the words.

"Bullshit! I've been staying in this shit hole for years because my company is too cheap to put me up in a better motel when I come into town for business. I'm more than familiar with your complimentary rodent-per-room standards. So what's changed? And since when does the DOH toss people out after hours?"

The manager shrugs. "Fuck if I know. Look, I'm just the manager, okay? I follow orders from on high, just like you do, so quit busting my balls."

"Dammit! So what am I supposed to do?"

"Hell, I don't know, find another place to stay and *expense* it?"

"Fuck you! I want a full refund, buddy, and I want to be compensated for the inconvenience. Or I ain't leaving."

The manager scratches his beer belly. "I can only refund seventy-five per cent of the remaining rate of your stay. You'll need to take up any further claims with the parent company."

"Are you fucking kidding me?" The guest is growing redder in the face.

The manager, who doesn't seem one little bit upset by the gathering crowd of disgruntled guests, shrugs. "Nope. Everything I've said is in the small print. Feel free to read it. Present your booking receipt when you check out and you'll be given what you're due." He takes a step back and addresses the crowd. "That'll be all, folks. Remember, the guys with locks will be here in an hour. If you ain't outta here, you'll be thrown out."

"Yeah, try it and I'll sue the pants off you." One guest, an aging woman with pink curlers in her hair, points an arthritic finger at the manager.

"I'm just doing my job, but go ahead, give it your best shot, lady," he sneers.

A few other patrons voice their anger, but the manager shrugs it off. I wait till he's heading back to his office before I sprint out from where I've been standing next to a banged-up Corolla.

"Excuse me, sir?"

He stops and glances over his shoulder. "Yeah?"

"I don't know if you remember me—"

"Sure, I remember you." His gaze slides over me. I pull my backpack across my body. He sees the action and his expression sours. "What do you want?"

"I paid you two hundred dollars this morning. To cover my stay till the end of the week?"

"Yeah. And?"

My grip tightens on my strap and I plead with karma to give me a break. "I…obviously, since I can't any longer, I need my money back."

His gaze slides once more over my body, slower, sleazier this time. A smile I've seen more times than I care to count eases over his pudgy features. "Of course, sweetheart. Like I said, bring me your paperwork and I'll fix you up."

The ice expands in my gut. "You know I don't have paperwork." My voice shakes and I despise myself for it.

His face contorts in a show of false regret. "Ah, I'm sorry. No paperwork, no refund. Company policy."

Anger dislodges the ice. I want to fly at him, claw that sick look of glee off his face, but I force myself to remain calm. For one thing, there are too many people around to witness it and possibly clock it on their camera phones if I do anything stupid. For another, I want no part of me touching the shit bag in front of me. My days of allowing men like him anywhere near me are over. Well…*nearly* over.

"Look, I'm asking you to show some…mercy." The word sticks in my throat. The idea of having to beg this piece of shit to give me back money that's rightfully mine burns a hole in my chest.

He steps closer, his gaze probing where I've crossed my hands over my breasts. "I can be merciful, sugar. Come with me to my office and I'll show you what Papa Bear can do for you." He smiles. His hand starts to lift toward me.

I step back, partly because the idea of him touching me fills me with severe loathing. But mostly because my knee is itching to make violent contact with the flabby Papa Bear parts between his legs. He accurately interprets the move.

"I guess you don't want your refund, after all." He waves a beefy hand in the direction of Union Turnpike subway where I've just walked from. "There's a homeless shelter that way. Or you can blow some homeless guy into sharing his cardboard mansion with you." He laughs and walks backward. "Either way, sweetheart, your *situation* is not my problem."

He disappears around the corner into his office and tears surge into my eyes.

I don't blink. Because, damn it, tears are of zero use to me right now. But, God, I want to succumb. I want to find the nearest dark corner and howl my eyes out. I want to beat myself for falling into a trap of my own making. With leaden feet, I retrace my steps to the motel room. My larger backpack sits where I left it this morning. At least the asshole didn't break in and help himself to my stuff as well.

I sink onto the bed and stare at the ugly wall until my vision hazes. Fat tears slide down my cheeks, shamelessly defying my will. Defeat throbs in my veins and I drop back on the bed, setting free thick sobs that rip from my throat loud enough to wake the dead.

I cry until I'm certain there isn't a drop of liquid left in my body. When I can bear to drag myself up, I make my way to the bathroom, blow my nose on coarse toilet paper and wash my face. My eyes collide with my reflection and I shudder in revulsion. My face is blotchy, the hair at my temples tear-soaked. Averting my gaze, I grab more paper and swipe at the damp spots. I throw the paper in the general vicinity of the trash. It misses. I don't pick it up. It can be my tiny *fuck you* to the cosmos for the unending deluge of shit-dumping.

I return to the room and catch the sound of an electronic ping. My heart trips in paralyzing alarm before I remember my new phone. In the tumult of being suddenly made homeless, I've forgotten my appointment with Fionnella and her team back in the Midtown apartment.

It's not for another two hours, but as I've found out in the last two days, Fionnella is nothing if not a stickler for punctuality. At midday today, I received a menu by text with a prompt to choose my preferred meal. The repeat of the burger and fries arrived within half an hour. I was in the middle of devouring it, when Sully found me and informed me of my new work status.

I nearly choked on a precious mouthful when he told me the two girls who contracted food poisoning last week had both quit, and that until they were replaced, I would be working in the executive restaurant. As if that wasn't intimidating enough, he calmly announced that my first task would be to serve Quinn Blackwood's lunch to him in his office.

A different emotion weaves through me as I pull out the phone.

What happened in Quinn's office still feels a little surreal. After a short exchange while I laid out his lunch, the man barely spoke more than a few words. Sitting at his dining table, watching him eat, was a weird experience, for sure. But it wasn't the sort of weird that made me recoil. It was a mind-bendingly fascinating weird. A make-your-heart-flip-flop-in-your-chest-with-each-move-he-made weird.

Watching him rendered me tongue-tied to the point where I was grateful he didn't want to indulge in conversation. But tongue-tied didn't mean paralyzed. My gaze was constantly drawn to him, although I didn't gather the courage to meet his eyes again—twice was more than enough. Especially when both times the sensation of sliding at rocket speed toward a dark, but blissfully fatalistic end knocked my breath out of my body.

And when my pathetic attempts to resist staring worked, I could feel him watching me, those piercing, soulless eyes probing me.

My breath draws out now in a long, shuddering exhale as I recall those eyes.

God—

Heavy fists pound the door. I jump and release a husky croak. "What?"

"Time to vacate, lady!"

I shove the phone into my back pocket and thoughts of Quinn Blackwood to the back of my mind. I quickly rebraid my hair and stuff it back under the baseball cap, grab my stuff, and open the door.

The manager smirks at me, flanked by two burly guys in dark clothing. They don't have any distinguishing badges. In fact, they look more like street thugs or bouncers than DOH officials, but then what the fuck do I know? I sidle past them, hurry down the stairs, and cross the parking lot, avoiding the gazes of other guests who're vacating the premises.

I lower my head and strike out toward the subway.

I'm still terrified to go anywhere near the Internet, which is why the first thing I did when Fionnella handed me the phone was to turn the Wi-Fi service off, regardless of her assurance that it was untraceable. If Clayton could track someone to Alaska, he could track me here. I know that. But that doesn't mean I intend to make it easy for him.

As my bag grows heavy in my hand, the subject of my homelessness looms insurmountably large in my mind. I consider asking directions to the shelter but even I know you can't book a place at a shelter in advance just to stash your luggage. And with my money almost gone, I don't even have a hope of finding a place to stay tonight. The rat-infested piss hole I'm walking away from cost forty-five dollars a night for the privilege. My only choice is to take all my stuff with me to my appointment and figure out what to do afterward.

I arrive with more than fifty minutes to spare. I find a spot under a tree in a park a couple of blocks away from the penthouse and drop down onto the grass. In order not to attract too many stares, I pretend interest in my phone. Time drags and with it a sudden intensity of hunger.

My stomach knows it's about to be fed and it has the temerity to grow impatient. When it growls and clenches one more time, I put away the phone and dig through my smaller backpack. I stashed an emergency chocolate bar in there a week ago and I almost moan in relief when my hand closes over it.

I'm on the run from Clayton Getty. I've just been evicted from my exorbitant hellhole. I'm sitting in a park, waiting to present myself to a team of strangers in a fuck-off apartment in order to begin a cycle of prepping to whore myself on film with a man I've never met, in return for a million dollars.

I figure I've earned an emergency chocolate bar.

10

FIRST TAKE

LUCKY

I arrive at the penthouse at the arranged time of six thirty. The uniformed doorman holds the door open without questioning my status, and calls the elevator for me. I make eye contact long enough to murmur thanks and breathe a sigh of relief when the doors shut. The relief lasts as long as it takes for me to tug the cap off my head and stuff it into my bag. I'm beset by a whole new set of nerves when I exit the elevator to find Fionnella waiting for me, minus her clipboard. For the first time, she's less than total sparkle.

"There you are. We need to get straight to it. The boss wants the first shots done tonight."

"Shots?"

She nods and falls into step with me when I reach her. "Yes. Todd can't start until we have you properly prepped."

I'm ushered down the hall to the great room and straight across to the grooming area. She introduces me to Angela, the technician who was absent on Monday and yesterday, when I met with the fitness trainer. The petite woman with a mop of dark brown hair beckons me into her section and pulls the curtain closed.

"I'll leave you to it. We need to finalize your lingerie choices." Fionnella stops when her gaze lands on my extra piece of luggage. She glances back up but doesn't voice the question lingering in her eyes. "Have you eaten yet?"

"No."

"Okay, I'll get you something for when you're done waxing. You can eat while your hair is being done."

Satisfied with her schedule, she nods and exits.

I drop my stuff in one corner and turn around to find Angela staring at me. I'm not sure whether she's assessing me for work purposes or her personal curiosity is getting the better of her.

"Your face, honey," she eventually says. "Are you temporarily blotchy or am I dealing with something else?"

Heat surges into my face. I'd forgotten about my epic crying jag among the detritus of everything else I'm dealing with. I swipe self-consciously at my cheeks. "It's temporary."

"Great. That helps a lot. Okay, get your clothes off, slip into the white gown and hop on the bed. Have you had a Brazilian before?"

I shake my head as I toe off my boots.

"What about a bleach?"

"No."

"Depending on your coloring down there, we may not need the bleach, but prepare yourself for the possibility."

She heads to the prepping table and turns on a machine that looks like a fondue set without the tower. I get rid of my clothes, tug the gown over my head and stretch out on the massage table. She returns with a small bowl, which she sets down at the foot of the bed. In the grand scheme of the huge obstacles I face, I'm mildly shocked to find myself nervous at the thought of having a patch of hair ripped off my pussy. But my nerves clearly filter through because she lays a hand on my knee.

"Relax, honey. The first time is a bitch, I won't lie, but tensing up will make it worse. I'll go as fast as I can."

Laughter spills out before I can hold it in. Even to my ears, I sound a touch off my rocker. "I'm sorry. This is all a little...surreal."

She nods as if she totally understands. Maybe she does. I wonder how often she does this for...the boss.

Q.

Did I really name him that? And what exactly did he mean by *bravo*?

My spinning thoughts refocus on the room and what's being done to my private parts. I take a slow, deep breath and force my limbs to slacken.

Twenty minutes later, I'm a full member of the Brazilian club, shock and pain-induced tears included.

Luckily, I pass the no-need-for-a-bleached-butthole test, much to my semi-hysterical relief. When Angela instructs me to, I get off the bed and hobble gingerly to the hair wash section of her domain.

The touch of firm fingers massaging heavenly-smelling shampoo into my hair takes my mind off the stinging in my crotch. And thanks to the miraculous hypoallergenic mist she sprayed down there, by the time I'm seated in front of the mirror with my dinner of fettuccini, garlic bread, and slice of cheesecake in my lap, the pain is almost gone.

The blow dry warms me from the outside and the hot food releases the chill inside me. By the time I'm done with both, I feel a little more able to form thoughts that don't start and end with abject hopelessness.

I need to find a place to stay tonight. That's my first priority once I'm done here. Fionnella has a laptop, but asking for it would involve too many questions. I toss the problem around while Angela combs and trims my hair.

Deciding I have no choice but to return to Queens and take my chances with the homeless shelter, I look up as Angela fluffs my hair one last time.

"There. We're done with your hair."

I look into the mirror and my eyes widen. My hair has always held a natural wave, but Angela has emphasized the curls with a hot iron and teased the layers so the caramel and blonde swirl around each other in eye-catching waves. I no longer have split ends and whatever product she used has left a shiny, healthy head of hair styled back away from my face. A few of the girls back at The Villa often attempted to replicate styles like these, but I've only ever seen perfection like this in a magazine.

My gaze lifts and catches hers in the mirror. "Thanks," I murmur. I can't summon more enthusiasm than that because, although I want to feel elated that my hair looks amazing, the purpose behind the makeover remains firmly locked in my mind.

The makeup session is even more dramatic than the hair, despite the subtle colors she uses. I barely recognize my own face by the time she finishes. I suddenly have noticeable cheekbones and my eyes are huge pools of deep green. I'm still staring at myself, stunned, when Fionnella walks in.

"Perfect, you're right on time." Her smile is back, although a touch strained at the edges. Angela excuses herself to tidy up and leaves Fionnella to judge her handiwork.

She makes pleased hums as she touches the curled ends of my hair.

"Come on, let's get you fitted for the shoot."

Her gaze follows me when I go to grab my stuff and when I return, she nods at my large backpack. "You look like you're going somewhere. Is there a change of address we need to know about?"

I need to be careful with my answer. "I...yes, but I'm not exactly sure what it's going to be just yet."

The smile leaves her eyes. "Is there a problem I need to know about, Lucky?" She cuts to the point.

My grip tightens on my backpack and I decide to come clean. "The place I was staying at was kinda...raided."

Her mouth purses. "Drugs?"

I shake my head quickly, although I can't exactly stop her from forming her own opinion. My motel address is scribbled down on one of her clipboards. She knows in which part of town I live. Or lived. "No, some other...vermin problem. Anyway, I didn't have time to find a new place because I had to come here." The half-lie slips out easier than expected.

She spears me with an incisive look. "We won't be done here for another couple of hours. You know that, don't you? That means you won't be able to start looking for a place to stay until almost midnight."

I nod. "I'll be fine," I say. The dull thudding of my heart states otherwise.

Fionnella turns away without responding, and I don't know whether my answer is satisfactory or not. Still in my gown, we head to Wendy's station. "Put your stuff over there." She points to the area behind her desk. "I'll go and see if Todd is ready."

But she doesn't head to Todd's area. She leaves the room for five minutes and when she returns her smile is back.

She inspects the lingerie on the table for a minute before she picks up a moss-green ensemble. "This one first."

To my surprise it's a simple lace-trimmed half teddy and French knickers set. Considering the nature of what I agreed to, I was expecting the pieces to be much saucier than this. With a touch of relief, I retreat to the curtained off area and slip the garments on, taking care to avoid messing up my hair. The silk feels warm and soft against my skin, and I let my fingers drift over it for a stolen second before I emerge.

"Great, we got your size right." She reaches for her clipboard and ticks a box, then cocks her head toward Todd's area. As we head over, the lights dim and I notice the three staged areas for the first time.

One area is set up to resemble a window of a suite or bedroom. A posh velvet chaise longue is set against roped-off, expensive curtains. The setting is classy and flawless, but it's clear the spotlight is on the chaise.

The other two areas follow the same design—one's a bed with sexily rumpled sheets, and the other the mirrored vanity of a black-and-gold bathroom.

Todd looks up from the piece of equipment in his hand and points to the chaise. "We'll start there."

Nerves attack me as I walk toward it. "What...what do you need me to do?"

"Just recline on it. Try not to exaggerate your poses. And look directly into the camera."

I recite the steps and nod. "Okay."

I climb onto the dais and walk to the chaise. The spotlight trained on the stage is warm but not uncomfortably so. I sit, place my hands on the seat and scoot back on the smooth velvet. It feels so natural to lie sideways and tuck my feet beneath me, so that's what I do. Taking care not to ruffle my hair too much, I tuck it over my shoulders and recline into the corner.

The first flash blinds me and I wince. "Sorry."

"It's cool, but try not to shut your eyes."

I take a breath and stare into the lens. Todd snaps several shots, taking a step closer with each one. After five minutes, he swaps cameras. This one doesn't need a flash, so I relax a little.

Staring into the lens, I'm suddenly reminded of another camera in another room down the hall and my first audition when I had to perform. Something stirs inside me—hot and urgent. I try not to fidget; the memory grows stronger.

Convince me that you're worth fucking. Convince me you're worth dying for.

The mechanical voice is so clear in my head, it feels like I'm back in that room again, giving myself over to commands that tap into fantasies I didn't know I harbored until I was challenged.

"Let's try another pose."

I slowly sit upright, my mind still in another room, and move to the middle of the seat. I plant both feet on the floor and bring my knees together. Hands on either side of me, I slowly lower my head until my nose is pointed to the floor and waterfalls of hair gently brush my cheek. As I lift my gaze and stare into the camera another voice, another room, slides into my mind frame.

Tell me, Elly, do I look like a freak to you?

It'll be our little secret...

Come here, Elly.

Sit.

The heat in my belly intensifies. My breath shudders in and out. My knees want to part. I fight them, fight the deeper tingling between my legs. Todd climbs the stage again, comes closer. My bare feet slide in opposite directions on the smooth wooden floor, but my knees stay glued together.

Quinn's low, gravel-rough voice replays over and over in my head as his deeply hypnotic, soulless eyes stare at me from the ever-advancing camera lens.

Come here, Elly.

Sit.

Elly...

Elly.

"I think that's it for this setup. Let's get you ready for the next one."

My body jerks into the present. I turn away from the camera and tighten my belly against the persistent heat. The sight of sour-faced Wendy waiting just behind Todd helps dissipate the electricity sizzling through my blood.

I stand and follow her. She hands me a russet-colored lace Basque and thong and I change.

Todd directs me to the bed and again allows me to strike my own poses. The sensations return, stronger than before.

My mind whirls with more than a touch of confusion. How can I be enjoying this? How can my body be this hot when everything about what I'm doing is wrong?

Yes, I'm doing this for a blindingly simple reason—to keep myself alive and to keep Clayton from discovering the secret I hold locked in my heart. But a part of me is also enjoying the thrill of dressing up in nice lingerie, wearing makeup, and playing minx with the camera. Because I know the man with the mechanical voice will see it?

Yes.

The answer slides deep into me, twists within my groin, and hardens my nipples as Todd snaps away. The silk sheets tangle around my body. I let my fingers glide over it, loving the texture, wondering how it would feel warmed by two bodies instead of one. I slide my hands up, rest them on either side of my head. I know my body is on show, my nipples clear to see beneath the lace, but I don't care. In fact, the idea makes me hotter. So much so, I feel a deep pang of regret when Todd calls a halt.

The third and final scene before the vanity mirror is simple. In a purple-and-black slip that barely covers my naked ass, I pick up the gold-cased lipstick, lean forward, and slide the tube across my lip. Without instruction, I allow my gaze to find the lens through the mirror. The faster clicks of the camera tells me I'm doing something right, and when Todd mutters, "Fantastic!" beneath his breath, elation spikes through me.

I'm sad when he lowers his camera. For the first time, he smiles. "That was good. Really good."

I return his smile. "Thanks."

He hands me the gown to cover up and I see a cheeky gleam in his eyes. "You're the kind of girl that gives people the idea that gay guys like me can be convinced to switch lanes."

I laugh. "Thanks, I think."

He grins and walks away.

Fionnella is waiting for me once I change back into my normal clothes.

"The boss would like to see you. Leave your stuff, you can get them after."

My heart leaps into my throat. I try to read her face but she's too good for me. I leave the room, my mind a chaotic vortex. He said we wouldn't speak again until my training was done. So why does he want me? Have I blown it?

Has he already seen the pictures and decided I'm no longer suitable? The thought of losing something I'm even now not sure was ever in my grasp fills me with so much anguish, my fingers shake as I turn the door handle and enter the familiar room.

Everything is the same, and yet I sense a difference in the atmosphere. A subtle shift I'm unable to pinpoint exactly.

"Lucky."

The way he says my name draws a shiver.

"Hi," I manage as I shut the door behind me.

"Sit down."

My movements lack perfect coordination as I move forward, and for the first time since this whole surreal situation started I experience real fear. Oh, I've been afraid for my life since fleeing The Villa. But there's nothing like being offered hope, and having it yanked away from you without explanation.

Fists balled in my lap, I stare at the surface of the table. Looking into the camera is too much. My desperation is too raw.

"Look at me, Lucky."

The request is absurd seeing as he's not in the room with me, but I know what he means. I want to pre-empt rejection with a plea. Or a *fuck you*. But words refuse to form.

I look into the camera.

"I'm told we have an accommodation problem."

Shock spikes through me. "I…what?"

"You've been evicted from your motel."

Fionnella.

My gaze drops. "Yes."

"Lucky." The demand is robotic, but no less intractable.

I find the lens again.

"A situation like this is potentially disruptive. Do you agree, Lucky?"

Potentially. All's not lost. Yet. I clench my gut against premature relief. "I won't let it get in the way of what I'm doing."

"It already has."

"How?"

"I'm here. Talking to you."

I ignore the sting of the words. "Right. I'm sorry for the inconvenience."

"You said you wouldn't fail me."

"I haven't," I answer, sharper than I intended. I wince and bite the inside of my lip. "Not really. I'm sorry Fionnella had to disturb you, but I had things under control."

"How?" He throws my question back at me.

My gaze drops again, even though I sense that doesn't please him. But I can't bear for him to witness my shame. "I was going to find another place tonight."

"Where? And before you think of lying or refusing to answer, know that I won't allow you to leave until I have an address where I can reach you."

I glare at him. "I wasn't going to lie."

"Good."

He waits.

I purse my lips, stomp down hard on my shame. It doesn't die a complete death but it's temporarily maimed. "I was going to find a bed at a shelter for the night, then hunt for somewhere else to live tomorrow."

Thick silence pulses through the wall, feeds through the lens. I'm not even sure if he's in this apartment or this building, never mind the same city as me. And yet I feel him. Around me. Above me. Inside me.

"A shelter."

I nod.

"Remember the guy in the bar, Lucky? The one who wants to fuck you more than he wants to live? Do you think that guy would want the woman he craves to be spending the night in a shelter?"

Who is this guy? Who the fuck is he to mess with me like this?

Fuck him and fuck this bullshit.

I charge to my feet and glare straight into the blinking light of the camera. "That was a made-up fantasy. This is my life! I'm sorry if I ruined your grand plans for the evening. You think I enjoy being made homeless? You think I enjoy being tossed out on my ass without getting my money back for the rat hole I had the privilege of calling home, or some dumb fuck telling me the only way I'm going to get my money is to suck his cock?"

I know I should stop, but my last nerve is shredded to pieces along with my hope. And if all I'm going to get out of this acid trip is a waxed crotch, nice-smelling hair, and a few free meals, then I deserve to rant a little.

Because, fuck karma.

"I know I'm nothing more than some expendable commodity to you, but you have no right to call me out for doing what I need to do to survive. I said I'll take care of it and I will. If that's not good enough for you, then too bad."

My chest burns with the need for air and I realize I haven't taken a breath throughout my outburst. Several quick breaths, then I toss the brand-new phone on the table.

Thank God I didn't throw the burner away.

"Are you done?"

I raise my chin. "I'm most definitely done."

"Sit down."

I don't want to. I don't want to be led by the nose into hope again. Besides, it's way past time to get off this crazy train. "No, thanks."

"I've spent time and resources on you, Lucky. Sit down."

"Or what?"

He doesn't respond. I walk backward until my ass hits the door, keeping my hands loose at my sides. So I can what? Make a quick escape if I need to? When every single person in this place reports to him? When I need a special passcode for the elevator to go either up or down?

If things head further south than they are now, I'm fucked. But I'll remain standing for the fucking, thanks.

"Would you like me to help you with your little problem, Lucky?"

My *no* surges up my windpipe and hovers on the tip of my tongue. I pause. Swallow down the *yes* that threatens to take its place.

This was too good to be true right from the start. Had I been reading this in the paper or watching it on some shitty documentary on TV, I'd be screaming at the brainless bitch for being so gullible.

But reality is a stark, terrifying place.

"You need help, Lucky. I'm offering it. All you need to say is yes."

The fight drains out of me so swiftly and so harshly, it actually resonates as physical pain within my bones. I want to drop where I stand, hand over the life I'm fighting so hard for to somebody. Anybody.

Him.

My booted foot kicks back against the door in a feeble attempt not to give in.

But he has all the time in the world.

Whereas I can count the grains of sand left in my hourglass.

I pick up my heavy head. Attempt to shake it, but it moves in the opposite direction.

"Say it, Lucky. If you want my help, say *yes*. Give yourself to me."

My heartbeat slows to a drugged thudding. I look into the camera. "Yes."

* * *

Q

She's mine.

And now she's exactly where I want her.

Fully under my control.

PART TWO

Lucky

11

FLASHBACK

5 March 2015
The Villa

My day starts like any other, with the alarm going off just after midday and bitching from a hungover Lolita, the girl I share a room with. She's twenty-four to my twenty-one. Those measly three years are one of many reasons she hates my guts.

The other reason is because she thinks I'm standing in the way of her promotion to become one of Clay's Entertainers.

To keep The Villa's Entertainers exclusive enough to attract wealthy patrons, Clay limited the girls to a cozy dozen and instituted a fancy booking system that involved said patrons going on a waiting list. Lolita was gagging to be promoted after one of the Entertainers fell down the stairs and permanently damaged her back. Clay promoted me instead, earning me an enemy for life.

But the truth is Lolita was overlooked because she sucks at giving blow jobs and she sucks at fucking, although she's moderate at hand jobs. The one thing she does excel at is pole dancing, courtesy of some fancy ballet training she received from rich foster parents before they decided she was the wrong side of adorably nuts and tossed her back into the care system.

For the last six months, I've endured her vitriol. Recently, after overhearing her tell one of the girls that she hates my hair and intends to cut it off while I sleep, I've taken to sleeping with my hair carefully pinned to my skull and secured with a swim cap.

It's uncomfortable as hell, but so far I've woken with my mane unmolested.

I hear her moving around in the room and pretend to be asleep. My first client isn't until two, so I have time to wait for her to shower and leave before I get up.

I also have time to go over my plan, make sure every angle is covered. It's only a matter of time before Clay discovers the documents in his safe are fake. I'm one of a handful of people allowed in his inner sanctum. He doesn't know I'm aware of the existence of his safe, but that won't matter. I need to be far away from here when he connects the dots, because then he'll know I'm the only one with the answers he needs.

Answers I promised to take to the grave.

Behind me, I hear Lolita disappear into the adjoining bathroom. I peel the swim cap off my head and moan in relief as I take out the hairpins.

Once all the pins are out, I sit on the side of my bed and massage my sore scalp. This is getting *really* old. I return the cap and pins to a different hiding spot, this time in the zip-up section of Lolita's least-favorite handbag. She found three of my previous hiding spots and slashed the caps to shreds. I would be amused by her antics if I weren't so goddamn fed up with wasting precious time to go to the sports store in Getty Falls to replace them. The last time I went into the store, the cashier looked at me funny. I could tell he was dying to find out what sex toy I intended to fashion from a swim cap. I remained silent and let him conjure up his own pathetic fantasy.

I'm in the middle of laying out my outfit for the day when I hear a knock. My grip tightens around the pearl choker my client favors.

The only people who knock on the doors of the North Wing are people who don't belong in the North Wing.

The North Wing is strictly out of bounds to patrons of The Villa and most of the male staff. It's where the girls in the upper echelons of The Villa hierarchy have their sleeping quarters. The only way to access it is through a set of double doors in the East Wing, via a security coded entrance, which is also monitored by two of Clayton's bodyguards twenty-four-seven.

At this time of day, before The Villa's doors open, the only person who could be knocking is—

"What, you're too good to answer the door now, are you?" Lolita pauses in the bathroom doorway, her wet hair clinging to her damp skin, a towel draped over her voluptuous figure.

I force my fingers to release the choker and walk to the door. I gulp down my relief when I see who it is, although it's short lived.

"Hey, Ridge," my roommate greets sultrily from behind me.

The mountain in front of me barely acknowledges her with a nod before his gaze drops back down to me.

Great, something else for her to hate me for.

I stare at Ridge Mathews.

Of all of Clay's minders, he's the one that frightens me the most, and most of them are ex-military or mercenaries and pretty damn scary to begin with. They're supposedly here for our protection, but I've seen the way Ridge's eyes follow me when we cross paths. I suppress a shudder and maintain a neutral expression.

"Clay wants to see you, asap."

Six words no girl at The Villa wants to hear first thing upon waking up. Or at any time during a twenty-four-hour cycle.

In the mirrored picture next to the door, I see Lolita's expression drop from sneer to sympathetic for a split second before she catches my gaze and normal service resumes.

"Oops, has Daddy's little girl been naughty?" she sniggers.

"Shut up, Lolita," I throw over my shoulder.

She laughs, drops the towel and walks bare-ass naked to her closet. "Come find me after if you need cooling cream for your paddled ass."

I don't bother responding to her. To Ridge, whose gaze is fixed on me the whole time with an intensity that is extremely unsettling, I say, "Tell him I'll be there in twenty minutes. I need a shower."

He nods, and although his gaze doesn't skim lower, I feel as if he's stripped me naked just by looking into my eyes. I step back and shut the door, then continue to the bathroom before Lolita emerges to deliver another dose of envy-laced snark I'm not in the mood for.

I intended to take a bath before work, but I rush through a shower and don a loose sundress and cowboy boots, catch my hair in a ponytail, and slide on a touch of lip gloss before I leave the North Wing.

The Villa is a grand residence, despite its soiled reputation. A Pre-Colonial mansion built by a baron with original Deep South roots, the rambling four-story has been revamped with questionable decor but top-of-the-line contemporary amenities, including a security-coded elevator that goes straight to the basement, where Clay's office is located.

I exit to the hum of photocopiers and computers and the occasional ringing phone.

Clayton Getty treats whoring like the rest of the legitimate businesses he inherited from his father. No one has the temerity to question him because he owns every single person in Getty Falls, be it through bribery or intimidation.

To my memory, the only person who ever dared to cross him was the man I grew up thinking was my father. And he paid dearly for it.

As if conjured up from my thoughts, Earl Gilbert—the man who was married to my mother for all of five minutes before he found out I wasn't his and divorced her—emerges from the door leading into Clay's office and slows to a stop when he sees me.

"The fuck you dressed like that for?" he sneers the moment he catches sight of what I'm wearing.

"I don't start work till two. You'll just have to contain yourself for a while longer before the slutty-outfit parade comes out, *Dad*."

His one functioning eye, the one not gouged out by Clayton Getty in retribution for daring to take what was his, blazes holy hell at me. "I told you not to call me that. You keep giving me lip like that, girl, you'll see what that gets you—"

"Enough of that, Earl. Bicker with her in your own time. Lucky, get in here."

For the thousandth time, I puzzle why Earl didn't leave Getty Falls after what Clayton did to him. I can only conclude that either Clayton spared Earl and turned him into a glorified lackey as an example to others or he believes in the *keep your enemies closer* mantra.

I don't skirt out of arms' reach the way I normally do when I'm within spitting distance of Earl because I know he won't lash out at me while Clayton's within earshot. Although he hasn't done that lately even when Clayton's not around. Not after seeing the way I handled a drunken client recently. Earl knows I'm not afraid to defend myself.

Still, he eyes me with icy malice as I walk past him and enter Clayton's office.

"Shut the door, Lucky."

I obey and turn around, the tendrils of fear I felt in Ridge's and Earl's presence giving way to the real, unadulterated McCoy.

Clayton Getty is tall and broad-shouldered, his frame more suitable to a farmer or a bounty hunter than to a brothel boss. His dark brown hair is kept neat and his beard trimmed by a once-a-week stylist.

Although Clayton uses the basement of his ancestral mansion as his office, he's very much the king in charge of his empire. He swivels his throne-like chair as his gaze sweeps me from head to toe.

"Earl has a point, you know? There's a standard dress code Entertainers need to abide by, even when they're off duty."

"Sorry, Clay. Ridge said it was important." I slip out the white lie.

He stares at me in tight-lipped silence for a full minute. Then he nods. "I wanted to personally let you know that Krakov expects first-class treatment today. He mentioned the last time he was here, you seemed a little...off."

My skin wants to turn itself inside out. I barely manage to hold it together. "I...didn't feel well. I think I was coming down with a virus."

"I explained something to that effect, but he's the customer, after all. Since you're feeling better today, I think we should go the extra mile to keep him happy, don't you?"

A boulder lodges in my throat. "W-what do you mean?"

"I mean, we can start off by meeting his plane when it lands shortly before two. We'll begin to wine and dine him as soon as his feet touch the ground and we'll continue to do everything in our power to make sure his experience is *unforgettable*. Can I rely on you to achieve that?"

"Of course."

"Good. Be dressed and downstairs at quarter to two. Ridge will drive you to the airstrip in the limo."

On the one hand, I'm two seconds away from emptying the bare contents of my stomach at the thought of going anywhere near Edward Krakov. On the other, I'm giddy with relief that this summons isn't to question me about the documents I took from his safe two days ago.

I nod and hightail it to the door. I grasp the handle, taste elusive freedom.

"Oh, one more thing, Lucky."

My heart drops to the soles of my battered boots. I hold my breath, clench my features to neutral, and turn.

"My security systems shows my passcode was accessed after hours two nights ago. You wouldn't happen to know anything about that, would you?"

A touch of confused surprise. The minute gathering of a frown. Then mild affront. I've practiced it in the mirror a thousand times. "Of course not." No inflection on any vowel. A perfect, terror-steeped delivery.

The gold-plated ballpoint pen in his hand rocks back and forth. Back and forth, as he watches me. Eventually, he nods.

"Okay. That's all."

12

CONTINUITY

I jerk awake, my racing heart on fire, a silent scream locked in my throat. Two nightmares in one night is a record even for me. The first one is now chillingly familiar—the sight of Ridge's face when I shot him through the chest and watched the life leave his eyes as he dropped dead in Clayton's office.

The second one is new. It's the kind of dream I hate. The one that starts with joy and the blindingly effervescent promise of happily-ever-after, and ends with you poised on the edge of some craggy ravine, knowing in your bones you're about to fall to your death.

It's clear that the ghosts of future past and present don't intend to leave me alone tonight, so I drag my fingers through my hair, resign myself to insomnia, and slide out of bed.

The moment I rock up to a standstill, I'm hit with another bout of overwhelming disbelief.

The room I'm standing in is bigger than the great room Fionnella's team uses in the Midtown apartment. In fact, it takes up three-quarters of the whole floor of the loft. According to Fionnella, this is the smallest loft in the complex where she delivered me after my breakdown six short hours ago. Despite having lived in a mansion of The Villa's proportions, I still find it difficult to wrap my mind around this place...this space...being all mine, at least for the next few weeks.

Provided Clayton doesn't find me first.

The under-floor heating warms my feet as I wander around the bedroom.

True to his word, Q has come through in helping me.

The Hell's Kitchen property is fully furnished, centrally heated, and more importantly, stocked to the gills with food, wine, and delicacies, some of which I've never heard of, never mind tasted.

I walk across the mezzanine floor to the railing that overlooks the cavernous space below. Contemporary furniture and an extensive entertainment center divide the living room from the dining area, with expensive-looking potted plants interspersed with paintings and eclectic pieces of art. The kitchen is a gourmand's dream, and I get the feeling I won't be brave enough to touch half of the gadgets in there.

After Fionnella's departure, I left a few lights on to brighten the darker corners. I'm not afraid of the dark, but I have more than enough to be jumpy about. I'd rather not add shadows in dark corners to the list of things to be concerned about.

Leaving the bedroom, I make my way slowly down the stairs, then just stand in the middle of the living room and stare around me.

Who is this guy?

Q...

Funny, the more I think about the name I've coined for him, the more it suits the stranger behind the wall. Except he won't be a stranger for much longer.

I realize I'm not dreading meeting him as much as I thought. Whether it's because my mind has exhausted itself on the possibilities of what he could be, or whether his treatment of me so far has been decidedly less monster-like than what I've been used to in the past, I'm not sure.

Either way, I know deep down that no matter what I'm feeling right now, dropping my guard around him, at any time, is dangerous. And yet, I'm standing in the middle of a living room, less afraid than I was a few short hours ago.

And once again getting...*hopeful*.

I squash the feeling and cross over to the double-wide fridge. I want to squeal with delight at being confronted with so much delicious food but I resist the need to gorge on a little bit of everything, and take out the ingredients to make a grilled cheese sandwich. I spotted a sandwich press earlier, and five minutes later am sitting cross-legged on the sofa with my sandwich in my lap.

I take a groan-worthy bite and reach for the TV control just as a beep emits from a sleek black gadget on the coffee table. There's a blinking green light on one end. Cautioning myself not to freak out, I pick it up. Beneath the light is a command that reads TALK/ON.

With my half-eaten mouthful of grilled cheese fast congealing in my mouth, I remain motionless, and will myself not to panic. The light flashes off after a minute. Just when my heart rate is beginning to slow, and I've almost convinced myself that this is nothing sinister, the light comes on again.

I rationalize why it can't be the worst-case scenario. For one thing, Clayton isn't the type of man to toy with his prey once it is within his crosshairs. If he knew where I was, I would already be in his clutches. Therefore the only logical, please God, conclusion is that this is something else.

I push the button. The light stops flashing but stays on green.

First, I hear him exhale. My head jerks up as the sound filters through the room.

"Lucky."

I drop the gadget. "Q?" I'm getting used to the smooth automation of his voice. Whatever tech he's using must be top-of-the-line, because he sounds less robotic and more human each time we speak.

"Yes."

I look around, spot the discreet speakers tucked into various corners of the living room.

"How are you doing this...I mean, how did you know I was up?"

"I have a state-of-the-art security system that alerts me when there's movement in the property at odd hours. It's three in the morning. You should be asleep. My system thinks you're an intruder. I wanted to verify that you were not." His voice flows all around me.

I take a couple of steps back and reclaim my sandwich. The explanation is reasonable. But I'm still a little creeped out, if a lot relieved. My gaze darts around.

"What about cameras? Do you have cameras installed in here, too?"

"Only on the outside. I can give you the code to disable both if it would make you more comfortable?"

I take small bite of my food. "Can you not do it remotely?"

"Of course, but I suspect you might not believe me if I said it was done?"

I bend my head to hide my guilty flush, even though he can't see me. Or at least I hope he can't.

I swallow before I reply, "That's okay. If you say it's done, I believe you."

"Thank you."

I take another bite and chew through the silence. "I'm sorry if my moving around woke you."

"I wasn't asleep."

"Oh, okay. Can I ask what you're doing awake at three a.m.?"

"Having a drink. And reviewing your shots."

A reel of the photo shoot flips through my mind and my body heats up. The thought that he's staring at those pictures right now makes a part of me tremble, while a definite part throbs. When he remains silent, I'm forced to ask, "And?"

"And I'm very much looking forward to fucking you, Lucky."

The matter-of-fact words, spoken softly through a mesh of tech, is hotter than anything I've ever heard in my life. My body grows heavy and a little weak, and I'm glad I'm sitting down.

"You...you don't think I'm too thin?"

"We're working on that, are we not?"

I laugh and the sound is the most natural I've heard in a long time. "Fionnella is definitely single-minded about fattening me up, that's for sure."

"She's following my instructions. I want you healthy and strong. I want you to be able to keep up with me."

My gaze skids to the far corner of the room where a treadmill and cross-trainer have been set up next to a yoga mat. "Can I use the equipment in here?"

"Everything in the apartment is yours, Lucky. You don't need to ask permission."

I pause for a moment and then ask the question that's been on my mind for a while. "So where will...the gig take place?"

"At another property of mine."

"So, not the Midtown apartment?"

"No."

I release a breath tinged with relief. "Okay. That's good."

"Why is it good?"

I shrug, feel a tad foolish. "Nothing. It's no big deal."

"It is, or you wouldn't have asked."

"Just that...Fionnella is not the kind of person I want to be doing that around."

He pauses for a moment before answering. "And why is that?"

"She just seems the motherly sort."

The pause is longer. "You don't strike me as naive, Lucky. Everyone wears a mask, even seemingly cookie-baking types like Fionnella. For all you know, hers is the thickest mask of all." There's something hard and sinister in his voice.

My skin prickles. "Like I said, it's no big deal. I would've done it either way."

"Glad to hear it." His voice still sounds clipped, more mechanical.

I warm my suddenly chilled arms with my hands and rise from the sofa. "I...uh, thanks for checking on me."

"My pleasure."

"I think I'm going to head back to bed now."

"You just ate—I heard you chewing. Going to bed so soon will give you indigestion."

For an illogical second, I wonder if he's lonely and trying to keep me here so he can talk to me. But then surely a guy like him, with wealth and power at his fingertips, would have more than enough to occupy him, even at three in the morning?

All the same, I find myself sitting back down. "I guess I can stay up for a little longer, maybe watch some TV…"

"If that's what you want."

I glance at the sleek gadget sitting in a futuristic-looking cradle that could be a remote and decide against it. "Or maybe not. I don't want to set off any alarms or anything."

"Tell me what sort of entertainment you require and I'll work it from here."

A tiny bit of that creepiness whispers closer. "I'm good, thanks. I prefer to just…" I stop when I realize the wish I'd almost voiced.

"Just what?" he encourages.

My twitching fingers grasp a strand of hair and toy with it. "I'd rather…talk, if that's okay. It's been a while."

A while is more than an exaggeration. The last person I talked to…truly had a conversation with that wasn't blatantly or overtly sexual, was my mother. And she's been dead for seven years. And in the last few weeks, the only person I've had more than a one-minute conversation with is Quinn Blackwood, and everything about that man terrifies me into near speechlessness.

I refocus when I hear faint sounds of feet on a hardwood floor. He's moving around. I realize this is the first time I've heard him do something other than speak.

My imagination fires up, trying to conjure up an image just from his electronic voice alone, trying to imagine where he is, what he sees when he looks out his window.

"I'm all ears, Lucky."

"Are you here? In New York City?" I blurt before I can stop myself.

The pause is long, uncomfortably so. "No."

I'm not sure why that dims my mood, the fact that we aren't in the same city. "Are we in the same country?" I press, despite knowing well enough that I should back off.

His answer this time is smoothly forthcoming. "Yes, I'm in the States. Does that please you, Lucky?"

My laugh is entirely self-conscious. "Why would you ask me that?"

"Because I sensed your unhappiness to find me not in the same city as you."

"You *sensed* it? What are you, psychic?" I play at being amused, but my gut clenches with trepidation at his astuteness.

"I'm surrounded by your pictures, Lucky. Your face reflects your mood beautifully, your body even more so. Your voice is merely another conduit of your emotions."

"Or I could be a very good actress."

"I don't think so, but if you insist, I look forward to discovering which version is more accurate."

"I have time to practice my poker face then."

"Good luck."

Like all his words, there's a thin trace of cruelty in them. I should be disturbed. But I find myself clutching a plump cushion, and when I turn my head, I realize I'm reclined on the sofa, the T-shirt I wore to bed now resting just beneath my panty line. "So, did you...did you like all of the photos?"

"Every single one. But one in particular captured my attention."

My breath catches. I suddenly feel too hot, and I want to peel the T-shirt over my head, but I don't want to move. "Which one?" I whisper, half of me hoping my voice is too low for him to hear and the other half yearning for an answer.

"You're seated. Your knees together, feet apart. You look... conflicted. Like you're fighting something you want to give in to, but won't allow yourself."

My chest vibrates with the strength of my agitated breathing. Beneath the T-shirt, my nipples are stiff, ravenous peaks. My stomach is hollowed out, and a wholly involuntary twitch of my hips clearly outlines my bare pussy against my thin, white panties.

"There's also a touch of guilt," he continues, "as if you don't think you deserve what you're not allowing yourself to crave."

"Wow, all that in one picture? You do fancy yourself a clairvoy-
ant," I dare to tease.

I hear a clink of ice against glass. "Tell me which part I got wrong,"
he commands.

I can't, of course, so I don't answer.

"There will be no guilt when I fuck you, Lucky. No guilt, no
fighting, only your complete surrender." The statement seethes with
purpose, and I'm caught in the web of sensation so strong I experience the tiniest of releases between my legs.

My hips twitch again and I turn and bite the cushion. Hard.

Fuck.

"Do you understand?" he demands.

I blink to try and regain focus. "Y-yes." My voice is a shamelessly
turned on croak.

"Lucky?"

God, the way that electric current vibrates through me! "Yes?"

"Time to head to bed."

My gaze roves over the room, takes in the stairs leading up to the
bedroom. "I don't think I can move."

"Why not?"

*Because moving will ruin what the sound of your voice is doing to
my clit.* "I'm…comfortable right here."

"I see. The sofa is comfortable enough, but I'd prefer it if you don't
make a habit of it. Uninterrupted rest when it's mandated will ensure
your continued health."

I should be pissed that he's instructing me on where I should
sleep. But the thick river of lust moving through my body is too delicious to ruin with a fight.

I tug the folded cashmere throw from the back of the sofa and
drape it over myself before I snuggle deeper into my makeshift bed.

"Right. Noted. Thanks for your understanding, Q." Saying his
name makes me smile.

"Goodnight, Lucky." I imagine I hear faint amusement in his
voice, too.

I turn my head and search for the black box. It's still on the floor where I dropped it earlier. The green light is still on. I stare at it as languor sweeps over me.

My sleep is thankfully dreamless. When I wake four hours later, my eyes immediately zero in on the box. It's still where I left it.

But the light has gone out.

And I'm once again left wondering if it was all a hallucination.

13

PLACES

The fitness instructor is done with me by nine. The intense two-hour session leaves me weak-limbed but wide awake as I exit the Wall Street subway and make my way to Blackwood Tower.

Today, I'm feeling a little less self-conscious—but no less vigilant—courtesy of the eight Bloomingdales shopping bags that arrived on my doorstep this morning. I opened the first one to find a note from Fionnella.

As discussed, dress rehearsal for clothes begins today. Find enclosed first selection.

As discussed? First selection?

Am I that unsophisticated to need a rehearsal for clothes? My frown stayed in place all through breakfast. I was a little out of it last night after my epic rant in the apartment, but I'm pretty sure I would've remembered a discussion about a new wardrobe. My brain may be a seething mass of fear-induced knots, but I'm sure I would also have remembered a planned shopping trip to Bloomingdales on my behalf. My eventual text to that effect garnered a one-line response.

Apologies. Instructions still stand. The Boss insists.

End of story.

I tug at the scarf around my neck as I hurry down the stairs to the basement and wonder if the problems I've managed to alleviate on the outside of Blackwood Tower will achieve the opposite effect inside.

Miguel's interest has been especially sharp the past couple of days, ever since I started working upstairs. He blithely ignores my evasive answers and probes with more questions.

And sure as shit, he's the first person I see when I walk into the break room. There are a couple of kitchen guys taking a break, but one walks out as I enter, and the other is absorbed in his phone and doesn't look up when Miguel spots me and gives a low whistle.

"*Hola, chiquita.*" Dark brown eyes rake me from head to toe. "Wow, looks like someone tripped and fell out of Vogue Magazine today."

I ignore him and attempt to walk past him. He grabs my wrist, his hold surprisingly rigid as he examines the label of my new black, waterfall-styled coat.

"*Valentino...*" He frowns as his speculative gaze moves from the label to my face and back again.

Panicked, I snatch my wrist so hard from his grasp I know it'll leave a mark. *Shit.* "You don't ever touch me without my permission, Miguel. *Ever.*" There's anger packed into every millimeter of that hushed sentence.

He raises his hand and steps back. "Cool it, sweet thing. Was only trying to compliment a lady, 's all."

Every instinct screams at me to walk away, but I see the questions swirling in his eyes. I need to defuse this new interest before it mushrooms.

I grind my teeth against the lies I need to tell to protect myself. But I have no choice. I can aggravate Miguel, or I can continue being laconic in the hope that he eventually gets the hint. Although from the way his eyes drop from my face to linger on my tits, I don't think that day is coming soon.

"It's...the coat...is a fake. And I have a thing after work. That's why I'm dressed like this."

He nods. "Like I said, we're cool. You could've just said that."

I notice he doesn't apologize for grabbing me. I choose not to inform him that the last man who touched me without my permission ended up with a bullet in his chest. In fact, I stash that memory firmly into the *don't go there* box and head for my locker. I can feel his eyes on me. When I look over my shoulder, I swear he's aiming his phone camera at me while pretending to be absorbed in it.

Jesus.

I quickly turn back around and grab my work gear. As I peel my clothes off in the changing room, I examine each label and my mouth drops open. *Valentino, Ferragamo, Balenciaga, Forever 21.* My new leather boots are stylish but look fairly standard. Until I check the label.

Manolo Blahniks.

My heart sinks further.

Shit.

Shit. Shit. Shit.

After the fitness instructor left this morning, I hit the shower and dressed in a hurry, knowing I needed to hustle or be late for my shift. When a quick examination of each bag revealed an entire ensemble, I thanked the Lord because I didn't have to waste time coordinating outfits. I just threw on the jeans, top, and coat in the first bag, dragged on the boots, and left.

The thought that I may have inadvertently painted a bull's-eye on my back through carelessness steadily claws through me for the next two hours as I finish laying tables and sorting condiment baskets in the Executive Restaurant. Once that's done, I take a quick break, then return to wait on the side of the counter for the chef to finish preparing Quinn Blackwood's lunch.

Even the thought of seeing him again doesn't erase the naked flame of terror at what my carelessness could cost me. I listen with diminished attention as the chef rumbles through the intricacies of serving the CEO's meal. I nod through it but have forgotten most of it by the time I wheel the trolley through Quinn's frosted double doors.

He's seated at his desk, as usual.

His gaze snaps to me the moment the door shuts, and stays riveted on me. As usual.

By the fourth or fifth step, my legs threaten to give way beneath the gravitational power of his stare. Nothing new there either. I arrive at the dining table without mishap, but still a little lost in my head.

"I thought we agreed on the general etiquette surrounding entering a room?"

My God. His voice.

It's deep, cultured, oiled with class and money and power and glory. The kind of voice that stops you in your tracks, that makes you want to throw your softness at his hardness, bruise yourself on his attention.

The complete compulsion of his voice and stare swivels me round to face him.

"I'm sorry. Good afternoon, Mr. Blackwood."

He recaps his black ballpoint pen and sets it down with a precise action. His eyes never leave my face. "Good afternoon, Elly."

I turn around and start laying his table. I know the moment he rises and walks to the front of his desk because the air thickens with awareness.

"Have you had lunch yet?" The same question as before.

A different answer today, courtesy of a text from Fionnella during my break to say she won't be feeding me this afternoon. "No. Not yet."

"Set a place for yourself."

I freeze for a moment, then curb the turbulent rush of emotion. "Ah, no thanks. I'm good."

I'm so attuned to him, I know the moment he straightens and heads toward me. His aura slams into me long before the spicy sandalwood of his aftershave wraps around me. "I hate to disagree with you, but no, you're not good."

I'm dying to look up into those piercing silver-blue eyes, but I fear it'll be my undoing. So I transfer dishes from trolley to table and check that the requisite distances are achieved. "I don't know what you mean."

"Have you been ill recently, Elly?"

The question surprises me enough to make me abandon my vow not to look at him. I meet electric eyes that trap mine for a second before raking over me. "No...I haven't."

"You don't like food, is that it?" he drawls. "Is that why you look so...breakable?"

"No, I love food."

He nods. "So, it must be me then?"

"You...what?"

"The idea of eating with me fills you with horror?"

My eyes widen. "I...no."

"Then set a place for yourself."

Sitting opposite him while he eats, waiting to collect his dishes is one thing. Despite the alarming intensity of it, it's what I'm paid to do. Eating with him, tasting the same food he's putting into his mouth...

I shake my head. "I can't."

He takes a single step toward me and I'm drenched in his substance. Today, he's wearing a navy suit with a navy shirt one shade deeper. A black pinstriped tie, black belt, and polished dress shoes complete the stunning ensemble. On his wrist, a streamlined silver watch gleams. We're still outside, arm's length of each other, but he may as well be binding me in ropes. Such is the power of Quinn Blackwood's force field.

He rests a hand flat on the table, next to his plate. "Whose name is at the top of the building, Elly?"

"Yours?"

"Then I believe that buys me a little sway in what goes on around here, don't you?"

"I guess."

"You guess?"

"I mean, yes, if you want to play that card."

"I don't want to play that card. But I will. Unless you tell me why you won't eat with me." His voice is conversational, but there's steel in there. Steel wrapped around six foot two of live electricity.

"I don't think it's appropriate. That's all."

Another step, and I can see the silver flares sparking the blues in his eyes.

"Look at the dining table, Elly, there are twelve places. Do you think I use all twelve places at once, all the time?"

"Of course not."

One more step. I lose the ability to breathe.

"What do you imagine I use it for then, if not to play musical chairs when no one's looking?"

My mouth twitches before amusement drops dead in his presence. "Business lunches."

He lifts the last dish from the trolley and places it on the table. Then he picks up a spare plate and cutlery and strides to the opposite end of the dining table.

When he's done laying it out, he pulls out a seat, just like he's done the last two times I've been here. "So, let's you and I have one."

"A business lunch? Why?"

"To air any grievance you might have."

"I don't have any."

"Either I'm doing something very right, or you're lying. I believe it's the latter."

I'm lying about a lot of things, but I don't like it pointed out. "You don't know me well enough to make that assessment, Mr. Blackwood."

"Don't I?" He whispers the two words in a way that sends a shiver over me. That deathly stillness that excited and frightened me the first time I laid eyes on him slides through the air, freezes us both in place.

We watch each other, his gaze never straying from its rigid focus on my face. Although his eyes…

God. There's something in there, something deep and dark and mercilessly horrifying. But whereas before it felt like an all-encompassing outlook, this time it's spotlighted on one thing.

Me.

"No." I use the word, but even I doubt the veracity of it. With each second in his presence I feel his stare like a paring knife beneath my skin, opening me up from the inside out.

"Then give me a chance to," he says. His large fingers glide slowly across the top of the dining chair. Then he grips the sides until his knuckles whiten. "Sit down, Elly."

* * *

Something happens between the moment I sit in the chair and when he places my food in front of me. It's almost like a switch has gone off inside him.

Conversation dries up and he's no longer interested in pursuing the imagined grievance he wanted to discuss.

The dinner of seared Wagyu beef strips on a bed of Caesar salad is cooked to perfection, but I barely taste it as I struggle to chew and swallow each mouthful.

All the simple but engaging conversation pieces I used on clients at The Villa to get them to talk dry up as I look up halfway through the silent meal to find his gaze locked on my wrist. Specifically, the courtesy-of-Miguel finger-marked bruise circling my left wrist.

His gaze moves from the bruise to my face.

His eyes are a thousand white-hot blades spiking into me.

I swallow wrong. My fingers fly toward my water glass.

He calmly sets his cutlery down, his meal abandoned.

I gulp more water. I chose water for the simple reason that I need a sharper-than-ever handle on my mental faculties. The consumption of alcohol was encouraged at The Villa during work hours, but I witnessed its ill effects on both clients and girls often enough to stay away from it.

But now I wonder if I should've asked for a glass of the Bordeaux Quinn poured for himself. The Bordeaux he's sipping now as he watches me.

"Grievances. Let's hear them." The question is clearly not one he wants to discuss. His gaze keeps moving back to my wrist. Each time the look in his eyes tips the volatility scale further toward what I imagine insanity looks like.

I glance at the door, wondering if I'll make it out in one piece. I haven't had a drink, and yet I'm tipsy with the sheer volume of high-octane emotions racing through me. "I don't have any. Honestly."

His hand closes around his wine glass. He picks it up. Sets it back down. He lays his palms flat on the table. "Hmm. And what about your coworkers? Are they grievance-free too?"

I try to shrug. My shoulder refuses to cooperate. "I don't know. I haven't been here that long."

"Perhaps a visit is required then, to stare into the whites of their eyes, as it were. Judge their contentment, or lack thereof, for myself."

"Surely you have people to do that for you?"

"A team of them."

I push a piece of beef around, before I spear it with my fork. "There you go. You can get them to put together an anonymous poll for you."

He considers my response for a second. "There are things I don't mind delegating. This isn't one of them," he breathes.

His gaze hooks into me again. Then my wrist.

God. He's serious.

My mind flies through the possible outcomes of the CEO visiting the basement three days after I start working for him. None of them are good. Aside from the personal attention it'll spotlight on me, there's Sully. I'm not sure how he's squaring away paying me in cash, but the last thing I want is scrutiny on him.

"Please. Can you not do that?"

His left forefinger taps on the table. I wonder if it's a grounding mechanism of some sort. "You don't want me to find out whether or not my employees are happy?"

"You can do that…without making a personal trip down there. When was the last time you went down there, anyway?"

"I've never had the privilege."

"But suddenly you want to? I've been serving you for three days. There's no way your visit won't make them think I'm some sort of…snitch."

"And the idea of being labeled as such distresses you?"

"Of course it does. Wouldn't it, you?"

A single tic flicks past one cheek, a ghostly sliver of a smile. "Are you asking me for a favor, Elly? Are you asking me to care about your comfort?"

The question is weird. Quinn Blackwood is, hands down, the strangest person I've ever met. He's also electrifyingly handsome and frightening enough to make me wonder how I'm still in one piece.

"I know I have no right to—"

"On the contrary, you have rights. Perhaps more than you know." Again softly spoken words, as if he doesn't want to spook me with whatever he's suppressing.

"Thanks. So, you won't come down there?"

His gaze refocuses from the middle distance of wherever he retreated to. Then it finds mine. And my leaping heart tells me I'm about to become intimate with the abyss.

I watch him rise from his seat, move toward me with measured, predatory strides that remind me of a sleek jungle cat. He stops next to my chair, and I have to raise my head to meet his eyes. My racing pulse is now screaming and I have to stop myself from full-out panting. Or bolting out the door.

He reaches out in slow motion, as if whatever his intentions are, he wants to draw them out for as long as possible.

His fingers find the back of my unbruised right hand. I flinch and gasp from the sizzling sensation. Something shifts in his eyes. A confirmation. Acceptance. Then his lids drop. He stares at his flesh touching mine. Tracing a tiny vein to my wrist and back again. His nostrils flare slightly before he closes his hand on mine and turns it palm up. Again, he traces his fingers over my palm. The sensation is a thousand times more potent. Lust and fire and the need to be fucked hard rush through my blood. My pussy clenches so hard I feel my juices wetting my panties.

He makes a sound and it jerks right through me. One finger rests on my wrist pulse as he raises his gaze and stares at me with stark, devastating hunger.

"I won't come down there, Elly. But you'll owe me."

14

HIATUS

Quinn Blackwood doesn't tell me exactly what I owe him. And I'm too chicken to ask. I leave his office in a deeper daze than ever before and lock myself in the bathroom as soon as I get a chance. For the first time in my life, the temptation to masturbate is born out of frenzied frustration rather than the adolescent curiosity that briefly gripped me before Mom died and my life went to shit.

I sit on the close-lidded toilet, rest my head against the cool tile, and, eyes closed, drift my fingers over my palm where he touched me.

I shudder, and the ball of fire between my legs threatens to rage out of control.

God.

My body is being prepped to fuck another man starting next week, and yet, I'm lusting after Quinn with a need that is beyond insane.

His face slides into my mind's eye and a moan slips free. Slowly, I open my legs and slide my hand underneath my panties. The force of need nearly sends me shooting off the toilet seat the moment my finger touches my engorged clit. Gasping, I glide my hand lower, to my blazing center. I'm hotter than a furnace and wet enough to feel my slickness on the inside of my thigh.

Getting myself off will be as easy and satisfying as jumping off a cliff. But a part of me resists. An innate knowledge that it won't be as satisfying as I imagine prevents me from succumbing to the need. I resort to massaging the outer lips of my pussy while trying to breathe through the terrible hunger tearing me apart. My brain finally relents and transmits the message to my cunt. Hunger recedes far enough for me to tear my eyes open, adjust my clothes, and stumble out of the stall.

The rest of the afternoon passes without incident, and I make it back to Hell's Kitchen in one still-dazed piece.

At seven, Bruce, my fitness trainer, returns to put me through another ninety minutes of hell. When he leaves, I strip and take a shower, luxuriating in the endless hot water and thankful that I'm too exhausted to tend to the dull ache still throbbing between my legs.

I dress in a brand-new set of lounge pants and top, and I'm on my way to the kitchen when the doorbell goes.

Before alarm takes full hold, I cross to the security screen and turn on the outside camera.

Fionnella.

I release the lock and wait for her to walk through the double set of security doors. Once the last one closes behind her, I open the front door.

Her hobo purse is slung over one shoulder, and she's clutching a large brown bag with a logo I don't recognize.

"Have you eaten?"

"No, but I was just about to make myself a sandwich." I can cook a few basic meals, but I'm no culinary expert by any stretch of the imagination, so having a fridge stocked full of food is a blessing but also a curse. Although I planned to make something other than grilled cheese or pasta this weekend, using a cookbook I discovered among the plethora of reading material in the loft.

She holds out the takeout bag. The aromas that waft from it are heavenly enough to make my mouth water. "To make up for the confusion over the clothes," she says.

I open the door wider with my right hand and reach out to take the bag with my left. Her gaze falls to my wrist. It hasn't gone purple as I feared, but the distinctive yellowing is clearly visible. Her gaze sharpens.

"It's nothing," I blurt, but my heart sinks at the resigned look on her face. "Please don't tell him."

She enters, shuts the door behind her, and regards me with a touch of sympathy. "It doesn't work that way, Lucky. If there's a situation we need to know about—"

"There isn't, I swear."

She reaches into her bag and pulls out her clipboard. "Give me the CliffNotes. I can't promise one way or the other how this will go. But I have a job to do, same as you."

"And that includes bothering him with something this minor?" I gripe.

A flicker of something hard in her gaze reminds me of Q's warning that not everyone's as they seem. "CliffNotes, Lucky. Who. How. When."

"Today, at work." I stop and grimace. "My new clothes attracted a little more attention than I expected. That's all."

She nods in understanding, but her gaze doesn't waver. "I'm waiting for the who."

"It's a guy I work with. Miguel. He's pretty harmless," I toss in hurriedly.

She finishes her notes and pulls out her phone. "Go eat."

"Fionnella…"

"The food's getting cold, Lucky. It's your favorite. You'll want to enjoy it while it's still hot."

She waits until I make my way to the kitchen before she retreats to the glass and brick wall at the far end of the living room. I plate the burger and fries and watch from the corner of my eye as she dials and presses the phone to her ear. Her voice is too low for me to catch her end of the conversation, but I don't need to. The slight ding in The Boss's one-million-dollar body has been duly reported.

The sanguine smile is back on her face when she joins me in the kitchen. We go through the next few days' schedule while I eat. Then she makes me stand on a scale in the bathroom for my weighing. She catalogues my five-pound weight gain with another bright smile, after which she promises to be in touch soon, and leaves.

He's going to call. But I don't know when, so I distract myself by trying to work out the elaborate TV/entertainment center controls.

I finally figure it out and I'm watching reruns of *The Big Bang Theory*, when the black box flashes green.

My heart climbs into my throat. I debate ignoring it. On top of the subject I don't want to discuss, I recall our conversation last night. My body is strung up on the attraction I feel for another man. I don't know if I want to add Q's brand of electronic hotness to my crazy right now.

But what choice do I have?

I slowly reach for the box. Before I can touch it, it flashes off. I jump back, relief and disappointment mingling through me. Five seconds later, the flashing resumes.

I pick it up and press the 'on' button.

"Were you thinking of not answering me, Lucky?" His voice flows around the room, like a living entity. "Think carefully before you answer."

My fingers curl around the box. "Yes, I was."

"Thank you for being truthful. Why?"

"The bruise is nothing. I didn't want it to become something."

"That's not for you to decide."

My shocked laugh is tinged with more than a touch of exasperation. "Excuse me?"

"Small fact you should know about me. Everything I own is precious to me. Everything I own is unequivocally mine, until such time as I choose to dispose of it. Everything I own I maintain in pristine condition. Do I own you, Lucky?"

My exasperation stands no chance beneath his obsidian power and the inevitability of my answer. "Yes," I whisper.

"Once again. With conviction. I need to know you've embraced the reality that I own you."

"Yes," I repeat. I toss the box on the sofa and take childish pleasure in glaring at it. "Yes, *you own me!*"

Silence seethes for several heartbeats. "Are you in pain?"

I'm not expecting that, nor the different cadence attached to the voice. He's just callously labeled me an object. A possession to dispose of eventually. Rich people don't care about the suffering of mere mortals.

And yet, he ensured you didn't end up in the shelter... or worse.

While my emotions sigh with gratitude for that, my brain holds back, cautioning me that everything happening to me could still be a twisted game in some rich man's fantasy.

The man I've labeled Q is a stranger. Until we come face-to-face and I'm able to assess him otherwise, he needs to remain that way, no matter how he makes me feel.

I tuck my feet beneath me on the sofa, noting absently that somehow the TV has been muted. "In the grand scheme of things, compared to what your fitness instructor put me through today, I'd say the pain in my wrist is a piece of cake."

"You think it's the same? Pain deliberately inflicted and pain endured for the purposes of honing your body?"

I frown. "Of course not. You just... I was trying to explain... okay, I get it. No, it's a bit uncomfortable when I touch it, but I'm not in pain. Can we get off the subject now, please?"

"We can. I have a prior engagement to attend to. If you would be so kind as to ensure I don't have to make another call like this, I would appreciate it."

The box turns black before I have a chance to respond. Or thank him for the clothes. Or just... enjoy the sound of his electronic voice.

I'm completely deflated.

When the TV miraculously unmutes again, my enjoyment in my favorite show is nil. I flounder on the sofa for another hour before I drag myself to the double bookshelf at the opposite end of the room. I halfheartedly settle for a psychological thriller that promises high jinx on a pirate ship and take it up to the bedroom.

Although I try to blank my mind and immerse myself in the story, I lose interest by the second chapter.

Two streams of conversation play through my mind, each with its own unique brand of mind-fuckery that sends my thoughts spinning.

I jumped out of the frying pan because my very survival depended on it.

But the fire licking at my heels might just consume me because the craving inside me, one that has grown without my even realizing it, has me locked in its terrible hold.

15

EXPOSITION

Q

I rip the voice distorter and the connecting earpiece from my face and crush the delicate tech in my fist. One piece of it breaks through my skin, but the pain doesn't register. It's buried far too deep beneath the Everest of deadly rage.

Striding to the trashcan next to my desk, I open my hand and let the fragments fall. Turning my hand over, I see three bright spots of blood dotting one finger. I rub at it with my thumb, smear it across my palm. All too soon the capillaries close up, my body's natural defenses rushing to seal the wound. Regret flickers like a heartbeat on a monitor before it flatlines. My gaze traces up my bare arm to the almost invisible scar on my inner elbow.

The doctors did a fine job. But they were instructed on pain of death to leave no evidence. Not even for me to find.

But at times like this I don't need a visual aid to feel the scar. It pulsates with a life force of its own, an open invitation to lose myself. To surrender to permanent darkness.

I reject the invitation, close my fist, and lay it on my desk. The other hand falls flat beside it. The strains of "Vissi d'Arte" fill my head. I count the sequences off one by one. Over and over.

Sweat pebbles my skin, drips down my face and neck and onto my bare torso as I count, my finger tapping faster and faster. But the dull roar in my head doesn't abate.

It started the moment I saw her wrist. That blemish, there on her skin, was nearly my undoing.

My true undoing came the moment I touched her. That flame, searing and illuminating ... hurt. It awakened. And alarmed.

Enough for me to contemplate giving in to the compulsion to end it all tonight, *now*. It writhes through me like a coiled snake, striking, ripping poisoned holes through me I make no attempt to stanch.

The temptation is overpowering.

But this isn't how it ends.

I can't let him get away with it.

I drop, drained, into my chair and stare into the gloom. In the near darkness my gaze finds her picture on my desk.

Mama.

Smiling. Always smiling. Trusting. So trusting.

I take a breath and it moves through me like a rejuvenating tide. Or as close to one as a soul existing in a vacuum can experience.

Except I didn't feel that way this afternoon with Elly. Not when she stared at me with defiance and surrender. Or when she begged me to draw her deeper into my obsidian web. The vacuum shifted then, attempted to make room for fuck knows what.

I don't want her soul. I have no use for her heart. Or her feelings. But her body is mine.

And she dared to withstand it being, hurt...marred. To brush it off as nothing, the skin I've touched, the skin wrapped around the body that will bring an orchestral ending to a decade-long plan?

I surge to my feet, once again fully enveloped in my most comfortable suit of moral bankruptcy and scalpel-sharp focus.

No, not quite scalpel-sharp. That edge was dulled today courtesy of bottomless green eyes and a plump, quivering mouth that just begged to be fucked.

I thought my focus was back. But the conversation ten minutes ago...

The poison is acid-sharp, eating at my control.

I need something specific. Something to take my mind off Lucky. And Elly.

XYNYC is closed on Wednesday nights. I think about the Punishment Club, the underground club Axel opened five years ago. It's most likely where I'll find what I need, but I don't think it's a good idea tonight. For one thing, I don't want to spend time hunting my prey. If I choose wrong, my state of mind will get worse.

For another, the Punishment Club is in Hell's Kitchen, a defiant three blocks from the loft where I stashed Lucky. Letting myself into her space and bringing everything to an end isn't a scenario I've mastered ruling out.

With my immediate respites out of the question, I reach for my phone.

Adriana Nathanson answers with a groggy, "Hello?"

"Your office. One hour."

"Quinn? It's...ten o'clock at night."

"That early, huh? Make it half an hour then." I hang up, stride through the apartment to my bedroom, and pull on a black tee on top of my black chinos. A battered leather jacket to keep out the chill and a quick detour to the bathroom to throw water on my face and clean the blood from my palm before I head out. I activate the valet app on my phone and my DB9 is waiting for me by the time I exit my building.

"Have a good evening, Mr. Blackwood."

I hand the valet boy a fifty and slide behind the wheel. Traffic is thankfully light and I reach Adriana's office with five minutes to spare.

She must have alerted her office security because I'm escorted up to her office and let in by a security guard. I pace until the click of heels sends me to the door of her office.

She sees me and stops in the middle of the hallway. Her gaze rakes over my all-black clothing and she takes a nervous breath without moving.

"Why, Adriana. Don't tell me you're afraid of me?"

A single shake of her head. "You're not violent. Not that way, anyway."

I'm not sure why that soothes me, but it does. "Are we going to conduct this session in the hallway?"

"So you're serious? You really want to talk?"

"Either that, or I want to fuck you up the ass. I haven't quite decided yet."

Her eyes widen and light up with suppressed excitement before her gaze drops. "Maybe we can do…both?"

I laugh. "You'd like that, wouldn't you? For me to send you back home to dear old Stanley with a sore ass and a heart brimming with fulfillment for all the good work you've done? Tell me, how is the darling husband doing these days?"

She resumes walking toward me. "Quinn, if you dragged me all the way here to toy with me, be warned, I'm not in the mood." The practiced sway of her hips beneath the wraparound dress she has on contradicts her words. I don't care enough to point it out.

I turn sideways for her to precede me into the office. She stops and stares up at me.

"Something's happened," she muses quietly. "What is it, Quinn?"

"Inside. Now."

She walks in, and I shut the door. I decline the drink she offers, cross the room, and drop into the sofa. Both hands spear into my hair and I search for words.

"You're right. I'm…affected."

"It's understandable, seeing as your father's back in the city—"

"It's not him. Well, it's not *all* him. But he's being a good demon for now and staying in his allotted box."

"Then who is it?"

"Names aren't important." I don't want to mention her name here, even the names that I know are fake. Not in this place of sickening filth and half-baked healing. For the first time, I wonder what her real name is. Where she's from. I catch myself and return Adriana's stare. "All that's important is how to get rid of it."

"Rid of what? What are you feeling?"

"The need to succumb." I say. My voice is barely a rumble. But with the time of night, and the quiet of the office, she hears me.

Her gaze moves over me. To the side. Down my arm. "Are you self-harming again?"

I silently commend her for not beating about the bush. She's in full shrink mode, and I realize I need that.

"No. That's not what this is about. Besides, harming implies an ongoing situation. Mine wasn't. It was a one-time thing."

"But you said you'd been thinking about it for a while before you did it, so there was forethought."

I shake my head once. "That's not what this is, Adriana. Trust me."

"Okay. Tell me in what way this person affects you, then."

Her image rises up. Defiant. Gorgeous. Fucked-up. Utterly fuck-able. Dangerous. I shrug. "They're poking holes in my black spaces."

"And this distresses you?"

"Hell no. I'm distressed for them."

"Why. Do they matter to you?"

I pause a second before I answer. "There's a potential they might fall through my cracks. I don't need the collateral damage. I thought I didn't care. I'm still not sure that I do. But it's…affecting me."

"Maybe consider cementing your cracks first? Put off involving this person in your situation just yet?"

I think of my fingers touching her satin-smooth skin, the white-hot flame on my desolate landscape. "It's not that easy. I'm already invested."

"Have you thought about setting yourself a hard limit?"

"It could be too late." I have a feeling it's already too late. For Quinn, anyway.

Q is another matter.

"Only you can decide by which point the investment will begin to lose its value. You're not afraid of making tough choices, Quinn. But you also enjoy the buildup of chaos. That has been one of the things you've refused to tackle. Maybe now is the time to start?"

"Timing's not good for me. Come up with another solution."

She sighs and sits back. "The only other alternative is to let them see who you are. Give them the choice to walk away. But I don't recommend that."

"Why not?"

"Because people see what they want to see. And because you're especially skilled at getting people to walk down a path they may not necessarily want to go but are unable to stop themselves from taking."

"Are we still talking about just me here, Dr. Nathanson?" I smirk.

Unease flits over her face. "I'm serious, Quinn."

I shrug. "So your solution is to save this person from my sociopathy before they hurt themselves through their own choices?"

"This isn't a game, Quinn. You wouldn't have woken me up at this time of the night if you weren't worried—"

"Seeking clarity doesn't equate with worry."

"Then let me be clear. Until you take steps to fix what's wrong with *you*, you're putting *them* in danger. You probably know this already, but have convinced yourself you don't care. But what you need to ask yourself is, do they deserve it?"

The stillness descends on me. It stops everything, including the roar.

I wanted clarity.

I've got it.

Will the demons let me keep it? Will the weight of my destiny let me even contemplate it?

I stand and walk over to her window. Down below, traffic on Lexington Avenue trips on as usual.

Through the reflection, I see Adriana stand. She hesitates for a moment before she makes her way to me. Her hand touches the middle of my back. No higher. She knows what that will earn her.

"I miss her too, Quinn. She was the best of all of us. That's why I want to do everything I can to help you heal. I know if anything were to happen to you, Adele would never—"

She gasps as I twist around, grab the hand on my back, and use it to propel her against the window. My hands close over her arms, and I lift her slight body up until we're face-to-face.

"Do not fucking speak her name, do you hear me? I don't want her name to ever pass your lips again. Not because she was your best friend and you *miss* her. Not because she made you my godmother, but you've taken delight in sucking my cock since I came of age. Do. Not. Speak. Her. Name. Because you know what happened. You were fucking there. And you did *nothing*."

Her face goes as white as the walls in her office. "Quinn, please—"

"Shut the fuck up. I don't want you to say my name, and I don't want to hear your excuses." My hiss is low, deadly enough for her to understand I mean business.

Her mouth snaps shut. I take a minute before I release her.

The roar is back. I want to slam my head against a wall to drown it back out. Instead, I shove my hands in my pockets.

"Goodbye, Adriana. I'm going out of town for a while. I'm not sure when I'll be back. Sorry about the lack of ass-fucking. I probably would've accommodated you, but you blew it by reminding me just what type of human being you truly are. I'm sure you'll find someone else to accommodate you in my absence."

Her face contorts. Before she can open her mouth, I'm headed out the door. I don't look back.

She knows better than to call my name again.

Back in my car, I pop the key in the ignition but don't start the engine. My fingers wrap around the steering wheel, eyes closed with my head against the seat rest. For endless moments, I'm lost.

The hate, the vengeance, and sex are instruments that oil my existence and keep my compass true. But thinking about her...my mother...always casts me adrift.

She was the purest thing in my life. The truest. A delicate flower in a nest of vipers. Her love was the closest thing that came to making me wish I was a better person. For her, I like to think I would've striven to be a less diabolical version of myself. Her every look once held that promise, that hope for me. And somewhere along the umbilical that connected a mother's love to her son, a seed dared to sprout inside of me. Until it was mercilessly destroyed.

A fragile seed in a nest of vipers. Adele Blackwood had had no hope.

The burning in my chest spreads wide, upward, past my throat, my nasal passages, to settle behind my eyes. I swallow the rancid taste of bile and let the black grief engulf me.

I should've done more. I should've saved her.

But you didn't.

My eyes fly open. I release my death grip on the steering wheel and start the engine. I drive aimlessly for an hour until I end up exactly where I shouldn't be. Hell's Kitchen. I park across the street and stare at the building.

The lamps she left on emit a soft and welcoming glow, the opposite of what I'm feeling right now. The opposite of what she'll feel if I let myself in and let hell break free.

Hell's attraction grows as I sit there, my engine idling. Without taking my eyes off the large square window, behind which my perfect poison lies, I hit the call button on my steering wheel.

"Yes, Boss," Fionnella, my homely ex-government operative and trusted team leader, responds. She's been with me from the beginning; is the only one who knows Q's identity and what the end game is. She also has a horse in this race, which keeps her motivated.

"Would you believe me if I apologized for calling you so late?" I inquire. Up above, I swear I see Lucky's shadow cross the window, but I accept my mind is in full chaos mode and could be making shit up.

"I believe remorse may have crossed your mind for a second, sir."

"If that counts, I'd appreciate an update."

"The only update since we spoke this evening is the results of her blood work. No surprises to report. She's healthy. Yours came back clean too."

My cock, pleased with the news, stirs and twitches. I relax my head against the seat and cup my dick. My last memorable fuck was a twenty-four-hour bender with a Latina spitfire three weeks ago. She'd welcomed my darkness, and things may have gotten a little out of hand, not enough for me to lose every shred of sanity, but close enough.

The clean bill of health brings a spike of impatience. "I need pros and cons of moving the schedule forward by a week."

"The setup at the property will be finished in forty-eight hours. The crew-vetting should also be done by Monday. Her birth control shot will be fully effective from Saturday."

"All pros."

"The cons depend on whether you intend to stay put for a while once you get to the property. She doesn't have a passport and her fake ID is the worst I've seen. Even a tenth grader would spot the flaws a mile away. She's not naïve, so I can only conclude she was desperate enough, for whatever reason, to accept the first one she came across."

My cock thickens, and I breathe out. The part of me that should be ashamed for getting hard at the thought of her desperation is blissfully bankrupt enough not to get in the way of my hard-on.

"If I need to take her out of the country, can you organize it?"

Fionnella sighs. "Of course, sir. But I'd appreciate as much advance notice as possible. I trust the people I work with, but I'm never comfortable with stuff to do with photos. Too much room for error."

"You'll have your notice."

"Thanks."

I hang up, pull my gaze from the window, and ease my foot from the brake pedal.

Lucky may well fall through my cracks, but I intend the experience to be nothing short of memorable.

16

TAKE TWO

Fionnella's text to me on Friday morning is the first warning that the dress rehearsal is over.

A driver will fetch you at seven p.m. Be ready. Please ensure all the relevant ties are severed with discretion.

I read and reread the text, wondering if she believed me about Miguel. Perhaps she thinks we're more than just coworkers? But the message makes me think of what to tell Sully. Granted, he never intimated his job offer would be permanent. He helped me out when I was in need. There will be a dozen others to take my place within a day.

But as I near Blackwood Tower, it's neither Miguel nor Sully who occupy my mind. Today will be the last day I serve Quinn Blackwood. Will he invite me to lunch again, or will he request just coffee, like he did yesterday, instruct me to serve it at the coffee table in front of the sofa in his office, and drink it while sitting far too close to me?

Even now, I recall the brush of his thigh against mine; the sandalwood and male musk that flowed from his skin. The way his lower lip curved on the cup, his strong throat as he swallowed.

He still hasn't asked me for the favor I owe him. And he won't get the chance after today. The thought produces a spike of regret that unnerves me more than I know is wise to allow.

It's enough to make me contemplate a different scenario for myself. One where I return to Blackwood Tower in a month's time, and ask Sully for my job back. But then in a month, provided the shit show of variables fall into place, I'll be too busy finding a way to talk Clayton into sparing my life in return for one million dollars to think about Blackwood Tower. And I'll be trying to do all that with Clayton without placing myself anywhere in his orbit.

Or divulging the secret that's locked tight in my heart.

Provided I manage to jump all those hurdles, then yes, I might give returning to Blackwood Tower and asking for my job back a try, so I can go back to lusting after its unattainable and questionably unstable CEO.

I half-snort as I change into uniform for my last day. Miguel is nowhere to be seen, which is a little surprising, but I secure my locker and head for Sully's office.

The middle-aged man listens to me, a thoughtful frown in place, and shrugs when I'm done thanking him. "It's no big deal. What I did for you, I hope someone else would've done for my kid. I'll have a job on my hands to get someone for Mr. Blackwood though. He seems taken with you."

My heart skips a beat. "I don't think so."

Sully smiles. "You know how many times the man's had lunch in his office since he took over from his father three years ago?"

I shake my head.

"Far less than you think. And certainly not every day for a week like he has this past week."

"I...I don't think that was because of me."

"Don't sell yourself short, Elly. The best things come in small packages. Or so my wife tells me." He waves me away. "Go on, now. Make the best of your last day. And don't forget to come pick up your pay when you're done."

The morning rushes by, probably because time, like the rest of my life, is determined to give me the finger, and before I know it,

I'm standing in front of Quinn's frosted doors. His EA, a sylphlike brunette with an expression as neutral as Switzerland, aims a remote at the door to release the lock.

"He's not in yet, but he's on his way up. He wants you to proceed as normal."

I start to nod, but she's already re-engrossed in her task. I wheel in the trolley and unload today's offering of sushi and accompanying dishes. I'm setting down the crystal goblet containing bluefin tuna topped with Osetra caviar when I sense him behind me.

"Elly. Hello."

I swallow and turn around. "Hello, Mr. Blackwood."

Eyes as bright and deadly as the sun rake me up and down before they settle on my mouth. "Call me Quinn, please. *Mr. Blackwood* is a man who has the unhealthy habit of wanting to make his employees do things they may not want to," he divulges in a stage whisper, sexy and pulse destroying.

My breath reacts accordingly. "Things like what?" I ask before I can stop myself.

He half-turns and throws his coat over the sofa. "Things I deem wise not to introduce before lunch, in case it turns your stomach."

"I'm not delicate."

For some reason, that reply invites that terrifying deathly stillness. Only his eyes move. He tracks my lips to my racing pulse. From my breasts to my hips to my feet and back up.

"Do you know how I feel about you, Elly?"

I actually gasp in shock at the unexpected question. "I…no, I don't."

He nods, as if we're discussing the price of Kobe beef. "That's fortunate because I don't know either, save to admit that every time I hear you speak, every time you look at me, I want to reach for that cheap garment that has the audacity to lay against your perfect skin, rip it off your body and spend a considerable amount of time doing terrible things to you. So I'm most relieved to learn you're not delicate."

The latent power behind his words, the fierce focus propels me back a step. My hip bumps the dining table. "You can't."

He strides forward, his gaze merciless. "Mr. Blackwood *most definitely* can. Quinn undeniably wants to. But he's prepared to listen to pleading arguments."

"Do you often think of and refer to yourself as separate entities?"

A whisper of a smile threatens to transform his face, but a stronger force, a frightening force, devours it before it can live. "My shrink probably thinks I am. She finds me…challenging. In fact, she may have had a hand in this little vignette."

My eyes widen. "She told you to tell me what you want to do to me?"

"She advocates laying one's cards on the table. The only card I'm interested in right now is the *I-want-to-fuck-you-blind* card. And since you're not running screaming out the door, perhaps her idea has merit, after all?"

Blood rushes through me at the speed of lightning. My tongue is so thick in my mouth I have to maneuver my jaw before I can speak. And each word I'm about to utter feels like it's riveted with spikes. "Mr.…Quinn, I'm sorry, but today's my last day."

He doesn't blink. "Your last day."

I swallow hard and nod. "Yes, I handed in my notice this morning."

"Why?"

My teeth worry the inside of my lip while I fight to maintain eye contact. Looking away will rat me out. "My position was never permanent and I…I need to take some time off for personal reasons."

"So, let me get this straight. You resigned this morning?"

Thoughts of being fucked by Mr. Quinn Blackwood recede a bit as panic flares. "Yes."

"I see."

He relieves me of the napkin I forgot I was holding and places it on the table. When his fingers wrap around mine, that flare unleashes harder but this time with a whole heap of lust. He escorts me to his desk and pushes me into the seat before it. He remains at my side as he hits a number on his phone.

"Mr. Blackwood, how may I help you?" a nauseatingly responsive female voice inquires.

"Nancy, can you tell me if this company has abandoned the notice-period-before-employment-termination clause?"

My breath slams out and stays out.

"No, Mr. Blackwood. The handbook clearly states the minimum of two weeks for junior employees and a sliding scale upward for senior employees."

"Illuminating as always, Nancy. Thanks."

He disconnects and leans against the desk, ankles crossed, thick arms folded as he stares at me. "Someone has dropped the ball downstairs. Would you care to enlighten me as to who that person is?"

Ice and lust and panic and the urge to kick my own ass, hard, fight for supremacy. I shake my head, both to dispel the forces, and to buy myself some time. There's no way I'm throwing Sully under the bus, but all it'll take is a simple phone call for Quinn to find out who hired me.

"I...don't want to get anyone into trouble."

"I feel as if we've had a variation of this conversation. Very recently."

I purse my lips but silence won't do me any favors right now. "Please, Mr. Blackwood."

Heat flares in his eyes. He remains silent for a full minute, before he stands. "Come."

He leads me to the dining table. The special containers holding sushi and the tuna on ice have done their job in not ruining lunch on top of everything else. Quinn doesn't seat me at the opposite end of the dining table this time. He sets one place at the head of the table and motions me to sit.

Wracked in trepidation, I take a seat. He takes the seat next to me and picks up the delicate fork, heaps up a mouthful of caviar-topped tuna and presents it to me. This room, this man, even the food has an insane effect on me. I open my mouth and take the morsel. Heavenly flavors burst on my tongue and I want to close my eyes and die at the bombardment of sensations inside and out.

As I'm chewing, he reaches into his jacket and takes out a business card. Or what I imagine is a business card. It's black with gold numbers on it, which he slides across the table to me.

"Do you have a phone?"

I hesitate. Technically, the phone in my possession is for a specific purpose, which I'm sure doesn't include the scenario I'm mired in right now. So I should say no. "Yes."

He waits.

I reach into my pocket and retrieve it.

He holds out his hand and I place the phone in it. A few taps later, a phone on his desk rings. He cancels the call and hands me back my phone along with the card.

I return them both to my pocket. The near silence of the whole thing fascinates and terrifies me.

Quinn's lids descend as he arranges another perfect mouthful. "Prior to today, you owed me...*something*, didn't you, Elly?"

"Yes."

"So now, you owe me something plus two weeks." It isn't framed as a question. I owe Quinn Blackwood two weeks.

"I can't give you two weeks. I have to be somewhere else."

He raises the fork again, feeds me another mouthful. "For how long?"

"A couple of weeks. Maybe three. I can't get out of it."

"Then we'll make a deal, Elly. You go do your thing that you can't get out of. Maybe I'll call you at some point, maybe I won't. Either way, when you're done with this thing, you come back here and give me two weeks."

"You want me to come back and work for you?"

"That is to be decided. After all, I'll have a couple of weeks, maybe three, to work out exactly what I want from you."

"What if I don't come back?"

He takes his time to feed me another mouthful, before cold blue eyes hook hard into mine. I have no doubt that the terrifying Mr. Blackwood is in residence. "If you don't come back, Elly, every single one of the sixty-eight people working down in your precious basement will be fired."

17

LIFTOFF

The windows at the back of the limo are tinted. Which is a good thing, because the fewer people to witness my meltdown reaching critical mass, the better.

For the last hour, I've been repeating three mantras under my breath:

One million dollars.

Save my life.

Keep the secret.

Each time a silent fourth reverberates at the back of my head.

Deliver yourself to Quinn Blackwood.

His threat wasn't idle. Not when he could buy a new set of catering staff once an hour every day for a year and barely feel a pinch in his wallet. But he was determined to make me see how serious he was. The chopsticks barely delivered the piece of tempura to my hungry lips when he added, "And I'll start with Sully Manning."

I give in to a hysteria-tinged chortle as the limo crawls through traffic. We left Hell's Kitchen at the stroke of seven. Besides a courteous greeting, the driver curtailed any attempt at conversation by putting up the partition in the limo, thereby sealing me in my moving luxury-padded cell. I lasted fifteen minutes before I texted

Fionnella to find out where the driver was taking me. She's not answering.

The first inkling of where I'm headed comes when I spot the signs for an airport. But it's not JFK or Newark. We're headed toward Teterboro Airport.

I've heard a few clients from The Villa refer to it so I know it is a private airport.

The hairs on my nape prickle to attention.

Airport means security.

Security means a name popping up and getting flagged on a database. Fear, hot and acrid, floods my insides. I claw for the abandoned phone and stiffen my shaking fingers long enough to call Fionnella.

This time, she answers. "Everything okay?"

"No! We're headed for the airport. I can't fly. I…I forgot my ID back at the loft."

"Don't worry, it's been taken care of."

My gut ices over. "What does that mean? You took my ID from the loft?" I've only used it once since I arrived in New York and that was to prove to Sully that I was over 18. We both knew it was as fake as the Elly Smith name printed on it, but he let it go. No way will it withstand a TSA check. I'll be in handcuffs before the scanner is done beeping.

"No, Lucky. Breaking and entering isn't my forte. What I mean is you're not leaving the country, so you're good."

"But…won't my name appear on some manifest of some sort?"

"What name?" she counters.

I fall silent.

"Exactly," she murmurs.

"Are…are you sure?"

"I'm sure."

The knot in my stomach dissipates a little. I remind myself that a lot of time and work have gone into getting me here. That my choices are abysmally limited. I can't trust anyone. But backing out is not an option right now.

"Okay. Can you at least tell me where I'm going?"

"That is not part of my brief. If the boss wants you to know, he'll tell you himself."

"Fionnella—"

"Piece of advice, Lucky. Don't sweat the small stuff or the things that are out of your control. You chose to do this. Your reasons are your own, of course, but if the end game is important to you, learn to surrender to the journey. It's the only way you'll come out the other side intact. Have a safe trip. And try the grilled shrimp when you board the plane. They're to die for."

She hangs up, leaving me with even more questions than I started the conversation with. I don't have time to dwell for long. The limo slowly weaves through an area peppered with private planes and pulls into a brightly lit hangar. It stops a dozen feet from a white-and-gold G650.

My jaw is too paralyzed to drop, and I stare at the aircraft as another boatload of *WTF-are-you-doing* punches me in the face.

"Miss? We're here."

I manage a nod, force my feet to move, and step out. I look at the driver. His face is politely neutral and I know I won't get any answers from him. Nor from the attendant and pilot waiting at the foot of the airplane steps.

I clutch my backpack and put one foot in front of the other.

"Welcome aboard, Miss." The pilot doffs his cap.

"Thanks."

"If it's all right with you, we'll be taking off in the next fifteen minutes."

I swallow a snort. We're taking off whether I freak out or not. We all know this. But it's cute how they make me feel as if it's up to me.

Silently, I climb up the steps and arrive in a different world. The Midtown apartment, the Hell's Kitchen loft, the makeover have all been indicators that Q is extremely wealthy. But the undeniable luxury of the private jet finally drives home to me the potential scale of what I'm dealing with.

If a man like Q has the power to buy me without once meeting me in person, he has the power to do other things. Like make me disappear.

And really, aren't those who fall through the cracks, or make an attempt to hide, easy prey to a ruthless predator?

My senses clang and I turn around. Before I can make a dash for the door, the steps lift and slide home, sealing me in the world's most expensive tube.

Panic cloys through me.

"Wait!"

The pilot bolts the door and turns. "I'm sorry, Miss, but we have to take off now or we'll miss our slot."

I eye the shut door. "Open the door. Please, I have to get off."

His eyes remain steady on mine. "I'm sorry. It's too late."

Although I hear the whine of an engine powering up, courtesy of the co-pilot, I know the pilot isn't just talking about the door. My thudding heart echoes the message in his gaze.

Somewhere in the last twenty-four hours, I've crossed an invisible line into the point of no return. Q may have chosen me a week ago, but everything that has followed has been a further test.

A test that I've passed, if the sudden ramp-up of activity is any indication. And now he's decided, there's no going back.

"Take a seat, Miss. The attendant will be along shortly with your pre-flight drink."

He heads off to the cockpit, and I hear the definitive click of the door.

I turn around. The attendant is pouring a glass of champagne, but I sense her attention on me. I have no doubt if I attempt anything foolish, like opening the door to the airplane, she'll be on me in a second. I can probably take her, but then what would that mean for me?

At least one thing is certain. If I don't make it out of whatever this fucked-up situation is that I've got myself into, Clayton won't get his hands on the secret. My fingers tighten around the handle of my backpack.

As I release the lock on my legs and head for the cream leather sofa in the middle of the plane, I let my fingers drift over the secret compartment I sewed into the bottom of the backpack. Perhaps it's foolish to carry the letter and document Ma gave to me. But it's only one half of the puzzle. I memorized the other half before I burned it in the hope that it'd buy me further time should Clayton catch up with me.

Thinking about him weirdly settles my panic. The fire I jumped into after escaping him hasn't consumed me yet. So while I still have breath, I still have hope.

... *surrender to the journey.*

I set the backpack aside, buckle myself in, and hold my breath for my first-ever ride on a plane.

Soon after a slightly dizzying takeoff, I accept a glass of champagne and the offer of grilled shrimp.

True to Fionnella's promise, the shrimp is divine. As is the pâté served on crackers and the mini burgers and accompanying sweet potato fries. When I return from using the lavatory, I curl up on the sofa and stare outside the window.

Geography fails me again, and with the outside shrouded in night, I have no clue where we're headed.

I try to blank my mind to what lies ahead so I accept another glass of champagne. A few sips in, I notice a subtle difference in taste, but really, what the fuck do I know about vintage champagne?

The bubbles are pleasantly tingly and the alcohol is easing the stranglehold fear has on me. I take a few more sips, and stare at the light blinking on the jet's wing.

It grows strangely hypnotic. I'm not sure if we dip, or if the swaying is just in my head. I try to take another sip, but my limbs feel heavy, lethargic.

My eyelids droop of their own accord. Just before they shut, I see the attendant lunge toward me.

Oops. I just dropped the glass.

* * *

A dull headache throbs at my temple. It's not bad, but it's uncomfortable enough for me not to want to open my eyes in case there's more pain lurking at my periphery.

Also, I sense sunshine. And wherever this headache stems from, I know it won't be a fan of bright lights. So I keep my eyes shut, breathe through it, and attempt to orient myself.

The limo. The airport. The plane. Champagne.

I'm hungover? From one glass of champagne? Or had it been two? My mind gives up on unraveling the hazy memory and moves on.

I'm in bed. The scent of crisp sheets and sea air register through my slightly foggy senses.

But how did I get here? And where the hell is *here*?

I suck in a breath and crack my eyes open. Yep, wall-to-wall sunshine. A bed wide enough to sleep a football team and a room large enough to accommodate their fans.

I drag myself onto my elbows, kick away the comforter, and glance down at myself.

The clothes I wore to the airport are gone. I'm wearing a crisp white T-shirt and my panties. No bra.

My heart lurches and I feel sick. I close my eyes and concentrate on the part of my body that would surely know if it has been violated. I feel nothing untoward. I don't allow myself to be relieved just yet.

I shift to the side of the bed. Besides the need to ease my bladder, I'm hoping a self-examination will enlighten me as to whether I've slept molest-free.

I emerge from the jaw-droppingly stunning marble-and-slate bathroom five minutes later none the wiser. A quick search for my things leads me to a dressing room. All my clothes and shoes from the loft are hung and arranged in neat rows. My backpack is in a small closet and a dressing table is set out with makeup and new accessories.

I grab a pair of lounge pants, slip them on, and return to the bedroom. Heavy, half-closed curtains conceal floor-to-ceiling windows on both sides of the room. I push one aside and peer outside.

Dark sand-and-pebble beach gives way to an unfettered view of water. Although the sun's shining, the dark-colored water makes me think we're still in the East. But the truth is I don't know.

Dropping the curtain, I turn and examine the room. The cream and gold decor is studded with expensive art and chandelier lamps that reek of elegance and class. It's everything an exclusive whore purchased for a million dollars would want.

Except this whore can't shake the notion that she was drugged and brought here so she wouldn't know where she is.

Insides beginning to quiver, I hurry across the room and throw the bedroom door open.

The soft exhalation that emits from a nearby speaker freezes me to a stop the moment I reach an arched hallway.

"Lucky. You're awake. Welcome to my home."

18

KANSAS, NOT KANSAS

My head jerks around, although I know it's highly unlikely Q would reveal himself if he's still choosing to talk to me through his speakers.

"Your home?"

"One of many, but yes."

I continue down the hallway, noting that he has a serious love of art. Each of the three properties I've seen so far has had a masterpiece or ten dotted around the place. I reach the landing and stop.

"Where exactly am I, Q?"

"You're here, with me. At last." His voice is low and throbs with enough anticipation for me to reach for the steadying support of the banister. He may have possibly drugged me to stop me from finding out where he's brought me, but his voice still does disgustingly filthy things to my insides.

"You know what I mean."

"How would knowing where you are change anything? You're not thinking of running, are you?"

I can't deny that the thought didn't cross my mind when I was in the bathroom. "I just want to know, that's all."

"All you need to know is that you're safe and will be well cared for while you're under my protection."

"And does your protection include *drugging* me? Because that's what you did to me on the plane, wasn't it?"

"Lucky—"

"Please. Tell me the truth."

Silence throbs for a minute. "You were given a light sedative to help you relax."

My heart lurches. "Why?"

"To calm you. My pilot reported you were slightly…agitated."

Anger ramps up my spine. "So your answer was to knock me out?"

"It wasn't supposed to. But combined with the alcohol—"

"It still wasn't okay."

"You were never in danger."

"That doesn't matter." My free hand slices into my hair in a futile effort to calm the soup of emotions bubbling through me. "This situation isn't a normal one for me. But as fucked-up as it is, I want…I *need* to be able to trust you on some basic level."

"I understand."

"Do you? Really? Somehow I find that hard to believe."

"Why is that?"

"I can't help thinking you're the type of guy who just takes what he wants."

"I am. But I never take by force. I haven't harmed you in any way, have I?"

I laugh. "So what was last night? A little harmless drugging between employer and employee? What happens the next time I have a complaint?"

"You will be reminded of what you agreed. Your body, your acquiescence in return for a million dollars." There's an edge to his voice, blades sliding into place.

But I can't let this go. "That didn't include being drugged. I'm most definitely not on board with that. And I want you to admit that it wasn't okay."

He remains silent for a long time. My gaze darts around the space, searching for where the speakers are hidden. I don't find any. It's like he lives within the walls.

His soft inhalation drifts out before he speaks. "That was not okay. You were only meant to sleep for the duration of the journey, not pass out for eight hours. Accept my apology."

My breath expels the relief locked in my chest, although there's a lingering sense of incompleteness in the apology. "Thank you. I accept."

He exhales. "I will resume full ownership now, Lucky."

My heart begins to race for another reason. "Okay."

"Good. Go downstairs. The kitchen is to your left. Your breakfast is ready."

Releasing the banister, I walk down a sweeping grand staircase carved out of solid light oak.

When I reach the bottom, I look around me.

The place is grand, the type of house you see in dynastic sagas on TV. Only with a contemporary decor and high-tech touches. For instance, there's a camera built into the chandelier that hangs in the magnificent foyer. And the same tablet-like panel set into the wall upstairs is fixed next to the double doors leading outside.

I take the left hallway and arrive in a chef's dream of a kitchen, complete with a double pantry.

On the breakfast island, fresh coffee, five types of juices and smoothies, bagels, and condiments in all flavors are laid out. Domed dishes reveal fluffy scrambled eggs, eggs Benedict, and sliced sausages.

My stomach somersaults with pleasure but I pause in the act of reaching for a warm plate.

"Are you here, in the house with me?"

"Not yet, but I'm on my way."

My heart joins in the circus trapeze act. While it tussles with my stomach, I grip the plate and contemplate another quandary.

"Eat, Lucky."

My gaze roams the kitchen until I spot a blinking light above the fridge. "You can see me."

"Yes. Something else is worrying you?"

I nod. "If you're not here, then who put me to bed last night?"

"Someone I trust."

That holds no reassurance value for me whatsoever, but I nod again and pick up a warm bagel. Spreading it with thick cream cheese, I bite self-consciously into it, stop myself from wolfing it down like a rabid animal. I finish off with orange juice and I clear my throat.

"Will you be staying here, in this house, with me?"

"In another wing, yes. But we'll only see each other when we fuck."

My breath stalls. I'm reminded that I'm not wearing a bra when my sensitive nipples form pellets against my T-shirt. I casually cross one arm across my breasts and lean my elbow on the island.

"Can I ask you something?"

"Go ahead."

"You're going to a lot of trouble to remain anonymous. So does that mean this…production isn't for your exclusive use?"

"Will it matter to you one way or the other?"

My head drops a little. I've sold my body for the better part of five years, not just to put a roof over my head or food in my stomach, but because I had no choice. From the moment I was born, Clayton Getty laid claim on me and there was no way I could've escaped Getty Falls if fate and felony hadn't greased my way out. But performing sexual acts was done in private, my humiliation saved for the depraved eyes of the paying client. The thought of performing in front of a camera, the act immortalized in a digital time capsule, threatens to send my breakfast back up.

"It…it shouldn't matter, but it's hard not to think about it."

"I can't help you with that. The very nature of what you're doing should prepare you for what you think is the worst-case scenario."

My breath shudders out and I nod.

I carry my plate to the sink and reach for the tap.

"I have people to take care of that, Lucky."

"Yeah, but they're not here, are they?" I yank at the tap and a torrent of water hits the center of the plate, sending it out in a drenching fountain. My front is soaked and heat rushes into my face. "Dammit," I mutter.

"I need you to stop being agitated."

"And I need to do *one little thing* for myself." I grab a rinse cloth and mop the countertop.

"You're not in control here."

Plate abandoned, I turn and glare at the camera. "You think I don't know that?"

"You need to accept it."

"Why?"

"Because I don't want to spend valuable time breaking you in."

My mouth drops open for a fistful of heartbeats before I clench my teeth. "I'm not a fucking dog."

"No. You're not. What you are, is wet."

A soft, deadly purr of sexual anticipation, his voice acts as an electrical conduit, charging straight through the camera to my body.

I knew my T-shirt was wet, but while I was arguing with him, it was a distant awareness. Now, I look down and nearly groan at the clear outline of my breasts, nipples, and stomach in the transparent cloth. My arms rush to cover myself.

"Stay." The command is low-voiced. Irrefutable. Exactly like a man to his pet dog.

I should call him out on it.

Instead my arms drop like leaden weights to my side. My nipples furl harder, the knowledge that they are under zoomed-in scrutiny charging them to painful, engorged points.

"Put your hands behind your back, Lucky."

My fingers find and interlink behind my back without more than a fleeting thought from me. His commands minutes ago were offensive, even though a part of me thrilled a little in anticipation of seeing him try to break me.

But right now, caught in the tense, explosive silence, I'm his to do with as he pleases. Because the sheer headiness of what is happening here is indescribable.

My breaths emerge in shallow pants. I can barely hear him over the racing of my heart.

"Are you turned on?"

"Yes."

"You see how satisfying it can be for you to let me have my way?"

My fingers twitch, but not with the need to cover myself. On the contrary I want to cup my breasts, relish the pleasure surging through me.

When I don't respond, he continues. "You have beautiful tits, Lucky."

"Thank you," I murmur.

"I look forward to fucking them."

More heat pours up my neck. A sound emerges from hidden speakers. I'm not sure if it's a groan or a grunt but it's deep and affected.

"I have to go."

Disappointment spears through me and my hands drop back to my sides. "Okay."

"The staff will be there at ten. They have my instructions. Work with them, please."

The faint buzz cuts off and I know he's gone. I sag against the sink, a little deflated, then alternately shocked and annoyed at myself. I tell myself it's because besides Fionnella, Q is the person I've spoken to the most in the last three weeks. But even more than that is the truth that I'm looking forward to what will happen tonight.

I'm looking forward to meeting the man who's paying me a million dollars to be his whore on camera.

* * *

Inevitably, the staff includes a fitness trainer and chef. The latter I don't mind at all. The former has me sweating and whining within minutes of the hundred crunches I'm required to do beside the pool. Turns out he's a yoga instructor too, so I'm stretched through numerous positions before he finally sets me free. I limp back inside and stop in awe once again. This place is beyond words.

I discovered the library next to the great room after breakfast. The room, complete with vaulted ceilings and a roaring fireplace, reeks with history. The great room is equally breathtaking, with silk wallpaper and two grand chandeliers that illuminate three groups of seating areas, each with a relaxation theme that invites guests to linger. The full tour on this side of the property yielded a fully self-contained guest house, a spa and cabana attached to the pool, a theater room, and wine cellar.

But a set of double doors behind the grand staircase was locked. And if the NO ENTRY sign above it wasn't clear enough, a seriously intimidating electronic panel next to the door convinced me to stay away from what was evidently Q's domain.

At four, the third member of the staff, Stephanie, knocks on my bedroom door. I assume she's a cross between a housekeeper and my personal stylist, because she enters wheeling a clothing rack, a portable massage table, and more grooming products.

I'm freshly showered and once she sets up, I lie on the table. The full body scrub is heavenly and the massage that follows equally divine. But the descent of the sun over the water and the unrelenting thumping of my heart signal the approach of something that has my insides in knots.

Finally, unable to stand the tension, I ask the question bursting on my tongue. "Is he here?"

"Yes. The boss arrived an hour ago. He's with his team."

I swallow. "Is he…is there any instruction for me?"

Stephanie indicates I turn over, and when I do, she rubs divine-smelling gel up my calf and over my thigh. Her fingers dig in with expert massage and I suppress a groan.

"He wants you in the wing at six."

Two short hours from now. Hours that pass quickly as I'm primped and prepped. Once Stephanie is done covering the birthmark on my thigh with a little concealer, she informs me that the boss has chosen the russet-colored lingerie, together with nude hose and garter set for tonight. I put it on without fear of messing my hair because it's been styled in simple wavy curls that hang down my back.

Russet-and-gold stilettos snugly cocoon my freshly pampered

feet, and on my wrist and throat, touches of expensive perfume scent the air with each heartbeat. My ensemble is completed when Stephanie steps forward with a stunning necklace and matching earrings.

"Are those real *diamonds*?" I stare at the single row of gems that circle the necklace.

"Of course."

Shocked laughter bursts from my throat. *Of course.*

The laughter dies when she steps back and examines me from head to toe. "You're ready." She hands me a floor-length silk robe.

"As I'll ever be." I belt the robe and follow her to the door.

19

We walk in silence to a small elevator I didn't see earlier on my tour. She inserts a key and when it slides open, she smiles at me. "You go alone. See you tomorrow."

I step inside, feeling like a gladiator at a Roman arena just before the steel gates rise up to spit them out to face their doom.

Except, I'm nowhere near gladiator-strong. My limbs are weak as kittens and my legs shake so hard, I fall back against the elevator wall. Only to immediately straighten because I don't want to risk staining the robe, or anything else that has been picked for this first meeting.

When the car stops, I step out into a dark carpeted hallway and immediately notice this place is as different from the rest of the house as night from day.

For one thing, there's tons of rigging. It begins at the door and runs along the walls both at waist and overhead level. Then continues along on either side of the darkened hallway and disappears into a room on the left from where a loud hum of electricity and machines emits.

The hallway ends before another set of double doors. They swing open before I reach them, and I step into yet another fantasy world. The decor in this section is bolder. Red and gold blend with mahogany. Darker Italian marble stretches across polished floors and expert stone masonry provides a backdrop for more stunning works of art.

My clicking heels draw to a stop at the counterpoint between two sweeping staircases, and I wonder just how big this place is and whether I'll ever be found if I manage to get lost.

I turn in a full circle. It's only then that I notice the cameras. Small, discreet. Some are rigged onto very thin cables. Others are stationary and blended into the decor.

But present. And numerous. And all trained on me.

Self-conscious in the extreme, I turn back to the stairs.

"Come upstairs, Lucky."

It's absurd that an electronic voice can grant me reassurance, but it's exactly the impetus I need to take the right set of stairs.

The royal blue carpet muffles my footsteps, but I arrive at the top without falling on my face. There are unlit hallways to my right and left, and another shorter, illuminated hallway in front of me. I follow the lights and arrive in front of an open door.

I step through and stop.

The bedroom is unapologetically male. The imposing bed is made of steel and wrought iron. The sheets are black, the carpet a deep burgundy. There are several other items of furniture dotted around the room. A chaise by the window. A rocking chair that is in no way meant for an aging man sits next to another commanding fire-place. A long, blood-red spanking bench with a matching ottoman is set against one wall. And at the foot of the bed, a backless double scroll-sided seat with a majestic and intricate design so beautiful, my breath catches. The plump seat is made of pure black silk, but it is the bronze carvings set into the arms that have me striding forward.

Halfway there, a scent fills my nostrils. Smoked cedar, a hint of sage, and the unmistakable musk of predatory male. I lose sight of everything else but that scent.

My gaze darts around the room, seeking shadows where he could be waiting.

Watching.

I come up empty. If he means for my anticipation to ramp up, he's succeeding. I make a full one-eighty, but I'm alone in the bedroom.

Alone with a dozen cameras. Now that I know what they look like, it's easy for me to pick them out, even though the ones in here aren't lit red yet.

Some are suspended overhead, two are fixed to the headboard. More blended with the furniture. Most of them are trained on the bed.

A soft whining sound behind me refocuses my attention. I look over my shoulder to see the doors swing shut.

"Your performance is about to begin. Do the cameras make you nervous?"

Duh? "Yes."

"If you can manage it, try to forget they're there."

I nod. "Okay."

"Remove your robe. Let me see you."

Shaky fingers pull the ties securing my robe. The silk slides off my shoulders with the barest movement and pools on the floor. I slowly sink down, pick it up, and lay it on the bed.

"There's a blindfold on the table next to the bed. Go and get it and return to the end of the bed."

I step back from the seat and locate the blindfold. It's set next to a huge lamp on a wide teak bedside table. My strides are slow as I obey the instruction.

The blindfold is made of heavy black silk. Although there's a bow design attached to one string, the two sides end with a metallic clasp design that would prevent accidental loosening. I run my fingers over the soft material, which is already warming in my hand.

With a firm hold on it, I return to the scroll seat.

"Sit down, Lucky."

I take the seat, rest the blindfold on my lap. The lights in the room dim a fraction, but the one directly above me brightens, throwing me into soft spotlight.

One camera slowly descends from the ceiling and stops a foot above my head. The blinking red light tells me it's recording my every blink. Every breath. I struggle to contain my nerves and stare straight ahead.

I remain like that for a good five minutes, before I see a shadow frame the closed frosted bedroom doors.

He's tall, broad shouldered, well-muscled. That's all I can tell from the hazy silhouette. My pulse takes a turn from jumpy to frenzied.

"Put the blindfold on. Secure it tightly. Then rest your hands beside you, palms down."

The thought that he's going to deny me sight further unsettles me enough to make me hesitate. I glance down at the blindfold, then back at his shadow.

"Do as you're told." A harder command that demands my obedience. It's also dangerous enough to trigger a state of excitement. But the warmth of the spotlight reminds me that I'm on a stage. That the cameras are picking up any signs of disobedience.

I only win this game if I play my part right. As much as I want to see the man who has been so expert at taking control of my emotions, I haven't come all this way to fail now.

I lift and place the blindfold over my eyes.

Immediately, my remaining senses scream with awareness. His scent is sharper, the soft air filtering into the room rushes louder. The black silk comes alive, each expensive thread leaping beneath my fingertips. My only deprived sense is a taste of what's to come. In anticipation, saliva floods my mouth.

But with all these sensations come a heavy dose of trepidation.

This is happening.

In front of cameras.

Apprehension eats away at the excitement. The trembling starts at my feet, works its way up to my knees. Seconds later, my whole body is engulfed.

And that's when I hear the soft parting of the doors.

He's here. In living flesh. Right in front of me.

My throat moves in a nervous swallow almost of its own accord, and my head jerks as I try to home in on him. But nerves have crossed to full-blown alarm, and he's uncontainable. He's all around and inside me. My rapid breathing is a whisper away from hyperventilation. Between my hands and the silk, a light coating of sweat forms.

The rush of blood through my veins grows into a roar, and the belief that I'm about to pass out becomes real.

"You're trembling." He's right above me, large and powerful and domineering.

"Yes." My response is a shaky mess, the blackness behind the blindfold seeming to thicken, even though rationally that is impossible.

"Are you afraid?"

I swallow hard. "A little," I lie.

"Of what?"

"Of the...unknown."

"Do you think I'll hurt you?"

I start to shake my head, but the naked truth slaps me in the face. "I don't know. Will you?"

A brief pause. "Would you like me to lie to you, Lucky?"

"N-no."

"Then I'll tell you I don't know either."

There's a note in his voice. Twisted tendrils of acceptance, regret, and elation at a state of being. My breath strangles.

Before I can form a coherent response, or think of a way to defend myself against the dark anticipation, I feel a drift of air, a shift of power from towering to enclosing.

He's in front of me. Like, right in front of my face.

"But I haven't forgotten your concerns. I may not succeed, but I'll do my best not to breach them."

I suppose I should be grateful for the consideration. But the dark delight and animalistic hunger in his electric voice—how come he still sounds like that when he's right in front of me?—warns me gratitude might turn out to be a useless commodity.

Another unstoppable tremble races through me. My thoughts disjoint as I wait.

Wait.

But he's in no hurry. His prey is caught. Hypnotized by his presence alone.

"You're beautiful." A heavy, unbiased compliment. A statement of pure ownership.

My breath is gone. I don't need air. Not right now. Not when he's so close I feel his body heat. Feel his breath when he speaks.

"I...thank you," I croak.

"I'm going to touch you, Lucky."

"Okay," I whisper.

The pads of two fingers drift over my collarbone along the line where the diamond necklace nestles.

My first flesh-to-flesh connection to Q.

I gasp at the raw, gritty sensation that simple touch yields. He slowly explores one collarbone and then moves, unhurried, to the other.

"I've dreamed of touching you like this. Feeling your pulse beat beneath my fingers. I've wondered what your skin would feel like."

"Now...you know," I whisper.

"Now I know, I want to taste it, lick every inch of it."

Equal parts desire and fear quiver through me. Desire because I want to be tasted. Licked. Fear because he still sounds like a sexy automaton, a fallen angel trapped in a machine. I can also hear the tiny whirrs of the cameras, can feel the lenses moving over my skin, documenting my every breath.

I'm a whore for his immediate pleasure, and will be a whore for his voyeuristic gratification for all eternity.

Suddenly, I'm grateful for the blindfold. It affords me a protection I know is only in my mind, but I welcome it just the same. Whether he had me wear it for that purpose or another, I'm grateful for it now.

I take my first complete breath since he entered the room. I focus on his fingers as they move back and forth, back and forth on my skin. Each slide sends sizzling heat to my nipples and clit.

"I've waited a while for this. So I won't stop at just tasting and licking. I'm going to devour you. Make you wet and wring you dry. And I'm going to do it many, many times, Lucky." Power and purpose and unfettered lust pound through his voice.

I have time to take one more breath before Q pounces.

20

8MM

Strong fingers sink into my hair. His grip is firm. Unbreakable. A tug that tilts my head back, exposing my face, jaw, and neck to the spotlight I feel burning into me.

"You're mine."

"Y . . . yes."

His thumbs graze gently over my cheeks as he angles my face this way and that. "Every inch of you belongs to me," he breathes.

The terrifying finality of the statement ratchets up my every emotion.

I feel another shift of air and the whirr of cameras as he rises, his hands still locked in my hair. Rough fingers gently massage my scalp.

"Open your legs."

My knees part. He moves between them, bringing his essence and magnificence even closer. He tilts my head farther back, secures me with one hand. With the other, he sets a trail along my jaw, my throat, pauses at my pulse, before drifting over my shoulder to clasp my arm. I sense him bend forward.

His smoky cedarwood scent intensifies. My belly quivers when his breath whispers over my face.

"I'm ready for your lips, Lucky. Are you ready for mine?"

The tingle that seizes my mouth is immediate. The russet-red gloss applied on them in no way alleviates their dryness. I slick my tongue over them. "Yes."

A low laugh, tinged with a whisper of the sinister. "I don't mean those lips, honey. Those can wait. The lips I crave are between those gorgeous legs." He takes a step back. "Stand up."

I totter to my feet. A little disoriented and drunk with heady emotion, I sway. He doesn't steady me. My arms flail for a second before I gain my feet. The impulse to reach forward, touch him, fires through me. But I intrinsically know touching is out of bounds until he gives me specific permission.

Or maybe I don't want to find out if he's human or not? I curb the absurd thought and bring my hands to my sides.

His hands land on my shoulders, trail down my arms to the tips of my fingers before he sets me free. I sense a huge height disparity between us. He must be thinking it too, because his next words, over a foot above my head, are, "So small. So fragile."

I shake my head, a spark of rebellion firing. "I'm not—"

"Shh. Hush, my little pocket firecracker. Take off your panties."

Using the back of the seat as my compass, I slowly turn around. I sense him take another step back. The immediate whir of the camera makes me think they operate on motion sensors. I try to block them out as I hook my fingers into the French shorts and peel them over my hips, but the sound grows until I can't block it out.

My fingers stall, one corner of the panties over my hip, the other below.

"I'm waiting, firecracker." There's a tense warning in his voice.

I swallow and force myself to keep going. I lean forward to step out of the scrap of silk and the scent of warm skin fills my nostrils. I'm not sure which parts of his body I'm closest to, but I know he's less than an inch from my face.

The knowledge lances me with craving, hot and fierce. My panties drop. I carefully step out of them, but I don't want to straighten. I want to lean farther forward. Taste him.

"Found something you want?" Q asks, his voice lending further fire to my heated core.

"Maybe," I whisper, my own voice weak.

"You have to wait, Lucky. Until my craving is seen to. Do you understand?"

You're not in control here. He said that to me in the kitchen this morning over the simple washing of a plate. I know it's a thousand times more so in this room.

"I do."

"Sit back down. Hands on the chair. Open your legs."

I obey.

"Open wider."

My knees part until the sides brush the seat and I'm exposed. Soft air rushes over my core, touching and attempting to cool the wetness forming there. Heat flares up my neck and into my face.

"Your pussy is beautiful, Lucky. So pretty, I almost don't want to spoil it. But it belongs to me. It's *my* property. So I'm going to desecrate it. You know that, don't you? I'm going to smack, eat, and pound it sore. Same with your ass."

I gulp in air. My thigh muscles quiver, but I'm unable to form words in the face of the powerful imagery he creates, so I remain silent.

He drops to his knees. "But first, I need my kiss. Lean back."

I slowly relax my body until the top of my back touches the end of the bed. I've been in a few positions before in my life, but I've never felt this exposed, this vulnerable before.

An exhalation of breath is all I get before firm, masculine lips bracket my bare pussy. My hips jerk and a hoarse gasp spills from my throat. Fire-hot sensation races up my spine, arches my back. The natural instinct to shut my legs, contain the flames, is curtailed when merciless hands grab my knees and hold me open.

Q doesn't concentrate on a specific spot like my clit or my furnace-hot center. He's making out with my whole pussy, drawing my lips between his and tasting me with the flat of his tongue.

The sensation is like nothing else I've ever experienced. Already, my head feels woozy. Deprived of sight, my remaining senses zero in on the sexy, dirty kiss being bestowed on me. He's eating me like I'm his favorite food. It feels good. So good.

A guttural purr, transmitted with a distinct electronic wave, fills the room.

God, how is he doing that?

He kisses me harder. The tip of his tongue flicks my engorged clit.

"Oh!" Breath rushes from me. I tilt my hips forward, seeking more of that singular pleasure.

He ignores my need and goes back to Frenching my pussy. Warm, firm tugs pull my flesh into his mouth, where he rolls my vulva over his tongue. The hood of my clit is pulled deep, strong, steady sucks further enflaming the turgid bundle of nerves. A long moan escapes me, and he raises his head.

I wish I could see his expression. I wish I could drown out the unmistakable hum of the camera.

I wish—

"Fuck, you're perfect. Taste so good."

Hands hook under my knees, throw my legs higher and wider. My head rolls back onto the bed and my fingers curl into the seat as he goes back for a deeper, longer taste. Pleasure spreads, thick and fast. My hips begin to writhe, my body caught in a relentless pursuit of its first bona fide, non-masturbation-induced climax.

"Oh God!"

Q stops without warning. My head surges off the bed, although I can't see anything.

"Please." I'm not sure why I whisper the word. Because I don't want the camera to catch my plea? Because even though I'm begging for it, I'm not sure I can withstand the explosion I sense heading my way?

"Do you want to come, Lucky?"

I swallow hard and nod.

"Whose body is this?" he asks.

"It's...yours."

He delivers another open-mouthed kiss between my legs. "Whose pussy?"

I have an inkling of where this is going. I don't like it. "Yours."

"Whose cum?"

My thighs shake with the force he has on my legs. "I…I'm…"

"*Whose. Cum?*"

"It's yours, Q."

Maybe I imagine the shudder that runs through him. Maybe in saying those three words, something shakes loose inside me. Maybe I'm out of my mind.

"*Mine,*" he growls. "So let me ask again. Do you want to come, Lucky?"

"Yes. Please. But with your permission," I reply. I'm a fast learner.

It earns me another kiss. Then another. The melting resumes, intensifies. My head falls back. My arms ache with the tight hold I have on the seat.

Hoarse sounds and electric hums mingle with my moans. I can't escape the humiliating thought that what's happening to me is being recorded. That I wouldn't be here if the promise of an obscene amount of money didn't wait at the end of my performance.

But I also can't stop the onrush of bliss gathering between my thighs. I gulp in air and exhale on a jagged moan. My nipples, already tights points of almost excruciating pleasure, chafe against the russet half-teddy as my breasts swell.

Q alters the mood of his kiss. He lets go of my knees, curls his hands around my thighs, and uses his thumbs to part my pussy. The hood of my clit is exposed to his warm breath a split second before he tongues it with pointed, determined purpose. Just as I think I'm about to lose control, he dips lower, stabs my entrance with his tongue. The alternating attention teeters me on the brink, until colors begin to swirl across my bound vision.

"Q…oh, God! Please," I gasp. "I want…I need to come."

I don't know if his deep grunt is permission or denial of it. He doesn't relent in his ministrations.

Knowing how close I'm skidding to damnation, I try again. "Please, may I come?" My voice is thick and rough. I'm gearing up to plead again, in case I was incoherent, when he hums against my pussy.

"So fucking good. Want to keep licking this perfect cunt."

A thunder-strong tremor moves through me. I'm not sure how long I can hang on. I try gritting my teeth, but the eruption is counting down in big, fat letters with each flick of that wicked tongue.

"May…may I come? *Oh God, please?*"

"Taste it…" His voice is a hoarse, jumbled mess. "I want to taste it. Every drop."

"May I?"

"Hmm. Yes, my little firecracker. Come for me…In my mouth."

A sob rips from my throat as I let go and surrender to the wave that slams into me. It rips me apart, and I want to drown in it almost as much as I want to protect myself from it. Q loosens his hold on me, but keeps my legs firmly open while he laps me up in hungry licks.

"Fuck," he mutters against me as I jerk through my bliss.

Several whirs penetrate my fog of pleasure, and I wonder how many cameras he's activated to record my climax. I start to stiffen, the idea that I'm enjoying this suddenly drawing ever-growing shame.

I don't know why I know he senses it, or why I know I've pissed him off. But when he pulls at me one last time, there's a touch of cruelty that makes me wince.

I feel him settle back on his legs. A second later he pulls off my shoes. "Crawl up on the bed. Make sure the blindfold stays in place." The mechanical tenor of his voice still transmits an aroused hoarseness, but there's implacable power as well as an edgy aggression that slices icy warning into my stomach.

My languid body is still thrumming, but I do as instructed, travelling a little slower when I reach the top of the bed to avoid bumping into it.

Plump satin pillows brace my body as I wait, hands once again at my sides.

I sense him prowling the room. I know he's watching me from the hyperawareness rippling beneath my skin.

After a minute, I hear his zipper lowering. The muscles in my belly bunch. I'm dying to know when the blindfold is coming off, but I dare not ask. He warned me he might not be able to help hurting me. I've just had a taste of his cruelty. I don't want to invite more.

21

NINE INCHES

He retreats and I hear a click, the sound a handheld digital camera makes as it turns on. My trepidation and shame return. My knees are together, but I feel the imprint of his hands vividly on my thighs, reminding me how wide open I've been to his digital eyes a few minutes ago.

The bed dips and he prowls close. "Lower yourself down a little; I want to take the rest of your clothes off."

I scoot down and silently raise my hands. I don't know if my initiative pleases him. He catches the hem of the half-teddy and gently tugs it over my head. The blindfold doesn't budge even a fraction. I hear a soft whoosh as the scrap of lace and silk is flung away. His breath catches. Then warm hands drift down the slopes of my chest to cup my breasts.

"Fuck, I love these. You have perfect breasts, Lucky. Perfectly fuckable." He squeezes and molds, his thumbs brushing back and forth over my nipples. My licked-dry pussy dampens, my breath uselessly frazzled.

"Lie back," he growls. "Arms above your head. I'm going to tie your hands."

I swallow the protest that rises to my throat. We agreed on a few hard-and-fast exclusions. But bondage, light or otherwise, wasn't discussed. Disconcertion ramps moderately high as I lie back and raise my arms to the headboard.

Firm ropes make short work of securing me to the bed before his mouth closes over one nipple. He sucks me hard and deep enough to flatten my nipple to the roof of his mouth. The sensation arrows white-hot flames straight to my pussy.

His appreciative groan as he suckles me fires me up even higher. Until a deeper hum of a camera impinges my consciousness. I stiffen.

He stills, releases my nipple. "You're going to have to stop doing that, Lucky."

"I can't help it. I can hear them moving."

"A few of them are programmed to track my motion. You'll have to get used to them." He catches my stiff peak in between his fingers.

I gasp. "I'll...try."

"You'll do more than try. I don't want you tensing up when I fuck you."

He replaces his fingers with his tongue and flicks a straining nub several times. My breath ruffles out and ends in a tiny scream.

Q continues to lick and squeeze my breasts as he trails his fingers down my shuddering midriff and stomach. "Open your legs. Unless I say otherwise, when you're with me, I want to see your pussy at all times. Is that understood?"

"Yes."

He trails lower, then pauses to caress my bare pussy for a spell, before he slides his hands between my legs. I'm wet and hot.

"Jesus. You're exquisite." One finger slides inside. My snug, greedy flesh closes around his digit. "And fucking *tight*."

He latches on to one breast as he slowly eases his finger back and forth. Within minutes, I'm back on the brink. He increases the tempo of the friction between my legs, his thumb mercilessly circling my clit.

At the back of my mind, it registers that besides his mouth and his fingers, my body hasn't connected with any part of his. I'm about to experience my second orgasm—subject to imminent permission sought and received—from a man whose face and body are still alien to me.

The thought is demolished beneath the juggernaut of my lust. Even the sounds of the cameras recede as I gallop toward my blissful end. "Q, may I come?"

"I want to make you wait. But I'm dying to fuck this amazing body of yours."

"Is that…permission?" I gasp as I try to hold on.

"What do you think?"

I shake my head. "Please. I don't want to guess. Tell me."

"Fucking hell, every inch of you is addictive. Come, Lucky."

My mind stops functioning. Every instinct is arrowed between my legs as pure sensation takes over. It's a full minute before I realize the keening sound in the room is from my throat. He continues to alternatively tease and lick my nipples until my convulsions quiet to tiny tremors.

Then he drops a kiss between my breasts. "Beautiful."

A small frown forms because the compliment sounds almost regretful. As if a precious thing is already losing its shine.

I give a small groan when his finger slides out of me. Then my frown gives way altogether when he moves and I feel the brush of his thigh against mine for the first time.

"You're warm," I blurt stupidly.

A low laugh. "Did you imagine me otherwise?"

"The…your voice," I whisper.

"You've felt my hands. My mouth. You're about to feel a whole lot more of me. Enough to know I'm not a robot."

"Can I…will I see you?"

"Not yet, firecracker. Tonight I just want you to *feel* me."

I wonder at the rationale behind that, but I deem it wise not to question it. He adjusts himself next to me, and I really feel him for the first time. As I imagined through all those meetings, his body is chiseled, hard from chest to thigh. In between, the thickness of his cock registers against my leg. Without sight, I can't guess accurately at its size, but the length is enough to make me miss a breath.

One hand caresses my bound hands. My lower arms. Elbows. Armpit. When his hand trails down my side, I jerk a little. I sense him pause, file the action away, before he continues. It's dawning on me with astonishing alarm how quickly he can take me from sensible woman to quivering mess.

His impatient hand parts my thighs, and I realize I squeezed them shut again after my second orgasm. I let my legs fall open.

"Wider," he growls.

I comply.

He makes a rough sound beneath his breath and leaves my side. In the next instant, he's kneeling between my legs, each ankle in his intractable hold. I'm yanked wider open, my legs pushed back at the knees. I'm bound and wide open to him and there's nowhere to hide. I swallow and go with it because I have no choice. When the camera tracking his move whirs, I struggle not to visibly cringe.

I feel him staring at me. Between my legs. My breath grows increasingly choppy as he remains silent for an eternity.

Eventually, his breathing gruff, he releases one ankle.

The head of his cock brushes my soaked heat. Up and down a few times before he slaps his heavy girth against me. That's the first inkling I get of Q's size.

The second is when he pushes his head inside me.

My body tenses against the thick, hard invasion. He pauses for a handful of seconds. The hand trapping my ankle pushes my leg back further, opening me wider.

He drives once more into me. Manages to insert himself just past the head. I wince and cry out. His chest heaves and the rattle of his exhales transmits electronically.

"*Motherfucker!*"

Behind the blindfold, my eyes water. My nasal passage tingles with an onslaught of shocked tears as he presses himself deeper inside me. "Ah!"

"I need to be inside you, Lucky."

"You're too big," I gasp when he subtly withdraws and attempts again.

"You're *too fucking tight*," he grits out. Fingers land on my clit and massage with pinpoint expertise that floods me instantly. But even the renewed wetness only affords him another couple of inches. "Jesus, relax for me, baby. That's it. Relax."

The combination of his voice and the massage releases some of my tension. The burn is still beyond intense, but Q's cock progresses along my channel. Deeper. Fuller.

"Breathe, Lucky." The instruction is terse, filled with a savage hunger that tells me one wrong move could see this thing spiral out of control.

I take a much-needed breath, and he pushes in to my hilt simultaneously. I'm filled to capacity, no more room at the inn.

"Fuck!" He releases my ankle and his fingers leave my clit to trail up my body to my breasts. I feel him rock forward just before he palms them both and rolls the peaks between his fingers. "I fucking love your breasts."

My moan ends in a hoarse gasp when he starts to fuck me. Long strokes that end in little rams, my whole body jerks with each penetration.

Moans turn into whimpers as another dimension of pleasure sidles alongside the burn. A mixture of pleasure and pain, it tramples through me, builds with every breath. I'm not sure what it does to my pussy, but Q groans as his mouth closes over one nipple.

"God, yes! Give it to me, baby. Give me every inch of that beautiful cunt."

I want to tell him he has it all. But my mind is fracturing, the feel of Q's cock inside me so unbelievably glorious, I can't form words. He fucks me fast and hard, drives me to the edge, then slows the tempo. My body doesn't care that it has already climaxed twice. Hunger I've never felt before ramps up my spine.

I'm twisting and turning. My hips surge up to meet his when he lets me. Which isn't for very long.

He releases my breasts after one long suck and hooks his arms under my knees. If I thought I was stretched wide before, this is a testament that I can be stretched more.

Clearly, the few yoga sessions were doing their job. Strong arms plant on either side of my waist. The camera follows his move. He pulls out all the way to the tip, then rams hard inside me.

"Q!"

"Who owns this pussy?" he grunts.

"You! You do."

"Fuck, yeah." He pulls out, thrusts again. Then the true pounding starts.

Q wasn't kidding about what he intended to do to me. The desecration will never see me whole again. I feel it in my soul as he takes complete control of me.

The intensity of his fucking registers on every inch of my body. My wrists throb where the rope secures me, but even that discomfort intensifies the pleasure. I'm near to combustion when he suddenly pulls out of me and flips me over.

The breath is knocked out of me and my whole body is quivering on the brink. I want to scream and beg for him to fill me again. Before I can do either, he's opening my legs and his mouth is on me again. He eats my hungry pussy, his tongue probing where his cock has possessed as he molds my ass in his big hands. For endless minutes, he feasts on my clit, his caresses growing rougher and the sounds from his throat progressively more feral.

Sharp predatory instincts know when I'm about to come because he rears up again and, keeping me pinned to the bed, rams back inside me.

"Agh!"

"Motherfucker!"

Powerful thighs planted on either side of my hips, he circles my waist in his hands. I'm completely immobile. Nowhere to run. Nowhere to hide. And he fucks the living shit out of me.

I'm a babbling wreck begging, screaming to come. Sweat from his body drips down my back by the time he snarls his permission. The convulsions that shatter through me trigger a shout from him. My insides are on fire, squeezing the life out of the thick cock buried inside me.

He withdraws and fights his way back through my rippling muscles with another animal grunt. And then, he's flooding me with jet streams of cum.

"Jesus!"

The hands banding my waist squeeze me to the point of pain I'm sure he isn't aware he's inflicting. His cock jerks wildly inside me and spasms rock the bed.

After an eternity, he lets go of me, falls forward, and catches himself on his forearms. The whir that follows reminds me of the cameras. But I'm too shattered to do more than chase my next breath.

Slowly, our breaths quiet. I feel his long exhalations between my shoulder blades. Fingers move my damp hair to one side to expose my nape. A kiss lands on my skin, sending a residual shudder through me.

"Next time, I'm coming on those perfect tits," he murmurs with the indolence of a satisfied jungle cat. "The time after that, it'll be all over that gorgeous ass. Say *yes, Q.*"

I struggle to work my vocal cords. "Yes, Q."

He jerks once inside me. Another kiss between my shoulder blades. Then another, lower. All the way to the end of my spine, and back up again.

He rears up a fraction away from me. I feel the power of his stare, his slow, deep breathing. He starts to lower himself again.

He lays his head on my back.

That's when I feel it. The touch of cold metal where his face should be.

22

FREEZE FRAME

It is a deliberate, chilling move.

Calculated to what? Frighten me? Remind me that I've let a total stranger fuck me senseless? Or that he's in control? That I belong to him and he has the power to do with me as he pleases?

Each thought sends a shiver rippling over me. Each shiver centers on the cold metal resting on my back.

Is he wearing a mask? That voice...the metal...Is he some sort of bionic man? But I felt his mouth, his tongue. His cock. Whatever he is, a greater part of him is human. But his face...

The more that the part of my mind not flooded with panic ponders the question, the more I steer away from the absurd. He's not a bionic freak. But it's possible he may be damaged somehow.

The voice, the mask, the need for anonymity...it makes sense.

My heart lurches.

"Are...are you okay?" I venture.

He tenses, but he doesn't move away. "I should be asking you that. Are you?"

My sex throbs as if a thousand drops of wax have been dripped onto it. I'll be sore as hell for a long while, but I shake my head. "I'm fine."

He lets out a small grunt of disbelief, but he doesn't vocally contradict me. His fingers trail down my sides, pause when I jerk a little in reaction to the ultra-sensitivity.

"The cameras are off," he says.

A thick knot of tension releases, and I sag deeper into the bed. We remain like that, my hands still tied above my head, his body bracketing mine. My eyesight still blackened.

"Can I take the blindfold off?"

He doesn't respond for several seconds. "No."

It's a definitive answer, but I swallow and try and find words that won't cause offense. "I...I don't care what you look like."

A harsh, metallic laugh that burns my skin. "Yes. You do." Again definitive.

This time I heed it and remain silent. He continues to caress me, even though the gentleness is gone. Both hands reach beneath my body and cup my breasts.

Inside me, I feel his thickness expand.

"Shit, I want to fuck you again."

My groan escapes before I can stop it.

"My body. My cunt." A harsh claiming, tinged with rage.

My belly quivers. He's angry. I'm not exactly sure why. He pulls out of me and slides his cock, slick with our mingled juices, upward between my butt cheeks. Back and forth he rocks, his hands still squeezing and teasing my breasts.

"If I decide to fuck you again, no cameras—just for me this time—would you object?"

Two parts of what he's just said jar me cold. What does he mean by *just for him*? And hadn't he reminded me a moment ago that my body belonged to him? My frown replicates the confusion twisting through my brain. "I..."

"You like to be fucked, Lucky. There's no shame in admitting it."

I shake my head because he's wrong. I don't like to be fucked. At least, I didn't until tonight. Until he gave me three orgasms I only ever managed by my own hand a million years ago, when sex was a cozy mystery, not a clinical reality with the sole objective of putting food in my stomach.

"You own me. For a month. Fucking me when you please is part of the deal." I use my best The Villa voice, even though deep inside I'm confounded by what he said.

"I do, don't I?" he purrs. The anger is vacant from his voice. As if whatever overtook him has been wrestled under control. He slides between my butt cheeks again and emits a groan. "I'm going to turn the cameras back on. It would be such a shame to miss capturing your next orgasm on film."

He rises, taking the cold metal and hot body with him.

Tension seizes me again when the hum returns. I'm still dealing with it when he flicks me onto my back again. His attention returns to my tits. Licking, biting, tweaking. I'm ready to fall into the vortex of sexual need, when he pulls away. He delivers attention to the rest of my body. When he reaches my thighs, he unclips the garters and slowly rolls the hose down one leg, then the other. The garter follows and I'm well and truly naked.

His thumbs trail up my inner thigh to rest on either side of my pulsating lips. "My body. My sweet fucking pussy."

A moan slips past my lips.

He laughs. "That turns you on, doesn't it?" The pad of one thumb brushes lightly over my clit, earning him a shudder. His laughter deepens. He bends close until his mouth hovers over my ear. "Did you think you wouldn't be?" he whispers. "That this would be a clinical fucking, a rutting exercise that you'd talk yourself through and then walk away from when done?"

Oh fuck. What did I do wrong now?

He's angry again. My head is spinning from the mercurial mood swings he's bombarding me with.

I lick my lips and whisper back. "Q, please tell me what you want."

"I want to fuck the shit out of you. And I want you to love it."

"I…do."

"You don't sound sure." The edge is sharper, the electricity from the voice distorter sizzling the last of my nerves. "If I remember correctly, you questioned our compatibility."

"I don't. Not anymore."

"Hmm. But I like to be thorough. So shall we be absolutely sure?" he rasps into my ear.

I don't get a chance to respond. His rigid cock slams into me, taking me from empty to full in a nanosecond.

I scream.

He grunts, sinister satisfaction lacing the sound. He slams through my slickness a second time. The intensity of pleasure smashing through me makes my heart race in wild alarm.

Q lifts away from me. "You like that." He's no longer whispering. Whether he's asking me for the cameras' sake or because he needs vocal confirmation of what must be comically obvious to him, I don't know.

But as I've been painfully reminded, he's in control. "Yes," I whimper.

"Louder, baby, I can't hear you."

"Yes!"

His strokes are sublime. I don't know whether to breathe or hold my breath and surrender to the impending explosion.

"I thought so. Your cream is threatening to drown me. Shall I make it so you can't walk tomorrow, Lucky?" he growls.

How the fuck do I answer that? I want to be able to walk. But how do I say no without flipping his switch back to anger? I settle for a neutral zone I fear may not exist. "Whatever you want, Q."

"What I want is for you to take more of my cock. I want all of me inside you."

Panic trickles down my spine, eroding a little bit of pleasure. How much more of him is there? The question barely flares to life before he flips me onto my side and throws one leg over his shoulder. Guess I'm about to find out.

He impales me, and my breath strangles. He lifts my lower half off the bed, and with almost effortless strength, begins to slide me up and down on his length. Unbelievably, each thrust seats him deeper inside me. The position must please him because he fucks me faster, his breath growing rattled and uneven. I wrap my hand around the rope fastening me to the bed and hold on tight for the insane ride.

Before long, the pressure builds to the breaking point. "Please...
come...I want...can I please..."

I'm a puppet on his string. The words tumble uselessly from my
lips as he bounces me into ecstasy.

"Q..."

"Wait," he grits. *Thrust. Thrust. Thrust. Thrust.*

Hot drops of sweat land on my leg and slide down toward my
core. His touch turns slick and I realize I'm drenched in sweat too.
I'm thinking the possibility of walking tomorrow looks like an unlikely event, when he grunts.

"Now, Lucky."

I squeeze my eyes shut tight behind the blindfold and glory in the
explosion of color across my vision and the detonation of pleasure in
my body. Q shouts out his own climax and once again, I'm flooded
with his seed.

This orgasm is short, sharp, and sublime. But it still blazes from
the inside out, and I'm useless by the time it's done with me.

Q pulls out of me almost immediately. I'm slick from head to toe,
but especially drenched between my thighs. I hear a click as he leaves
the bed. I remember the cameras, and I try not to grimace at the
sight I must make.

I'm still catching my breath when firm hands release me from the
rope. He massages my wrists in silence then brings them to my sides.
He retreats for a couple of minutes, then I sense his return.

"Sit up for me," he instructs. His voice is neither harsh nor gentle.
He's settled for a middle ground that throws me into even more confusion.

I raise myself up, and he slips something around my shoulders.
My robe. I push my arms through the sleeves and secure the belt.

"I'm going to take you back now. Don't remove the blindfold until
I tell you to."

Questions crowd my brain, but I nod. "Okay."

He lifts me into his arms easily, and I'm once again intimate with
hard abs and tensile strength. When he starts to walk I reach out, in-
tending to secure my arm around his neck.

He freezes. "No."

I snatch my hand away. "Umm...sorry."

"I won't let you fall, if that's what you're worried about."

"The blindfold. It's just...I'm not used to it."

"It won't be on for much longer," he rasps as he resumes walking.

Too much has happened to me tonight. I don't possess the brain power to ponder if he means that statement in reference to right now or to the immediate future. His strides are sure and fast as he heads for the wing where I slept last night. The fact that he doesn't need to open or close doors makes me wonder if there's someone else aiding him. I skitter away from that thought. I have enough things on my mind to drive me crazy.

He enters what I assume to be my bedroom and the sound of running water mingled with the scent of bath salts permeates the air. The sound grows louder as we enter the bathroom.

"A bath will help with any discomfort."

He lowers me down and takes the robe off my shoulders. He takes my hand and leads me a few steps to the edge of the tub. "Test the temperature."

I bend cautiously and touch the warm water. "It's fine."

He picks me up and gently places me in the tub and holds on to my hands. "Sit down."

I lower myself in, and give a small moan when the water and bubbles engulf me. The scent is a heavenly mix of lavender, eucalyptus, and aloe. He lets go of my hands, and I lower them to the water to resist the temptation to indulge in one brief touch.

He helps me remove the diamond necklace and earrings, but he doesn't leave immediately after. My breath freezes, and I know I'm dying for him to tell me to remove the blindfold. When he doesn't say anything for a full minute, I tilt my head toward him.

"Q?"

"Goodnight, Lucky. Stephanie is nearby. If you need help call for her. Let her know how you feel tomorrow. If you need medical attention it'll be provided."

My insides recoil. I'm proud of myself for not letting it show on the outside. But I'm also kicking myself for entertaining the thought that there could ever be a connection between us.

I'm here to be fucked ten ways to Sunday, every hour of every day if he chooses. Whatever extracurricular scenarios my brain is conjuring up need to be stopped. *Right now.*

"Goodnight, Q."

He leaves immediately. Only the possibility that there could be hidden cameras in the bathroom stops me from removing the blindfold the moment the bathroom door shuts. Five minutes go by before I hear a soft click.

"You can take the blindfold off now."

I release the clasp and blink in the thankfully low light of the beautifully decorated bathroom. I stare at the blindfold, a million more question piling on the ones already crowding my brain, but one punches through.

The possibility that Q isn't doing this for himself.

That all this has been staged for someone else's benefit scrambles my brain.

The soothing water of the Jacuzzi begins to work on my overused muscles. I toss the blindfold on the vanity and relax in the water, then I weigh the pros and cons of tonight in my mind.

Pro. He fucks hard and he is borderline insatiable. But he's not a sadist. He seems to be considerate and cares about my comfort.

Con. He's not a sadist. But the potential is there.

I pick up a sponge and wash myself. When I touch myself between the legs, my breath shudders out and my mind loops back to the final fucking.

That brief exhibition of a darker character lurking in the shadows scared the crap out of me. My instincts warned me to tread carefully with Q. I ignore that warning at my own peril.

I linger in the bath until the water turns cool. The temptation to warm it up again and linger for a while longer is strong. But I'm worn out and can't risk falling asleep in the bath.

Although…he might be watching. And what, he'll come save me? What if watching me drown in the bath is part of this bizarre deal?

The macabre thought and the full knowledge that Q has me twisting in a quagmire of confusion send me out of the bath.

My eye on the prize is what I need to concentrate on. I've made it through performance one.

Only nine more to go.

Despite that thought planted firmly in my mind, I still stagger to a stop when I reenter the bedroom.

Because sitting on the bed is a small open case.

Inside it, ten stacks of ten thousand dollars arranged neatly in the case.

Performance one.

One hundred thousand dollars.

For sex with a man whose face I still haven't seen.

* * *

Q

I watch her sleep from one of the large monitors gracing my living room. I wonder if she always sleeps in the nude or if she's choosing to do so tonight because she's sore. I resisted the temptation to turn on the monitor in her bedroom until the need got too strong to deny. The reason for resisting in the first place escaped me the moment I flipped the switch. Wait. No. It was because I was torn between either watching her, or waking her up and summoning her back to the bedroom in the south wing.

Tonight was...

I take a sip of whiskey as I contemplate, but an accurate description fails to come to me.

I can't describe how tonight went.

One thing is painfully evident though. I'll be repeating the experience tomorrow, whether she's sore or not. Because, fuck it, she's as addictive as the black hole I've spent the last ten years feeding.

I relax in the armchair, wrap my hand around the raging hard-on that shows no signs of abating and squeeze myself.

What the fuck? The volcanic arousal that engulfs me is like nothing I've ever felt before. Hell, the last time I staged a performance, I was forced to resort to a little blue pill halfway through the week, such was my lack of pleasure in the whole thing. I get the distinct feeling I won't be needing any such enhancer this time around. Unless it is to ensure the pleasure already fully present achieves its maximum benefit.

Twenty-four hours buried fully inside her. The idea isn't without its enticing merits.

I toss the idea in my mind as I watch her toss and turn.

She's not resting comfortably. I want to think it's because she still feels my presence between her legs—*Jesus*, she was ridiculously small—but I caught her expression when she walked out of the bathroom and saw the first installment of her payment.

Like the confirmation of the one-million-dollar payout during her second interview, she didn't react predictably to the sight of the money. Her predecessor had leapt with joy, tossed a handful of the bills in the air, and then quickly darted around, gathering them up before, God forbid, they disappeared.

Lucky merely shut the case, looked around the room for a secure place, and ended up shoving it on the high shelf in her dressing room. She totally missed the typed note on top of the first stack, recommending she put the money in the bedroom safe and instructions for using the safe.

Whatever she needs the money for, it isn't for personal satisfaction. Or perhaps it is deeply personal?

I step away from examining that unpredictable reaction and return to what happened in the south-wing bedroom. To certain facets that need analysis.

Purely on a pleasure scale—because there's no other parameter for me to measure—fucking her was a singularly gratifying experience. She's reminded me again how much I like to fuck. How much I enjoy that sweet place between a woman's legs. And that's a tick in her favor. Hell, for a minute, I might even manage to let myself indulge.

The next few weeks will be bearable because of it. The reminder of why I'm doing this does very little to cool my jets. I'm still as hard as fuck, growing harder with each passing second. She turns again, murmurs in her sleep. She tucks one hand beneath her cheek and other between her thighs. The one-part-innocent, one-part-filthy action sends me to my feet. I toss back the rest of the drink and slam the glass down.

I should turn the monitor off.

Same as I should've stopped myself from issuing that ultimatum back in my office about her coming back to me.

But the compulsion now, as it was then, is total.

I want to storm through the dozen rooms separating us. I want to wake her up. I want to pound into her until I'm drowning in her cum, then come inside her over and over until we're eyeball deep in filth.

Then I want to start all over again.

The possibility that I'll damage her irreparably is high—Q has already decided against taking his shrink's advice—there will be no saving Lucky from him. As for Quinn...I mentally shrug. My cracks have gaped wider in the forty-eight hours since I talked to Adriana Nathanson, so the risk to Lucky is greater.

Adriana was right. My father's presence in the city has triggered an escalation of the darkness inside me. Enough for me to contemplate whether I should remain here for the entire time I need with Lucky or try and handle a few more birds with one stone.

For one thing, Delilah has redoubled her efforts where I'm concerned. She needs to be dealt with. Ignoring her for much longer means risking the potential to blow this thing wide open.

Maxwell also needs to be handled. He's still not thrilled about the Miami situation. He's going to be even more pissed when he realizes I've given away two more of his precious properties. And although my consenting to participate in his campaign has slowed down the flames racing toward the inevitable nuclear meltdown, the end result hasn't altered. He may be governor of New York State, a post that is demanding at the best of times, but he's also a Blackwood. Keeping a finger on the pulse of the empire he's no longer king of, but holds a good portion of, is a must. Especially when he's making secret moves to regain that kingdom for when he's no longer governor.

It's not a great time to be out of New York. But I have a little leeway.

My gaze returns to the monitor and I walk closer. She's turned again, lying on her front, the spill of caramel, blond hair brushing her delicate spine.

My cock throbs harder.

Three days.

No. Four.

I need four uninterrupted days with my firecracker. Minimum.

Then I'll take the short break I need to ensure my enemies remain in my crosshairs.

23

CLOSE-UP

I wake up sore. No surprises there.

My legs shake when I try to walk from bed to bathroom. The bath I had last night went a ways to soothing the throbbing between my legs, but it wasn't a miracle cure by any stretch. There are faint red marks on my inner thighs and around my waist. I wince as I pee and touching my swollen lips brings back a flood of erotic memories of what Q did to me last night. What he plans to do to me today.

The orgasms he drew so effortlessly from me. The thought hadn't even crossed my mind to put together the sequence of fake moans and groans leading to fake orgasms I mastered back at The Villa.

This was supposed to be a technical exercise. A clinical exchange of body for money. But I knew the moment he touched me that he had the ability to make it something else.

It's that something else that lingers on my mind when I dress in yoga pants and a Lycra tank and head outside to the designated exercise area. I'm a few minutes earlier than the appointed nine o'clock workout, so I walk to the end of the sun-splashed terrace and eye the high wall signaling the end of the wing. A similar wall rises up on the other side of the great room, but there's a huge garden, and pool, and a gate that leads down a steep path to a jetty overhanging the water. I haven't ventured down the garden yet, but from the high position of the house, I can see the craggy rocks against which the waves pound.

The walls do an effective job in obscuring just how big this place is. I also haven't found a door that leads outside besides the ones that bring me to the garden. Which means my only escape, should I need one, is via the water.

I'm a gilded, well-fed, diamond-wearing prisoner, with absolutely no clue where I am.

In some ways I'm reassured that if I don't know where I am, neither will Clayton or my father. But I know that's a pipe dream that has no basis in reality, but for a moment I let it wash away a little of the fear that clings perpetually to me.

I stop pondering the wall and let the view of the water soothe me. I have my first hundred thousand. Nine more days like last night and then I can allow myself to think of the possibility of a future.

Maybe in New York.

Maybe Quinn Blackwood.

I startle when I realize I haven't thought much about him since arriving here. It's almost as if when I'm with Q, I stop thinking about the enigmatic CEO with the wastelands of hell in his eyes. And when I'm with Quinn, the man with the hypnotically sexy mechanical voice ceases to exist. I don't deny that they both have profound, albeit different, effects on me. But one is a finite means to an end.

While the other…

I settle on the top step and fold my hands across my knees. To be honest, I don't know what Quinn Blackwood is. Or whether he's even anything to me.

But you want to find out…

"There you are. You ready to get limber?"

I startle and glance up at Fred…or Freddie. Or was it Eddie? Fitness Trainer. Here to prepare my body for another night of fucking. My face reddens as I nod.

If he sees my reaction, he chooses not to comment. He nods approvingly at my half-finished bottle of water, and we get started.

After we're done I head back in. Stephanie's laying out breakfast in the kitchen and I wolf down a plate of bacon, eggs, and hash browns, topped off with a glass of juice. She's stacking groceries in the fridge when I finish but stops and intercepts me as I head to the sink with my plate. For some reason my head snaps up to the camera above the fridge.

It's blinking red. I hand over my plate without protest. As I turn to leave, Stephanie's voice stops me. "I'll be up in an hour to help you get ready."

My eyes widen. "In an hour? I thought I wouldn't be needed until tonight."

"My brief is to get you ready by noon," Stephanie replies.

My gaze returns to the camera. It continues to blink. I feel him watching me. "I see."

I leave the kitchen and head up the sweeping stairs with my heart rate uncomfortably higher than it was twenty minutes ago. One hour. Then I'll be in that room with him again.

The nerves that climb up my spine should be because I'll be stepping back into the unknown. But I recognize part of the emotion as excitement. In the hallway leading to my bedroom, another camera blinks at me. My steps slow to a stop. I want to say something, but I can't think of anything to say that won't betray the slow sizzle burning in my pelvis. Like the cameras back in the Midtown penthouse, these burn into me.

I swallow and lower my gaze. As I enter my room, I swear I can almost hear him purr, "One hour, Lucky."

* * *

I retrace my steps to locked double doors. This time, my outfit is a black lace slip with a matching thong. No garters or other undergarments. My finger- and toenails are painted red to match the red-soled black heels on my feet, and between my breasts hangs a blood-red ruby on a gold chain. The stone is twice the size of my thumb. I'm almost too scared to look at it or even touch it.

With my hair worn up and the absence of a robe today, I feel exposed as I walk through the dark corridor and enter the foyer of Q's wing. I wonder if this is a clever ploy to put me at a disadvantage. I snort beneath my breath.

Was I ever at an advantage?

I pause between the sweeping stairs, same as I did yesterday.

"Right staircase. Turn left at the top."

That voice haunted my dreams last night. It made me do things that drew emotions so strong, I woke up covered in sweat and shame. Which led to worse dreams. About Clayton. About Ridge. My Father. Ma. Death. Destruction.

My mind and body are far from rested as I climb the stairs. But thoughts of respite evaporate from my mind, when halfway up the stairs a camera swings into view.

It's suspended on a pulley, the lens trained on me.

Without the robe I know it can pick up every inch of my exposed skin. The combination of cool air and blatant focus ripens my sensitive nipples. They peak to attention beneath the lace and with each moment, chafe with a shamefully delicious friction that makes me bite the inside of my lip.

I've barely made it to the top of the stairs and I'm aroused. My fingers curl around the wooden banister to steady myself.

"Pick up the pace, firecracker."

I'm not sure how I feel about that nickname. On the one hand, it has a hint of take-no-prisoners that appeals to me, but on the other, I can't help but think he's mocking me, toying with me the way a cat toys with a mouse.

I reach the top and turn left. Sunlight pours through tall cathedral-like windows on either side of me. I want to stop and look through them, get my bearings. But I know he won't like that. I content myself with a quick peek out the right window, but all I see is water. Frustration trickles into the cocktail mix of emotions. And then I arrive in front of another set of doors, and two emotions reign supreme.

Trepidation.

Excitement.

I enter. Unlike the one we used last night, this room has no windows. But the decor is equally bold and masculine, stripes of navy and ocher dominating the large space. Again, the focal point is the bed, with cameras trained around the four posts bracing its king-size majesty.

There's no seat at the end of the waist-high bed, only the blindfold and the pair of gold-colored ropes.

He's going to tie me up again.

The thought should fill me with strong misgivings. Perhaps even a flat refusal. But even though I know he's watching, listening, I don't speak.

I walk to the middle of the room and rest my hands on the bed.

"Good afternoon, Lucky."

I shiver at the formal greeting. We both know his civility is a guise. But guise or not, now that I know the savagely demanding male attached to it, that voice is extremely effective in setting my pulse alight. "Hi."

"The blindfold, please. Then place your hands back on the bed."

I pick it up with shaky fingers and secure it around my head. The clasps click into place and my world turns black.

He doesn't mess around this time. I hear him enter almost immediately. The whine of the camera follows, drawing closer with each passing second. The moment the door snicks shut, strong, shackling arms imprison me.

My breath leaves my lungs when his hot, hard body imprints against mine. He's naked, and the erection he's sporting is monumental against my back, the hands that find my breasts, rough and demanding.

"Missed these." He teases urgent thumbs over the stiff lace-covered peaks, then catches them between his fingers and squeezes. The continuous tug at my nipples sends arrows of lust straight between my legs. In under a minute, liquid heat floods me. It scents the air and he growls deep in his throat.

One hand leaves my breast, pulls up the slip, and slides into my panties. "Missed this beautiful pussy more. So fucking wet." His finger finds my clit, and mercilessly flicks.

I hear the camera track his movement. The shame the mechanical sound induces is ever-present, but the blanket of arousal is growing thicker. My moan, when he slips one finger inside me, is raw and unguarded.

"Are you sore?" he demands, his voice a charged vibration above me. "Don't lie."

"Yes, I am."

The answer seems to please him. His cock jerks against the small of my back. "Would you like me to be gentle with you, Lucky?"

Another shiver racks me as my mind tears in different directions. I should say yes, ask him to go easy on me. But I sense that wouldn't please him.

The fact that I want to please him rips my mind into further pieces. The pressure between my legs intensifies. I gasp. My fingers curl into the silk sheets. "Answer me, firecracker." The thick finger that plunges into me sends me to my tiptoes.

"Your body. Your pussy."

A loud breath explodes from him. I sense his approval in the caress of my breast and the fingers that massage my pussy. "Yes," he purrs. "So fucking right."

He releases me abruptly, and I nearly groan at the absence of his finger inside me. The slip is tugged up and off my body. The thong goes the opposite route, and I'm left naked but for my heels and blindfold.

His tip finds my entrance and my breath strangles to nothing.

"*My body.*"

He penetrates me with a thrust so raw and rough, my feet leave the ground. I scream and my fists claw at the sheets.

"*My pussy.*"

I get a repeat of the same. I scream harder. By the third thrust, he's crammed me full. Fuller than he managed yesterday if his groan of triumph is any indication. "Love that you're taking more of me, baby." He fucks me in sure, long strokes for a full minute, before he bends over my shaking body. "By the time the weekend's over you'll take all of me, won't you, *my little firecracker*?" He punctuates the last three words with harsh animal thrusts.

"Oh!" I struggle to find my stolen breath. "Yes."

"And why would you do that, Lucky?"

"Your body...your pussy."

Those four words send him crazy. My feet don't touch the ground again. One thick arm circles my waist and I'm lifted off the floor. His rough instruction to wrap my legs around his muscular thighs secures my position before he proceeds to rip me apart from the inside. Every thrust hits my end with a sharp intensity that drives the little breath I manage to catch straight back out of my lungs. He works me like an expert conductor, delivering pure, unadulterated ecstasy straight into my bloodstream.

I almost forget to ask him for permission. My internal muscles tense and quiver, the anticipation of pleasure almost unbearable.

It's his shout, followed by the thick, "Fuck!" that warns me that I can't come without his say-so.

"M-may...I?" My brain and my tongue can barely form the words.

"What was that, beautiful?" he growls above me.

"Come...please, may I...Q?" Every atom of my being is poised and ready. My channel is tightening harder, the need to come almost preventing his thrusts.

"My God, you feel incredible!"

"Pleeeeeeaaaase!"

I won't last one more second. I know it. I don't know what my punishment will be if I go against his wishes. I suck in a desperate breath and hold it, knowing I'm about to damn myself. My mouth goes slack and I prepare to let go.

"Yes," he grates out, his voice a primitive roar that bursts me wide open.

I come so hard I feel my juices saturate my pussy and flow down my thighs. I can't find my breath and my already black vision dims further. I lose strength in my arms and legs, and I sag and flop around like a useless creature.

The arm around me tightens as Q takes control of me. He carries me around the side of the bed, and tosses me down before he climbs over me. My wrists are caught and trapped in one hand, my legs are parted once more, and he's seated fully inside me between one fren-zied heartbeat and the next.

My back arches off the bed as he fucks me with renewed vigor. Dirty, decadent sounds of wet flesh slapping against flesh forms the background music to this lewd coupling. I hear the cameras. The wash of shame builds. But so does the onslaught of sensation.

Above me, Q's breathing turns even harsher. His cock thickens in-side me. I'm stretched to my absolute fullest and strung as tight as a bow.

Thick, mechanical words flow over me as he falls into his own pleasure trance. *"Fuck you for days…you milk me so good…mine… fucking mine…motherfucker!"*

The words are like torch paper to my fire.

I shouldn't be enjoying this. I am literally under a spotlight, stag-ing a performance for an audience of one or an audience of a million. The words falling from his lips could be words practiced in front of a mirror in a room somewhere in this strange place.

I shouldn't be enjoying this.

But I am.

24

FRENCH HOURS

My body has a mind of its own. It revels in the power it has over the mysterious man taking such thorough and expert possession of it.

It prepares to fall apart again, crash with mindless frenzy on the shores of bliss.

"Come for me, firecracker. Kill me with that pussy."

Convince me you're worth dying *for.*

The words from our first meeting slam into my head. It triggers a strange sensation inside me. Suddenly, I don't want this to be a forgettable fuck he tosses over his shoulder the moment he leaves the room.

I may be selling my body to save my life. That doesn't mean my pride is dead too.

My hands are shackled in his, but I have my hips. My legs.

I throw them around his waist. He's lean, superbly honed. Perfect to lock my legs around. Thanks to my recent fitness regime, my thighs are stronger. I use the purchase to lift myself, meet his thrust midair. I almost black out from the overload of sensation that hits me.

"*Fuck!*"

The roar blisters my ears. This one is for me. Not the cameras recording our every move. Shame is still a live wire twisting inside me. But alongside it, there's also pride. *This one is for me.*

His next thrust drives me back into the bed. But I've unleashed something within myself. An animal that needs to be fed.

I execute the move again, and a strangled moan leaves his chest.

Between the pressure building inside my body and the pleasure-pain high of meeting his relentless thrusts, I know I won't last long.

Sweat drips off his body onto mine. The heat between us is combustible. I'm about to perish in the inferno. I'm not sure where the words come from. They must have been building from that single memory.

His rough keening growls from his chest. His free hand digs into my hips, guides me into his final thrust.

And I murmur into his ear, "Am I worth *dying* for?"

Q tenses as if he's been shot. Then he's coming like mad, flooding my insides with thick, hot semen. His release triggers mine. My body jerks and twists beneath his and we fight for air. Several minutes later, he's still twitching inside me.

My mind staggers beneath the lessons my body has thrown at me. I've never known anything like this. I want to hate it, but it feels good. I battle with myself for a full minute, then abandon the fight. I breathe out, and let myself revel in the moment.

His head falls on my chest.

The touch of cold metal freezes everything inside me. From one instant to the next I'm reminded of everything that is wrong about this situation.

As if he senses my withdrawal, he tenses. Then rises off me.

My wrists are released from his hold. Before I can lower them, he growls, "Stay."

The bed dips for a second, then levels when he steps away. As quickly as he entered, I hear him leave.

A minute ticks by. Two. I'm frozen in a twisted tableau of shame and satiation. The blood still roaring in my ears means I can't tell if the cameras have stopped rolling. My senses won't calm and I can't stop the onslaught of emotions that batter me. I'm not sure how long I lie there, before his voice flares into the room.

"The cameras are off now. Take the blindfold off."

My hands shake as I free myself. The lights are low enough not to cause my eyes discomfort. I'm alone in a sea of silk pillows and indignity. I raise my gaze, and thank God, the cameras have receded. I throw the blindfold to the side and stare down at my body. The evidence of his rough possession is everywhere. My thighs, my breasts, my wrists. I look around the room and spot a door to one side.

"The bathroom. Use it if you have to, but don't clean yourself up."

My eyes widen. "Why not?"

"I want you dirty. When I come back, I want you smelling of me." The primitive possession in that statement holds no apology.

I feel the stamp of it all over my body. "When will you be back?"

"In a few hours. Don't leave the suite. Are you hungry?"

I'm ravenous. For more than just food. Although how that could be when he's commanded such powerful orgasms from me, I can't fathom. A flush creeps up my neck as I nod. "Yes."

His laugh holds a tinge of cruelty. "You'll have me again soon, Lucky. Rest for now. Your food will be brought to you shortly."

That he can read me so easily when I don't know the first thing about him irritates me. "Thanks. You're far too kind."

"No. I'm not." There's a deadly ring to the three words that immediately chills my spine. They also tweak a part of my brain, attempt to make a connection that flounders for a brief moment, then fizzles and dies.

I catch a corner of the heavy coverlet and draw it over me. Whether he takes that as conversation over or he has nothing else to say, I sense the instant he clicks off.

Tiredness seeps into my bones. I'm the kind of sore that draws a moan each time I move, but not ones of distressing pain. I sink into the bed and surrender to the conflict raging inside me. When it exhausts itself without my help, it releases me long enough for me to fall asleep.

Stephanie wakes me gently what seems like five minutes later.

Without windows, I can't tell how much time has passed. She tells me I've been asleep for four hours.

The large tray she sets on my lap contains a steaming bowl of linguine in a creamy sauce. The cutlets of Parma ham melt in my mouth and I polish off the meal in minutes, soaking up the remaining cream with thick focaccia bread. I leave the wine alone, and settle for a club soda. Once she takes the tray away, I slide out of bed and make my way gingerly to the bathroom. Like everything else Q-related, the bathroom is huge, every luxury and amenity within reach. I stare with a little longing at the multi-headed shower before I shake my head.

I return to the room after I take care of business, but I don't get back into bed. There's an entertainment center with a sleek-looking MP4 player sitting on a glass surface. This remote, unlike the one I used in the Hell's Kitchen loft, looks simple. I press the power button and strings of an Italian operetta fill the room. I grimace and hit the next button.

Imagine Dragons's *Demons* slowly pounds into life. My eyes widen and my shocked gasp ends in laughter. A tiny part of me is thrilled that I like the first thing I've learned about Q. No, not my first thing. This is the second. The first thing I like about him is stamped inside and outside my body. Q is extremely skilled when it comes to a woman's body.

The song is halfway through when I sense him again. My skin grows feverish and my belly rolls with trepidation and excitement.

Was this some form of early-onset Stockholm Syndrome? The remote slips from my hand onto the floor and I don't bother to pick it up.

"Lucky." He's outside the door.

I return to the bed and put the blindfold back on. I'm not sure where he wants me so I remain standing by the side of the bed and place my hands on top of the rumpled sheets. I don't need sight to confirm his purposeful stride toward me. The very air seethes with thick, sexual intent.

He reaches me, pulls me back against him, and runs his hands all over my body. Each powerful caress pulls a shiver from me. He bends his head and sniffs the curve of my shoulder. "Was that amusement at my choice of music I heard a few minutes ago?"

"Ah…no. It was unexpected, that's all."

"Why unexpected?"

"They're my favorite band." I let out a self-conscious laugh. "I was just surprised that…I don't know what you look or really sound like but we like the same music."

He slides his hands beneath my breasts. "And that pleases you?" he rasps.

I shrug. "It helps make this a little less…weird."

He pauses for a second. "What else would help?"

Instinctively, I know a request to take the blindfold off will be denied. That courtesy, *if* it happens, will come from him. "I would like to touch you. With my hands. Maybe see you?" I throw in there anyway.

My breath hitches when he picks me up. Since I haven't been given permission to touch, my hands hang down by my sides as he strides away from the bed.

A few seconds later, he settles on a seat that I remember looks like a leather-studded La-Z-Boy recliner next to the fireplace, and he arranges me over his lap so my feet are on the floor either side of him. The thick rod of his cock lies snug between my pussy lips, but he doesn't penetrate me. He lies back and grabs my hips, slowly grinds me into his hardness. I'm slick and wet and he groans at the delicious friction.

After about a minute, his hands caress up my sides. I jerk a little, and he chuckles.

"You're ticklish just there."

"Yeah…" My hips move over him, the desire to pump almost unconscious.

"I'm going to let you touch me now."

My breath expels in a burst of excitement. "Okay."

His hands trail up and over my breasts. For a long moment, he just plays with my mounds. Then he cups my shoulders, draws his hands down my arms, and captures my hands.

I stop breathing altogether when he brings our entwined hands to his abdomen and lays my palms flat against his skin. I can't help my soft gasp at the hard, hot sleekness of him, the tight muscles shifting beneath my touch. His hands stay on mine for a minute before he lifts them away. I tentatively explore him, hear his sharp intake of breath when my short nails scrape over his skin. Between my legs, his cock thickens, extends a little more. My hips continue their slow grind as I trail my hands up over his ribcage. Flat nipples harden at my touch, drawing another sharp breath from him.

When I reach his pecs, he settles his hands over mine. "Stay," he commands.

I've had my fun. But already it's over. Disappointment tears through me, but the feeling doesn't last for long. His hands leave mine, grasp my hips, and elevate me long enough to position himself at my entrance. Between one breath and the other, I'm impaled. I scream as *Ready, Aim, Fire* blasts through the speakers. And even though I'm on top, Q totally tops me with relentless drives into my pussy from below.

"Love hearing you scream…"

My nails dig into his skin as I try to hold on. But it's no use. I stop screaming long enough to ask the question that'll fling me into nirvana. Permission is granted. I throw my head back and surrender to the fireball exploding between my legs.

When I collapse forward, he allows me to rest on his chest. But the thrusts never diminish. He draws another mind-bending orgasm from me before he roars his own release.

I'm a useless, boneless mess on top of him, when he murmurs, "Tomorrow, Lucky. I'll let you see me."

25

OUTTAKE

On Monday, I wake up midmorning to the news that I'm to have my first colon cleanse. What I expect will be an unforgettable experience has been scheduled for four in the afternoon, according to Stephanie, to allow my body a little time to recuperate from last night's activities.

I wasn't carried back to my suite until almost 3 a.m. But unlike the night before, Q left me in the care of Stephanie, who supervised my bath and helped my weary body into bed. I snuffed out in seconds, my mind shutting down from sheer exhaustion, which thankfully left my dreams undisturbed.

I'm wide awake now, though, and to stop myself from thinking about what awaits me this afternoon, I decide to go for a swim since I've been given a pass from fitness training today. The white bikini set is part of the new wardrobe. As I put it on, I glance at myself in the mirror. Stephanie has taken over Fionnella's health tracking duties, and reported this morning that I've put on eight pounds so far. I can see where my hips and butt are a little plumper and other bones a little less jutting. There's also a vibrancy to my skin that could be attributed to the lotions and potions that've become a part of my pre-sex regimen.

Thoughts of sex predictably steer my mind to Q's near-frenzied ravishing of my body long into the night. He didn't leave after returning the second time. Nor did his stamina dim even a little bit.

He swore to defile my pussy. And he stuck to his word.

And tonight, he's moving to other parts of your body.

I push the thought away, turn away from the mirror, and pause when I see the other thing that awaited me this morning. The stack of money on my bedside table.

The means to my freedom.

So why does the sight of it sicken me?

Ignoring the question, I pick up the money, return to the dressing room, and place it with the stack from yesterday.

I stare at the crisp bills. Two hundred thousand dollars. Probably more than enough to buy myself a deep enough hole to hide in. Except I'll never be able to stay hidden. Not with the knowledge that Clayton is hunting me.

Certainly not without a means of ensuring that the other secret he's hunting stays a secret. To do that I, ironically, need to stay in the open.

Going into hiding means I can't keep an eye on her.

My sister.

Petra.

The daughter Clayton suspects is his. The fifteen-year-old I *know* is his.

The deathbed promise I made to my mother to protect her from Clayton at all costs still burns fierce in my heart. I hadn't planned on *at all costs* involving murder and arson, of course. But I had no choice.

I killed for Petra.

I don't want to do it again, but there's no way I'm letting Clay get his hands on her. Petra escaped the fates my mother and I couldn't. I don't have a single doubt that should Clay lay his hands on her, he will drag her into his vile world. I don't intend for that to happen. She's the reason I had less than a hundred dollars to my name when I fled The Villa. Most of the money I painfully scraped together went into helping her stay in hiding.

The rest bought me a hacker's services to alter records and forge documents to throw Clay off her scent.

I knew he wouldn't lose the scent for long. Clay is too clever to be fooled indefinitely. But my efforts bought me three months, until Ridge dropped his bombshell.

26

BACK LOT

5 *March 2015*
The Airport

The plan starts to unravel as we stand on the tarmac awaiting Edward Krakov's plane.

Ridge is two feet from me, doing absolutely nothing to respect my personal space. The plane is taxiing into the private hangar, but his eyes aren't observing the client's safe landing. Nor is he doing anything remotely security-like, as is his job description. In fact, he's barely even glanced around since we arrived.

No, those flint-colored eyes are as firmly fixed on me as they have been since we left The Villa. God only knows how he managed to drive and keep his eyes on my tits and bare legs without crashing into a tree and killing us.

I tug at the disgustingly short ice-blue tube dress I'm wearing, and barely stop myself from reaching up and ripping off the pearl choker. Even in March, the California sun throws off enough heat to piss off an armadillo, and I'm no different.

Toss in Clayton's parting words in his office this morning, and the sight of the vile Russian exchanging last words with his pilot on the steps of the private plane a few dozen feet away, and my nerves are shot to pieces.

I don't have room for the ominous look lurking in Ridge's eyes or the waves of creep bouncing off him.

My attempt to step away from him backfires when he immediately shadows my move.

I should be scared of him. I am, on some self-preserving level. But my temper has been known to give reason a finger at the worst possible times.

"For fuck's sake, Ridge. If you come any closer, I'll become intimately familiar with what you ate last week."

"Watch your mouth, little girl," he growls. But he reaches into his pocket and pops a mint into his mouth. Then moves even closer.

"Look, Ridge, I don't want to give Krakov another excuse to report me to Clay. You know how possessive he gets. You practically breathing down my neck isn't going to go down well."

"Fuck the commie asshole. He doesn't deserve to touch you."

My breath hitches, both at the blistering possessiveness in his voice and the waves of animosity pulsing from his massive frame. My shocked stare makes the mistake of catching his, and I glimpse blatant intent in his gaze.

A ball of trepidation knots in my gut. From the corner of my eye I see Edward Krakov approach. Ridge takes a half-step away from me, but he counteracts that move by folding his thick arms and staring with cold, dead eyes at Krakov.

My brain reels with the extra problem just dumped in my lap, but I shove a thin lid over it and produce a blinding smile for the man I'm supposed to make feel like a king.

"Eddie, I'm so happy to see you again."

He takes the hands I hold out and kisses me twice on each cheek, even as his small arctic-gray eyes slide to Ridge.

"As am I to see you, *babushka*. I hope you're fully recovered from your little…ailment?"

I nod and smile brighter. "I am, and it's so sweet of you to ask."

The snakelike gleam that always sends chills down my spine enters his eyes. "I am sweet only for you, *'bushka*. Because you're my special one."

"And I appreciate you all the more for it."

We false-banter all the way to the car. Behind us, Ridge's mountainous presence hulks ominously. I can't shake the feeling that something's about to go down. Something that involves me.

In the limo on the way back, I do my best to entertain Krakov. Bile rises up my throat when his hand slips underneath my dress. Swallowing it down, I blank my mind and let my gaze wander. Unfortunately, it wanders to the rearview mirror, and I catch Ridge's impenetrable gaze. He locks on me for uncomfortably long seconds before his attention switches back to the road.

The knot of fear in my belly expands.

Definitely something going on.

We arrive at The Villa and enter the large, boldly decorated foyer. A handful of guests are mingling in the space that doubles as a selection area, and Entertainers are busy chatting up clients. A server carrying a tray of champagne approaches and Krakov helps himself to a glass. I select a watered-down mimosa and try not to tense when I see Clay approaching.

Greetings are exchanged before he says to Krakov, "I've reserved a room at the casino in town for a few selected guests. It'll be an honor to have you as my special guest."

Krakov's mouth twists and he shrugs. "I may be too busy with my *babushka*, tonight. I'll let you know."

It's a poorly kept secret that Clayton part-owns Getty Casinos and likes nothing better than to help The Villa's guests offload even more of their money at his gaming tables. I can almost see the dollar signs in his eyes as he attempts to reel in Krakov. "Of course. And naturally, Lucky will accompany you if you do decide to join us."

I will my stomach not to turn as I smile at both men. "If you'll excuse me for a second, I'll just go a take a quick peek at the schedule." Edward Krakov, like most men, have their Villa favorites—in his case, me—but he also likes to sample other wares during his three-day stays. Remi, Clayton's long-time PA, who also doubles as a receptionist, keeps an electronic schedule on her discreet mini tablet. If I'm lucky, Krakov will have booked two or three other girls, leaving me free of his vile attention for five or six hours per day.

Edward Krakov holds the dubious honor of having been my first client at The Villa. To date, I'm not sure how much he paid Clayton for me, but judging by Clayton's smile as I was delivered to Krakov's room the night of my seventeenth birthday, it had to be a small fortune. For his part, Krakov took pleasure in using my body to satisfy every sick perversion, the Russian's proclivity for pain-edged sex a rough and shocking introduction to a world far removed from the fumbling teenage efforts that robbed me of my virginity two months before Ma died.

His only saving grace is that Krakov has a pencil-thin dick, which causes discomfort but not lasting hurt. Of course, what he lacks in the cock department, he more than makes up for with his hands, his mouth, and a copious amount of sex toys.

I suppress a shudder and start to turn away.

Clayton catches my arm. "Did I not mention it earlier? Edward has booked you for the whole three days."

This time, I don't quite manage to keep my horror from showing. A cold look enters Krakov's eyes. I need to appease or I'll pay for it later.

I return to his side and slide my hand down his arm. "In that case, I'll just go powder my nose. You must also be getting hungry. Shall I have the chef prepare you some *borscht*? Or would you prefer *pelmeni* this evening?"

His beady gaze slides over me and he licks his lower lip. "You can help me decide a little later, *myshka*."

"Okay. Let me pop into the little girls' room and I'll be right back."

My smile stays on my face until I enter the lavatory. Then I cling weakly to the sink and struggle to keep from throwing up.

Three days with Krakov. I can barely stand him for three minutes, never mind three days. My feigned illness during his last visit was because he wanted to fuck me without a condom. For an extra five thousand, Clayton allows that. The thought of him inside me with no barrier caused me enough distress to become physically ill, a fact that didn't please him.

Today, I know both he and Clayton are on board. That I can't stop it from happening without causing serious issues with Clayton. Issues I can't afford to bring down on top of my head with suspicion already aimed at me.

I stumble into the bathroom and try to calm my racing mind. Five minutes pass without a clear resolution as to how I can avoid being bare-backed by Edward Krakov.

I flush the toilet and exit the stall.

To find Ridge leaning against the vanity, arms crossed.

Naked fear freezes me for precious seconds. Then I step back into the stall and slam the door. Or I attempt to. He blocks me easily, his superior strength making a joke of my efforts. And he's not even expending much energy.

"Easy, girl. I'm not here to hurt you," he rasps.

"Then let go of the door," I reply, fear making my voice and body shake.

"I'm just here to talk, but I'm not talking to a fucking closed door, Lucky. You come out, or I come in." The sick relish in his voice is at variance with the *just talk* line.

I kick myself for picking the rarely used, less posh toilet nearest the kitchen, instead of the snazzy one the girls prefer nearer reception. I wanted to put a bit of distance between myself and Krakov, totally forgetting Ridge and the loaded looks he's been sending me all day.

"I can hear you just fine from here," I say, injecting as much power into my voice as my shaking will allow.

"Not happening. Come out and let's get this over with. Clay's gonna come looking for you soon."

"Yeah? And what do you think he's going to say when he finds you in here?" I challenge.

"I heard you in here, crying. Came to investigate." I hear the shrug in his voice. "You locked yourself in here because you don't want to fuck that asshole. I'm trying to talk you out."

The answer sounds pat. Well thought through. My heart lurches as I wonder how long he's been planning this.

"Come out, Lucky. You can't stay in there forever."

My arms quiver from the strain of trying to keep him out. Mild terror threatens to scramble my brain. I tell myself he could've entered by now if he wanted to.

Slowly I release the door and step out. The look on his face hasn't changed. I don't know how to accurately describe it. It's a cross between lust, possession, pity, and anger. The first two I understand. The last two baffle me.

I quickly measure the distance between the door and me. He spots and intercepts any move I might try to make.

My fists ball and I force my gaze to meet this. "You want to talk. Well, talk."

He doesn't speak immediately. Those flint eyes rake me from head to toe, lingering on my bare legs and my tits. "Christ, you're so fucking pretty." His voice is thick with hunger.

My terror mounts. "Ridge—"

He clears his throat and gives a single shake of his head, as if he's clearing his thoughts. I sure as fuck don't want to know what those thoughts are, so I remain silent. Vigilant.

"I know what you did."

Tension roars up my spine. "Excuse me?"

"You went into Clay's office two nights ago. Took something. I know it was you."

"I have no fucking idea what you're talking about."

"Watch that mouth."

I bite back another curse and try to keep my voice even. "I don't know what you think you know, but I didn't go into Clay's office."

He ambles over to my side, crowding me again. I breathe in his excessively applied aftershave and try not to gag. "I did two tours in Fallujah. Did you know that?"

"I didn't. Thank you for your service."

He smirks for a second before his features return to their gut-freezing intensity. "You know what my specialty was?"

I shake my head.

"Computers. Electronics. Anything with a chip or a motherboard, I can dismantle and put together." He reaches into his pocket and pulls out an electronic card. It looks like the security pass we use to get between buildings. Only it's the wrong color. "Clay had me design this special baby for him. It records everyone's movements between the buildings, including his, and it's also connected to face recognition software on his laptop. Clever thing about this card is, it also flags discrepancies. For instance, if the camera spots you say, in the North Wing, but your card is swiped at the front gate two minutes later, it sends an alert. Do you get where I'm going with this, Lucky?"

My heart climbs into my throat. "If…if that belongs to Clay, why do you have it?"

"Good question. He *thinks* he's misplaced it."

"And?"

"I have until tomorrow to find it or I make another one for him. Either way, we both know what he'll find once he gets a hold of this card again."

I swallow hard. "What do you want, Ridge?"

His features twist with a blend of anticipation and triumph. He slips the card back in his pocket and takes out something else. It's a tiny pouch, containing about three pinches of white powder.

Oh shit.

He steps forward and holds out the pouch to me. "Slip this into the asshole's drink tonight."

I step back. "No."

He closes the gap between us. "I'm not giving you much of a choice here."

"What is it?"

"It's not poison. Much as I want to wipe him off the face of the fucking planet, for one thing I won't put you in that position."

I eye the white powder. "So what position is this, then?"

He shrugs. "It'll knock him out till morning. He'll wake up with a mild headache and no recollection of the night before. But not much else." He shakes the baggie. "We both know you hate fucking him, Lucky. I'm giving you a way out."

"But you're not, though, are you, Ridge? You want something."

He attempts a smile that doesn't make it past the naked hunger cleaving his features. He reaches forward with the hand holding the bag and runs his forefinger down my cheek. "I dream of you when I go to sleep. Every single night. You know that?"

When I don't answer, he removes his hand.

"I know you took something from Clay's office. He hasn't worked out what it is yet. He's leaving for the casino at eight thirty. Make sure you spike Krakov's drink before then. I'll make sure Clay knows the asshole's not coming. Once Clay leaves for the casino, come to his office. Bring whatever you took, and I'll make all your little sins go away."

"In return for…?"

His gaze lands on my mouth. His Adam's apple bobs. "You know what I want. What I've wanted since Clay hired me two years ago. You've denied me for long enough, Lucky." He holds out the bag. "Make it happen."

He doesn't need to add anything else. I know I'm caught between the proverbial fucked rock and a fucking hard place. I take the baggie, tuck it into the tiny zipper compartment of my clutch.

I return to the foyer with profuse apologies and my best acting skills firmly in place. But Clay still stabs me with a hard, speculative stare. That stare strays to me with alarming frequency for the rest of the time Krakov stays in the lounge and cocktail bar. Contrary to what I thought was coming my way, Krakov draws out the moment he takes me to his suite. My relief is palpable when he requests dinner at seven. I pander to his every wish, while inside I'm a sticky hot mess.

My instincts warn me that climbing into bed with Ridge to save myself from Clay is the worst possible solution to my problems.

But when Krakov takes my hand after dinner and starts to lead me away from the dining room, I'm out of options. Clay raises his glass to Krakov as we pass his seat. The Russian, alarmingly sober despite the premium vodka he's been knocking back for the better part of four hours, slaps him on the back.

Clay's gaze meets mine, and my heart somersaults at the peculiar look in his eyes. Earl, who's also lurking nearby, sends me a scathing look as I leave the room. I want to tell myself it's my imagination, but the voice in my head won't allow me.

When Krakov stops in the bar for a nightcap, I take my chance and drag him to a dark booth. While his head is buried between my breasts, I slip the powder into his drink. My heart stops beating in the time it takes for the white powder to dissolve, and I'm a whisper from fainting when he accepts the vodka and knocks it back.

I don't know how long I have before the drug takes effect, so I stand, put on my best pout, and bend over so my cleavage is on full display. He takes the bait. I hurry to the elevator, grateful when he dismisses his two bodyguards.

His gait starts to weave as we reach his suite. I slip my arm around him and almost frog-march him inside. The bed is within easy distance. Krakov is out before his head hits the pillow. The part of me that's grateful I don't have to endure his touch tonight is woefully feeble against the greater evil lurking in my future.

Heart racing, I undress him, scatter his clothes around the room, then with a quick prayer, take out my travel-size perfume and spray two puffs over his body. I don't know what will happen when I go to meet Ridge, but on the off chance Krakov wakes up, my scent in his bed might buy me some credibility.

I hurry out of the room and head for the North Wing. I have ten minutes to grab the encrypted thumb drive I took from Clayton's safe before Ridge's eight-thirty deadline.

My heart is racing out of control by the time I make it to my room. I sit on my bed and take a minute to control my shaking. My gaze lands on my closet. I'm not sure why I stand and head for it. Not sure why I drag out the backpack containing my sacred-things-not-to-leave-behind.

I want to believe that a higher power is looking out for me, prompting me in this direction. But I've been crapped on too many times for the hollow belief to sustain me. Nevertheless, I shove my purse and smaller backpack into the larger one. I know it's unlikely any of the girls will be up here at this time of night, but I still make my way cautiously along the corridor and breathe in relief when I make it to the elevator without encountering anyone.

I swipe my card for the basement and peer out cautiously when the doors open. Most of the area is shut down for the night, but the small corridor leading to Clay's office is lit. I stash the backpack under the desk nearest the elevator and make my way to Clay's office.

As I near it, I smell cigar smoke. My heart stops.

Clay.

He's the only one who smokes the Cubans. But Clay left for the casino. No, wait, I didn't actually see him leave.

I'm rooted on the spot, unsure whether to flee or confront my fate.

The office door opens and Ridge walks through. "I thought I heard the elevator." He attempts a smile and holds up a lit Cuban. "I hope you don't mind the smell. When the boss is away, and all that, right?"

"C-Clay's not here?"

He frowns. "No. I told you, he's gone to the casino." He stands back and beckons me in.

My feet unfreeze and I enter.

Ridge shuts the door and I hear a distinct click. I whirl to face him, and he shrugs. "No one's going to come down here, but I don't want us to be disturbed. Is that okay?"

I jerk out a nod, because what the fuck else can I do?

He takes a long pull from the cigar, blows dirty rings toward the ceiling before he walks to where I'm standing in the middle of the office. "First things first. What you took from Clay's safe. Let's have it." He holds out his hand.

Slowly I take out the thumb drive. It's the same drive I stole from the safe earlier in the week, replacing it with a blank one. The one I'm handing back is the real thing containing details Clay's PI dug up on Petra's whereabouts, but I've had the hacker put a virus on it. Should

Clay or anyone not too tech-savvy try to access the information, the drive would corrupt. I thought of destroying it, but something held me back. Maybe that higher power that foresaw this moment?

I mentally shrug.

Ridge takes the drive from me and goes to the safe. He inputs the code, but instead of placing the drive in, he removes the blank one and places them both on the desk. He walks back without shutting the safe and perches on the edge of Clay's desk. "Take your hair down," he murmurs through another cloud of cigar smoke. "I hate it when you wear it up like that."

I try to blank my mind, the way I do when I'm with a client. But this situation is different. Petra's safety is on the line.

Hands shaking, I remove the clips holding my hair up. He murmurs his approval when my hair cascades down around my face. He props the cigar on the edge of an ashtray and approaches me.

For a long moment, he stares down at me. "Sweet heaven, you're gorgeous."

He picks me up and walks me to the wall. I feel the suppressed strength in his arms. I can tell he's trying to be gentle, but gentle isn't in his nature. I look into his eyes and I'm amazed he's held back the torrid hunger for this long.

He props me up with his body and runs his hands over me. "Do you know how long I've waited for this?"

"Uh...no. Ridge?"

"Hmm?" he murmurs, but his attention is absorbed in the hands molding my breasts.

"Clay. Are you sure he doesn't know?"

His gaze doesn't lift from my chest. He pulls my dress down and cups me again through my lace bra. "Let me worry about Clay."

"What does that mean?"

"Exactly that. If you give me what I want...if you *keep* giving me what I want, he'll never find out what you did." His head descends and he delivers open-mouthed kisses across the tops of my breasts.

Something is wrong. I know it in my gut. I recall Clay's stare as I left the dining room earlier, and my breath strangles. Ridge hooks his fingers beneath my bra. A livid eagerness sparks his features. I close my eyes and brace myself.

His cell phone rings.

"Fuck!" He looks from my chest to my face and for a second I fear he's going to ignore the call.

But he sets me down. "Hold that thought." He pulls out his phone. "Yes, boss."

I stop in the act of adjusting my dress and hold my breath.

Ridge paces to the end of the office and turns to face me. "Yes, I have both drives."

My eyes widen in alarm.

He smirks. "No, I haven't had a chance to check them yet. It'll need careful handling if there's a worm on it."

I'm aware my heart has stopped beating, that my fear is naked and raw.

"Yes, boss. I should have the information for you by morning. No problem. And Clay? Thanks for giving her to me tonight." His gaze locks on mine. "I know how special she is to you."

My vision blurs. I sway against the wall and I know I'm going to pass out. But I can't.

Petra. Have to save my sister.

I lurch toward the door. I make it, but it won't budge. I recall Ridge locking it. He must have the key in his pocket. I yank at it again, desperate and consumed with terror.

Strong arms lift me clean off the floor and yank me toward the desk. "Wrong move, little girl."

"Why?" I hate the fear ripping through my voice but my mind is spinning from the sheer deadliness of the trap I've walked into.

"Ask yourself the same question. You're trying to keep a father from his child! You know how the care system fucks you up?" He tosses me on the desk and holds me down with one large hand. The gentleness is gone. "No child deserves that."

I open my mouth to refute the claim, but stop just in time. I'm not going to tell him that Petra is with a loving family. A family, who agreed to relocate, go into hiding just to protect her.

"We came real close last month, Clay and I. That shit farm in Idaho where she was stashed? We missed her. But you know why I love working for Clayton Getty? 'Cuz he's fucking *relentless*. He was only my CO for a year, but he's the leader I dreamed of serving."

Clay served for a spell in the Army before his father's death brought him back to Getty Falls. The bond between the two men finally makes sense. My fear triples.

"You don't know anything about her! Why would you want to bring her here, to this place?" I scream.

"You want her mucking out horse shit, rather than be treated like a fucking queen?"

He's delusional.

"We're whores. I'd die before I let you or Clay lay a finger on her!"

"It's not really up to you, princess. I've seen pictures of her. You're fucking stunning. But your sister…she's something else. She could *own* this place." The light in his eyes sickens me to my soul.

I struggle against the hand pressing me down. But he restrains me easily. Slowly, he bends down. My legs flail as I try to find purchase. His mouth lands on mine and he moans. Against my belly, I feel the thick ridge of his erection.

I fight harder, but he raises his head and laughs. "I'm going to have you tonight, little girl. Tonight and every night until your sister gets here. Then I'm going to have her too."

The thick roar that erupts from my throat blinds me for a second. But it's not just the roar. Smoke drifts into the air and enters my lungs. The cigar. It's set alight papers on Clay's desk.

I search blindly for something, anything to defend myself with. My fingers find the thick ashtray made of solid glass. I grab and swing. It connects with his temple.

Ridge staggers off me. Rage fills his eyes. I scramble off the desk and race away from him. He lurches toward me, retribution and lust burning in his face.

Fear threatens to paralyze me, but I can't afford to let it. I search the room and my gaze lands on the open safe.

Inside it is a black, gleaming piece. Clay's gun.

I grab hold of it. Point it at him. "Stop. Please."

He laughs. "The only way you're going to stop me, little girl, is to shoot me."

My mind blanks.

Then it refocuses on one thing.

Petra.

I lift the gun.

I shoot.

* * *

I stare down at the money.

I remind myself again why I'm doing this.

My beautiful, innocent sister. The only one who matters in all this.

I'm doing it so Clayton doesn't turn another daughter into a whore.

Yes, Clayton Getty is my *biological father*. Finding out I was his and not Earl's is partly why he spared Earl's life.

But he's also the man who took bids from strangers as to who would be the first man to defile his seventeen-year-old daughter.

I shot Ridge Mathews to keep him from going after my sister. I'm going to offer Clayton Getty one million dollars to forget Petra exists.

If he doesn't accept, I will shoot him too. Because there's no way I'm allowing him to do to Petra what he's done to me.

PART THREE
Quinn

27

THE MARISLASIS

The first time I heard the term I was twelve years old.

The Greater Good.

The definition seemed strange to me.

How could sacrificing what you want in favor of what someone else wanted be a good thing? It's possible it was the first time I realized something was wrong with me.

I was a spoiled, pampered, only child. The male offspring of two powerhouse dynasties who could make grown men cower before me from the moment I realized what true power was. Sacrifice wasn't in my vocabulary. Neither were words like *reasonable* or *considerate*.

One particular word that was totally alien to me was sharing.

I didn't share. Period. The fact that I had to share my mother with my father was a huge problem for me from the day I was born. Learning to swallow that bitter pill on a daily basis was enough of a sacrifice in my opinion.

So imagine my surprise when I realized this *sharing* nonsense was truly a thing. That people actually participated in it. Of their own free will.

But even then, I was jarringly aware that what he was asking of her that night didn't seem right.

Mothers and fathers were supposed to love each other. *Only* each other. Right?

So seeing him lead her down the hallway to the guest suite was disturbing enough. Odder still was the super skimpy nightie she wore. Mama's nighties were always long and flowing, with a robe over it with a train that made her look like a queen.

Not tonight, though. Tonight she looked like one of those girls in the cheap magazines Wesley, my driver, hides beneath the car seat when he sees me coming. The idiot doesn't know I have my own, superior, collection thanks to Armand, our gardener.

But I digress.

Mama. Looking un-queen like. In the part of the house that's far away from the bedroom suite she shares with my father.

I should be in bed. But I'm rarely able to sleep when we have guests. For one thing, everyone wants a piece of Mama, and sometimes my annoyance at having to work for her attention keeps me up at night. She's mine and mine alone.

Her sole attention is what makes my world turn.

Call it what you will…some fucked-up Oedipus complex? Yeah, I know what it means. I looked it up after I heard some asshole joke about it in reference to me and Mama when we were at the country club the other day. Maybe that's what I have. There's nothing remotely sexual about the connection I have with my mother, but who cares what other people think? All I know is that I'm never happier than when she's smiling at me. Hugging me. Laughing at the jokes I meticulously scour books, TV shows, and magazines to find and tell her. Watching her face blossom with happiness when she sees me is like seeing the sun come out after a horrible thunderstorm.

I hate those. Thunderstorms. I also hate it when she's not smiling. Tonight, she's not smiling. She crying.

The sound triggers a series of memories. I frown when I realize I've heard it before. The sound of her crying. I never thought much about it because I always assumed it was Mrs. Harper, our overly emotional housekeeper who cries at the drop of a hat, especially when she's with Mama. The few times I heard the crying, it would turn out to be Mrs. Harper, not Mama. Mama would always smile a happy smile when she saw me.

But tonight her cheeks are wet. Her shoulders are hunched over as Maxwell, my father, leads her down the hallway to the double doors of the guest suite.

Captain Harrington's suite.

My concern for her makes me leave my hiding place behind the huge grandfather clock in the guest wing. I creep closer along the wall, making sure to stay in the shadows. My heart bangs against my ribs in fear and confusion as Mama holds her fist against her mouth.

"You agreed, Adele. You don't want to let me down, do you?"

Mama shakes her head.

Maxwell nods in satisfaction and kisses her gently on the forehead. His gentleness with her makes my anger with him abate a touch. But my heart is still racing, my brain utterly perplexed at what is happening.

"Remember the end goal. Remember this is for the greater good."

A sob catches in her throat. I'm ready to lunge out of my hiding place when Maxwell turns the door handle and pushes it open. Mama stumbles forward, her high heels catching on the carpet. She turns and looks at Maxwell. Her face looks...pleading, her eyes great pools of distress. His jaw tenses and he jerks his chin at her.

"The greater good, Adele."

Why is he saying that? From my hiding place I can tell what's going on is the opposite of good. Mama is crying. That's *bad*.

I have to save her.

I step out. Then immediately shrink back when I see the two men coming silently down the hall. They're Captain Harrington's assistants; they arrived with the Captain and are staying for the weekend at our plantation mansion in South Carolina. They both give me the creeps, the big, muscly one especially.

Maxwell sees them and steps back from the doorway. They're both dressed in their pajamas and one of them is holding something in his hand. Like the video camera Mama got me for my last birthday. They enter and shut the door without speaking to him.

I plaster myself against the wall as Maxwell walks past me and returns to his bedroom. My gaze swings back to the guest suite door.

Mama is in there, doing something. Something she doesn't want to do. Something that makes her cry.

And she's doing it for *the greater good*.

I stay in my hiding place for hours and hours, the three words playing in my head. Eventually, my eyelids begin to droop. I want to go knock on the door, see if Mama's all right. But my feet won't obey me. They want to run in the other direction, back to my room. I don't let them. Because I don't want to leave Mama in that room.

Mrs. Harper finds me in my hiding place at sunrise. She hassles me back to bed. I want to ask all the questions bursting through my mind.

But the old biddy is crying again, sniffing into that damn white handkerchief she always has tucked in her pocket.

She promises me pancakes for breakfast, as if she's offering me some rare, magnificent treat. It's stupid, because I'm Quinn Blackwood. If I want pancakes, I'll have pancakes. She has zero power over the delivery or withholding of pancakes. What I want her to do is to return to that room and get Mama. I'd do it myself but I can barely keep my eyes open. But Mama can't stay in that room no matter what she agreed.

Because from where I'm standing, it's very clear that the greater good sucks.

28

BOOM SHOT

The sound of her footfalls pulls me from the Blackwood plantation mansion hallway to the present. The only greater good in my immediate future is what I'm planning to do to her in this room.

The larger plan is already taken care of.

My gaze moves over the items on the table. Half of the toys I thought I'd need I've discarded. Pure, undiluted chemistry has taken care of the need for extra stimulants. We still have several days to cover, and those items could well come in handy.

For now, Lucky's body is enough. Just the thought of her supple form and I'm hard as a fucking rock.

I turn from the French windows from where I've been staring across the water at the Blackwood mansion. I haven't set foot in that place in years. For a second, I think of Mrs. Harper. And her disgustingly addictive pancakes.

Footsteps draw near, and my thoughts scatter.

The room I'm in is dark. But the dining room is staged and lit to my specification. She enters, and the inferno in my groin rages higher.

The body chain circles her neck and drapes her figure to perfection. The gold chain fringes that fall over her breasts play peekaboo with her aroused nipples. Lower, another chain circles her waist, with a fringe over her pussy. With each movement beneath the lights, her body glows and highlights her beauty. I grit my teeth against the pounding in my cock.

Added to the edge riding me, I grapple to find control. I force myself to stay put, take several beats before joining her. I stride closer to the doors dividing us and watch as she picks up the note next to her place setting.

Barely an hour ago, I thought tonight would go differently. She wanted to "see" me. I arranged to make it possible. But that was before memories set my blackness on edge. I shouldn't care about the effect I have on Lucky. But I remember Elly's reaction the first time she looked into my eyes. I was calm then and she was barely able to look at me.

I'm not calm now.

My hooded gaze tracks Lucky's movement as she leans forward and lifts the dome off the first "dish." She's disappointed to see the blindfold. The twinge in my chest suggests I care about her disappointment.

Curious.

I finger the control in my hand, debate for a second, then press the play button. Her head snaps up at the sound of the familiar music.

And she smiles.

Her fingers caress the piece of silk in her hand, but she doesn't move to put it on. My rigid cock protests at the delay.

"Is there a reason for your inactivity, Lucky?" I drawl.

She startles, then a trace of hurt crosses her face. She quickly blinks it away. "Hi to you, too."

"The blindfold, please," I insist.

She tenses for a second. Then she moves the dish away as instructed and climbs onto the table. She settles on her knees, the dangerously sexy stilettos tucked against her bare ass. Raising her hands, she secures the blindfold in place and rests her hands palm up on her thighs.

I open the French doors, enter the room, and take my place at the head of the long banquet table.

"Good evening, Lucky. You look stunning."

She catches her inner lip between her teeth before she answers. "Thank you. Wish I could see you so I can return the compliment."

The ploy almost makes me smile. "The night is still young. I could change my mind before we're through."

"I...hope you do."

That little telltale of her wants jars me in an unfamiliar way. A way that makes me want...again...absurdly...to offer her what she desires.

I change the subject. "How were your preparations this afternoon?"

Heat flares into her cheeks but she doesn't turn away in embarrassment. "They were...different."

"How do you feel?"

She grimaces. "Can we talk about something else besides my butt, please?"

"No, Lucky. Your...butt is the focal point of tonight's entertainment."

Her lips purse and she looks away for a second. "Are you okay?"

The unexpected questions jars. "Am I *okay*?"

She nods. "You sound a little...off."

I laugh. "A curious conclusion."

"Scoff all you want. You don't have to answer if you don't want to. I'm just...I don't want to spend the evening wondering if you're all right. That's all."

"I'm..." I stop when I realize I'm not in the mood to lie. Nor am I willing to have my thoughts recorded on camera. This part will need to be edited out, anyway. "Your concern is noted."

Another trace of hurt passes over her face. I ignore it and focus on the space between us. She's too far away.

"Come to me, Lucky. Don't be afraid, I'll guide you."

She takes a breath, then reaches forward. When her palms connect with the surface of the table, she tentatively crawls forward. The chains sway against her body, offering me a view of her beautiful, pink-tipped tits.

Behind the fly of my black pants, my cock engorges and throbs painfully. I squeeze the base to alleviate some of the pressure, and will her closer.

"The second dish is in front of you. Stop...now."

She pauses and gingerly reaches forward. Her fingers brush the silver dome and she lifts the lid and sets it behind her. Searching, she finds her gift and picks it up. Her head cocks to one side as she investigates. Then her breath hitches.

"Do you know what you're holding, firecracker?" I murmur.

"Yes, I think so."

"Turn it on."

She adjusts her hold and twists the gadget to its first setting. A low hum joins the music.

"Open your legs. Put it in."

Her lips part on a single pant. Slowly, her knees slide apart on the table. Watching Lucky slide the silver vibrator between her legs, her hips jerking and a full-body shiver gripping her as electricity hits her sensitive folds, is beyond sexy. The cameras are picking up her every move, and I know this is a shot I'll be replaying for a long time.

"Close your legs. Move a little to your right, and come forward. Don't let it fall out."

Another shiver as she traps the vibrator between her pussy lips. Lifting and setting the dinner plate behind her, she crawls forward once more. Her movements are inhibited by the gadget between her legs, and her breath catches whenever the vibrations hit her right.

She's two-thirds of the way to me. I want to surge to my feet, move the last dish out of the way, and penetrate her hard, the way I did the second time yesterday. I can't afford to get carried away. As much as I love fucking her, this production is for a specific purpose. The enjoyment of it, though surprisingly mind-altering, can't outweigh the end goal.

Her crawl has brought her close enough for me to hear her agitated breathing over the music. Her nipples are hard points and her arms tremble as she stretches forward. The last dish is set in front of me. With admirable accuracy, she finds and lifts the dome.

Her fingers search over the gadget and hot color flares into her cheeks.

"Would you like me to help you with it?"

She swallows hard and shakes her head.

"Make it wet," I instruct, curbing my disappointment and contenting myself with watching her lick the black butt plug from tip to base.

I shift in my seat and lower my zipper to ease the tight pressure. My cock springs out. I grip it hard, pump it a couple of time, and bite back a groan. I lean forward and move the dishes out of the way, then subside back into my chair. "Turn around. I want to see you put it in."

Her nostrils quiver in reaction to my command, but she shifts around on her knees until she's facing away from me. Her hair is hanging in a wavy curtain down her back, the soft lines of her figure flaring to curvy hips, making me itch to get my hands on her once more. My breath locks in my throat as she leans forward on one hand. She widens her stance and I see her perfect little cunt framed around the vibrator.

She starts to edge the butt plug toward her puckered entrance. I surge to my feet and seize her wrist. "I've changed my mind. I'll take care of this part."

Her breath falls out. She releases the plug and braces both hands on the table.

I set the plug down, unable to resist touching her beautiful skin. My finger traces the delicate line of her spine from nape to tail bone, my blood thrumming at her minute shivers. I palm her ass and squeeze the firm globes, knead her until she moans. I want to reach for her tits, but I'm already leaking, and I'm yet to go anywhere near her back passage. I hook my hand on the underside of her ass and caress her clit with my thumb. Another loud moan rips from her throat.

I flick the vibrator to the second setting and her back arches as pleasure curls through her. "Oooh…"

"Do you like that, firecracker?"

"Hmm…yes."

Wetness coats my thumb. I trace it up to her butt hole and spread it around. She tenses slightly but relaxes when I don't apply pressure. I take my time, apply moisture between the two holes. I resist for as long as I can stand, then spread her wide and taste her.

A tiny scream unfurls from her as I rim her with my tongue. I want more of that sound, so I pile on the pleasure. Readjusting my stance, I slip one hand under and between her legs to massage her pussy as I lick her puckered hole. Her whole body shakes.

"Oh God…Q," she pants.

"Come for me when you're ready, sweet thing. No permission needed tonight."

My words seem to open up a wider avenue of pleasure for her. Her body softens even more, her pussy grows wetter and I'm offered her heady deliciousness on a plate.

"Jesus, you're unbelievable."

I tune in to her breathing, the jerky roll of her hips, the spasming of her hands on the table. I pick up the plug when I manage to fit the tip of my tongue in her tight channel.

When I feel her on the edge, I give her clit a few hard taps. Her head snaps up, and she gives a loud scream as she climaxes. I ease back and place the plug against her hole. The moment her ride starts to slow, I push it in. She bucks wildly against the pressure, then screams again as it slides home and another orgasm catches the tail wind of the first.

She gushes against my hand, and I nearly lose my mind. I drop my head between her shoulders, momentarily regretting the presence of my mask, and absorb her shudders through the metal barrier.

When she quiets, I remove my hand, coat my dick with her slickness, and arrange her face up on the table. Her breathing is still labored, but I'm done waiting. I pull her forward so her head hangs over the table, and move the chains aside to free her breasts.

My stance widens to fit her head between my legs, and I trap her beautiful globes in my hand and slide my cock between her breasts.

The feeling is exquisite enough to make me pause for a teeth-clenching breath. My reeling senses puzzle what it is about her that fires me up so high. I've fucked more women than I can count. Each one, bar one or two, was a pleasure-filled experience. I love pussy. Have done since my very first taste.

Lucky is something else. I sensed the anomaly the moment she lifted her gaze to the camera that first day.

I take a beat to ponder why.

Is it because she is the denouement in this fucked-up play? The crowning glory in what I intend to be a rousing victory? Or is she, like my fucked-up self, a version of her own anomaly, created to blend with mine?

She knocks my hands, and thoughts, out of the way, and cups her breasts around my cock. I want to berate her impatience, for the control-taking. But I'm too fucking turned on by the move. I stare down at her petite, perfect figure, her creamy skin against my darker one. The sight is unbelievably engrossing enough to draw a tight groan from my throat. I slide my hands down her sides to cir-cle her waist. Using the leverage I pump myself harder, faster. Her moan tells me she loves it. I keep up the pace, feel my balls tighten in readiness for the wild ride to my black bliss. Her hips start to pump, the vibrator still doing its job. I slide one hand between her legs and she's soaked. My eyes fight the urge to roll as the rush grows more intense. I want to see her body; I'm addicted to her every movement. Her thighs clamp around my hand and she jerks.

"Q!"

"Yes, baby. Let it fly."

She lets go and the sounds from her throat are the headiest I've ever heard. It connects straight to my balls. I pump hard once, twice, then grab her hands and lift them away. Her beautiful breasts are ex-posed to me. I stagger back, vision blurred, and blow my load all over her tits. The force of the orgasm weakens my legs. I brace one hand on the table and continue to spurt over her body. The sight of my semen on her skin does something to my brain. I want to stain her in it, make it so she'll never be free of me.

I exhale harshly, my thoughts veering down a road I should leave alone. But the hunger for secrets claws through me. I want to know who Lucky is, what makes Elly tick. I need to know why she's here beneath me, and why the potential of a million dollars makes her look fearful rather than ecstatic. Why she, a chance face and body in a sea of faces and bodies, has this effect on me.

I want to know everything about this creature.

I decide then, that's a job for Quinn, not Q.

"I'm going to get a pink diamond for this pussy." My fingers drift over her lips, eliciting a shudder from her oversensitive body. I rest my touch at the hood of her clit. "Same size, same color as your beautiful clit. I'll rest it right here." I ease my caress and she moans through another shiver.

"I don't like piercings."

My mouth twitches. "Neither do I. I'll work something out." I step back and adjust her on the table so her head isn't hanging anymore. Bending forward, I place a kiss on her flat belly. "Stay."

I zip myself up and head to the bathroom next door. I grab a couple of towels, run them under warm water and return to the dining room. Lucky is lying on her side, her lips caught in her teeth as she suppresses a moan.

The sight of her rings all my sexual bells. Loud and hard. Already, I want to fuck her again. I hit the remote to stop the filming and clean her up.

"Q?" Her voice is soft and languid.

"Hmm?"

"Can I take the vibrator out?"

My body is still recovering from my orgasm. I should give her time to recover too. "No. Not yet." *Told you I'm not nice.* "But I'll decrease the vibration."

I lower the setting and she stops shuddering. "Thank you."

I stare down at her. My cock is waking up again. I want to fuck her ass, like right now. But her soft body on the hard table also jars. "Would you like me to make you comfortable, Lucky?"

Her nod slides her silky hair over the table. "Yes, please."

I look around. Tonight's shoot was set to happen in here. But I can improvise a little. Sliding my hands under her, I pick her up, carry her into the living room, and place her on the sofa. There are no lit lamps in here, but there's enough light spilling from the dining room that I catch her shiver, despite the ambient temperature.

"Are you cold?"

She shrugs. "A little."

The robe she was instructed to leave outside the dining room door is on the floor. I retrieve it and drape it over her shoulders.

"Would you like a drink?"

She swallows and a tiny moan falls from her lips. "Umm...Q?"

"Yes?"

"The...the vibrator—"

"It stays, firecracker. So does the plug. Drink?"

She nods.

I pour myself a whiskey in the dining room and fix her a light alcohol-based cocktail. From the way she reacted to the champagne on the plane, I can tell she's a relative lightweight. I don't want her drunk for the next session.

When she senses me coming toward her, she holds out her hand. She's mastering adjusting to the deprivation of sight. Were I of the inclination or if I had the time, I would enjoy training her into my little slave. A smile twitches my lips and I choose to keep that morsel away from my firecracker as I place the drink in her hand.

I retreat to the end of the living room and take the armchair by the darkened fireplace.

She takes a sip of her drink, licks her lips. After a moment of silence, her hand drifts up to touch her blindfold.

My release has taken the edge off my savage anger, so I change tactics again.

"Do you still want to see me, Lucky?"

Her body stills. She's probably trying to work out if it is a trick question. "This isn't a you-can-see-me-but-then-I'll-have-to-kill-you scenario, is it?" she ventures tentatively. There's a throb of anticipation, but there are also many terrible emotions in that question.

"No. It's far less lethal than that."

"Then, if you don't mind."

I mind. And yet the alien need to *give* needles me. Enough so I remain silent, sipping my drink while I contemplate the emotion. The last person who triggered a need such as this was—

My thoughts screech to a halt. My inhalation is sharp and ragged enough to make her twitch.

"Umm, we don't have to do this if you don't—"

"Take off the blindfold, Lucky."

I'm aware my voice is a frozen lake she risks falling into if she's not careful.

"Q—"

"Last chance. The offer expires with your next breath."

The breath in question catches, locks in her lungs as she contemplates the icy danger beneath her feet. Seconds tick by. Her free hand slowly creeps up to the back of her head.

I'm curiously anticipatory. Hell, my pulse is elevated in a nonsexual way, another peculiar first.

She releases the catch and draws the blindfold away from her face. Her beautiful green eyes blink and I realize I've missed seeing them. Not that I can see them to my satisfaction in the near-dark room.

The moment her sight acclimates, she finds me. I know she only has the faintest impression of me, that my black pants will be near invisible, my unbuttoned white shirt marginally so. All the same sensation crawls over my sprawled body as her gaze pierces me in the dark.

"Lucky."

She exhales in a burst of air, as if my saying her name has set her free. "Hi. Nice to meet you."

I smirk cruelly. "Is it?"

Her laugh is a touch nervous, and her gaze searches harder in the dark. "Definitely. I was beginning to think you were a figment of my imagination."

"Do all your imaginary men fuck you the way I do?"

The glass wobbles in her hand. Her gaze lowers and I imagine I see her face redden. But she doesn't answer. I'm mildly stunned by the searing need to know.

"Answer me, firecracker."

Her lids rise. "You're my first imaginary man."

Unsatisfactory. And yet not. I want to applaud the clever answer. I also want to punish her for it. "You're no longer wearing the blindfold. Do you not believe that I'm flesh and blood?"

"I know you're in the room with me. But your face...your voice...You're still a mystery."

"There's a price to pay for being too curious. Are you willing to risk it?"

A shiver passes through her. I'm not sure whether it's the effect of the device still wedged between her legs, or my answer. Either way, it's vaguely stimulating, this game we're playing.

She takes a large sip of her drink, licks her lips before lowering the glass. "No. But I think you are."

Kitten-strength talons of surprise hook into me. Their presence isn't disturbing, but they've grabbed my attention. "Is that an attempt to reverse-psych me, sweet thing?"

She shakes her head. "No. I'm just going on what I feel."

"And what is it exactly you *feel*?"

"You're...getting off on this. Your privacy is extremely important to you, but so is the danger. You can probably go through this without letting me see you, but I don't think you'll be totally satisfied with that."

"Why do you think that is?"

A shrug lifts one shoulder. "I don't know. But what I do know is that I don't take risks unless I have to. So whatever secret you're keeping, it's safe with me. I...don't think the price you're talking about includes hurting me—"

"You willing to bet the farm on that?"

One corner of her plump mouth lifts. I want to kiss it. Why haven't I kissed her yet?

"I don't have a farm to bet. And you could probably prove me wrong. Are you going to?" Her jaw is thrust out in challenge.

My mouth twitches. So small. So fierce. "No, firecracker. Physical abuse doesn't turn me on."

She exhales. "Then, yes, I want to see you, and you have my word I won't tell anyone."

I reach for the controls that I always have at hand. My finger finds the appropriate button and tiny beams of yellow light overhead transform the room from near darkness to twilight gloom.

Leaning forward, I place my elbows on my knees and capture her gaze.

"Can you see me now?"

29

TILT

LUCKY

Imagination is a wonderful, peculiar thing.

It makes up shit and furiously fills gaps to feed itself. From the first time I crossed paths with Q, I've imagined him in many ways. A god. A monster. A disfigured psycho. A withered octogenarian desperately clinging to the back door of the Playboy Mansion—okay, maybe not that. But my thoughts have veered between a few extremes.

None of them prepare me for my first sight of Q.

He's...beautiful. Roman statue, fallen angel, prince of darkness, beautiful. And that is just from seeing his body.

Because, of course, his face is covered. I knew he wore a mask the first time he fucked me. And with all his talk of risks, my instincts told me a man like him wouldn't reveal himself on a whim.

But even more than the visually stunning magnificence of his body, it's the mask that commands my attention. It covers ninety-five per cent of his face, a masterpiece of bronze, gold and black metal that looks like it's a living, breathing part of him. There are subtle inbuilt ridges that disguise the true shape of his face and jaw, and the only parts of his face visible are his eyes, and the inch-wide slashes that extend from beneath his cheekbones down to his mouth.

His full, sexy mouth.

Between my legs, the vibrator and butt plug make their presence felt. A shiver twitches through me. I've only ever used a plug once. A version much smaller than the one currently residing in me. And even though the size is a fraction of Q's cock, the feeling of fullness is overwhelming. I'm trying not to imagine what it will be like to have the man across the room from me inside my back passage.

The man with the ripped body and dark blond hair.

Dark blond.

For some reason that makes me frown. In every version of my imaginary guy, his hair was dark. Brown or black. But I'm not distracted from the splendor of him for very long. I already know he's tall from our severe height disparity. But his body is sleek and rangy, his open shirt giving me a glimpse of a thick chest and hairless torso. Without seeing his face, I can't guess his age accurately, but I can tell he's young, either late twenties or early thirties.

"Lucky."

My pulse jumps and my gaze falls to his lips. Lips I haven't yet had the privilege of kissing. My mind reluctantly lets go of images of kissing and devices, knowing what the thick murmur of my name means this time. "Y...yes. I see you. Even without the"—I indicate his mask—"I don't have to imagine you. Thank you."

He doesn't move. Or acknowledge my response. Not for a full minute.

When my nerves get the better of me, I glance around.

"Where are we?" I ask. Something tells me to keep my voice soft, to not disturb the peace.

Nevertheless, he tenses. His head tilts like he's weighing the pros and cons of divulging our location. "South Carolina," he responds.

"Oh, okay."

"You seem relieved. Did you think I'd taken you to the ends of the earth?"

I attempt a smile, but my mind is grappling with how he's still doing that with his voice. Is there some sort of implant? "Something like that."

"The end of the earth is beautiful this time of year."

"I'm sure it is. But I need…I prefer to stay put for now."

I sense him pondering my small slip, prodding at it like a predator prods its prey.

"To most people, a million dollars is literally a life-changing sum; the means to achieve a bigger and better lifestyle. That almost always means a geographical relocation. For you, I'm assuming an upgrade from homeless shelter to something else?"

I'm not expecting the direct volley of opinion. My mouth drops open a second before I collect myself beneath eyes of indeterminate color probing me. "Something else, yes. Not ends of the earth something else, though."

Again he doesn't respond immediately. His eyes remain pinned on me for another minute.

"Finish your drink and come here, Lucky."

He's bored with talking. I feel his hunger rippling toward me, tearing the ground beneath my feet open like a devastating earthquake.

In direct response, my pussy and butt hole clench hard enough to make me moan.

He hears it. Exhales sharply. "Now, firecracker."

I raise the glass and drain the sweet, tangy cocktail. The faint taste of rum and strawberries lingers, but the buzz in my veins as I drop the robe and rise shakily to my feet has nothing to do with alcohol. I'm still slippery from my earlier orgasms. The vibrator threatens to slip out. I slide my fingers between the fringe of the body chain and in between my legs to hold it in place.

"Fuck," Q curses under his breath.

He tracks my slow approach with dark, sizzling eyes. They're a dark gray or hazel, I can't tell. Every few steps I take, he hits a button on the remote and the room grows darker. By the time I'm three feet from him, I can hardly see him. But I hear his rough breathing, see his gleaming eyes.

Up close the mask is even more magnificent. I want to touch it, feel its beauty beneath my fingers.

He reads me like a book. "You want to touch me, Lucky?"

"Yes. Can I?"

He contemplates me for a stretch. Then he nods. I take a cautious step forward because my instincts are clanging with enough force to tilt my world on its axis. He warned me about risks. I don't know why touching him feels like I'm risking my very life.

I reach out and cup his jaw. The metal is hard and smooth, but not as cold as the first time against my back. It warms beneath my fingers as I caress upward. Over his nose, cheekbone, forehead. His breath washes over my wrist and I shiver. I should step back from the force threatening to consume me.

I step forward. His eyes unpin me, track greedily over my body. I sense more than see his hand lift. Warm fingers trail from my throat to my breast then lower to flick my nipple.

My full-body shudder makes him exhale roughly again. My fingers sneak up and curl through his vibrant hair. When my nails lightly scrape his scalp he hisses under his breath.

His hand leaves my nipple, drags over my skin to capture my hand that is still between my legs. He stares at my glistening fingers for a second before he draws them into his mouth.

Between one breath and the next, he's licking my essence, groaning as his mouth pulls hungrily at my digits. His long legs part, and he draws me in between them. Before I can give in to the burgeoning wish to touch him, he circles my wrists, draws them behind my back, and imprisons them with one hand.

Disappointment blossoms through me, but I don't have time to dwell on it. His mouth and tongue are working insane magic on my skin. Teeth nip the sensitive skin above my navel. Hot kisses, rough teeth, jagged breath. The smoky cedar scent of him. Everything about Q is a heady enough experience that I'm not left wanting for long. His wicked tongue licks up the slope of my breast and flicks incessantly over one nipple. When my knees start to buckle, he flicks the vibrator to a higher setting and grabs a hold of my hip.

Then he keeps me there, trapped between his legs, trapped on the precipice of bliss as my body catches fire.

My vision loses focus and I burn inside and out. My legs give out, but he's there, propping me up with effortless strength, never for a second letting up on what he's doing to me.

"It's too much, Q! Please... Oh God, I'm coming!" Did he give me blanket permission to come? I can't remember. But I know I won't be able to stop myself this time. *I'm coming!*" I warn and plead again.

He doesn't stop. Doesn't berate me. His guttural groan wraps hot around my nipple, and he pulls hard and relentlessly at my flesh.

I surrender to the explosive force ripping up from my toes. White-hot convulsions rip through me, clenching deep in my pussy and around the plug in my ass. I'm vaguely aware I'm falling. I'm going to crash hard, but I don't care. This feeling is too incredible to worry about where I land.

I bump against something hard. His body. He grunts but doesn't let go. The hand on my hip releases me and I hear a hurried fumbling. My vision is still shot to shit and I'm still caught under waves of pleasure. I gasp when the vibrator is tugged out of my pussy. He releases my wrists and tugs me forward to place my hands on the armchair on either side of his head. Rough hands lift me over his lap and his thick head breaches my core. Dark eyes stare up at me, absorb my every breath as he forces my hips down to receive him.

Another scream rips through the room.

The plug in my ass leaves very little room for him. I'm full. Crammed tighter than I've ever been, sending the pleasure-pain dichotomy to optimum levels. My eyes water and I can't breathe.

My senses reel in silent, stunned wonder. Suddenly, I'm conflicted by how much I like being fucked by him. I'm a whore. I'm not supposed to enjoy this.

But I love it. Oh God, how much do I love what's happening to me right now?

Q, attuned to me with frighteningly sharp acuity, probes me deeper with his eyes.

"Good?"

"*Yes!*" My response ends in another scream as he withdraws and crams me full again.

"More?" he demands with his electric voice.

"Uh-huh."

The grip on my hips tightens. I'm sure I'll have a few bruises to show in the morning.

He gives me more. And somewhere in between being fucked to death and pure ecstasy, I become aware that something is missing. Something vital, that pertains to my whole reason for being here.

The whine of the cameras.

We're in near-total darkness. He's not filming this.

So this is for him alone?

The thought pleases me way more than it should. It makes me grip the chair tighter, clench my pussy, and slam harder into him.

"*Motherfucker,*" he growls. His voice is so thick it's barely coherent.

A smile curves my lips, almost of its own accord. I feel him shudder beneath me, and I grind into him, harder than before. The move resonates deep inside me, the thickness of him hitting me in a spot that makes color explode across my vision.

"Pleased with yourself, are you, my little firecracker?" he drawls after another deep groan.

The sound draws my gaze to his throat, then up to his lips. I want to kiss him. The need pounds me so bad my lips tingle. I lick my tongue across my mouth. "Hmm." I lower my head, desperate for a taste.

He draws back from me. The move is subtle, but definitive. It causes actual pain to resonate inside me.

What the fuck is wrong with me?

I push the sensation away, close my eyes, and concentrate on other pleasures.

"You don't want to see me anymore, Lucky?" he taunts. "You don't like what you see?"

On the contrary, I like it too much. I shake my head. "It's not that."

"Open your eyes," he commands. "You may not want to see me, but I want to see you."

There's an odd timbre to his words. A thin layer of cruelty underpinned by…vulnerability. My eyes pop open. His stare is bold and carnal, his dark eyes at odds with his tone.

"I want to see you," I murmur. My gaze drops to his hard torso. "Touch you."

"Fuck me?"

My head jerks up and down. "Yes."

His hands release my hips, fall to his sides. "Fuck me," he commands. His eyes have taken on a different gleam. "Earn your money. Make me glad I picked you."

My breath catches at the savage cruelty behind his words. The pain that lances me is deeper, sharper. I don't know why his words have this power over me, but tears sting my eyes. I blink them away, struggle to regain common sense.

Because he's right, after all. I'm here to fuck him for a million dollars. Just because the camera isn't recording us doesn't mean anything about this is different. I belong to him until I've earned my money.

So I fuck him. Stroke his hard, thick length with increasing pumps until I'm bouncing in a frenzied, relentless rhythm. I don't stop when lust and pain rip through me. I don't stop when he bares gritted teeth like a shark ready to devour me.

I don't stop when he reaches around and tugs on the plug, drawing a tortured scream from me. Even when I start to come hard, harder than before…even when he shouts and digs his fingers into my hips once more and his cock ripples along my clenching channel, I don't stop.

Not until I'm wrung completely dry.

Not until my vision churns through an ocean of color then flames out in a sea of glistening black.

Then everything falls away.

I wake up in a different room. Facedown on a bed.

The blindfold is back on my face and my ass is in the air, supported by pillows.

The plug is still in place.

The cameras are back.

Q is hunched over me.

My heart lurches.

His fingers tug intermittently at the plug. Every few seconds, he licks my pussy, my taint, the puckered skin of my hole.

I imagined I had nothing left to give. Unbelievably, I grow wet. When I moan, he pauses.

"You're awake." His voice throbs with dark anticipation.

I remember how our last session ended, and I fight the hurt that scrambles up toward my heart.

He reminded me that I was a whore. Big deal. I'd fuck an army of Qs to save Petra.

"Yes," I reply, bleeding my voice dry of emotion.

I sense a shift in the air. He's displeased. Big *fucking* deal. I refuse to be an emotional mess for him to play with. He wants a whore, he's getting one.

"Are you going to fuck my ass, Q?" I purr. "I want you to so bad, baby."

The grip on my ass tightens. I choose not to heed the warning. I push back against his hand. "Take it, big man. You own it."

The hard smack comes out of the blue. The sound ricocheting around the room adds to the sting on my flaming ass. Behind the blindfold my eyes water. I bite my lip and turn my gasp into a moan. "Hmm…more. Your naughty little firecracker wants more."

He spanks me again, harder than before. Twice on both cheeks. My ass hurts like a bitch. But the good thing is the hurt in my ass has overshadowed the foolish hurt in my heart.

So I continue. I throw every filthy, evocative sexual cliché I can at him. The smacks keep coming. I get wetter. His exhalations grow darker with fury.

"Yes, Big Daddy. Make me scream for it."

With a vicious growl, he pulls the plug from my ass. A dribble of warm oil lands on my stinging flesh, between my legs. His fingers caress lube into my hole.

Then he's there.

One fist plants next to my head as he looms over me.

His hot, whiskey-and-mint breath washes over my face. "Shut the fuck up. Now. Or this won't go well for you," he blazes in my ear, low enough that I know he doesn't want the camera to pick up his words.

"Why, Q? I thought you wanted a whore? Am I doing it wrong?" I whisper back.

His breath hisses as he pushes against me. His control is on the edge.

I'm dancing with fire. But I can't seem to pull back. "You don't have to worry. I'll be your good little whore. It's my true area of expertise."

He freezes for a flaming second. I'm forever grateful I don't have my sight.

When he pushes inside my ass, my scream is for the pleasure, the pain, and the colossal admission of what I am that I've just detonated at his feet.

His low, long grunt is filled with fury, lust and a red-hot retribution. I barely have time to absorb the impact of his full, rough invasion before he's coming back at me. The lube helps ease his way, but he's huge. And he's locked in his own all-consuming vortex, his strokes harder, his hips pumping mercilessly into me.

"This what you want, Lucky?" I hear the dark relish in his voice. And my sphincter clenches shamelessly around him. "It is, isn't it, you filthy little thing?"

Oh God! Despite the blindfold, I squeeze my eyes tight, praying it will block out the greed and shame flaying me. My mouth drops open on breathless pants, my hips rising of their own accord to meet his terrible invasion.

A series of epithets fly from his lips. "*Jesus… Oh, fuck. Motherfucker!*"

My empty pussy creams shamelessly with each helpless curse. I raise myself onto my elbows and his masked face slips into the crook of my neck. Q fucks me deep and long and hard. He slows down long enough for me to slide into a screaming orgasm, then picks up the punishing pace.

I lie beneath him and take every greedy second of it.

Time ceases to matter. We're caught in a cycle of wrath and cruelty and sex.

He's unleashed his darkness, and I'm the sex-hypnotized recipient of all of it. Even after he roars his climax, he keeps going, keeps flaying me.

I probably pass out again. At some point my mind ceases to be my own. Like my body, my brain waves are absorbed by him…into him.

When I collapse, he catches my head and turns it sideways so I don't suffocate. But he doesn't stop. He never stops. Not until my vision turns black again.

The second time I wake up, I'm in my own bed in my wing of the mansion.

Bright light filters through the gap in the curtains. I blink for a few dazed seconds, then raise the covers to glance down at myself.

My hips, thighs, and breasts are covered in dark pink bruises. My ass feels like it's gone ten rounds with Godzilla, and I can barely lift my legs.

But I'm filled with a deep sense of satisfaction. Almost as if…as if I've never been more sated in my life.

I'm absorbing the disturbing revelation when Stephanie knocks and enters the room, carrying a breakfast tray. It's heaped with all my favorites—bacon, eggs, waffles heaped with whipped cream and strawberries, and a bowl of diced fruit.

She sets it down on my lap with a smile. "Did you sleep well? You were pretty out of it last night."

My face flames and I pretend to be absorbed in pouring a glass of orange juice. "Yeah," I murmur.

She crosses to the curtains and throws them open. Then returns to me.

"The boss mentioned you might be a little stiff. Would you like a light massage when you're done with breakfast?"

My cheeks burn hotter, and I shake my head. "I'm okay."

She nods. "I'll go and run you a bath."

I force the food down a throat clogged with embarrassment and when she returns to take the tray away, I catch her eye. There's no point beating about the bush.

"So what's on the agenda for today?" Sodomy? Deep throating? A *soupçon* of Shibari, perhaps? I find myself holding my breath.

Stephanie smiles. "Nothing."

"I…what?"

"Nothing. The boss has left."

I'm totally unprepared for the breath-stealing pummeling that attacks my insides. "He's *left*?"

She nods. "Fionnella will be in touch at some point today with further instructions. Until then, you're free to just chill."

She sails out with another smile.

I pull the sheet up to my chest, acutely aware that the light has just gone out of my day.

And bracingly aware, too, that this feeling is totally, fucking, *wrong*.

* * *

The soothing bath turns out to be anything but. I'm on tenterhooks, wondering why Q has left. Wondering if I crossed a line last night with my over-the-top porn-star narrative. Wondering why, if that was the case, he left twenty stacks of ten thousand dollars instead of ten. Would he pay me double if I displeased him? Why would he pay me double at all? Was it his way of telling me to fuck off?

My mind churns relentlessly until it propels me out of the bath. I dry myself and throw on the first thing that comes to hand—a cream, butter-soft pantsuit that feels heavenly against my still sensitive skin.

I leave my suite and as I walk down the hallway, my gaze locks on the cameras above my head. No blinking red lights.

Downstairs, I pace restlessly through the living room, kitchen, out to the terrace and back again. It suddenly occurs to me that I haven't used my phone since I got here. Haven't needed to. I press the home button. Nothing happens. I race back upstairs and plug it onto the charger.

Excruciating minutes pass before the wheel stops spinning and it powers on. I startle as three pings announce e-mails.

My finger trembles as I slide it across the screen.

I haven't missed a call from Fionnella.

But I've missed three calls from Quinn Blackwood.

Each one sent at some point in the middle of every night since last Friday.

Each call is followed by a text one minute later.

Each text bears the same message.

You're in my head.

30

THE MARTINI SHOT

"Is it done?"

"Yes. She's on her way back. The plane lands at Teterboro in half an hour."

"Good. And the apartment?"

"The tech guys are setting up as we speak. They'll have to work through the night."

"I want it done by morning, Fionnella. Double their pay if you have to."

"I already did. And added a little sweetener on top because of the back-to-back work on the other project."

I tuck the phone against my neck and do up the buttons of my black shirt. "You have my undying gratitude. You know that, of course."

She sighs. "I would prefer waking up without more gray hairs than I go to sleep with. And please don't tell me it suits me. No woman likes to hear that," she says crisply.

"Wouldn't dream of it. Not that I don't think it, though."

She chuckles. "You were always too smooth for your own good. Knew it right from the moment I met you."

We both pause a couple of beats, the circumstances of our meeting temporarily stalling conversation. I have no doubt my life would be on the same course without meeting Fionnella Smith. But I'm aware the path I've taken has been less...lonely with her on board.

"We're almost there, Nella," I murmur.

Her breath catches on a hook of suppressed pain. Then she clears her throat briskly. "Yes. Okay."

I snap out my sleeve before I start to fold it back onto my forearm. "So, did you meet any resistance?"

"You mean was she full of her usual twenty questions?"

"Hmm."

"Of course, she was. You just had to confuse the hell out of the girl by paying her double for one night, didn't you? Why the hell would you do that?"

Because I was rough with her. Because I loved every second of taking her ass. Because she was so fucking tight my cock still bears strangle marks.

"Was it not well received?"

"Was the bubonic plague well received? You'd think you'd sent her a case of anthrax instead of an extra hundred grand. She wants to know why, and I don't think she'll let it go. I spent the better part of an hour yesterday fielding her questions. So you better find a damn good reason for going off script."

My blood thrums through my veins at the thought of going head-to-head with my firecracker. "I'll take care of it."

Fionnella exhales. "Thanks." The response is a touch weary. She's been waiting as long as I have for this to end. If I had a functioning heart, it would go out to her. All I can promise is the retribution that has been over a decade in coming. "I'll be in touch when the place is all set."

I hang up and finish dressing. The all-black attire cements my mood, and I firmly place the past weekend's activities in a compartmentalized box by the time I gun the engine of my rarely used, nondescript Ford Mustang out of the underground garage and onto the street.

The brownstone in Brooklyn is another one I own, along with

the identical unoccupied properties on either side of it. But these ones don't come under the Blackwood umbrella. They're untraceable purchases, procured through two dozen shell companies. I drive past the houses and park at the end of the street. I would've preferred to park on another block altogether but I can't risk being recognized.

I wait until I'm sure there's no one around, and climb the steps to the brownstone. I let myself in and lock the door behind me. Unlike most of my other properties, this house is fully decorated. Artistic Tiffany floor lamps light the wide hallway, but the custom-designed living room and kitchen are dark.

Music strains through the house from the single bedroom upstairs. I had the upstairs of the house modified to a specific layout, one that announced the space as fit for only one purpose.

The giving of pleasure.

I stride up the stairs in measured steps. Sultry laughter designed to entice weaves through the air as I enter the empty bedroom. The bed, the center of attention in the vast space, is emperor-sized, custom built to accommodate multiple partners. Bespoke sheets and linens drape the bed and weave around the four posts, expertly intertwined with soft lighting. In one corner, a spanking bench waits decadently next to an elevated silver bucket holding three bottles of vintage champagne. I take it all in with dark satisfaction, sliding my hands into my pockets as I cross the room to lean in the bathroom doorway.

She's the center of attention even in the extra large Jacuzzi bathtub. One foot is extended out of the water, clutched in the large hands of the man in front of her as she enjoys her foot massage. Behind her another man rubs her shoulders in smooth, firm circles. He must be the teller of the jokes, because her head is tilted back, her hungry eyes moving over his as she listens to his low, deep droning.

He delivers the punch line. She laughs. Then moans her approval at the foot rub before taking a sip of her champagne.

Foot rub guy's gaze cuts to me, silently announcing my presence.

Delilah turns and gasps in delight when she sees me. "Oh, Quinn!

I'm so happy you're here. I thought you weren't going to show." She sets her glass on a nearby vanity and stretches out both hands to me.

I walk farther into the bathroom but ignore her outstretched hands.

"Are you having fun?" I ask.

Her eyes flash at the snub, but her smile stays in place as she relaxes against the man beef behind her and strokes his jaw. "Derek and Kyle have done a great job of keeping me company. But seriously, Quinn, do we have to meet all the way in *Brooklyn*?" Her pout is artificial and irritating.

And her statement is rich considering she was born and bred in Queens.

"A small price to pay for all of this, don't you think?" I say.

She rolls her eyes and proffers her other foot to Derek. Or is it Kyle? I never stopped long enough to work out which twin was which. "I hate it when you go all practical on me. You're here now, baby. That's all that matters." Her gaze locks hard on me, before she conducts a ravenous survey of my body. "Are you going to join us?"

I stroll to the vanity and lean, cross-legged, against it. "Sorry, sweetheart. I had a shower half an hour ago."

"Hmm…shame." Her gaze climbs up and rests on my hair. "Interesting color. You revisiting a boy band phase?"

I slide my hand through the dirty-blond strands I haven't had time to alter. "I never had a boy band phase. But yes…I'm experimenting."

Her eyes lock on mine again and she licks her lips. "My favorite word…experimenting."

My skin wants to crawl away from my body. But even it knows what's at stake, so it stays put.

I straighten and start undoing my shirt. "When you're done frolicking in the bath, I'll be in the bedroom." I walk back out, return to the bedroom. I hear her instructing Derek…or Kyle…to help her out.

I tug my shirt off and toss it into a chair. Shoes and socks come off next. My pants stay on, though. As does the vintage Patek Philippe watch on my wrist. It has a special significance in the Maxwell/Delilah game.

I ignore the low, excited laughter behind me and crawl onto the bed. Lounging in the midst of a dozen pillows against the massive headboard, I fold my arms and wait for her to come out.

It's a production, of course.

She's beautiful. She's powerful. As wife of the incumbent governor, she commands the greatest state in the world. But Delilah Black-wood has danced in the palm of my hand since the day we met. That's not to say I don't give her fair due.

She walks out with the strut of a regal queen. The Chinese silk robe is untied, and drapes to the floor. She's naked underneath it, of course. The jet-black hair that was pinned up in the bath is now flowing over her slim shoulders. She walks three steps in front of the identical twins, who follow, buff slaves, towels draped around their waists. Her gray eyes grow dark, a feverishly carnal gleam stoking the depths as her gaze runs over my body. She licks her lower lip and I can tell she's a breath away from panting like the bitch she is.

When she stops at the bottom of the bed, each twin helps her slide the robe off her shoulders. At thirty-five her body is still youthful enough to not require the attention of a surgeon's knife. And yet her boobs hold an unnatural perk.

I move my gaze from her tits and watch her run her hands over her thighs.

"I've missed you so much, Quinn."

"Then what the fuck are you doing all the way over there?" I ask.

Her pleased smile lights up her whole face. She hitches a knee onto the bed and crawls sinuously toward me. When she reaches my legs, she runs both hands up my inner calves and thighs. I lounge back against the headboard and allow the caress. Her fingers tremble as they approach my cock. She's highly turned on but also nervous. She doesn't know which version of Quinn she's going to get. Her gaze darts up at me as she struggles to overcome the nerves.

"God, you look so serious," she half laughs.

"This is serious business, my sweet," I reply.

The endearment eases her tension a touch, like it's designed to. She grows bolder and cups me through my pants. I'm chubby enough to please her. Her smile widens. Her stare returns to my crotch and her mouth falls open as she gets caught up in increasing my girth. I look up and nod subtly at the twins.

They drop their towels and get on the bed. Delilah jerks a little in delight when twin hands caress her body. But she doesn't pay them much attention. It's me she wants. Me she's dying to fuck.

I unfold my arms, giving her silent consent. Her hand leaves my cock and inches up my torso. Her touch on my bare skin makes my gut clench hard.

"My God, Quinn, you have no idea how much I've needed this, darling."

She crawls closer and replaces her hands with her mouth. Her tongue licks greedily at my flesh, then her teeth join in the fun. She's growing more frenzied by the minute. Behind her, one twin trails a flogger down her back as the other works a hand between her thighs. Her eyes drift shut and she shivers in anticipation. I nod at the flogger bearer and he brings it down hard across her back, then repeats it every five seconds. Delilah's guttural moans are pure bitch in heat. The pungent scent of her arousal coats the air, and her teeth sink into my pecs as her excitement escalates. She kisses her way up my body to my neck. When she opens her mouth over my pulse, I grab her by the throat. Her pulse beats a frenzied tattoo against my fingers.

"Hickies will get you no cock," I warn. My voice is a blade of ice.

She shivers and strains against my hold. "Kiss me, please."

"All in good time."

She pouts and grabs my face in both hands. Her thumb drifts over my lower lip, the ravenous look in her eyes all-consuming as she jerks through the flogging. "God, you're so sexy, Quinn. I…think I'm falling in love with you."

I lift one eyebrow. "The sex is that good?"

Her expression dims. "You know it's not just the sex. I care about you."

I believe her. After all, who wouldn't care about an heir to an unimaginable fortune with a huge experienced cock to boot? She cares enough to have aided and abetted Maxwell in his endeavors, while spreading her legs for younger men whenever his back was turned.

"I know you do, darling. Thank you," I murmur.

Her face softens, right before she moans as another strike lashes across her back. I let go of her neck and her mouth strains for mine.

In a swift move, I catch her around the waist and flip her beneath me. She gasps in delight and curls her legs around my waist. I reach behind me and snap my fingers. A leather choker is slapped into my palm. I slide it up her skin and she shivers.

"Is that for me, baby?" she asks sultrily.

"*Everything* in this room is for you. You're a queen. You deserve it." I loop the choker around her throat and tie it tight. Her breath truncates and her pupils dilate.

Easy. *So fucking easy.*

Another snap of my fingers and I receive the ropes. In under a minute she's secured to the bed. I trail my hand from her throat to her tits. I toy with each globe before sliding lower. Her eyes stay on me, hungry, greedier with each passing second. I slip past the triangle of groomed hair at her crotch and touch her leathery clit.

"Oh, yes!"

I play with her for a minute, then remove my touch. "Not wet enough. Clearly you're not as pleased to see me as I thought you were." I remove myself and perch on the side of the bed.

Her head jerks up off the pillow. "No! Please, Quinn. I'm wet. I promise."

I stretch out beside her and trail my fingers over her cheek. "Shh, it's okay. I'm not offended. It's been a while for both of us. Why don't we let Derek and Kyle have a go at that sweet pussy? And I can just…bask in your beauty."

I don't need to signal the twins. They're already buried between her legs. They take turns licking and flogging her pussy. When her eyes begin to roll, I hook my fingers beneath the choker and pull. Her whole body jerks. I take turns pulling and releasing. She climaxes in under a minute. I continue stroking her cheek as Kyle puts on a condom. Before she's fully recovered, he penetrates her.

"No," she moans weakly. "I want you, Quinn."

"You'll have me. First we need to reward the boys for their beautiful work on you, don't you think?"

She nods grudgingly, then inhales sharply as the thrusts get harder, rougher. Derek climbs higher up the bed and plays with her nipples. When they're erect, he clips tiny pegs to the peaks. Then he goes to work with the flogger. A scream rips through her throat with each strike.

"Am I losing you, sweetheart?"

She shakes her head vigorously, her gaze struggling to stay on mine.

"Good." I lean in closer, brush my nose against her cheek. She turns her head and nuzzles me. "Where does Maxwell think you are tonight?" I ask.

"At…a Women Librarian focus group in Midtown."

I laugh. "How very naughty of you, abandoning the women like that. And where is the governor tonight?" I press.

She shudders and moans before answering, "Fundraiser for veterans at Lincoln Center."

"And here you are, his precious gem, getting your rocks off behind his back," I taunt.

Her gaze starts to harden, and I catch the glimpse of the Delilah who didn't blink twice about committing a felony in order to take out a rival. A series of merciless thrusts from Kyle dissolves the look. "I make a better governor's wife when I'm well satisfied." She turns her head and meets Kyle's gaze. "Harder!"

He complies. Her head rears back, and she screams as another orgasm flays her. The twins switch places. Derek is the rougher of the two. Before she has time to recover, he takes control of her.

When she catches her breath a little, her gaze seeks mine. She wants to protest my noninvolvement, but she's enjoying herself too much. When Kyle pulls roughly at the nipple pegs, she groans deep and surrenders to the hedonistic pleasure.

An hour later, she's bathed in sweat. Her screams roll into each other.

When she climaxes for the fourth time, I turn away, suppress a shudder.

Baste myself in darkness and purpose.

"Quinn, you...I need you," she slurs, her multiple orgasms making her near delirious.

I stand, pull down my pants and boxers enough to take out my semi-hard cock. I remount the bed and position myself between her thighs. Derek and Kyle are taking turns kissing and flogging her tits and midriff. She's trying to see me, but they're in her way. I play with her soaked pussy for a while then reach for the toy I need. She moans deliriously as I cram her full with the dildo. It does its job superbly, but it's the ever-tightening choker Kyle is working that gives her the autoerotic experience she craves. This time when she comes, she passes out.

I hop off the bed, and zip up my pants.

"Don't untie her until I'm gone."

"She's gonna be pissed," Kyle says.

"I'm sure you can handle her. If she's extra work, let me know. I'll see that you're compensated."

I take off the watch and lay it facedown on the bedside table so the inscription underneath is visible.

From Delilah to Maxwell. Fidelity and Love. Everlasting.

The twins grin at each other as I re-dress and leave.

My stomach rolls hard against the iron clench I have on it as I rush out of the brownstone and head toward my car. The seething bile bubbling up inside me rises with each step. I get to the Mustang just as it surges up my throat.

Bending over, I vomit on the sidewalk.

31

AXIS OF ACTION

I find the nearest bodega, grab the first bottle of water I see, and tear off the lid. I slap a twenty on the counter and rush back out. In the nearby alley, I rinse my mouth and spit it out. Rinse and repeat until the bottle is empty. I still taste bile and disgust.

Whiskey. I need whiskey.

Or Lucky.

My mind spins at the second thought. I slow it the fuck down and swipe my hand across my mouth.

No, not Lucky. *Whiskey.*

The more expensive the better. And I know just where to get it.

I slide back behind the wheel, slam the door shut, and stomp my foot on the gas. I arrive at XYNYC half an hour later. The crowd is healthy, especially for a Thursday night. Axel runs the place on a tiered membership system. Platinum members get in on Fridays and Saturdays. Sundays are for gold members. The remaining days are free for all, but with a keen eye on who he lets in the door.

The paparazzi are camped outside as usual. I flick them the finger, guaranteeing them a front tabloid exclusive and make my way inside. I wade through fourth-generation *trustfundistas* to the bar, ignoring the sly camera phones pointed my way.

The bartender catches my eye and immediately heads my way. "Macallan. Triple. Neat."

He brings me the drink and I swallow it in one go. I indicate with the glass for another. When he fills it, I take a smaller mouthful, breathe through the burn, and will it to deaden my insides. Only a hint of the numbness returns. I finish the drink and am contemplating a new one, when Axel joins me at the bar.

"You know there's a better blend reserved for you in your VIP room, right?" he says.

I slam the glass on the counter. "Too far," I rasp.

Axel is the same height and build as me, so his speculative gray eyes meet mine full on. The shit we've both endured means there's also no fear or hesitation in his eyes as he stars into my soulless ones. After a minute, he looks away. A few women dance close, try to catch his eye. He ignores them and after a minute looks back at me. "That bad, huh?"

I grit my teeth and breathe deep. "Worse."

"Need any help?"

I shake my head. "It's done. I have what I need."

He nods again, but I sense his distraction. When his gaze tracks across the room, I follow it to the woman standing alone at the place reserved for Axel's guests. She's leaning against the railing, glass of champagne in one hand. At first sight, she seems to be just one of the many beautiful women enjoying XYNYC's exclusive atmosphere. But at second glance, I sense her tension, even from across the room. I look past her to the two club bodyguards on either side of the lounge, blocking her exit. "If you need anything else, let me know," Axel says, without taking his eyes off her.

I glance at him. "Looks like you have your hands full with your own situation that needs taking care off."

"Yeah," he growls. "Fucking tell me about it."

I look back at the woman. She looks familiar, but my brain is too wired to accommodate anything other than the need to dig myself deeper into my abyss, wipe the last two hours from my immediate memory.

"Thanks for the taking care of the other situation," I say.

He shrugs. "My guy at the DOH says they've had a hard-on for that chain of motels for a while. Greasing the right palm just… *encouraged* them to bump it to the top of their list. All it needed was a phone call and a few of my bodyguards to get the place evacuated." He flicks a glance at me before the woman commands his attention once more. "Did the right person end up where they needed to be?"

I nod. "Yes." The thought of Lucky suddenly makes my skin itch in a better way, but the underlying disgust remains from my encounter with Delilah. "Is the apartment occupied right now?"

Axel drags his gaze from the woman. "No, it's empty."

"Can I hit your shower?" I ask, aware that my voice is bleeding pure black void.

His eyes narrow. "Sure. Take as much time as you need. Change of clothes in the closet too. I'll get one of the girls to bring up a bottle."

I jerk out a nod and head for the side of the bar. I slam my hand against the AUTHORIZED PERSONNEL ONLY door and stride to the small elevator tucked in the back. The apartment belongs to the club, so technically it's half mine, but since Axel spends most of his time in XYNYC, he uses it more than I do.

My clothes come off long before I make it to the shower. I turn the temperature to scalding, scrub myself three times in quick succession. It barely makes a dent. Bile rises again and I throw up. With a hint of unfamiliar desperation, I wrench the knob to freezing cold. The ice settles me and I welcome the shivers that race over my skin.

I'm not sure how long I stand with my hands braced on the shower wall. The knock on the door forces me to switch off the water. Snapping a towel around my waist, I wrench the door open.

The female bartender, dressed in a tight sleeveless black dress, stares back at me with wide blue eyes. Both her arms are covered in elaborate ink, and her blue-black hair is cut in drastically sharp angles. She's pretty, in a pixie sort of way.

"Yes?" I hiss.

Her sharp inhale doesn't stop her gaze flicking over my body. "Uh,

Axel sent me up with a bottle. I knocked on the door a few times, but you didn't answer…"

I walk past her into the bedroom. The Macallan M is sitting on the silver tray next to an ice bucket and a glass. I pick it up, pull out the cork with my teeth, and take a long swig. I turn around. She's still standing in the bathroom doorway, her eyes telegraphing a look I'm all too familiar with.

Striding to the bedroom door, I kick it hard enough to slam it into the wall. "Thanks for the delivery, sweetheart. Be sure to tell Axel to give you a nice tip from me. But sadly, there's nothing else on offer tonight."

She rearranges her features from disappointment to nonchalance, and walks out with her chin in the air. I take another swig, slam the bottle down, and head for the closet. I'm tugging a black tee over the borrowed jeans when I hear the ping of a text.

I leave the bedroom and hunt for my discarded clothes. I find the phone on the floor next to the coffee table in the living room and swipe it awake.

The text message produces a reaction that makes me question whether the heart I thought was dead is actually still alive, somewhere in the seething mass of emptiness inside me.

I take a step back and sink into the sofa. Then I read the message again.

You're in my head, too.

* * *

I shouldn't do it.

The session with Delilah tonight has thrown a bracing perspective on my intended goals. Or rather my goal *posts*. They need shifting. Fast. Or I risk every plan I've put into place over the last ten years unraveling.

Maxwell unofficially announced his intention to run for a second term this morning, partly necessitating my return from South Carolina on Tuesday. I stood next to him and Delilah, dutiful son and stepson, and applauded after his speech at the governor's mansion in Albany.

The time and place I have etched on my mind are months away. All I need to do is bide my time.

So I shouldn't do this. Shouldn't draw Lucky further into this soulless circus. My cracks are wide open, unassailable crevasses. She has no idea what she's risking if she allows me to see her again.

But…I'm Quinn Blackwood. Selflessness is an alien concept.

I want her. I…need her. She's mine. Thinking about her makes my body itch for a completely different reason. Besides, contractually, for another seven fucks, she belongs to me.

I own her.

So I dial the number.

The ringing echoes six times, then clicks.

I hear her breathing, but she doesn't say anything. Not for several seconds. "Uh…hello?" The acute trepidation in her voice reminds me that I'm not the only one with secrets in this game. Whatever demons she's battling consume her just as mine do.

Common ground feels…good.

"Elly." Saying her name soothes another layer of the hell circle.

She exhales softly in surprise. "Quinn? I wasn't expecting you to call."

"You prefer me to remain in your head?"

"I…no. I mean, all your texts were sent in the middle of the night. I thought I wouldn't hear from you till later. Not that I expected to hear from you, of course. I mean…" She stumbles to a halt.

I'm lying back on the sofa without realizing I've moved. My hand is resting on my, thankfully, no-longer-roiling stomach. The blackness is still churning, but I no longer want to crawl out of my skin. "Midnight is twenty minutes away. We can continue this conversation then. Will I still be in your head?"

"Umm, maybe," she answers. I catch a ghost of a smile in her voice. Or it could be in my razed imagination.

"Maybe is not good for me. Keep talking. I prefer not take the chance that I might not be come midnight."

"Do you like me in your head, Quinn?" she asked softly.

My teeth grit for a second. "More than is good for you."

A short inhalation. "Why isn't it good for me?"

I simply laugh.

"Do I amuse you?" Her sexy voice is stiff with growing affront.

"You do a lot of things to me, Elly, and you know it. Isn't that why you responded to my text? Isn't that why you're at the end of the phone right now, when your instincts scream at you to run?"

"I don't know what you're talking about," she replies. "Why am I in your head?" she blurts.

Because I spent far too many nights when I wasn't fucking you, watching you sleep. Wanting to drag you into my cracks.

"Because you see me. You know you should be afraid, but you don't run."

"Quinn...are you okay?"

Same question, different version of the woman whose last name I don't even know.

"Tell me your name."

This time the inhalation is sharper. "What?"

"What's Elly short for?"

She stays silent for a long time. "I don't think this is a good idea," she eventually says.

"For you to tell me your name? You don't think you can trust me?"

She laughs. "The guy who tells me to run? What do you think?"

"I think you shouldn't trust me. But I want to know anyway. Eleanor."

"No."

"Eloise. Ella. Arabella. Petronella. Mariella."

"No."

"Hmm, I'm running out of options. Elephant."

Her husky laugh washes over me. "Wow. Elephant. Really?"

"Tell me. Is Elly even your name?"

Her laughter stops. "Yes," she says.

"And it's short for?"

"Why do you want to know, Quinn?" Her voice is just above a murmur.

"I want to see you."

"No, you don't. You want me to run."

I let my eyes drift shut. "I want both."

"That's impossible."

"That word doesn't exist for me." *Never has, never will.*

"It does for me."

"Then you shouldn't have called."

"I can hang up now."

"You called. That door is shut. There's no going back from that."

"And the only way is forward?"

An alien need pounds through me. "Let me see you. Are you done with your *thing*?"

She hesitates a beat. "No. Not yet." Her voice has changed. There's reluctance in there. And excitement.

My cock stirs. "You owe me, Elly."

She breathes out again. "I know, but this thing I'm doing…it's complicated."

"Complicated is if you're shackled to a wall in a dungeon in an underground castle somewhere in the South China Sea. Are you?"

"No, not exactly."

"You're shackled to a wall in a dungeon in New York?"

"I'm not shackled anywhere. But I'm locked *into* something."

"Something that prevents you from having dinner with me?"

She gasps. "You want to take me out?"

"I want. You sound surprised."

"Well, I've never been…" She stops. Seconds tick by. "I can't go to dinner with you, Quinn."

"On account of those shackles?"

"Something like that."

My hand travels down to lie on the bulge in my pants. Just hearing her voice makes me hard. "I want to see you."

She sighs. "Maybe…I can come to your office. Have lunch…?"

"No."

"Right. Okay." She sounds hurt.

"No, because I'm not there. And lunch is too short. I want dinner with you."

"I don't—"

"Don't say no to me, Elly." I harden my voice, give her a glimpse of my obsidian heart. "I don't like it."

Her breath catches. Silence thrums. "Can you give me half a day? I can't promise anything, Quinn, but maybe I can work something out?"

Despite the cruel game I'm playing, I'm intrigued. "I can do that."

"Okay."

We don't speak for a minute, but the silence is easier. "Tell me," I encourage.

"No. You sound better."

My laughter takes me by surprise. "Better?"

"Yes. Less...anguished."

Laughter ceases. I open my eyes, stare blankly at the white ceiling. "That's a shame."

A huff of surprise. "You're sorry you're feeling better?"

"I'm sorry you believe me to be anything but what I am."

"I...don't know what that means."

"Sure, you do," I respond. "You see me, Elly. Don't you?"

"I see that you're in pain," she whispers. "That for some reason you're locked into the suffering and choose to stay in it."

My breath doesn't catch. My dead heart doesn't skip a beat. Truth is truth. Truth from Elly is...something else. But I'm not going to examine it right now. "Yes," I respond simply.

"Why?"

"Ask me why I need breath to exist."

"Quinn..." Her voice drifts away together with, I suspect, her attempt to understand. "I'm so sorry," she eventually says.

Then my breath catches. Because in that moment, right then, I'm ablaze with the need to wrap myself in that sympathy, devour it until there's nothing left.

"Call me tomorrow. Early. And, Elly?"

"Yes?"

"I'll need a yes."

I hang up and quickly redial.

"Fionnella, is the apartment ready?"

A deep sigh. "No, you said you wanted it done by morning. Twelve twenty-eight a.m. is *not* morning."

"Technically—"

"No. It's not." I hear muffled sounds, probably her sitting up in bed. "What's gotten into you, Quinn?"

Ghosts dance on the ceiling. I squeeze my eyes shut once more. "We need to bring the schedule forward."

She doesn't pause a beat. "By how much?"

"Weeks, not months."

"I can make it happen. But are you sure?" There's cautious optimism in her voice. But also palpable relief. The end is in sight.

"I'm sure. It's time."

"Does this have anything to do with Lucky?"

"Will it matter?"

"Not to me. But will you let it matter to you? Or is that question already redundant?"

"You see too much."

"Isn't that why we're in this thing together? We saw too much, *felt* too much. And we paid the price. Is that what's happening with Lucky? Is she—?"

"About the apartment—"

"No. Morning is morning. I'm going back to bed. And Quinn."

I remain silent.

"You better not do anything stupid."

I hang up and stand. I root around for my car keys and wallet, then shove the discarded clothes in the trash.

The Mustang isn't as fast as my DB9, but it still gets me back to my apartment in under half an hour. I go to the second bedroom reserved for Q and pick up the things I need.

The DB9 has me outside the Hell's Kitchen loft in record time.

I key in the code, disable the alarm, and let myself in. A single lamp softly illuminates the living and kitchen area, but upstairs is shrouded in darkness. I adjust the mask, make sure the needle-thin wire of the voice distorter is tucked inside my cheek.

On silent feet, I walk up the stairs.

Tomorrow, I'll have Elly. Tonight, I need Lucky.

* * *

LUCKY

I'm dreaming that stupid dream again. The one where happiness mocks me with its sheer fucking brilliance. I want to shove it out of the way, skip to the terrifying bits, and just be done with it. But no, the death by happiness continues its fucked-up play-by-play.

Quinn's smile.

His voice.

His laughter.

I want you, Elly.

You see me, don't you?

I begin to reach out. And my wish is granted. His face catches fire. Begins to turn to ash right before my very eyes. I want to recoil, but that means letting him go. I don't want to let go. I try to cling, but my hand comes away with the blackest soot.

Soot. Everywhere. Climbing up my body, invading my mouth, my ears. My nostrils. I can't breathe.

I jerk awake with a silent scream.

Then realize the dream isn't over.

He's found me. He's in the room with me.

A louder scream as I launch out of bed. My shin smacks painfully into the bedside table as I scramble backward.

"Don't hurt me! Please don't hurt me, Clay. We...let's work something out."

"Lucky—"

"I have money! Four hundred thousand dollars. It's yours. I can get more. Just give me some time—" *Wait.* The voice. The smoked cedar aftershave. "Q?" I squeak.

"Lucky."

The adrenaline high releases me with a gorging whoosh. I stagger from the relief, my hand pressing against my chest to calm my hammering heart. Then the implication of the last minute pounds into me. *"What the fuck is wrong with you?"*

I lurch toward the bed again, intent on throwing some light, literally and figuratively, on this situation.

"Stay," he commands with a low, deep voice.

"No, I won't fucking stay! I'm not your goddamn dog. You can't creep into my bedroom and scare the living shit out of me, then tell me to *stay.*"

"My bedroom. My body. My pussy."

"My sanity. My terror. My fucking cardiac arrest!"

"Do you want me to leave?"

"Would you, if I said *hell* yes?"

"No."

"Then why bother asking?"

"To make you feel calmer."

I dig shaking fingers through my hair. "Jesus."

"Get back into bed, Lucky."

"Why?"

"So I can make you feel better."

My breath shudders out as other sensations replace fear and anger. The bombshell I dropped will need addressing. But right now, I see his hulking shape against the wall in the darkness, and I can't think beyond the fact that *he's here.*

He must sense my shifting mood, my building excitement. He detaches himself from the wall. "The bed. Now."

I haltingly retrace my steps, slide between the still warm sheets. I can't turn on the lights without permission, so I watch the shadow disrobe. A minute after I get in, he gets into bed with me. One large hand grabs my hips and pulls me into his body.

He's fully aroused, his cock a solid column between us. I catch the gleam of his beautiful mask as he begins to explore my body.

Fear recedes.

Lust builds.

My sigh contains more than a hint of contentment as he parts my legs and kisses his way down my body. He reaches his destination, throws my legs over his shoulder, and precedes to make out with my pussy.

The extreme emotions have me careering toward orgasm in three minutes flat. He licks me clean and prowls up my body. His thick cock finds my core and he rams deep and hard inside me.

"Oh!"

"Feel better?" his electronic voice demands.

"Maybe."

He rams hard again and strokes in and out a few times. "How about now?"

My hands reach out, tentatively caress his muscular arms. When he doesn't stop me, I glide my hands up to his broad shoulders. "Y...yes!"

He fucks me till every last shred of fear evaporates. Bending low, I think he's going to kiss me. Finally. But he leans against my cheek.

"I frightened you. I'm sorry."

"I...it's okay."

"My body. My pussy."

Laughter startles out of me, despite the climax bearing down on me. "Yeah, champ. I haven't forgotten."

He grunts in satisfaction. Fucks me deep. Deeper than ever before. My body is a teeming morass of sensation. But a thought impinges.

"Q?"

"Hmm?"

"No cameras?"

"No. Not tonight. This is for you...for me...for *us*."

Well, shit if that doesn't make my treacherous body sing. Shit if that doesn't make me come harder than I've come in my life.

32

SCENE 2—VIAGRA NIGHTS

PART ONE

LUCKY

"Can I have a friend over?"

Fionnella looks up from her clipboard. "A *friend*?" She says the word like it's an STD.

I nod, calmly spoon another mouthful of cereal into my mouth.

"Male or female?" she asks from across the kitchen isle.

"Does it matter?"

She sets the clipboard down. "Don't be naive, Lucky."

"Fine. Forget I asked."

"No, I won't forget it. Where did you meet this *friend*?"

"What makes you think they're not someone I've known my whole life?"

Her stare is direct and cynical. "Are they?"

I shrug. "It's no big deal if you don't want me to bring anyone here."

She plays with her pen for a minute. "It's not up to me. You asked. I'll run it upstairs, see if there are objections to you having a *male* friend over."

I bite the snappy comeback off my tongue and swallow it. I've been a little cranky since I woke up and found Q gone and another hundred thousand sitting on the dresser. In the space of five days, I've made more money than I know I'll make at any other point in my life. I don't even care about the stigma attached to how I came by it.

No, what's got me cranky is the way my heart feels…bruised each time I think of Q. How can I have such weighty feelings for a faceless stranger? The way I felt two days ago in South Carolina, when I woke up and Stephanie told me he'd left, disturbed the hell out of me. Those feelings doubled this morning when I woke up to an empty bed. How can his absence leave me with a hollow feeling inside when I don't even know what he looks like, what his real name is?

What baffles me even more is that I have similar feelings toward Quinn, the man who's barely touched me, never mind fucked me.

A part of me admits the feelings are attachment borne out of the circumstances I find myself in. Quinn, Fionnella, and Q are the only people I've had the most prolonged contact with in the past five, harrowing weeks. Out of those three, one is becoming a friend, one is fucking me, and the other is mind-fucking me. And in some weird way, I'm getting addicted to the friendship and both brands of fucking.

My mind skates over the conversation with Quinn last night, and the desire to see him again intensifies. So instead of telling Fionnella once again to forget I asked, I look at her, smile and say, "That would be great. Thanks."

She gives me a peculiar smile in return, and goes back to her clipboard. "Your weight is much improved. How do you feel generally?"

"Great."

She ticks a box, then looks at me. Her eyes are speculative. "Anything on your mind you want to talk about?"

I tense. "Not particularly, no."

Did Q mention Clay to her? If so, what is she going to do about it? What can she do about it? The fact that she's here, conducting her routine check-in, suggests nothing has changed. But then, what do I know?

"When will I be returning to South Carolina?" I ask, trying to read her face.

She gives nothing away. "You won't be."

My breath catches and I lose my appetite. "Is...something wrong?"

"No, nothing's wrong. The boss has commitments in the city, so there's been a change of venue, that's all."

Relief eases through me. "Oh, right." I stare around the loft, but I can't see any obvious changes to the layout. "Will he be meeting me here from now on?"

"No."

"He was here last night."

A flicker of something crosses her face, but it's gone almost instantly. "It's his place, Lucky. He can come and go as he pleases. Just as you can. No need to stay cooped up in here all day." Her gaze probes mine, and I'm thinking she does know what I let slip last night.

I get up from the counter, take my bowl to the sink to avoid looking at her. "I don't like the cold. No need to go out if I don't have to."

"It's not that cold today. Besides, you have warm clothes. I can organize a car service for you if you want."

I pour the uneaten cereal down the garbage disposal and turn on the tap. "No, thanks. I'm good."

"Are you?"

My spine tenses ten times harder than before. I grab a sponge and scrub the bowl. "I'm not sure I know what you mean."

She stays silent for a short spell. Then sighs. "Okay, Lucky. Have it your way." I'm not sure why there's a hint of sadness in that response.

I look over my shoulder, but she's gathering her things, shoving them into her giant bag. She looks at me as she hitches the strap over her shoulder. Her smile is back. Only this time, after witnessing a few variations of it, I can spot the cracks.

There's tightly furled grief. Icily controlled anger. Determination.

My gaze stays on her as she makes her way to the door. I want to say something, but I don't. We're all, in our own way, locked in compartmentalized codes of silence we dare not breach.

She opens the door, but pauses. "Your next appointment is tonight, but I suspect the boss will be in touch sooner than that. Enjoy your day."

True to form, the moment I emerge from the shower twenty minutes later, I see the blinking green light on top of the dresser. I'm not exactly sure how the box moved from the living room into the bedroom, but I've stopped questioning the way things work in Q's world. He probably has invisible elves hiding in the closet.

The thought is both disturbing and funny, and I chuckle as I switch the gadget on.

"Something funny?"

"Just bemused at the workings of your world."

"Elaborate."

My towel still wrapped around me, I hop into bed and sit crosslegged with the gadget in front of me. His voice emanates from speakers around the loft, but I feel our connection through the box. "Your little black box moved upstairs. I was debating whether leprechauns were at play or just modern technology."

"It's always been there. I just moved it into your line of sight."

"Oh, right."

"How are you this morning, Lucky?"

The question is couched in civility, but for some reason, I shiver. "I'm fine."

"Do you want to try that again?"

"I'm *fine*," I stress. "You scared me last night, that's all."

"Your distress has been addressed. The content of your response hasn't."

"And it won't be. That's my business, Q. Please leave it alone."

"Fionnella tells me you won't leave the loft."

"Fionnella needs to mind her own business too," I respond, suddenly feeling decidedly less friendly toward my maternal minder. "Whether I go out or not should be my choice, surely?"

"Of course, but the reason you won't isn't the cold, is it, firecracker? California may be the sunshine state, but it gets just as cold there sometimes, doesn't it?"

My gut clenches in shock. "What…how do you know?"

"Wild guess. Which you just confirmed."

I don't believe him. I lift shaking hands to my mouth and swallow hard. "Please…Q, leave this alone." My voice is a naked plea.

But of course, he doesn't. "Who is Clay?"

"He's nobody! Forget the name."

"Why is he after you, Lucky?"

I launch off the bed, my agitated feet pacing away from the black box, as if I can escape him. "Are you even listening to me? I don't want to talk about it!"

"You belong to me. You're in danger from this individual. Tell me what I need to know, or I'll takes steps to find out on my own."

I freeze in the middle of the room. "*God, no!* Please don't do that. Promise me you won't do that, Q?"

He counters immediately. "I'll give you my word, if you tell me what I need to know."

I lick my lips, wrestle down the correct words that'll satisfy him and keep Petra and me safe at the same time. "He's someone I owe money to, okay? I put some distance between us because I didn't have the money to pay him."

"That's why you came to me."

I nod, remember he can't see me, and clear my throat. "Yes."

"How much?"

Too damn much. "About a million dollars."

"You're not sure how much you owe him?"

"I'm…I'm hoping he'll accept a million dollars."

"What if he doesn't?" he counters, his voice growing harsher with each question.

"Then it'll be my problem."

"Wrong answer, firecracker."

I throw my hands up. "Why? Why is it a wrong answer? How is any of this your problem? And don't say it's because I belong to you. Our time together is finite. Once we're done, I walk away. You won't need to think about me, or take on this…this *crusade* you don't want to keep out of. What, are you bored with your own life?" My chest heaves as I resume pacing. "Because I'm sure there are a thousand other things you could interest yourself with besides me. Especially when I don't want you to be bothered!"

"You're right. I can be in a million other places, doing a million other things. But here I am."

That does something dangerous to my foolish, hopeful heart. "Because I fascinate you? Because I'm your little lapdog you can command to *stay*, and I will?"

"The former is true. You fascinate me. The latter you respond to because you want to. I doubt I can make you do anything you don't want to, firecracker."

I hop back on the bed, and stare hard at the black box. "I've told you what you wanted to know. Do I have your word that you'll leave it alone?"

"I'll think about it. Take off your towel."

"I...*what*? How do you know—*you can see me*?" My gaze darts around the room.

"Yes."

I jerk upright onto my knees. "You said there were no cameras in here," I snap.

"There weren't until you mistook me for someone who wants to physically harm you."

My brain staggers beneath the weight of what he's saying. "But, I haven't left the loft since last night. How did you get a camera in here?"

"Accept that I'm extremely resourceful, Lucky, and take off the towel."

I shake my head, my gaze still searching the room. When I don't find it, I glare at the box. "Where is it?"

"Why do you want to know?"

"Because I want to find it and rip the damn thing out."

"Why?"

"Are you seriously asking me that?"

"You're still distressed," he observes coolly.

My breath puffs out in disbelief. "I wasn't when I came out of the shower."

He doesn't say anything. Not for a good minute.

Exasperated, I look around the room again. "What, you don't like me pointing out that you're the cause of my distress?"

"No. I regret that I'm not there to...see to it."

The brief hesitation in his words convinces me he doesn't mean soothing my distress in the normal, *comforting* way. The thought of how he would comfort me makes my heart skip a few beats. Not enough to abandon the totally fucked-up set of situations he's ramming down my throat right now.

"Q—"

"Take off the towel, Lucky. I prefer not to ask again."

"I prefer that you give me your word that you won't do anything about Clay."

"You have my word."

I exhale in relief. "Thank you."

"You're welcome."

I stay seated, stare at the box for another ten seconds. Then I slowly lift my arms and let the towel fall loose into my lap.

His breathing alters. "Fuck, you have the most perfect tits, firecracker. I can fuck them all day, you know that?"

My breath shortens and my fingers slide into my hair just to give me something to do with my hands. "You'd need a couple of pills of Viagra for that," I joke.

He pauses a beat. "Hmm, it's not an unappealing idea."

I freeze in place. "What? You take Viagra?"

"Not normally. But I would with you, to minimize the recovery periods in between fucking you. The thought of giving it to you, making you come continuously all day and all night blows my fucking mind."

I try to control my breathing, but the imagery he's projecting is messing with my ability to think. Hell, it's messing with my everything. I'm aware my nipples have turned into tight, painful points and my hairless pussy is growing damp. My mouth dries, then surges with saliva as decadent thoughts flood my brain.

"Does it turn you on, Lucky?"

A short, torn moan is my answer.

"Shall I make it happen, firecracker?"

I want to say no. I'm dying to say yes. On the one hand, I'm certain I won't survive the experience. On the other, I can't wait to get started. My head shake lasts two seconds before it bobs into a nod.

He laughs. "I'm not sure how to take that. We'll reassess in a minute. Get rid of that towel and lie back for me now, baby."

Refusing doesn't cross my mind. It's what I want, too. I lie back and spread my legs like he taught me to.

His hiss of approval flows through the room. I get the sense that the camera is either above me or directly in front of me. But the loft ceiling is too high, with thick beams where he can hide a camera. So I stop looking.

"You know how much I wanted to fuck you again before I left?"

My breasts are heavy. I cup and squeeze them. He groans. "Why didn't you? Your body, your pussy, right?" I half tease.

"You were sleeping like an angel. Against my better judgment, I chose to leave you alone."

"Why against your better judgment?"

"Because now I'm aching for that tight pussy. Touch it, Lucky. Open yourself wider and show me what I'm missing."

One hand glides down and into my folds. My back arches as sensation buckets down on me.

"You're so fucking beautiful," he growls, low and hoarse. "Work that clit for me. I want to see you come."

I go to town on my body. The fact that he's watching me ceases to disturb me. I revel in his low hisses and thick groans, use it to shamelessly ramp up my own arousal until I'm past the point of no return. I scream as my release tears through me. I hear Q's harsh breathing as I settle back into normal rhythm. Sublime lethargy drifts over me and I want to surrender to it.

"Lucky."

I groan in response.

"We have something else to discuss."

My eyes drift shut. "What?" I slur.

"The subject of your *friend*?"

I become instantly alert. "Uh…yeah?" I sift through the cadence of his voice. Is he pissed off? Indifferent? "You okay with me having him over?"

"That depends."

"On what?"

"Do you like him?"

I frown. "Why do you care?"

"Because I care if you intend to fuck him."

"Does liking automatically equal fucking?"

"Don't women think so?"

"What about men? What about you?"

"I like fucking you. A lot. Enough for me to wonder if you're planning on giving that body I own to this friend who's coming over."

"No, I don't plan on fucking him."

"Tonight or at all?"

I shrug. His tone suggests he's not pissed. But there's something there. Q is fucking with my mind again. "Not while I'm yours."

"So you do like him then?"

"I don't know how I feel about him. He's…it's complicated."

"In what way is it complicated?"

"Wow, you're full of questions. Are you bored, Q?"

"You want me to give you permission for some guy to come sniffing around what's mine. He may be a mind-fuck artist for all you know. Give me satisfactory answers and I'll consider it."

My frown deepens as my confusion escalates. "I was just thinking the same thing about you."

"What?"

"The mind-fuck part."

"Your friend and I have that in common?" he asks.

Shocked laughter erupts from me. "I see you're not denying it."

"You've proven yourself adequate to the challenge of being mind-fucked."

"Seeing and calling your bullshit doesn't mean I enjoy the aggravation, Q."

"Then why are you smiling?"

I wipe the smile off my face and glare around the room. "Where is the camera?"

"Cameras, plural. Headboard and floor lamp."

"I'm going to rip them out. You know that, don't you?"

"Yes."

I raise an eyebrow. "You won't get pissed off with me?"

"They were meant to be temporary. I've put in place a more robust protection detail."

I surge upright. "What sort of protection detail?" The last thing I need are more people digging into my business.

"None that will compromise your privacy. Or put you on any radar you wish to avoid."

I'm a little reassured, but all the same. "Q—"

"You won't come to any physical harm, Lucky. Not while you're with me."

Something about that statement bothers me. Badly. Enough to make my heart lurch and my stomach hollow out. Before I can think of an adequate response, he speaks.

"You have my permission to see your friend."

Umm...right. I'm a little put out that he's not jealous. I expected more resistance from him, what with the *my body, my pussy* edict he's so fond of throwing down.

"Okay. Thanks."

"You're welcome. But, Lucky?"

"Hmm?"

"Make sure you get enough rest. You come to me at midnight. And Viagra Night is happening."

33

REEL

LUCKY

After Q hangs up, I go in search of the cameras. I realize I'm not as upset by their presence, but I act on principle alone. They're both wireless and connected via blue-tooth. There are no switches on the high-tech looking gadgets, so I throw them into a drawer and slam it shut.

Then I fall back into bed and pull the covers over my head. My nap lasts two hours and I wake up refreshed.

Languishing in bed, I think back over the conversation with Q. The man has a way with words. And a formidable iron will. To say I've never met anyone like him is an understatement.

To say my feelings for him are a little murkier than whore and client? Also an understatement. The only person who ever looked out for me was my mother. And that was when she wasn't off her head on cheap liquor to drown out Clayton's cruel monopoly of her life. But it hadn't all been bad. The nine months she stayed sober while she was pregnant with Petra were the happiest of my life.

I still don't know how she managed to hide the pregnancy from Clayton, but I guess it was a combination of deliberately putting on weight so he'd keep his hands off her, and the very genuine illness and subsequent death of her mother, the grandmother I never met, necessitating my first out-of-state trip to Nevada. Petra was born while we were there, arriving a month early. Ma must have laid plans beforehand, because one minute, she had a baby in her arms, the next we were on the bus back to Getty Falls, minus said baby.

The raw anguish and tears in her eyes when she swore me to secrecy made me take the pledge seriously. I kept up my end of the bargain. But Ma, unbeknownst to me, kept a picture of Petra the day she was born, along with Petra's hospital bracelet. Items that eventually fell into Clayton's hands.

And now here I am...

I jump when the cell phone rings. Plucking it off the table, I check the screen.

Quinn. My epic mind-fuck impresario.

"Hello."

"You were supposed to call. Early."

I pull the phone from my ear and check the time. 2:10pm. "I was..." *Getting myself off on camera for my faceless lover.* "Asleep."

"Dinner." The command is tight.

"Yes," I answer simply.

He exhales. "I'll pick you up at seven."

I open my mouth to suggest that we have dinner here. I can't go out. I *shouldn't* go out. But Q's voice is in my head. *You belong to me. I've put in place a more robust protection detail.*

For some reason I trust the offer of protection. He and I are not done. And I believe him when he says he won't let anything happen to me while I'm his. I may be being epically stupid, but I clutch the phone closer to my ear. And I say, "Yes."

"Give me your address."

I experience another twinge of uncertainty, then I tell him.

"Good," is all Quinn says, before he hangs up.

I drop the phone on the bed and cover my face with my hands.

The sensation of having fallen into the Twilight Zone builds. I calm myself and think things through rationally.

Before I quit working at Blackwood Tower, I was using public transport and exposing myself daily to street cameras that Clay could track. My disguise was good, but he has the might of a whole law enforcement precinct behind him.

Quinn's picking me up and we're going to dinner in a restaurant. Surely, that's safer?

My mind bares its teeth in a cynical sneer.

I drag my hands down my face, then I pick up the phone and dial.

Fionnella answers on the first ring.

"I...uh, I've decided to go out after all. Dinner tonight. With my friend."

"Good for you. As long as you're back by eleven to get yourself ready, we're good. I'll have the stylist come early to help you out. Saves preparation time later."

"Okay." I hesitate for a second. "Umm, Q said something about protection?"

She doesn't miss a beat, or ask questions. She's already moved on from our exchange this morning. I love her for that. "Text me the details of where you're going before you leave the loft. I'll take care of it."

"Fionnella?"

"Yes?"

"Thanks.

She exhales softly. "You're welcome."

I spend the rest of the afternoon lazing about. I watch TV, play a little music. And try not to be craptastically nervous about what is essentially my first-ever date.

When the stylist arrives at six, I'm already showered. She checks out the smoky-gray halter-neck dress and black Blahniks I've laid out and applies matching makeup. My green eyes look huge and mysterious when she's finished, and my hair is blow-dried and styled in layered waves down my back.

The confidence boost of looking good helps with the nerves as I wait, cute clutch in hand, for Quinn to arrive.

The security buzzer goes five minutes early.

My lack of dating etiquette bites hard. Should I go down? Should he come up? I press the intercom to release the door and watch him enter.

I pick up my fur-lined black leather jacket and open the front door.

Quinn enters the hallway, sees me, and freezes to a halt. I have very little idea how much I've missed seeing him until that moment. He's dressed head to toe in custom-made black with his shirt open at the throat. His dark hair gleams under the hallway light, and broad shoulders fill my vision. When those almost inhuman silver-blue eyes meet mine, everything inside me clenches tight.

"Elly." His voice, like sandpaper on velvet, sets me alight.

"Hi."

He stares at me for an age, drinks me in, returns for seconds, thirds. Then, still standing in the hallway, a good dozen feet from me, he holds out one hand.

For some reason I'm terrified to step over my threshold.

"You don't want to come in?"

"No."

"Why not?"

"Because you look like that." His gaze devours me from head to toe. Then he beckons me with his hand. "We need to leave, Elly. Now."

I nod, retain enough brain matter to enter the alarm code before I shut the door behind me. He's still holding out his hand. When I reach him, I take it.

His sharp puff of breath echoes my silent gasp. Touching him is like touching an electric current. There's no other description. He feels it too, and he stares down at me for another minute.

"Why? Is there something wrong with the way I look?" I ask to fill the tight silence.

"Is there... Hell... You look..." he stops. Then turns and leads me down the hall.

I laugh nervously. "Are you going to finish that sentence?"

He glances back at me as we exit the building. "Whatever you've been doing since I last saw you agrees with you. I thought you were beautiful before. Now you're...perfect."

My blush stains my cheeks. He sees it and the corner of his mouth twitches. "If you blush at that, then I'm glad I didn't tell you what I *really* thought."

"Try me," I return with a daring I find from somewhere. I don't want him to try me. Not really. Time played tricks and lessened the magnitude of Quinn's dominating presence in my mind. Seeing him again, I'm reminded that I'm dealing with a man whose power and glory seeps from his pores.

His hand tightens almost painfully around mine as we round the corner to where a low-slung sports car is parked on the street. He reaches for the passenger door handle, but he stops at the last minute and turns to me, still holding my hand.

Again he stares down at me for a long time, before his free hand lifts to my face. He brushes a finger down my cheek. "I'm tempted, Elly. So very tempted to try you. But maybe later."

He opens the door, and I slide into the buttery-soft seat. Heart jumping, I watch his long, sexy stride as he comes around to take the wheel.

He doesn't look at me as he guns the engine and hits the road. Our conversation from last night replays in my head and I swallow. I don't want to be mind-fucked again by asking him how he's feeling. But the silence is eating away at me. I watch his finger tap on the steering wheel and something twinges through my brain. Before it forms properly, I remember I need to text Fionnella.

"Where are you taking me?"

Piercing eyes slice into me. "Why, do you regret this date already?"

"Is that what this is? A date? Only I thought that involved talking."

"Aren't we talking? Aren't we already saying the things that need to be said?"

"I don't know, Quinn. I'm not as fluent as you in cryptic-speak."

"You understand me, Elly. More than you want to admit."

I grimace. "Can we at least pretend I don't, and speak like normal human beings? And about where you're taking me, I need an answer."

He speeds through an amber light, then rattles out an address. I catch some of it and quickly text the Gramercy Park location to Fionnella. She responds seconds later with a "got it."

"Refresh my memory. Normal speak is where we ask each other about our backgrounds, try desperately to find what we have in common. Do you really want to waste time doing that?"

"Yes. I need…a little normal." When the words fall from my lips I realize how true they are. My life the past several weeks has been a mixture of fear-induced flight, followed by almost mind-bending surrealism. Even Miguel and Sully seem like hallucinations I dreamt up.

"Fine. You first. Tell me your last name."

Shit. I walked into that one. I toy with withholding it for a few seconds, then blurt out, "Gilbert."

He looks over at me, and the gleam in his eyes spikes the hairs on my nape. "Elly Gilbert."

"Elyse. My first name is Elyse."

Eyes on the road, he slowly reaches out with his right hand and captures mine. He brings it to his mouth, and kisses the back of it. "Elyse Gilbert." He tests my name on his tongue, his voice sexily coarse. "A pleasure to meet you."

I shiver at the darkness in his tone as he says that. All around us, civilization pulses through the heart of the most vibrant city in the world. Inside the powerful car, I'm caught in something savagely primitive. And I don't know if I want to escape.

"Your turn. I know the top-layer stuff, so don't give me those."

"Are you sure you're ready for me to go deep?" he asks, eyes still on the road, my hand inches from his mouth.

I clear my throat. "Maybe it's better if I ask the questions?"

A tic appears in his temple, but he nods. "Shoot."

"Where did you grow up?"

"All over. Summers in the South, winters abroad. But mainly New York."

"Were you born here?"

"No. I was born in my mother's ancestral home on Kiawah Island."

I make a face. "Don't know where that is. I'm not great with geography. But it sounds exotic."

He lowers my hand to his thigh, but keeps his hand on it. "It sounds more exotic than it is."

"Are your—?" I stop and laugh. "You know I don't even know how old you are?"

He glances sharply at me. "Does it matter?"

I shrug. "Not really. I can roughly guess your age, but I was just about to ask you about your parents and it occurred to me I didn't know how old you are. Not that I naturally assume your parents are—" My words dry up when a viciously arctic look crosses his face. Beneath my hand, his thigh bunches in rigid reaction. I've stepped on a huge, throbbing nerve. "I'm sorry, we can skip the family history if you prefer."

He remains silent for a few blocks. I can tell he's reeling himself back from wherever he's at. "My mother died when I was fifteen." The answer is completely devoid of emotion. "My father..." he glances at me. "You don't know who my father is?"

I shake my head.

He pulls the car to a stop in front of a building in Gramercy Park. Black-and-gold double doors front the restaurant and the sign etched in gold on the wide black awning reads *Juniere's*.

A valet jogs over to the car, but Quinn's focus stays on me. "My father is Maxwell Blackwood."

I stare back blankly. "Sorry, no clue who he is, although I think I may have seen his picture on a magazine that first day I served you."

Another gleam weaves through his eyes, but it doesn't stay for very long. "Maxwell Blackwood is the incumbent governor of New York."

My eyes widen and my mouth drops open. I try to adjust both quickly before I make a complete idiot of myself. "I. Wow. You must be proud." The second the words leave my lips, I want to take them back. My clanging instincts scream *no*, he's not proud. Far, far from it. "Or not?"

He squeezes my hand then lets go. The valet opens my door, and I join Quinn in front of the restaurant. He passes the keys to the valet and slides his hand around my waist.

We enter the split-level restaurant and are led upstairs by a smartly dressed maître d' who addresses Quinn by name, tells him how honored he is to have him revisit after so long. Quinn's nod is curt, enough to dissuade further conversation.

The smoky mirrored ceilings and gray marble decor bleed class and exclusivity. There are about a dozen tables on the second floor. We're led to the table in the middle, which involves passing several tables with diners who obviously know Quinn Blackwood. Ergo, he gets respectful nods and smiles and I get the *who the fuck is she* looks. One particularly potent one makes me miss my step. Quinn's hand tightens on my waist.

When we reach the table, he helps me with my jacket, which he hands to a waiter, then pulls out my chair and leans close behind me. "Stop looking so wide-eyed and beautifully lost. It pushes my manic button."

My whole body is caught in a tremor as I settle into my seat. When he sits down, I glance at him and grimace.

"Sorry, I—"

"Please don't say you can't help it." He arranges his wine and water glasses a short distance away from his plate. "That's worse."

I purse my lips, aware that the words flowing from him are almost an afterthought to whatever is going on behind his eyes. And something's going on. Something so dark and deep, I'm too scared to even look directly at him for too long.

I toy with my water glass and on a wild whim, nod when the sommelier arrives with a chilled bottle of wine. I have a feeling I'll need the rare alcohol boost to survive the evening.

"You never told me how old you are."

He takes a large sip of wine and his eyes hook into me. The outer ring of jagged black around his iris seems to be eating up the blue. "Old enough. Maybe even too old."

"What does that mean?"

He just shrugs.

I set my glass down. "I'm sorry if I broached a touchy subject. You should have stopped me if you didn't want me to ask."

"You wanted to see beneath the layer. Don't blame me if you don't like what you see."

"Is this how your dates normally go?"

"This isn't a normal date."

For some reason alien to me, I try harder. "Tell me how your other dates go, just for the hell of it."

"A fuck for a starter, a fuck for the main, and a fuck for dessert," he murmurs, loud enough for me to hear, low enough not to be overheard.

Heat surges through me. "So I'm the exception to the rule?"

"None of them were in my head. *Ever*," he says in that damn even, sinister voice.

I'm more than a little alarmed. "Quinn—"

"I want to remain civil. For you. Don't ask me why. So tell me something that doesn't make me think of all the terrible and fantastic things I want to do your body, Elyse. Tell me now."

"What do you want to know?"

"Will you be coming back to work for me at Blackwood?"

My breath hitches. "Do you want me to?"

"No."

"You don't think I was good at my job?"

"You were great at it. But I have bigger plans for you than the need for you to serve me food."

"You have plans for me?"

His gaze drops from my eyes to my mouth. "I want you, Elyse. My time is limited, but I want to *keep* seeing you."

"I...don't know if that will be possible."

His jaw hardens for a second. Then he frowns and shakes his head. "What will it take? State your terms."

For the second time in a very short half hour, my jaw threatens to drop. People like Quinn Blackwood don't ask people like me those questions. I think of all the things I did in my life prior to five weeks ago, what I've done since. No way in hell are we compatible on any polling system.

"You don't want me," I say. The words hurt.

"Those are useless words."

I open my mouth, to say what, I don't know. The waiter approaches with menus. The food is French fusion. The menu is in French. I have no idea what I'm looking at. My gaze rises, collides with Quinn's.

"She'll have the herb and truffle risotto to start, and the braised lamb with potatoes. I'll have the same."

I hand my menu to the waiter with a smile. When he departs, I glance at Quinn. "Thanks."

He nods. "You were saying?"

"I'm not from New York. Maybe you've already guessed that. I ended up here because…my choices were limited. Those choices mean I can't start anything with you."

"You already have."

The naked truth shames me a little. "Maybe. But it can't last."

"Give me a time frame to work with."

"What?"

"We're both constrained by time. I want to know how long you can give me."

I frown. "Are you going somewhere?"

His gaze sweeps down. "Something like that."

"Oh. Umm…maybe a couple of weeks?" The regret that pounds me with those words staggers me.

He leans forward in his chair, bringing the towering force of nature with him. "So what we initially agreed on? No more?" His spectacular eyes devour my face.

"That's all I have," I say.

He slowly sits back. "I'll take it."

I tremble in my seat, wondering what I've let myself in for. Then I remember Q. "I may not be available all the time."

"Neither will I."

I stare at him, teeming with questions. Questions I can't ask because I don't want to answer any of his. Our food arrives. We eat mostly in silence, both focusing our turbulent emotions on food. Once the plates are cleared away, I glance at him. His eyes are still churning with demonic hell. "Why do you want me, Quinn?" I blurt, repeating the question boring a hole inside me.

None of this makes sense. Not really. Not when you take the time to think it through rationally.

The fingers resting on the table straighten out till his palm is flat. Then his finger starts to bounce. "Maybe I want a little...relief."

Something cracks inside me. Because I get that. I reach out, lay my hand on top of his. His finger stills. "Okay. I'll be your relief. It's okay, Quinn."

"You don't know what you're letting yourself in for."

I sigh. "Make up your mind. You want me to stay or you don't."

He exhales sharply. For a moment he looks...lost. "I do." He glances down at our hands. Then back up. "Are you done eating? Do you want dessert?"

"Yes. No."

He pulls his hand from beneath mine, takes out his wallet, and throws a few hundred-dollar bills on the table. "Let's get out of here."

Outside, I turn to him. "Where are we going?"

"I'm taking you back."

Disappointment swells high. I want to spend more time with him. I want to start being his relief. Like right now.

But Q is waiting. And little slut that I am, I need what he gives me too. So I nod, and get in Quinn's car.

It's a quarter to ten when we get back to the loft. Quinn walks me to the door, his hand linked tightly with mine. I key in the outer code and he walks inside with me. We walk down the hallway in silence, and he waits till I open my front door. I turn to him.

Suddenly, his fingers are spearing into my hair. He's thrusting me against the wall. I have a nanosecond to gasp before his firm, delicious mouth is on mine. He roughly parts my lips with his tongue, then he's invading me. *Oh God.* Quinn Blackwood tastes amazing. I moan deep as my fantasy becomes a reality. He kisses my mouth the way his eyes devour me: with single-minded, near demonic intent. He brazenly licks the inside of my mouth, then bites my lower lip hard before soothing it with his tongue. My clutch falls to the floor along with my jacket. Urgent hands scramble for purchase on his hard, hot body. They land somewhere on his chest, and I cling on for dear life. When my gasps turn to desperate pleas for air, he pulls back, stares down at me, and slowly pushes his thumb into my mouth. I don't know whether to bite or suck. So I do both.

His breath hisses out. After a minute, he yanks his digit out. Then he's back to kissing me. My fingers find his hair. I pull and scrape as my panties grow stupidly, shamelessly wet. His hands move roughly over my body, searching, imprinting, but his mouth never leaves mine. It's as if he's starved for it and doesn't intend to let up until he's engorged.

My need to breathe becomes increasingly frantic, and I gulp in desperate lungfuls when he lets up. He rests his forehead against mine, rocks his hips into mine. The thick outline of his cock makes me struggle not to salivate like a hormonal teenager. But I can't stop my hips from rocking forward too, from cradling him for a mad minute against my pelvis.

He groans. "God, I want to fuck you till you break. I may not be the right person to put you back together, but I want to do it anyway."

I lift my gaze and am immediately annihilated by piercing silver-blue pools of hell.

"I can't," I breathe into his mouth.

He kisses the words away, but doesn't protest.

I can't have sex with him while I'm fucking Q. Even if I could get away with it, it feels wrong. But the temptation is there. *God, how I'm tempted.* Because if he fucks half as good as he kisses, I'm in for a wild ride. I lick my lips and attempt to step back. His grip tightens, and he growls under his breath.

"Not yet."

"Quinn…"

"Don't go yet, Elyse. One more minute."

His ragged plea makes me melt back against the wall. "Okay."

This time his kisses are gentler. Like he's feeding his depleted soul instead of the demons riding him. We stay like that for a long time, his mouth sipping and nipping at mine.

Eventually he tears himself away with a harsh curse. He stares at me with a thousand horrifying emotions seething in his eyes.

Then he walks away without a backward glance.

34

SCENE 3—VIAGRA NIGHTS

PART TWO

"She's on her way."

"How long?"

"Depending on traffic, half an hour."

"You're angry with me."

Fionnella sighs. "I don't know what I am. But I do want to know what the hell you're playing at. She wanted to stay at the loft. That was perfect. Why take her out? And why Juniere's for God's sake? Maxwell and Delilah could've been there."

"They weren't."

"Would you even have noticed if they were?"

My jaw grits. "Yes."

"Quinn, we've come too far for you to hit the self-destruct button prematurely when we're this close."

I grip the phone tighter. "I need her, Nella."

"What about her? Paying her for a job she undertook with her eyes wide open is one thing. This... whatever you're doing on the side with her... I can't talk you out of it, I know. But her baggage is as heavy as yours. Take a moment before you drag both of you down."

"It's too late."

She sighs again. "How did I know you'd say that?"

"Because it's always been too late."

"Quinn…" She stops and exhales. "Don't take her to Juniere's again."

I turn away from the Fifth Avenue view and rest my back against the cool glass. I hadn't meant to take Elyse to Mama's favorite restaurant or sit at her favorite table. That it happened at all is a puzzle I'm grappling with. "Okay."

"Okay," she responds.

"What about the Clay situation?"

"I'm on it. I should have something for you by Saturday."

Fionnella is normally quicker than that, but I know what day tomorrow is.

"Want some company tomorrow?" I offer.

"No. But thanks." Her voice is bleak and cold with long-suppressed grief. "You know I prefer to do the drive on my own," she adds roughly.

The drive to Maine. To the grave where Michael, her son, is buried. It's the anniversary of his death tomorrow.

Michael Smith was my age when Adriana Nathanson got her claws into him. A two-tour Marine suffering from acute PTSD, the good doctor fucked with his mind, while fucking him every chance she got.

I met Fionnella Smith on the last day her son was alive. She accompanied him to Dr. Nathanson's office because she was worried about his treatment. A chance meeting by the water cooler. A desperate confession of her fears for her son. My biting advice to take Michael and run. An e-mail from her a month later that Michael had committed suicide. My own confessions of what those who were supposed to love her had done to Mama.

Those events brought about this unlikely partnership. I may be fucked-up beyond repair, but I'm not fucking this up for her.

"Call me when you get back," I say.

"I will."

She hangs up, and I turn, lean my head against the glass. I want to blank my mind, but the voices won't stop. Neither does the raw hunger that's been plaguing me since I walked away from Elyse. Dinner was a bad idea. It opened me up to…a lot. I said things…*felt* things I can't take back. Like telling her about Kiawah Island. She'll only need a quick Internet search to connect the dots and find out that where Q took her and where Quinn was born are two properties within the same estate.

Maybe I want her to make the connection? Maybe I'm tired of giving her one persona without the other. Of fucking her without showing my face.

And that kiss. Fuck, that kiss.

I groan, lift the glass of whiskey, and take a sip. My cock is harder than fuck. But my mind hasn't stopped reeling through events. Her hand on mine on the table. The sympathy in her eyes. The unexpected jolting of that charred lump in my chest. And this relief that I suddenly want? What the fuck is that about?

How can I want respite now when it's all coming to an end anyway?

I drain the glass and toss it away, not caring where it lands. I press both hands against the glass and breathe, searching for a center I know isn't there.

I'm grateful when the concierge's buzzer sounds. "Your guest has arrived, sir. Shall I send her up?"

"Yes," I croak.

She's here. The sharp edges of my lust glisten, readying itself to cleave. I step back from the window, go to the far side of the living room where the mask is waiting on the cocktail bar. Next to it is a solitary blue pill. I swallow the pill and put on the mask. The voice distorter goes in my mouth and I adjust the lighting. The cameras are already rolling.

I open the door and wait for the elevator to arrive. This apartment is by far one of the most expensive of my New York portfolio. It's also a Blackwood Estate apartment. Once going back to South Carolina became unviable, I chose this apartment.

The elevator arrives and I see she's heeded my instruction. The weather is cool enough for her to get away with a light coat covering her body. But I'm more interested in what she has on underneath. Or what she hasn't.

"Lucky."

Her head jerks in my direction, the blindfold I asked her to wear in the elevator firmly in place.

"Hello, Q," she responds huskily.

I step forward to stop the doors from shutting and toy with the idea of sliding my fingers through hers like I did earlier this evening. Would she recognize Quinn's touch?

A part of me wants her to; the part of me that confessed to needing her to Fionnella. The part I haven't been able to block out effectively since.

Another part of me wants the game to continue forever.

I catch hold of her wrist. Her perfume, the same one she wore to dinner, wraps around me as I walk her into the apartment.

The moment the door shuts, I come up behind her, slide my arms around her waist to untie the coat. I release the single button and the coat slides off her shoulders.

She's naked, except for the lace-topped stockings, the diamond necklace, and her heels. I cup her shoulders and she shivers.

"Did you enjoy your naked-under-the-coat ride across town, Lucky?" I growl in her ear.

"A little bit," she mutters.

"And when you talked to the concierge downstairs? Did you blush?"

She bites her inner lip and her nostrils flare. "Possibly."

I turn her around, my movements a little rougher than I can control.

Her mouth. *Holy fuck*, her mouth. Still swollen from my rough kisses a couple of hours ago.

I pass a rough thumb over her bruised lower lip, the need to experience the kiss again making my cock throb painfully. I silently despise Quinn for taking what I can't have.

Shit. I'm jealous of myself. That's how fucked-up I am. The fact that I'm dying to kiss her again, but can't in case she recognizes me, makes me want to lash out and cuddle her at the same time. Jesus. I don't know what the fuck I want.

"Come here," I growl, walking backward. "Follow the sound of my voice."

She comes immediately. As I walk deeper into the living room, I can tell she's aroused, already panting lightly. I clench my teeth against a moan and the need to take her, like right fucking now.

The apartment is a minimalist's dream of space and glass. The only significant pieces of furniture are the extra large, L-shaped white designer sofa and the floating fireplace. The soaring glass windows offer a stunning view of the city. The strategic lighting offers a modicum of privacy, but it's not total. Anyone with a powerful set of binoculars can witness what's happening in here.

I lead her to the sofa and I sit down, spread my legs. "Stop."

She halts, her hands twitching at her side. "You haven't had the privilege of sucking my cock yet, have you?" I rasp.

Her panting increases a notch. "You know I haven't," she mutters.

"Would you like to?" Why am I asking when I should be commanding?

The answer ceases to matter when her head bobs and her tongue darts out to coat her upper lip. "Yes."

"Get on your knees. Slowly."

Her descent is smooth, measured. Her tits bounce lightly when she rocks forward onto her knees. My mouth dries as I gorge myself on her stunning beauty.

"Come to me, Lucky."

She prowls forward and positions herself between my thighs with unerring accuracy. Her hands lift, pause. "Can I touch you?" she asks softly.

"*Fuck, yes.*"

My forceful answer brings a hint of a smile to her luscious mouth.

"Does it amuse you, firecracker? To know how much I'm becoming addicted to your touch?"

Her smile widens and her small hands find the inside of my thighs. "Not amuse, no. But I...like it."

I catch her hands in mine and drag them to the fastening of my pants. "Take me out. See how much you like sucking me, too."

Her fingers go to work. The moment she has me in her hands, her whole body tightens. She gasps softly and I watch her areolas break out in goose bumps.

"Something wrong?" I ask redundantly.

She swallows. "You're so big. So hard."

"I've been inside you. You know how big I am."

She shakes her head as her hands tentatively explore me. I bite back a groan and take a deep breath. "This is different. Oh God, you took the Viagra?"

Despite the tortured pressure in my balls, my mouth twitches. "Did you think I was joking?"

Heat rushes up her neck into her smooth cheeks. "I wasn't sure."

I grunt. "Now you know. You're going to have me like this, all night. Jack me, Lucky. Don't stop until I tell you to."

Her hands close over me and work me up and down. The expert little flick of her wrists intensifies the pressure in my balls. Her lips part and her breath emerges in tiny, erotic puffs.

I move my gaze from her mouth before I go insane. "Tell me. Did you enjoy your date?"

Her movements halt for a nanosecond before she resumes her task. "You sure you want to talk about that?"

"Why not?"

"Because it's not…appropriate."

"By whose definition?"

Her mouth purses and she concedes the argument. "It was good."

My gaze fixates on her hands. I grit my teeth as her thumb catches a drop of pre-cum and spreads it down the underside of my cock. "Just good?" I grate.

"Okay, it was better than good."

"Do you like him, Lucky? This guy you're seeing behind my back?"

"It's not behind your back. And…yes, I like him."

I allow myself a smile. The sensation of it feels strange but I let it linger, and something lightens in my chest. Her hands tighten around my cock and the smile turns into a groan.

"Are you trying to distract me, firecracker?"

"Yes."

"You're doing a superb job," I growl. "Jack it harder."

Her grip firms and my vision blurs. My head slams back into the seat, and I can't help the muted roar that rips through my throat.

I'm about a minute, tops, from coming. "Mouth, baby. I want your *mouth*."

Her soft lips close around my thick head, and my hips buck in wild response. Once I'm wet with her saliva, she attempts to take more of me. She works me in like a champ, her tongue circling and flicking like little flames of torture. In moments, she takes me to another plane.

Fuck, she's perfect.

As sensation reels through me, I crack open a strange new door, and I contemplate what my life would've been like had I not been set on this path. Would I have found happiness with a woman like Elyse "Lucky" Gilbert? Filled her cute little womb with my babies and let her shower them with love? She's capable of it. Tonight I witnessed her compassion for Quinn. Watched her soft eyes drench with sympathy for his insanity.

The picture grows. Its vividness threatens the obsidian foundations of my destiny. Enough to trigger a thick vein of desperation, which in turn triggers anger.

I buck harder into her mouth. She gags and tries to raise her head. I plunge my fingers into her hair and hold her still. "Take it!"

I tense in anticipation of her refusal. Instead, she takes a deep, noisy breath through her nose. Then opens her throat.

"*Fuck!* Fuck, fuck, fuck!" Fire shoots through my balls, and I explode down her gorgeous throat. I come like a torrent, my curses ripping through the room as I buck like a fucking demented thoroughbred.

She swallows every single drop, a sultry little smile of triumph teasing her lips.

I don't have the energy to call her on it. Instead, I bask in it as she gently massages my balls. I take five to catch my breath, then pat my thighs. "Come here, baby."

Lucky rises and climbs onto my lap. I'm still erect, and my cock rests between her pussy lips when she spreads her legs on either side of me. Her hips circle in cute little jerks as she fights the need to plunge down and fill her snug cunt with my cock.

"Stay," I warn.

She whimpers, but her hands rise to rest on my shoulders. Her fingers play with the hair on my nape as I take turns licking and sucking her beautiful nipples. Her wetness soaks the head of my cock, but she doesn't go beyond teasing herself with my tip.

"My little firecracker, you're so good," I murmur against her skin. "Do you want to be rewarded for being my excellent little slave?"

"I'm not your..." She stops. I look up to catch her biting her lip. "Yes," she blurts.

I laugh. Another titanium string anchoring me to my blackness snaps free. My laughter strangles.

What the fuck is going on?

"Stand up. Turn ninety degrees to your left and walk forward in a straight line. Slowly."

She tenses at my hard tone, but she does as she's told. I get off the sofa and kick off my pants. My dick is rock-hard again. The sight of her, black stockings caressing her legs, swaying sinuously on those heels, turns me harder still.

I prowl after her. "Hands out in front of you now."

She reaches out, touches the cool glass wall. I stop behind her. She's so fucking small. I want to protect and possess. I want to absorb her into me and make her fly at the same time.

I shut off my increasingly disturbing thoughts and plant my hands on either side of hers. Our bodies are so close I feel the soft heat vibrating off her. I want to bask in it so bad, my vision blurs. "You know where you are?"

She shakes her head. Her hair is styled up. I lean forward and bite lightly at her nape.

"You're in front of a glass wall. The light is dimmed, but the glass is still see-through. We're on the thirtieth floor, but anyone who's really looking can see you. What do you think about that, fire-cracker?" I whisper in her ear.

Her throat moves. "I...I don't care."

My cock jumps, slapping her lightly on the ass. "Why don't you care?"

"Because I just want you to fuck me," she replies shakily.

"So you don't mind who sees me cramming that tight little pussy?"

She moans, a soft and needy sound that makes my cock slap her again. "Your body. Your pussy. However you want it."

A red haze blankets me. "*Jesus.* Where the fuck did you come from?" The raw question burns my throat. Another million alien sensations lance me as I place my hands over hers.

I don't even need to tell her to part her legs, pout her sexy rump toward me. I bend my knees long enough for my cock to find her entrance. An upward thrust sends her to her toes. Her scream is fucking ambrosia. She turns her head and places her cheek against the glass. And I fuck her long and hard and deep until she comes and collapses into my arms.

I carry her sweet weight to the rug before the fireplace. Wait for her to catch her breath. Then I take her ass.

The living room becomes our dirty little playground long after the horizon tinges gray and orange.

She's almost comatose when I slide into her pussy once more. Her back to my front, I wrap both arms around her shoulders and waist. Trap her to me. I revel in her shudders as I rock in and out of her slick channel.

Words fill my head, rattle around, gather speed. Before I know it, they're spilling out.

"I would keep you, Lucky. If I didn't need to do this. If my life wasn't a fucked-up wasteland, I would keep you. Make you mine for-ever."

She trembles at my words. I fuck her some more, absorb her

weary little cries. She begins to unravel. Her inner clenches are as potent as her first orgasm, milk me just as firmly.

"I'm coming for you, firecracker. Coming so fucking hard…"

Her breath hitches, like she's catching back a sob.

As release grips me in its relentless talons, I touch my fingers to the blindfold over her gorgeous eyes. They come away damp. She's crying.

My own eyes sting with the torment of suddenly, for the first time in my life, wanting something I can't have. Something I'm not worthy of.

And I don't know what to do with all these fucking feelings.

PART FOUR
Elyse

35

WALK & TALK

I would keep you.
  Make you mine forever.
The words pound through my head. The anguish, the bewilderment lacing his tone continues to haunt me two days later. I haven't heard from Q since the early hours of Friday, when I awoke in the penthouse alone. Fionnella tells me he's tied up with other matters and that until I hear from him, my time is my own. To be honest, I'm grateful for the reprieve. The combination of marathon sex and ragged emotions has left me in a state of shock.

Thursday night was the most intense night of my life. Every single moment was overwhelming. And deeply personal. So much so, I barely noticed the cameras. And when I remembered they existed, I didn't care. In hindsight I realize what's happened.

Sex with Q has stopped being a transaction and turned into something else. Something more. I'm falling for him. Probably already have.

The enormity of that revelation has turned me into a half-zombie. I haven't left the loft. I miss him, want that damned black box to light up. At the same time, I'm scared that he will get in touch. Because on Friday, after I managed to find the energy to walk and leave the apartment, I came home to find three hundred thousand dollars on my dresser. I'm now two hundred thousand shy of my goal. Two more "normal" sessions. Or one intense fuck away from never seeing Q again.

The anguish that knowledge brings terrifies the shit out of me.

To take my mind off my terror, I do something equally terrifying.

I begin to make plans on how to contact Clay once I have the money.

I can't just show up back at Getty Falls and expect him to forgive and forget. I also need to find a way to make him accept that the million dollars is better than attempting to wrestle Petra's whereabouts from me.

Handling Clay Getty will be a delicate task. He didn't rise to his position of power by letting people like me get away with wronging him. And by destroying his ancestral home, his prized possession, I've placed myself in the prime position of number-one enemy.

I pace the loft for a couple of hours before I summon the courage to flip on the Wi-Fi to connect to the Internet.

A quick search of the Fresno newspapers tells me very little about what's happening in Getty Falls. I don't refine my search because I once heard Lolita mention something about a geo-locator on websites that tracks searches. I have no clue how many people search Getty Falls, but I don't want to take the risk of shining a spotlight on myself.

What I do is hit Twitter and search for the Getty Falls Sheriff's Office page. On the main page is a short bio and picture of the sheriff with his shit-eating smile. I scroll down and read through the feed.

Acting Sheriff Daniels responds to a burglar alarm...suspect apprehended.

Two days prior to that...*Acting Sheriff Daniels and Officer Pratt respond to reports of a domestic altercation.*

I go back as far as I can to when the sheriff was last on duty. I hold my breath when I find what I'm looking for.

Sheriff Clayton Getty on a temporary leave of absence to deal with private matters. Deputy Rick Daniels will act as sheriff.

Officers attend the funeral of Ridge Mathews. My breath catches and I click on the attached link. ...*Sheriff Getty confirmed his death was a tragic accident.*

God, Clay covered it up. My heart continues to race as I scroll back up and stare at Clayton Getty's picture in the bio.

Yes, my biological father isn't just a third-generation brothel landlord, he's also a corrupt sheriff in charge of law enforcement at Getty Falls. And he took a leave of absence the day after I burned his whorehouse down and skipped town.

I'm staring at his picture when a retweet pops into the feed.

Person of interest sought in Getty Falls fire. Elyse Gilbert, 5'4" has been missing since the fire. If seen, contact the Sheriff's Dept. There's a link beneath the message along with my picture. The phone clatters to the ground as ice drenches me from head to toe. My heart bangs against my ribs, and I struggle to breathe.

I scramble for the phone again. I turn off the Wi-Fi and jump up from the sofa. But the truth is inescapable. If I needed confirmation that Clayton was coming after me, I have it.

But would he have put my name and picture up on social media if he knew where I was? Does the fishing expedition mean he's lost my trail? I force the fear aside and try to think things through properly. Since quitting my job at Blackwood Tower, I've been off the radar for a week. Even if he knows I'm in New York, my not using public transportation right now may be working to keep him from finding me.

All the same, I need to bring this to a head sooner rather than later. Every day he wastes time trying to find me and doesn't means his attention might shift to locating Petra.

I glance at the phone, debate whether to call Fionnella to tease out a more specific date for when I'll next see Q.

The phone vibrates just then, making me jump.

Quinn.

My heart leaps for a different reason. Hands shaking, I answer the phone.

"Hi."

"What's wrong?" The coarse rasp of his voice holds a layer of concern.

I suck in a deep breath. "Nothing's wrong."

"Don't lie to me, Elyse." Steel layers over concern.

I rub my forehead in agitation. "I did something. And it's catching up to me."

"Are you in danger?"

I squeeze my eyes shut for a second. "I'm trying my best not to be."

"And how are you doing that?" he fires back.

How can I tell him that I'm selling my body to pay off the pimp whose empire I destroyed? "I'm still trying to work that out."

Quinn stays silent for a minute. "Would you consider my help?"

My heart flutters like mad. "Thanks, but no."

"You would offer me relief, but won't take help in return?" he presses.

The differences between us charge up like an invisible wall. I'm not sure exactly what his issues are, but mine will land me murder and arson charges should they ever get out. "This... it's not the same. You advised me to run not too long ago. I think it's only fair that I tell you to do the same."

"Why?"

I rub my forehead harder. "I'd hate for you to be caught up in my shit, Quinn."

"Too late." The way he says it, soft, deadly, like a coiled, poisonous snake fat with venom, just itching to sink its lethal fangs into something.

I shiver despite the ambient temperature. "It's not—"

"We can table this discussion for another time, but don't waste more words on this. I want to see you today."

I should say no. I *should*. I should stay inside, hide from Clay.

A broken piece of me picks itself up off the floor, stabs at the fear. "Okay. I'm not sure what kind of company I'll be though."

"Leave your mood to me. I'll pick you up at eight."

He hangs up, leaving me with yet another head full of questions.

I don't call Fionnella. And I slap a *to be continued* sticker on my puzzling feelings about Q and shove it to the back of my mind.

But there's one call I've been putting off. I dig out my backpack, pull out the picture of Ma and me, and turn over the frame. The alphanumeric code I wrote translates to a phone number, and I dial it with shaking hands.

"Hello?" A tentative voice answers.

"It's me. Elyse."

"Oh, it's so good to hear your voice. We've been so worried! Are you okay?"

"I'm fine, Mrs. Ringwald."

Her laughter is tinged with relief. "I told you, call me Doris."

"Doris…is she there?"

"Of course. Hold on."

The phone clatters softly, then it's picked up again.

"Elyse?"

My heart leaps and tears burn. "Petra. How…how's things?"

"Good. Well, good with a *heavy* dose of boring," she amends.

I laugh. And it feels so good. "The farm not keeping you busy?"

"I love the horses. The home-schooling, not so much." She lowers her voice. "Doris likes to repeat the same lesson over and over, like I'm thick or something."

I grin at the eye roll in her words, then I sober up.

"Don't give her a hard time, okay? This is all new to her, too."

Petra sighs. "I know. I think her and Paul are thinking of swapping. Hopefully he's better at the teaching thing." She pauses for a few heartbeats. "Am I going to see you soon?"

My heart lurches. "I won't lie to you, Petra. I don't know. For now, it's best I stay away."

I've met my beautiful baby sister only once. A year ago when Clayton started asking questions, I took steps to track her down and warn her adoptive parents about the threat he posed. Paul and Doris Ringwald took the warning seriously and relocated from Nevada to Idaho. My second warning call two months ago forced them to head north to a farmhouse outside Vancouver. It helps me sleep better at night to know they're as invested in her safety as I am.

"Are you sure we can come back when I turn eighteen?" Petra presses.

"Yes." Clayton would no longer have any rights to claim her then. "So please hold on a little longer, okay?"

Another sigh. "Okay."

"I'll call when I can. I promise."

She passes me back to her adoptive parents and I reassure them that everything's okay before I hang up.

Once my heart resettles, my thoughts return to Quinn.

What exactly does *leave your mood to me*, mean? And where is he taking me this time?

I take a long scented bath, puzzle over the questions a little more, then abandon them. Quinn is electrifyingly cryptic. And autocratically hard-headed.

Almost as much as—

The sponge I'm running over my arm pauses. I frown.

Am I in danger of blurring the lines by comparing the two men in my life? They aren't that alike. Both are seriously alpha, sure. But Q doesn't ask. He takes. Whereas Quinn asks persistently until he gets what he wants.

My frown clears for a minute, then returns.

But they both set me on fire, and I fear more exposure will only make things worse. Except I'm not in a hurry to walk away from either.

I try to shut my thoughts off as I zip up my sleeveless black jumpsuit and strappy heels. On a self-comforting whim, I dig into my backpack and bring out a small jewelry box. Inside nestles a delicate silver chain with a heart locket given to Ma by her father for her sweet sixteenth. It's the only thing I kept from Ma's belongings beside the picture and I intend to give it to Petra. But I can't resist wearing it now, to feel closer to the mother I lost and the sister I've turned my life inside out to protect.

Quinn rings the buzzer at eight. This time, he comes to the door.

Those eyes dig into me, and I make sure to keep my smile carefully pinned into place. I make no effort to resist when he cups my nape and tilts my head up to kiss me. Somewhere between the bath and getting dressed, I decided to take this evening as it comes. I'll give him as much of my truth as I can without endangering my sister. What he does with that information will be his problem.

For now…the kiss. God, I love the way he kisses.

I'm moaning like a whore in church by the time he lifts his head.

"I've fucking missed doing that."

I laugh. "Me too."

He doesn't smile exactly, but I can tell my response pleases him. "You ready?"

I nod. The weather has turned warmer in the last couple of days, so I bring a wrap with my clutch.

We head to a nightclub—XYNYC—in Soho. Even before we reach the valet parking area, the paparazzi are upon us. They shout Quinn's name, fire questions about who I am and what we are to each other. Lights blind me and I stumble when I get out of the car.

Quinn tries to protect me from the more aggressive of the paps and that sparks an even greater frenzy. By the time we stumble through the VIP entrance, I've swung from easygoing about our date to regret.

"Sorry about that." Quinn's jaw tightens and he gauges my reaction carefully once we're inside. "They normally keep their distance."

My shrug doesn't fire on all cylinders because my mind is busy churning out worst-case scenarios of what this could mean for me in terms of Clay finding me. I shudder.

What the fuck have I done?

Quinn frowns. "Elyse, are you okay?"

I meet his gaze, take a breath and go with the truth. "There's someone looking for me. Someone I'm hoping won't find me until I'm ready to be found." I wave a shaky hand outside. "Those paps—"

I stop speaking when he steps toward me and cradles my face in his hands. "I'll take care of it. I promise."

My eyes widen. "How?"

His thumbs brush down my cheeks. "I won't bore you with the details, but I want you to trust me. Can you do that?"

Nodding is stupidly simple, if seriously unwise.

I taste his approval in the kiss he seals on my lips. And when he links his fingers with mine and leads me into the nightclub, my fear is reduced to dregs.

He takes me to his personal roped-off VIP area, and we order burgers and fries. I'm sipping a glass of champagne and checking out the glitterati on the dance floor when we're joined by a dark-haired, drop-dead gorgeous hunk of beefcake. With his gelled-back hair, carefully cropped stubble and sharp designer suit, he looks like he's just finished a photo shoot for GQ magazine. Except the deadly look in his eyes and the granite-set jaw tells me he would chew up and spit out anyone who dares come near him with a camera.

He nods and rumbles a response when we're introduced. I catch his name as Axel Rutherford, owner of the club, but not much else. He conducts a low, terse conversation with Quinn, then leaves.

From across the lounge, Quinn stares at me.

Something about the way his head cocks to the side tweaks a brain wave. But then he starts moving and I'm lost in the animal grace of him, the sheer sexiness of the man who seems as absorbed in me as I am in him. He reaches me, cups my shoulders, and leans down to whisper in my ear.

"Tell me what song you like."

My smile is a little shy. "Why?"

"I want you to dance for me."

Not with me. *For me.* Way to throw a self-conscious vibe on a girl. "I don't really—"

"Please."

My eyes goggle at the intensity behind the plea. I blurt out something like Maroon 5. He beckons the bouncer and relays the information. Two songs later, the club mix of "Animals" pounds through the speakers. I recall the lyrics and inwardly grimace.

But he's looking at me, expectant.

And I start to sway. He takes my glass from me, steps back, and gives me a little room. I should be cringing with embarrassment. The look in his eyes won't let me. It's like he needs me to dance. He slowly circles me as I move, throw myself into the throbbing beat. I feel his eyes everywhere. On my throat, my arms, my ass, my breasts. Halfway through, he lifts my glass and gulps down half my champagne. The sight of him drinking from my glass is so intimate, my breath catches. On his next rotation, he drifts his fingers down my arm.

The touch singes me right to my pussy.

Fuck. I bite my lip and circle my hips to the beat. He's behind me when the music blends into another tune. Firm fingers plunge into my hair, and he kisses his way from my neck to my jaw to the corner of my mouth.

"You take my fucking breath away," he croons into my ear.

Flushed with horny vibes, I turn and throw my arms around his neck. Our kiss is what force-ten gales are made of. Mouth-fucking at its most intense, we go at it until a throat clears loudly from the lounge doorway.

I hide my face in Quinn's jacket and let him deal with the intrusion. His chest rumbles with whatever he's saying. After a minute, he whispers in my ear. "Our food's here."

Food. Okay. I can do food. He leads me to a small bar area where our plates are waiting. I can't quite look him in the eye after attacking his mouth like it was my favorite toy, so I concentrate on sating my other hunger. I polish off the burger and fries in minutes, then look up when I hear his dark chuckle.

"Always knew you were a voracious little thing."

I glance at his plate. He's barely taken more than a few bites. Such a waste. "I have a great relationship with food."

He picks up a fry, dunks it in ketchup, and holds it to my lips. I take the food and give an exaggerated little moan. I'm rewarded with something that vaguely resembles a half smile. He shares the rest of his food with me, feeding it to me like he fed me in his office what feels like a lifetime ago. God, was that only last week?

When we're done, we head back to the edge of the lounge. I work off some of the calories over the next few songs. Quinn doesn't join me in dancing, but he stays close, eyes always on me. More drinks are served. We take a break an hour later, and head to the sofa, where we mouth-fuck a whole lot more.

At some point, I end up in his lap. His big hands cup my ass and he grinds me into the thick rod of his hard-on. But by mutual agreement we don't take it beyond that, although I know deep down, if fate and circumstances allow, it's only a matter of time before I fuck him.

We leave the club in the early hours. Outside, there's no sign of the paparazzi. We get into the back of a limo, Quinn having drunk too much to drive his DB9. In the back seat, I find myself once again in his lap. His hands are on my ass, but we're not kissing. His piercing blue eyes survey me from where he's leaning against the headrest.

"I have a thing tomorrow during the day."

"A thing?"

A sliver of ice crawls over his features. "With Maxwell."

"Your father?"

A curt nod. "It finishes in the afternoon. I'll come to you after."

"Okay."

"Good." The pressure on my ass increases. "Kiss me."

We make out all the way back to Hell's Kitchen.

When he leaves me at the door, I'm disappointed, but a little grateful.

Because I know I'm falling in love with two men. And my head feels like it's going to explode from the pressure.

* * *

QUINN

I'm in the shower, jacking off—yes, I'm fucking masturbating for the first time in years, to the memory of Elyse's ass in my hands, her tits, her pussy grinding into me at the back of my limo—when my phone rings.

I turn off the spray. "Answer." When the voice activation kicks in, "Yes?" I growl.

"We have a problem."

My back knots in tension. "What is it, Nella?"

"Clayton Getty. We've lost his trail."

"Where?"

"Private airport in Reno. He hired a plane. Flight plan said he was headed to Tallahassee. He never landed there."

My wood dies a quick, merciless death.

36

NOIR

One Week Later

For the first time in forever, I wake up with a smile on my face. I've seen Quinn every night for the past week.

Last night was the best night of all. He took me to dinner at a posh restaurant on top of some tower whose name I can't recall. Our table was the only one on the terrace. And after dinner, we danced under the stars. We ended up at XYNYC after that, of course. He confessed he was part owner and enjoyed going there to relax, which isn't a bad thing considering I like the music and food there, too. There were fewer paps this time, for which I was grateful.

I replay the previous magical seven days in my head as I bask in my warm bed. Among the many little pockets of awesome, the one I find most precious is the fact that Quinn is willing to give me time, to take things at my own pace.

I've never had that. Every significant encounter I've ever had to date was on someone else's terms. What makes it even more special is that I know he wants to fuck the hell out of me. The anticipation alone has my hands moving down my body, wondering how it will feel to have him inside me when the time comes.

My brain rolls through a clutch of superlatives, some of which have me laughing out loud. Until that happens, I intend to enjoy his world-class kissing.

Hunger eventually drives me from bed, after which I laze around, watch a movie. The phone stays silent and I breathe an inward sigh of relief as the hours tick by without a summons from Fionnella or Q. I don't know how to take Q's ominous silence, but by two, I know I probably won't hear from either of them, so I'm free to spend the afternoon with Quinn as we planned.

Perversely, that acknowledgement slows time right down. I amble listlessly from bedroom to kitchen to living room. Eventually I turn the TV back on, channel surf aimlessly, and stop at an entertainment channel. Some celebrity or other is skydiving naked off a mountain in South America. I roll my eyes and am about to flick to another channel when I freeze.

Quinn.

On TV.

My breath rushes out for two reasons.

One, *dear God*, the man is beautiful. Almost impossibly so. It hurts just to look at him full on.

Two, the look on his face chills my blood. It's the same look he wore the first time I saw him. The deathly stillness, the soulless stare. But behind it, I see ravaging anguish. He's standing at a podium of some sort with a group of people. My gaze moves to the man giving the speech, and I note the uncanny resemblance between father and son. I stare at Maxwell Blackwood for a moment before Quinn once again absorbs my attention.

When his father finishes speaking, he claps, but his expression doesn't change. Amid the smiles and handshakes, his face remains a rigid mask. He leans sideways as the person next to him, a stunningly beautiful woman with straight black hair and piercing gray eyes, whispers in his ear. He straightens without answering or looking at her, but as they turn to leave the stage, Quinn's hand slides around her waist.

Then, I watch, stunned, as his hand moves lower to her ass. The squeeze is lightning quick, over before it even begins, but my insides congeal.

I launch off the sofa, my hand fumbling with the control. I hit rewind, hoping, praying that I saw wrong. But yes, there it is. His hand. On her ass. *Squeeze.*

Oh God!

I stagger backward, force myself to listen to the rest of the newscast. Maxwell Blackwood intends to run for a second term as governor, blah blah blah....support of his second wife, Delilah Blackwood, and his son, Quinn Blackwood.

My heart drops to my feet.

He was copping a feel of his stepmother's ass on live TV?

The remote drops from my numb fingers as I'm hurled once again into the Twilight Zone.

What the fuck?

Nausea rolls through my stomach. I return to the sofa before my legs give way.

I try to control my breathing. *Calm the fuck down.* There must be an explanation. But what, though? How do you explain something like that away?

I look back at the TV. The segment has moved on, but it's still about Quinn. The caption *Chameleon Blackwood* is now slapped across the screen. Next to his normal clean-cut, suit-wearing picture is another one in which he's sporting a lighter hair color, a chilling frown, and giving the picture taker—most likely a paparazzo—a finger. The background in the second picture looks like the outside of XYNYC. There's no sound so I can't hear what the segment's about. The mute button must have activated when the remote fell. I frown at the two pictures.

My brain is firing warnings at me, but my mind is too fixated on that image of his hand on his stepmother's ass to accommodate anything else.

The program moves on to another celebrity. I lie back and spike my fingers into my hair. I want to grab my phone, call him, and demand an explanation.

But when it comes down to it, what rights do I have? We fell into this...*thing*...without rhyme or reason. And Quinn has been aware from the beginning that I have something else going on. Something *he* has accommodated. So really, I don't have a leg to stand on.

That bracing reality drags spikes of pain through me. I'm still sitting on the sofa, staring into space, when he buzzes the door.

He's wearing the dark gray suit from TV, minus the tie.

I try to smile when he walks in. I fail. I try to throw myself into the long, beautiful make-out session he stages with my mouth. I succeed. But only just.

Silver-blue eyes pierce me when he lifts his head. "Something's wrong."

No shit.

"I saw you on TV."

That deathly stillness engulfs his whole body. "And?"

What could I say? *You had your hand on your stepmother's ass and besides the actively eww factor of it, I don't know what to do with this insane jealousy riding me?*

"Quinn, are you seeing someone else?"

The only reaction I get is a slight flare of his nostrils. "What sort of question is that?"

"A normal one that I should've asked before this...whatever *this* is, started."

"I'm seeing you. Am I fucking someone else? Not right now. But I love to fuck, Elyse. I won't deny it. I fuck when the urge takes me. I'm hoping to fuck the shit out of you when you're done with your thing. When that happens, I intend for you to be the only one I fuck. Does that answer your question?"

Not even close. But I nod, because I can't bring myself to ask the other question.

"Good, then let's go."

I glance down at my jeans and cream cashmere sweater. "Do I need to change?"

His eyes, still containing jagged shadows, fly over me. "No, come as you are. Maybe bring a scarf."

"Where are we going?"

"For a drive. I need to clear my head. Do you mind?"

"No." I could do with some head-clearing myself.

I hurry upstairs, slip my feet into new tan knee-high boots. I loop a long blue-and-silver scarf around my neck, glide on some lip gloss, and leave my hair loose. I shove some money and my phone into one of my new cross-body purses and check myself out in the mirror one last time.

His jacket is off and he's pacing the living room when I return. The moment he catches sight of me, he holds out his hand. A tight knot inside me eases. When I reach him, he takes my hand, pulls me close, and kisses me long and hard before he walks us out the door.

He's not driving the DB9 today. Sitting on the curb is another low-slung sports car. A silver Mercedes-AMG. It looks scarily powerful.

He helps me into it, tosses his jacket into the back, and walks around to his side with stilted movements. The throaty engine roars to life and he burns rubber as he leaves the curb. He doesn't talk as we endure the late afternoon traffic out of Manhattan, but he catches my hand, kisses my knuckles a few times before resting it on his thigh. Jazz and rock anthems blast from the speakers.

It's not until we hit the outskirts of New Jersey that he lowers the volume.

"Whatever you saw on TV…it's complicated." His voice is low, coarse as gravel.

The nausea threatens again. "There's complicated and then there's *complicated*. Which kind are we talking about?"

He doesn't even blink. "The second kind."

My heart drops. "I don't know what to do with that, Quinn."

He stays silent for a mile or two. Then he glances at me. "That relief you offered. I'm asking for it now."

God.

"Tell me I didn't see what I think I saw on TV?" I press.

His eyes leave the road for a second. The black shadows have multiplied. "I'm not into anyone else, Elyse. Right now, you're the only thing I want."

Right now. What about last week? What about *next* week?

The words stick in my throat. I remind myself I don't have any rights here.

"You can't live like this, Quinn." Whatever's going on, it's taking a dangerous toll on him.

I'm surprised when he nods. "It'll be over soon." They're more than just words. They're a dark, solemn pledge that vibrates through the car.

My breath shudders out and I nod in return. "Okay. Then, whatever you need, I'm here."

His chest rises and falls in a deep exhale. He turns the music back up and shoves his foot on the gas. We fly up interstate highways and eventually emerge into the countryside. In the late afternoon sun, spring colors bloom. The roads are relatively traffic-free, and Quinn's smooth driving lulls us both into calmer states.

An age later, I see signs for the Catskills. We stop for an early dinner at a local pub. Conversation is light and limited, but Quinn remains attentive, his gaze running over me several times as we eat.

After we're done, we head back to the car. He kisses me before I get back in, and my hand returns to his thigh as we drive deeper into the Catskills.

Alpine countryside and historic B&Bs whizz by as the Mercedes eats up the miles.

Eventually, he pulls to a stop in Catskills Park. When he leaves the car, I follow. We hike a short distance to a still lake. Quinn shoves his hands into his pockets, walks off by himself, his shoulders hunched as he stares into the water.

I want to hug him, but the vibes he's throwing off make me keep my distance. After about ten minutes, he retraces his steps to me.

"My mother loved it here," he says without looking up from the lake. "When she wanted to get out of the city, we would drive up here, spend the night at a B&B, and return home in the morning. Just me and her."

My heart squeezes at the raw anguish in his voice. "That must have been special for you."

"Yes. I thought so."

I frown at the odd note. "You don't think it was for her?"

He shrugs. "I wish she would've trusted me."

"With what?"

He looks at me and his eyes are terrifying again. "Enough to tell me why she needed to escape. Enough to let me save her."

"How...from what?"

"From him. From Maxwell."

Shock stabs me. "Your *father*?"

He doesn't respond. His face turns desolately bleak and he stares back at the water. After five harrowing minutes pass, I give in to the urge and hug him.

He stiffens and pushes away from me so violently, I stumble.

He immediately curses and lunges toward me. "Elyse, I'm sorry... I didn't mean..."

I hold out my hands and dive out of his reach, my heart hammering. "It's fine. I'm fine."

His hands ball into fists, and his chest rises and falls in ragged breaths. We stare at each other for a fistful of heartbeats, then I slowly hold out my hand.

He takes it, clenches his fingers tight around mine, and we walk back to the car. We drive around a little more and end up outside a quaint, centuries-old white-and-blue clapboard house with a B&B sign on the outside.

Quinn parks on the curb and looks broodily at the property.

"This is where you used to stay?" I venture.

He nods and points to the tiny turret jutting out from the roof. "Right at the top. It was my own personal castle for a night."

On impulse, I step out of the car, go around to his side, and hold out my hand. "I'd like to see it," I say with a smile.

He hesitates for a moment, but then steps out. We climb the small hill and enter the parlor reception area. A woman in her fifties emerges from a back office and smiles at us. Her chest tag reads MANAGER.

"How can I help you folks?"

I exchange glances with Quinn. He raises an eyebrow, his eyes gleaming with the barest hint of amusement. "Uh…this is a probably an odd request, but my uh…friend here used to stay here with his mom." I look at Quinn, but he doesn't seem inclined to help. "We…he wants to see the room upstairs…where they used to stay?"

The woman looks from me to Quinn and back again. "You mean you want to book it for the night?"

"Um, well, not exactly—"

"Yes. Is it available?" Quinn asks.

My eyes widen in a *what-are-you-doing* query, but he ignores me.

The woman nods with a slight frown. "It is, but the beds in there are two singles, not a double. Are you sure you don't want another—?"

"We'll take it." Quinn pulls out his wallet and slides his black card and ID across the desk.

She picks up the ID, sees his name and her eyes widen. "Quinn? You're Adele Blackwood's son?"

He nods tersely.

Her face softens. "I was sad to read about her passing. She was a lovely woman."

Stillness engulfs him. "Thanks."

She senses the subject isn't one to linger on, so she enters his details, and hands back his cards. "If you'll wait a moment, I'll grab the keys and take you up."

The moment she disappears, I turn to Quinn. "This isn't a good idea."

His eyes hook into me. "Why not? Do you have someplace else to be?"

"No. But—"

"It's just for one night, Elyse."

37

BLUR

I could come up with a million excuses. But the truth is I want this precious time with Quinn. So I say nothing. And I nod.

He exhales.

And we wait for the manager to return with the keys.

He takes my hand as we're escorted upstairs.

The room is charming, with flowery bedspreads and cute paintings of mountains I can't imagine the Quinn I know now, loving. But as I look around at the rocking chair in the corner and the log fireplace, I realize it wasn't the place that held meaning for him, it was the person he was here with.

I turn from the window and look at him.

He's staring at the bed on the right, his gaze shadowed again. The manager retreats silently, and I go to stand next to him.

"Do you want to take that bed?" I murmur softly.

"Yes."

"Okay, I'll go and wash up."

He catches my arm before I can leave. "It wasn't you, Elyse. Earlier, when you tried to hug me. It was me. I don't like to be hugged. The last person to hug me was my mother."

My heart staggers with pain for him. "It's okay. Really."

He shakes his head. "No, it's not. She knew she was going to die. It was her way of saying goodbye. I loved her, but I absolutely *hate* her for it."

My insides shudder hard. "Oh, Quinn—"

He turns abruptly and shackles me with his arms. "Give it to me, Elyse. The relief. Please. I need it."

The internal conflict that churns lasts all of five seconds. I know somewhere along the line, guilt and shame for not keeping my promise to Q will sting, but right in this moment, I can think of nothing I want more than to give myself to Quinn. So I don't protest when he pulls me tighter into his hard, lean body.

Our kisses over the last week have grown progressively more frenzied, our mouths attempting to sate what our bodies need. This time, the kiss is pure, heavenly foreplay, tinged with the desperation and desolation raging through Quinn.

My hands slide up his neck. He picks me up and walks me to the bed. He lets go for a minute, and I lean back, stare at the god before me.

Without taking his eyes off me, he sinks down and tugs my boots off, then his own. Feverish eyes rake over me as he joins me on the bed, and takes my mouth again. We tumble back against the pillows. His tongue flicks against mine and I moan. He goes deeper, his caresses growing more intense with each passing second. Firm hands slide under my sweater, fingers stroke my skin. I'm furnace-hot, melting from the inside.

After an eternity of kissing, his mouth leaves mine, trails to my jaw, my earlobe, my pulse. I go on an exploration trip of my own. Quinn's body is unbelievably honed. Tight muscles jump beneath my touch as I pull his shirt free of his pants and glide my hands up his back.

His weight on me feels solid, even a touch familiar. I realize that before Q, I never voluntarily explored a man's body, so I wonder if all men who take care of their bodies feel the same.

I look up at him. He's staring at me, his gaze probing in watchful, almost dreading silence. I shut out my conflicting thoughts against comparing the two men I've interacted with recently, and revel in the fact that I'm here, in this place and time, with Quinn Blackwood.

I smile.

He exhales. His hands trail up my midriff, then with impatient movements, he rears up and pulls my thick sweater over my head. His jaw drops at the sight of my braless breasts.

When he looks up, there's a dangerous light in his eyes. "You always go out without a bra, Elyse?" he croaks.

I shake my head. "We...you looked like you needed to leave in a hurry."

One finger trails from my collarbone to the top of one breast. My nipple puckers, the areola breaking out in goose bumps.

He cups one mound and groans. "So fucking soft. So responsive. Need to taste you." His mouth closes over one peak, pulls it hard into his mouth before swirling his tongue around it.

Fireworks spark off in my brain. When I clutch his head, Quinn raises his gaze, gauges my pleasure with an avid intensity that makes me gasp. Without releasing me from the stare, he flicks his tongue over me, then kisses his way to the other peak.

"Oh God!"

"Tell me how you feel, Elyse," comes his raw command. The coarse gravel of his voice is almost incoherent.

"Good. *So, so good!*"

He lavishes attention on me for the longest time, and with each appreciative gleam of his beautiful eyes, I become wetter.

My nipples are bruised rose by the time he kisses his way down my body. Even then his gaze lingers on my breast. Quinn is clearly a breast man.

Like Q.

I frown.

Stop it.

The warning takes care of itself when Quinn opens the fastening of my jeans. His gaze captures mine as he slowly pulls down the zipper. He licks a path from my navel to the top of my panties, then rubs his stubble against my covered pussy.

"I can smell you, baby. Are you wet for me?"

"Yes," I gasp.

The hands that rid me of my jeans are a little rough, a lot unsteady. He rises on his knees to toss them away, then stares down at my body.

"Breathtaking. So very beautiful."

My panties follow the same path as my jeans. Then I'm bare to Quinn. And his ravenous eyes. Where his hands don't touch, his eyes devour. And when he parts my thighs and delivers both conduits of attention, I'm a fucking goner.

"Need to taste," he says again, before capturing each thigh in his big hands and spreading me wide open. His thumbs part my lips and he licks me from hole to clit.

My hips want to surge off the bed. He pins me down, repeats the action, but this time lingers on my clit. More fireworks explode. Liquid heat pours out of me.

"Fuck!" He laps me up with almost embarrassing enthusiasm.

That single-minded concentration and the borderline feral sounds from his throat are such a damn turn-on, I know I'm going to go off in a second. I clutch my breasts and squeeze my eyes shut.

"Quinn…I'm coming."

"Look at me when you come, Elyse. I want you to see me," he rasps.

My head feels almost too heavy to lift, but I struggle onto one elbow, and spear my fingers into his hair. "Yes. Whatever you need, Quinn."

His eyes darken and his eyelids flutter before he regains his purpose. He sucks my clit with a hard, merciless pull, and sends me over the edge.

"Oh, yes! Oh God…" My nails dig into his scalp and my gaze fuses with his as my release smashes through me.

The connection between us is soul-searing. He lets me see his pain, his fury, the desolation that has eaten away at him. I also see entreaty and regret.

As I come down from the most incredible high, I cup his face in my hand. "Quinn," I murmur, dying to give him more. Dying to give him everything.

He rears up and rips his shirt over his head. "I need to be inside you, Elly. Need you."

His motions are truncated, his eyes desperately clinging to mine as he removes his pants and briefs.

"You have me."

His nod is almost sorrowful. My heart bleeds as I take him in my arms. Our kiss holds a mixture of desperation, lust, and my flavors as he settles between my thighs. I feel the head of his cock at my core and a persistent thought intrudes. I attempt to break the kiss. He's set on denying the disconnection.

"Quinn?" I mumble.

"Hmm?"

"Uh, do you... have a condom?"

He freezes. Eyes that have insisted on a connection breaks away from mine. He sucks in a huge breath, then shakes his head. "No," he says.

The idea of stopping fills me with pain and dread. What I'm about to do may be right up there on the epic stupidity scale, but the thought of being denied is unbearable.

"I...can I trust you with my health, Quinn?"

He nods immediately. "I won't force you if you don't want you, but yes, you can."

I suck in a breath. "Okay. I'm clean, by the way. And I'm on birth control."

"So am I."

"You're on birth control?" I tease, desperate to allay any impending disappointment.

"I'm clean," he says. "I won't lie about something like that. I promise."

My heart lifts. "I believe you."

He smiles.

Quinn Blackwood smiles for the very first time since we met. And the sight of it is so fucking magnificent, my mouth drops open.

"Wow."

"What?"

"That...your smile. Wow."

It grows wider.

And just like that, my heart decides.

Once I give myself permission to, falling in love with Quinn Blackwood is as easy and as terrifying as falling off the edge of a cliff. The crash is inevitable but goddamn, I intend to enjoy the exhilarating descent.

So I return his smile. Slide my hands over his beautifully sculpted arms and lock my fingers at his nape. "Now that we've got that cleared up, what are you waiting for?"

His smile slowly fades away. I don't mind, because it's replaced by that feral hunger that electrifies my soul. Braced on his elbows, he spears one hand into my hair and the other beneath my ass. He tilts my hips upward and thrusts, hard and deep and gloriously into me.

Dear God. Either the men I was unfortunate to sleep with before were all woefully underendowed or I've lucked out and found two men with cocks designed to send a woman to heaven!

My mind veers once more to the similarities between the man who owns me and the one I want to belong to.

Once again, I'm not allowed to dwell on the thought.

Quinn slams into me. I scream, then pray there are no occupants around us. Then scream again as he fills me tight. His deep answering groans roll into one another.

Then the filthy words start.

"Love. Seeing. Those. Fucking. Tits. Bounce.

"Pussy so good. *Fuck*, you hold me so tight, Elly.

"Wanna feel you come all over my cock. Will you be a good girl and do that for me?

"That's right, baby. Scream for me. Want everyone to know how fucking good this is."

I'm way past the point of caring how raw and needy I sound as I scream some more, beg him to keep fucking me.

His eyes never leave mine as he pounds into me.

The connection is so sizzling and intense, much too soon, pressure builds again. My pussy clenches harder around him and he growls.

"*Yes!*"

I take that as permission and I fly.

Seconds later, Quinn lets out a primitive roar and shoots thick, hot semen inside me. He buries his face in my neck, his breathing hoarse and ragged as endless convulsions roll through him.

My arms come around him for a few seconds before I clock that I'm hugging him. I hold my breath, but he doesn't push me away. Instead, he rolls us over and hugs me tight in return. We stay like that as we battle for air.

I kiss his skin. Breathe him in.

Beneath his fading sandalwood scent, his musk flares, wraps around me. Again it feels familiar. Again I hate myself for blurring one man into the other.

I push the thought aside and look up. He's watching me. He leans down and presses his lips to mine.

"Thank you," he rasps.

I fall harder. New words of love trip over my tongue. I barely manage to hold them back. "Tell me about your mom," I say instead.

A wave of sadness rushes over his face. "She was beautiful. And funny. She loved me. She was my everything." He doesn't say more than that. The tight lid he keeps on his emotions won't let him.

I have a million other questions, but I limit it to one. "You said she was saying goodbye...with that hug? Did she...?"

"Take her own life? No. That was Maxwell's job."

I gasp. "Your father killed her?"

He drags his gaze from mine, his face a frozen landscape once again. "She ended her life in the technical sense, but Maxwell took her life long before she died."

"Oh, Quinn."

His arms tighten painfully around me. After a few minutes, his gaze finds mine, digs feverishly into me. "Things are going to get intense over the next week, Elyse. You won't like me very much when it's all over. But I hope you'll understand."

Panic claws up my spine. "I—what—?"

He kisses me hard. "Don't ask questions. I won't answer them. And nothing you can say will change anything. The course is set. But I need what's happening here, right now. I hope you want it too." He stops and sucks in a breath. "If you don't I'll...try to understand."

I have two options. Say no and destroy the finite time we have together. Say yes, endure the uncertainty of what's coming...while loving and making love with Quinn in the time we have together. The choice is laughably easy. "I want what you want."

The answer earns me another earth-shaking smile. The cock still buried inside me begins to harden. I gasp with the wonder of him filling me up. When I attempt to sit up, Quinn holds me down. He spreads my thighs with his, and with one hand on my lower back and one hand around my shoulders, he pistons inside me.

My eyes roll and I lunge for his mouth. We stay like that, kissing and fucking until another climax breaks over us.

Eventually, he lets me up so I can use the bathroom. I'm sticky and sweaty, so I hit the shower in the small en-suite. The need to return to the bedroom, to Quinn, makes me rush through washing.

When I'm done, I don't bother to dry off. I wrap the towel around me and enter the bedroom.

Quinn's not there. His wallet is on the bedside table, but his clothes are gone. I force down the tiny spurt of alarm and open the bedroom door. He's not in the hallway or the landing. I shut the door again and look around for a note or a clue of where he is.

Nothing.

Okay...

I hurriedly dry myself off and tug on my clothes, minus panties, which are too embarrassingly damp to put back on. I snatch my phone from my purse, the keycard from the dresser, and leave the room. Besides the parlor, there are two more rooms—a small dining room and adjoining reading room. They're both empty. I finger my phone, and am debating whether to call him, or go out and see if his car is still outside, when I hear a low, harsh curse.

I look through the dining room window. He's outside. His phone is clamped to his ear and he's pacing the lawn while frantically rubbing his temple.

"It's been a goddamn week! You have everything you need. How fucking hard can it be? Never mind what I'm doing. *Just do your goddamn job*…Shit, I'm sorry…of course…I know that wasn't part of the plan…no, everything is still going ahead…Wednesday is fine. Start with their e-mail and phone contacts, as agreed. Send everything. Then as many networks as possible. *Nothing has changed,* you have my word. Just…I need this thing handled too."

He stops and listens for a minute. My heart is racing like a wild mustang on crack and I don't even know why. My whole body freezes when he lets out a blood-curdling laugh.

"My *soul*?" he seethes, before his shoulders hunch forward in abject, harrowing dejection. "Please don't waste your time worrying about something you can't change. Yeah…bye."

He slides the phone onto his back pocket and balls his fists. He's turned away from me so I can't see his face, but his body language is chilling.

He must sense my regard, because he tenses and whirls. His gaze zeros in on where I'm standing at the window.

We stare at each other, the earth cracking beneath our feet, doom blasting its imminent arrival. Quinn slowly uncurls his fist and walks back inside. He finds me at the window, unmoving. Hands cup my shoulders and he slides his face next to mine.

"No questions. Please, Elyse."

"It really is going to be a temporary thing for us, isn't it?"

His breath locks, then he exhales in a rush. "Yes. I'm sorry."

I nod calmly, even though my newly loved-up heart is screaming. "Yeah. I'm sorry too."

I let him lead me back upstairs. Undress me. Put me in bed and slide in next to me. This time our lovemaking is near silent, our only communication with our eyes. Afterward, he pulls me into his arms. And we sleep. I don't dream. I don't know if he does.

We end up staying two more days. When Quinn goes out to get toothbrushes and a few supplies, I text Fionnella. She comes back with a pass to live my life. The worry that Q may be done with me grows, but not enough to derail my time with Quinn.

For a hefty extra, the manager, Cindy, makes our meals and brings them up to the room. In between eating and sleeping, Quinn Blackwood fucks me like he's a raging addict and I'm his last-ever line of coke.

When we eventually leave the memorable B&B, my heart weeps all through the drive back to Manhattan. At one point, the pain gets so bad that I dig the hand I placed on Quinn's thigh into his skin without conscious thought. That earns me a detour to a deserted lay-by and a quick, rabid fuck over the hood of the Mercedes with my jeans wrapped around my knees.

Worry and the afterglow of sex eventually lull me into sleep. I wake up from a murky dream with my heart hammering. We're a few blocks from the loft in Hell's Kitchen.

A few blocks from possibly not seeing Quinn again.

I glance at him. His jaw is rigid, the hand over my own on his thigh gripping me tight. When we arrive, he turns the ignition off. I release my seatbelt and open the door, but he doesn't let me go. He stays put, his hand still trapping my own. My searching glance meets turbulent silver-blue eyes.

He opens his mouth. "Elly, I need to tell you—"

Something's coming. Something bad. This might be the only chance I get, so I pre-empt him.

"Quinn."

"Hmm?"

"I love you."

His eyes flare wide. Wider than I've ever seen. His face loses all color and he starts to shake his head. "Elyse...Jesus—"

The mobile in the console blares through the car. We both look at it and freeze. Three rings. Four. He looks at me and shakes his head. But he picks up the phone.

The voice is female. And it's agitated. Quinn's eyes dart to mine and I read his icy trepidation. He throws his door open, then freezes.

"What are you talking about?" he fires. His eyes search the

rearview mirror frantically before his head swivels round. The glance he throws at me is filled with dread and black fury. "No, dammit. Where are the damn bodyguards? I don't see them. I don't see anything. Are you sure?"

A different sort of fear grips me. Whereas I feared for my emotions a few seconds ago, now my terror is expanding. Sinister forces are looming large and unstoppable. What terrifies me more than anything is that all my senses are screaming that my already deeply precarious situation is about to get a whole lot worse. And that somehow Quinn is involved. I don't want to believe it.

But...karma. And the look in his eyes leaves little room for ambivalence.

The voice on the phone is getting even more agitated. But I force myself to speak his name. "Quinn."

He's still searching the surroundings. For something. Something that shouldn't be here. Something dangerous. And he's firing more questions into his phone.

"Quinn!"

As he's turning back around, his thumb hits the speaker button. A female voice floods the car.

"Yes! I'm telling you, Quinn. You need to get Lucky the hell out of there. Now!"

Fionnella's voice.

Fionnella!

For a few seconds, my mind freezes in blessed self-preservation. Then shock sucker-punches me, along with the wrecking ball that is my own epic stupidity.

Quinn stares at me, the regret, dread, and alarm finally beginning to make sense. The hand I have on his thigh turns to ice, along with the rest of my body. I want to move it, but I can't. His grip is locked tight on me as we stare at each other.

My mouth drops open. "No..."

His eyes flare with a desperate, pleading light. "Elly, I can explain..."

"No! *God...no.*"

"Please...hear me out—"

Of course, fate decides not to give me time to process it. I'm still locked in the shock vault when rough hands grab my shoulders and yank me right out of the car. Quinn lunges for me, but his seatbelt prevents him from gaining any traction. His filthy curse rips the air as I hit the sidewalk sideways and pain ricochets through my bruised hipbone.

Quinn surges out of the car with a furious roar and vaults over the hood of the Mercedes as I'm dragged backward and tossed over someone's shoulder.

"*Elyse!*"

The otherworldly sensation of what's happening forces a scream from my throat. But it emerges as a gargled croak.

Quinn's heavy footsteps charge after me and my captor.

"Put her the fuck down, right fucking now, asshole!"

"Or what?" I hear a taunt from the voice that has given me nightmares for the better part of seven years.

I twist my head to see several men rushing alongside those of my captor. My heart sinks.

"She belongs to me. You get to take her over my fucking dead body!"

Everyone freezes. "I can make that happen, friend." The very distinct sound of a gun being cocked cracks through the air. "Just say the word."

I hear a garbled shout, probably from Fionnella. My brain is spinning. From shock. From fear.

"You shoot me, right here, right now, and you won't get down the block before my security take you down. Your best outcome is to leave Elyse. Take me instead. I'm certain I can make it worth your while."

Quinn's voice is devoid of emotion, eerily calm and sourced from the very depths of hell. Whereas my brain is desperately twisting itself free of the shock so I can do something other than stare at the sidewalk from my upside-down position. Another scream bubbles up. This time it makes it and rips free.

Unfortunately the sound galvanizes my captors. "I'd love to stay and negotiate, but I simply don't have the time. I came for Lucky. I have her. I promise you, if you take another step I will shoot. Take her to the van," Clay instructs the man holding me.

"*No! Elyse!* Jesus. Let go of her. I swear to God, if you hurt her—"

"Dammit. Earl, take care of him, please?"

No...no...no...

I don't know what or who I'm pleading for. I turn my head in time to see Quinn jerk sideways and launch himself after me. Earl steps in his way and takes a swing at him. He ducks and jabs a blow to Earl's gut. Before he can regain his step, Gordon connects a right hook to his jaw. There's a sickening crunch as Quinn's head swivels to the side, and it strangles another scream inside me.

Quinn staggers for a nanosecond before his gaze zeroes in on me, his face set with deathly intent as he attempts to shake off his attackers. He barrels into Gordon with deadly, streamlined force, and even though the man is built like a Sherman tank, he's propelled backward into the concrete wall that forms the outer perimeter of the loft.

My vision is beginning to blur, and for a second, I wish for unconsciousness. I need a moment's respite from the tsunami of hell raining on me.

The distant screech of tires pierces my dazed senses before I can pass out.

"Shit, we've got company. Earl, leave him. Let's go!"

I jerk myself upright, attempt to twist myself free. Beefy hands and iron-like arms grip me tighter.

I'm tossed into the back of a van. My head cracks against the side and my tailbone wails in pain as it connects with the bare metal floor.

The driver's door opens and shuts. "Gordon, Let's go now!"

The last thing I see before the door slams shut is Quinn rising up off the ground and flying toward the van. I hear the slam of his fists against the moving van. His roar as the vehicle accelerates away is unlike any sound I've ever heard in my life.

I stare into the blackness. I want to scream again.

But I'm locked in deeper shock.

Quinn is Q.

Q is Quinn.

This has been one twisted game for both of them all along.

Fuck.

My.

Life.

* * *

QUINN

I pry my eyes open. Faces are swimming above me. Some hold concern, others rabid curiosity. Pain radiates from the side of my head, from my wrist and ribs. I know the metallic taste in my mouth is blood before I swallow. Someone mentions an ambulance. Someone takes a picture.

Cars screech to a halt beside me. Pounding feet rush at me. A voice I recognize asks if I'm all right.

I struggle to sit up. Look around.

Memory returns in a blinding flash of cold fire.

38

CUTTING-ROOM FLOOR

QUINN

Fuck.
　　Fuck.
　　Fuck. Fuck. Fuck, *Fuck!*

39

IT'S A WRAP...OR NOT

Q is Quinn.

Quinn is Q.

My shock is wearing off.

As I'm bitch-slapped with reality, the truth becomes glaringly obvious.

Dear God, I must be the stupidest woman on earth. Even when my brain force-fed me the information, I ignored it.

I believed myself in love with two men. Ha!

What I am is addicted to two sociopaths who are actually one person, thus ensuring I'll doubt my sanity for the rest of my life.

If I have a life left to live, that is.

The black cloth over my head is stifling. Even more so than the tape across my mouth. I'm not sure exactly how much time has passed. A day? Two? The gnawing hunger eating my intestines tells me it's closer to the latter.

The whole production meant to scare the living shit out of me has so far bounced off my armor plate of shock.

The ominous footsteps. The hands tied behind my back. Feet bound. The bright light in the face one moment, then the black bag over the head again? Rinse and repeat. It's so cliché I want to laugh. Except I suspect I'll choke, what with the tape and all. So I plead with my brain to hold on just a little bit longer. *Breathe, Elyse. Just breathe.* The terror will probably return in good time; I don't need to help it along.

Clayton won't like it when I refuse to divulge Petra's whereabouts. And an angry Clayton is—

"Well, young lady. Quite the merry-go-round you've led me on, isn't it?"

The bag is whipped off my head. The action drags my hair in front of my face. I look around, try to orient myself. Not quite the dungeon under a castle in the middle of the South China Sea, but it's dark and dingy all right. We're in a basement. Eight feet above, small, filthy rectangular windows reflect streetlights. Somewhere in the distance, hip hop blares from loudspeakers.

The naked bulb above my head burns into my skin and blinds me, but I'm able to make out Clay, sitting on a chair six feet from me. Our gazes collide, and I see hate blazing from eyes the same color as mine.

I shrug.

He lifts an eyebrow. "That's all I get? After hunting you for six weeks? *A shrug?*"

I stare back at him. He has the nerve to look disappointed.

"I see you haven't let all that time go to waste, though? Quite the industrious little bee you've been. Such a shame you didn't think to work that *enthusiastically* for me back at The Villa."

I let my gaze radiate boredom. It's the only way to get what I want, the tape off my mouth. Sure enough, he snaps his fingers impatiently. A figure appears from the circle of light. Earl, his one eye glaring hate and condescension.

"Didn't I tell you you'd end up like this, you filthy slut?" he crows, then he rips the tape off my mouth.

The rippling trail of pain it leaves forces a gasp out of me. "No, actually, you were wrong. I'm not screaming and I'm not naked. I'm also sure as hell not dead."

"We'll see about that—"

"Enough, Earl."

Earl sneers and moves out of the way.

Clayton smirks. "You were saying?"

"Go fuck yourself?"

He grimaces. "Ah, she lives. I suppose I've had that coming for...what? Two months? Ten years? More?"

"I'm never going to tell you where she is. Never!"

He nods. "I know. But I'll find her. I'm a patient man. I'll find her and bring her home." He leans forward, elbows on knees. "I just want us to be a family, Lucky. Is that so bad?"

"Are you fucking kidding me right now? I may be in shock but I'm not insane."

His head tilts. "You sure about that? From the circus blowing all over the news, I say you inherited some of your mother's mental instability."

"She got that way because of what you did to her!"

"What? Treat her like a queen? Give her the best that money can buy only to find out she's screwing that dimwit behind my back?"

Earl grumbles. Clayton ignores him.

"You really are delusional, aren't you?"

He regards me steadily for a minute. "Ridge didn't deserve what you did to him."

Now the fear invades. So does the rage. "He tried to rape me, with your blessing."

"Now, let's not sling unfair accusations around. You went down there of your own free will. Like your mother, you thought you could pull the wool over my eyes when I was two steps ahead of you the whole time."

"If you were you would've foreseen what happened to your lapdog."

Fury shrouds his face. "Watch your tone. That man was a veteran, a defender of his country. He didn't deserve to be barbecued by a second-rate whore."

My eyes widen. "My God, you loved him, didn't you? What, he was the son you never had, while the daughter under your nose deserved to be passed around like a Sunday afternoon buffet?"

"I kept you fed and clothed—"

"While keeping me under guard twenty-four hours a day and whoring me off seven days a week. Yeah, I felt *really* loved."

"This isn't a father-daughter bonding session, Lucky." He reaches into his suede jacket and pulls out a folded document. "This is a warrant for your arrest, signed by my good friend, Judge Tolley, you remember him? You gave him a birthday treat to remember last year. All I need is to act on this, and you'll be back in Getty Falls standing trial for murder."

Despite the quaking inside, I lift my chin. "Are you sure? I'm pretty certain the authorities will have something to say about a sheriff three thousand miles from his sand pit randomly slapping handcuffs on a citizen."

"You assume anyone knows I'm here. I have a private jet on standby. I could have you back home and in jail by nightfall. And while you're awaiting your trial, I'll continue my search for Petra."

Her name on his lips liquefies my insides. "There are billions of girls in the world, Clay. Thousands who will buy the Kool Aid you're selling, unfortunately. Why her? Why can't you just leave her be?"

He staggers to his feet, his face livid. *"Because she is mine!"*

He's not going to stop looking for her. Never. "I have money. I'll give it all to you if you promise to give up searching for her. That's what you want her for, isn't it? To be your next star attraction? Tell me what she's worth, I'll pay it."

"How? You think that rich asshole you were cavorting with will bail you out? Even if I wanted to take him up on his offer to make all this worth my while, I say it's too late, seeing as he has enough problems of his own right now."

The vise around my heart tightens. "What are you talking about?"

He snaps his fingers. "Right. You've been in the dark, literally for the last two days, haven't you? Earl, bring the laptop. Show Lucky here all the excitement she's missed. If you ask me, you're the star attraction everyone's interested in now." He waves the document at me. "Maybe I should revisit my decision. You're an Internet sensation now. Your premium has gone up—"

"What the hell are you talking about?" I demand louder.

Earl steps back into the light, a laptop clutched in his hand. He snags a chair and sets it down with the laptop a few feet from me. With a nasty smirk, he hits the button, stands back and folds his arms.

At first I'm not sure what I'm seeing. The camera is shaking badly, the person holding it hiding behind a curtain or drape. The shot gets better when a woman walks into view, accompanied by a man. The footage is years old, but I recognize a younger Maxwell Blackwood immediately.

He walks the woman into a bedroom suite. On the bed, two half-dressed men wait. The expressions on their faces are ones I'm unwillingly familiar with. Maxwell murmurs in her ear, then turns to leave. She tries to grab him, her sobs escalating. He pushes her back toward the bed. When she protests, he reaches into his pocket and pulls out a set of handcuffs and secures her to the bedpost.

"You can't go back on your promises, Adele. I'm disappointed in you." He leaves her there, walks out. The men rise from the bed, and move toward her.

My heart shreds as the name registers. Adele. Quinn's mother.

The camera cuts to another, similar footage of Adele with other men. On and on. Six in total. Then to a different scene. Maxwell is sitting on a sofa with Adele. He's wearing a suit, she's in her night-gown. Again there are hints of a drape in the corner of the screen. He talks in a low, insistent voice. She's weeping softly and nodding. After a minute, he nods to someone off camera. A woman walks onto the screen and hands Maxwell a vial of pills.

As she turns away, I see her face and my breath catches.

It's Quinn's stepmother, Delilah Blackwood.

Maxwell carries on talking to Adele, one hand soothing her back. The footage is fast-forwarded to where he sets the pills down in front of her and kisses her temple. She rises, goes to a drawer, and returns with a black-clothed lump. When she sits down, he pats her hand.

"You're doing the right thing, Adele. It's for the greater good," he says.

He leaves the room. Adele reaches for the pills, shakes them out into her palm, and swallows them with a glass of water. Her movements are slow when she parts the black cloth and picks up a gun.

No!

The camera wobbles. "Mama?" The cracked voice of a boy not quite yet a man.

Adele's head turns slowly toward the voice, the gun rising in her hand.

The camera swings downward, then falls to the carpet. Feet rush in and out of the shot.

"No, Mama! *No!*"

The still-rolling camera records the sound of the shot.

Then the endless screaming starts.

I absently note the sobs ripping from my throat, the wetness on my face. Somewhere beyond the buzzing in my head, I hear Earl chuckle.

The footage moves on. Quinn in his early twenties, sitting on a sofa. He's being asked questions by a woman with her back to the camera. They're about the state of his mental health.

His shrink.

His answers are monosyllabic. Every now and then, he smirks at the camera over her shoulder. The video rolls forward, until, unbelievably, she gets up and begins to undress. Quinn issues instructions, which she follows, all the way through giving him oral sex. And through it all, his eyes stare soullessly into the camera.

Fast-forward again through the shrink's footage. At one point it stops at a plaque in her office. Adriana Nathanson.

Then comes the one that sends a spike straight through my gut.

Quinn and Delilah. Nausea punches through my diaphragm. My whole body heaves and I prepare to hurl. At the last instant it subsides, but I can't take my eyes off the depravity happening on-screen.

Delilah and Quinn.

Sometimes on their own. Other times with multiple partners.

Fast-forward to two days ago. Breaking news. Maxwell and

Delilah's ashen faces when the footage is projected onto a large screen at a gala they're attending. Friends being interviewed. The mayor giving his opinion on the scandal. The footage shown again.

The police leading Maxwell away in handcuffs. Then Delilah in handcuffs.

Different footage of Quinn. He's also with the police, but there are no handcuffs. Cameras are shoved in his face. The look in his eyes...soulless.

Then Q, masked. Q, unmasked. Q with other women.

Q with me. I have my blindfold on for all of the footage, unlike the other women.

I now understand the need for the blindfold, but that brings zero relief.

A sound bubbles up from my throat. My vision blurs with raw tears and burning humiliation. The footage rolls forward and ends with the caption: *The Life & Times of the Notorious, Murdering Blackwoods.*

Earl smirks as he retrieves the laptop.

I feel dead inside.

"Your man is quite the Internet sensation, just like you." Clayton shakes his head. "What a family. All that money. Not a single sane brain cell between them."

"He did it for his mother." That much is glaringly obvious.

But why the fuck am I defending him?

"He's a sick freak. The only reason he isn't locked away yet is because of all those Blackwood billions. But I see he got his claws into you." His eyes gleam with malice, then turn contemplative. "What did you make out of this shindig? And don't say nothing. I taught you better than that. I also heard when you said you had money."

I use the only bargaining chip I have. "Eight hundred thousand dollars. It's yours if you let me go and promise never to go after Petra."

Earl snorts. "She's lying."

Clayton eyes me. "What's to stop me from taking the money and going after her anyway?"

I force myself to remain calm. "I'll give you half of it now. Then a hundred thousand every nine months for the next thirty-six months."

He smiles. "You're a clever little thing, aren't you? You think I won't go after her once she turns eighteen?"

"Think about it. You make half a million from *all* the girls combined in a year—yes, I've seen the books. I'm offering you eight hundred thousand for one girl."

"What about you burning down my *family home*? You expect me to just forget about that? And Ridge?"

"The insurance will take care of The Villa. As for Ridge, you've already had the coroner rule his death an accident. Use the money to mourn him."

He rushes forward and seizes my chin in his hands. "You have it all figured out, haven't you?" he seethes. "I should teach you an unforgettable lesson. Fortunately, for you, incest isn't my thing."

I don't answer. Fury blazes in his eyes. He's on the edge. All I can do is count on cold hard cash saving my life. And Petra's.

"Where's the money?"

I shake my head. "I'm not telling you. Not until we have a deal."

He stares down at me for an age. Then he hands the warrant to Earl. "You and I are going to get this money. Earl will sit on this for two hours. If we're not back by then, he'll happily put the wheels in motion, won't you, Earl?"

Earl takes the warrant and stuffs it in his pocket. "With pleasure."

My hands and feet are untied. I stagger to my feet, then stumble as blood rushes back into deprived areas of my body. My purse and phone are nowhere in sight. And at some point my boots were taken off, so I follow Clayton out of the basement in my soiled socks.

"Can I have my boots back?"

He shrugs. "I have no clue where they are. Besides, if no shoes will keep you in line, I'm all for it."

We reach the top of the stairs and I look around. If anyone lives here, they've long since given up on any need to keep the place tidy. There's a soiled, ripped futon sofa shoved up against one wall, actual holes in the carpet, beer bottles and pizza boxes discarded everywhere, and the fridge door is hanging on one screw.

Before I can ask who lives here, a rake-thin man emerges from the single bedroom. His eyes are bloodshot and track marks trail down both gangly arms.

Clayton passes him a hundred-dollar bill, which he pounces on with rabid glee. "Remember what we talked about. Keep an eye on things and you'll get another one of those."

The junkie nods. When he cracks open the bedroom door and dives back in, I see my boots tucked against the door.

I have a fair idea how much they cost, and what the resale value means to an addict, especially if he has my purse and phone as well. I'm not prepared to die over my possessions, so I keep my mouth shut and follow Clayton out. Two of his henchmen are guarding the hallway, another two the stairwell.

We head up dark stairs, across a series of hallways, then down ten flights of stairs in a weird relay formation. The van sitting on the curb is different from the one Clayton used to capture me. That he's managed to hold me for two days without anyone finding me strikes a peculiar note in my heart. With everything I've found out about Quinn/Q, I don't know whether to be frightened or relieved. One way or the other, this is about to be over.

A signal is received and we step out into light rain. My feet are wet and cold in seconds but I barely feel it. I pray for my senses to remain numb.

I'm shoved into the van once again, and Gordon climbs in, his black eyes transmitting pure malice. The blackened windows stop me from seeing any signs, and after a few blocks, I stop trying to guess which direction we're headed. For all I know, Clayton could be taking a roundabout route to the loft.

My head pounds, and pain claws me to my very soul. Every time my brain veers toward thoughts of Quinn, I pull myself back. That wound is nowhere near ready to be tended, and I'm content to leave it sore and throbbing for now.

I lose track of time and only focus when I notice the van has pulled over. There are distant sounds of traffic but nothing close. Up front, I hear Clayton talking, then what sounds like a brief scuffle.

Gordon stares at me, his gaze daring me to do something. I don't have the strength to tell him I have very little fight left. I shift my gaze to the dirty floor as the back door opens.

We're parked in an alley. And Clayton is holding the body of an unconscious woman in his arms.

My heart kicks, and the fight I thought was gone surges back.

"Who is this? What the hell are you doing?" My voice sounds bleak and feeble despite my best effort to project strength.

"This is Colleen." He drops her next to Gordon. "She's supposed to be at a blind date across town in forty-five minutes. Isn't that nice?"

Fear freezes my heart. "Then what is she doing here? You can't just kidnap her!"

"You really didn't think I'd let you waltz into your fancy loft and risk you alerting the authorities, did you? Or did you think I'd come along and walk into a trap?"

"No. I swear I wasn't—"

"Miss Colleen here can be your little incentive. You get me my money...*all of it*...and she makes it to her date in one piece. You don't..." He peers down at the woman splayed on the van floor. "Well, I can always do with a mature redhead in my stable."

The shock of what's happening keeps me quiet as the van moves off again. Ten minutes later, a soft knock sounds against the front partition. The van stops and Gordon shoves the back door open. We're a block from the loft.

Clayton shoves back the partition. "You have ten minutes, then Colleen's fate is out of your hands."

The moment I step out, the van moves off. I'm alone on the quiet Hell's Kitchen street, but I'm far from free. A complete stranger's life hangs in the balance right next to Petra's.

Fear propels me forward, and I arrive in front of the security door of the loft. I enter the code and the door unlocks. I release my trapped breath. The thought that Quinn hasn't had time to change the codes because of his self-induced shit storm brings me little comfort. My frozen feet march me through the doors and up the stairs into the bedroom of the disturbed stranger I thought I knew well enough to fall in love with.

Tears surge hot and acrid into my eyes. I let them fall. The only energy I have is reserved for another stranger's life. I shove the money and my precious keepsakes into my battered backpack. Everything else I leave behind.

I walk with soiled socks and a shredded heart back to where I was dropped off. Clayton turns up a couple of minutes later. He hops out and snatches the backpack from me. I watch with numb interest as he rips open the zipper and greedily flips through the crisp bills.

Inside the van, the redhead moans as she regains consciousness. Clay zips up the bag and jumps into the back of the van with me. We drive for a few blocks before we pull into another quiet street.

Gordon hops out with a groggy Colleen.

He freezes in midstep when loud sirens rip through the air.

Clayton pounces and drags me against his body, and starts fumbling for his belt.

Even though everything inside me is numbed with pain, I know I can't miss this chance. My sister still needs me. The authorities can have me, but not until I make sure Petra's safety hasn't been compromised. I bite down hard on the arm restraining my shoulder.

"Fucking bitch!"

The moment his grip loosens, I break free, fly out of the van, and run for my life. I only get two blocks before another siren whirls behind me.

"FBI. Stop!"

Heart as heavy as stone, I stop, thrusting my hands into the air.

Heart hammering, teeth clenched, I wait.

"Are you Elyse Gilbert?"

I tentatively turn my head. "Y…yes?"

One male and one female officer approach. "Was Clayton Getty holding you against your will?"

"Yes. Where am I?" I ask.

"You're in the Bronx. Put your hands down, Miss. We'll be taking you in for questioning, but you're not under arrest."

"I'm not?"

The female officer who approaches shakes her head. "Are you all right?"

I stop and think about the answer. Everything inside me shakes. "No. I'm not."

She nods, and her assessing gaze lingers on the bruise on my temple. "Well, let's see about reversing that, shall we? The ambulance is here. We'll get you some medical attention." She beckons me closer.

My numb feet move toward her.

"Oh, and your people are here."

"My *people*?"

The male officer thumbs a black limo idling on the curb. "Yeah, one of them had the clever idea to put a tracking device in the cash. It took two days, but the moment it was moved, we followed it..."

His words fade away as the back door opens and a sharp-suited black guy I've never seen before steps out. Closely behind him, Fionnella steps out.

Then the door on the farthest side opens.

Quinn steps out. Rushes around to where the other two are standing.

Across the street, rabid silver-blue eyes spear into me. His hair is spiky, his unshaven face holding a million more shadows. In his eyes I read remorse, fear, determination.

He starts to cross the street toward me. "Elyse, are you okay? God, please tell me you're okay." His gravel-rough voice is grittier. Bleaker than I've ever heard it.

I don't want to hear it now.

"*No!*" I take a step back.

He keeps coming. Hands outstretched.

"Did he hurt you?"

"*Stop!*"

Everything I saw on the laptop in the basement rushes back. I stagger back until my shoulder bumps hard into an iron railing. Both FBI officers halt, their gazes swinging between me and Quinn.

Q.

Whoever the fuck he's decided to be today.

"Elyse, baby. Please, let me explain—"

"Stay away from me!"

The female officer's hands fly out toward Quinn in a halting gesture.

The male officer frowns. "Miss Gilbert—"

"Officers, I don't want those people anywhere near me," I yell shakily. "Especially him." I point at Quinn. Q. *Jesus...*

Quinn's eyes flare in alarm. One hand spikes through his hair. "God, please! I need...please, don't do this...Elyse."

The sound of my name on his lips freaks me out harder.

"No!" Hysteria ravages my voice, but I'm past caring. "I don't care if you have to arrest me, but please keep Quinn Blackwood away from me!"

40

AFTERPARTY

Three months later

I stand at the fence, coffee in hand, and watch horse and rider canter in a perfect circle. It's far too early on a Sunday morning to be inhaling horse manure, but the opportunity to spend time with Petra is a godsend. An impossibility I never dreamed would come true.

My baby sister laughs as her mare throws her head. I find myself laughing too. How can I not? Her laugher is the most beautiful sound in the world.

Doris and Paul join me at the fence. I smile at my sister's adoptive parents and we watch her in silence for a few minutes.

"She's a natural, isn't she?" Doris's voice radiates pure maternal pride.

I nod. "She sure is." I look over at her. "Thank you."

The older woman squeezes my arm. "Thank you for all you did to protect her. At least now that man is behind bars, we can all rest a little easier."

That man.

Clayton Getty.

The road to his incarceration wasn't easy. He had too many officials in his back pocket and tried to call in favors far and wide, stalling for as long as possible the FBI's attempts to bring multiple charges.

Eventually, it was his own deputy who proved instrumental in putting him away.

Turns out, the FBI'd had their eye on what was going on in Getty Falls for a while. Sadly, none of the cops were willing to stand up to Clayton. Not until Deputy Rick Daniels stepped into Clay's shoes and decided he never wanted to take them off.

Daniels convinced a few key people to come forward with the promise of immunity from prosecution. After that, Clay's corrupt empire started to tumble. He's now behind bars for fraud, prostitution, racketeering, and kidnapping. There were a few dozen minor charges thrown in too, but suffice it to say, he won't be breathing free air for at least thirty years, which is fine by me.

For myself, the FBI decided not to press charges after I confessed to what happened at The Villa. As it turned out, Ridge Mathews wasn't the golden boy Clay made him out to be. He was dishonorably discharged from the Army for raping an underage girl in Iraq. And with Clay having already documented his death as accidental, the authorities were happy to let the matter rest in return for my testimony.

Now that the danger is behind me, I know I have to come to terms with killing a man.

Being here, in Vancouver, with Petra, helps me a little in thinking I did the wrong thing for the right reasons.

Petra waves from across the field. I smile and wave back, and my soul settles a little bit. She canters over with Winnie, her favorite mare, the newest gift to arrive at the farm.

"Are you sure I can't tempt you into riding with me?" Her light green eyes blaze with enthusiasm and happiness.

I wrinkle my nose in mock horror. "Uh, no. After falling off three times last week, I need a *huge* ego boost, and several layers of padding before I'm tempted to try again."

She laughs and trots off again.

"Breakfast in half an hour," Paul shouts after her.

As they discuss what to have for breakfast, the phone in my pocket buzzes.

My heart wobbles, but I make no move to reach for it.

I know who it is. I also know it's time to change my number. Again.

Four times in three months. Each time, it takes about a week before he discovers the new number. I probably shouldn't bother.

Maybe it's a game we're playing.

Maybe this is destined to be my life.

When the buzzing continues, Doris glances over at me. "Everything okay?"

I nod.

She doesn't push.

We drift into the warm, sunny kitchen for breakfast, then I head upstairs to take a shower. In my room, I sit on my bed and take out the phone.

Fifteen texts from Quinn, the first one dated five days ago, two days after I got my latest phone. The texts aren't requests for communication or pleas to be heard. They're bite-size letters, detailing his life, past and present.

Sometimes he calls me Lucky. Sometimes Elly. Other times Elyse. I guess I'm all those to him. He never calls me firecracker. Maybe that time is over for him.

Regardless of how he addresses me, the information is inexhaustible. At first I didn't want to read them.

What he did was unforgivable. I don't care that I was partly responsible for my epic downfall; Quinn and Q manipulated me with the cunning and talent of Machiavelli.

I can never trust him. And I can't entertain the idea of being with someone I don't trust.

The phone buzzes again. I glance at the screen and read the latest message.

6 July: Elyse,

Delilah was charged today. Yesterday Maxwell was formally charged with manslaughter. The DA is ecstatic. She doesn't have to wait for Maxwell and Delilah to divorce before compelling her to testify against my father. Delilah also finally confessed to lacing Mama's anti-depression pills with Benzo over a six-month period when she was Mama's assistant. Those were the pills Mama took that day. The day my life changed forever. I should feel vindicated. Triumphant. Avenged. I feel nothing. I don't even hurt anymore. But my cracks keep growing. But it's fine. I'm fine. I'm fine.

Quinn.

I hate myself for the lurching of my heart. Just as I hate myself for scrolling through, reading his other texts...

3 July: Elly,

I wanted you to see me. You saw me. A part of me wishes you would forgive what you saw. A part of me hopes you never forgive. He destroyed her just to gain more power and money. The Blackwood billions and the thirty-billion inheritance from her family clearly weren't enough. How greedy can one man be? He called me from jail last week, asked to see me. I went because I needed to tell him why. Needed to not leave him with a sense of righteousness that he's free of guilt in all this. I sat across from him. And I told him my plan all along was to humiliate him in the worst possible way. Make him want to kill himself like he made her kill herself. If that didn't succeed I was going to kill him myself. But...Elyse...when it came down to it, I couldn't kill him. I was a coward.

That's why he's still alive. He's breathing and she's not. That kills me, Elyse. But I take solace in one thing. I've destroyed the one thing he loves. The Blackwood name. No one will ever speak of it with pride or awe again. That too was my plan. It was the right thing to do. FOR THE GREATER FUCKING GOOD.

Quinn

* * *

2 July: Lucky,

I wanted to be a movie director. Did I tell you that? No, I don't think I did. That camera...the one...it was my first, a gift from Mama. Anyway, I guess in some way I got to direct the movie of my life. Given another chance I would change one cast member. You didn't deserve your role. I knew it long before your love touched me for one blissful second. I play that moment in my mind over and over. If I could have one thing in this miserable life, it would be to freeze that moment in time. Forever. Forgive me.

Quinn

* * *

1 July: Lucky,

I saw an ad today. For waffles. I thought of you. Just thought you should know. Forgive me. Forgive me.

Quinn

* * *

28 June: Elly

I hope you'll accept the horse for Petra. I hear she loves horses, that she's a talented rider. In another life I would've loved to meet her. Get to know her. But this is my life. I accept it. Don't send the mare back. Let her enjoy it. Please. Forgive me.

Quinn.

* * *

26 June: Elyse,

It's Mama's birthday today. She would've been forty-nine. Mrs. Harper, our housekeeper, would've baked her a cake with pink frosting and daffodil flowers. Mama would've wrinkled her nose, laughed, and said she wasn't eight years old. But she would've secretly loved it. I miss her. I miss you. I miss you.

Quinn

* * *

20 June: Elly,

Found out today that Maxwell might never face charges for what he did. He has too many people in his back pocket. I don't know what to do with that. I'm not giving up though. He has to pay. But...I hurt everywhere. I haven't hurt like this in...forever. He killed her. He killed her. I tried to save her. I tried to save her. I tried. So hard. She told me to let her go. Why would she do that? Why would she want to leave me? It hurts, Elly. So damn much.

Quinn

* * *

15 June: Lucky

I never told you my age. I'm twenty-eight.

Quinn

* * *

30 April: Elly,

Charges were brought against Dr. Nathanson today. She's lost her license. Jail is too good for her for abandoning Mama, the woman supposed to be her best friend, when she knew what Maxwell was doing to her. Like me, she could've saved her. My efforts came too late. But she chose not to. For her own selfish reasons, she condoned Mama's suffering. I hope she rots in hell.

Quinn

I drop the phone on the bed, lie back, and swipe at the tears dripping down my face. I should be done with these damn tears. Done with Quinn. I should throw my phone away and not buy another one. After all, if I don't have a phone, he can't contact me. The thought spears me with anguish so ravaging, I jerk into fetal position. I'm not sure how long I lie there, calling myself a thousand kinds of fool.

The distant rumbling of a vehicle sends me to the window.

The farmhouse is remote for a reason. As is the clear No Trespass sign half a mile down the dirt road. I don't need to look down the driveway to know Paul will already be meeting the car, his shotgun tucked into the crook of his arm. He scared the living shit out of a bunch of joyriders who took the wrong turn onto his property last week.

Although, looking at the sleek black SUV approaching, I have a feeling these aren't joy riders.

The driver slows when he spots Paul. When Paul cautiously beckons, the vehicle rolls forward. The passenger-side window winds down and a conversation takes place. Paul nods once and looks up to my bedroom window.

A tingling seizes my nape as the door opens.

Fionnella steps out.

I bolt out of the room and charge down the stairs. Paul and Fionnella are on the porch by the time I wrench open the front door.

"You're not welcome here, Fionnella." I switch glances to Paul. "She's not welcome!"

He nods. "I told her that. She wanted to hear it from you."

I turn back to Fionnella. "You're not—"

"Five minutes, Lucky." She holds out her hands. "That's all I'm asking for."

I'm shaking my head before she's halfway through the sentence. "No."

She sighs. "I have something from him, for you." She reaches into her pocket, pulls out an envelope, and holds it out to me.

"I don't want it, whatever it is. He already manipulated me into keeping the horse. That's it, I don't want anything else from him."

Fionnella glances at Paul, who's still hovering. Whatever she signals him, he casts me a supportive look, but retreats back into the house. Through the window, I see Petra and Doris staring at me. I try a reassuring smile, but I'm sure it misses the mark.

"It's the money you're owed, Lucky. You earned it. Don't refuse it because of stubborn pride."

Humiliation reddens my face. "Thanks for the reminder." I snatch the envelope out of her hands and rip it open. My jaw drops at the sum written on the check.

"Is this some sort of joke?"

She shakes her head. "The two hundred thousand is the remainder of what you agreed. The five million is for reparations."

"Well, tell him to take his reparations, and shove it."

Fionnella's mouth tightens. "Lucky—"

"My name is Elyse. So what else does he want? Please don't insult me by telling me you flew all the way here just to deliver this." I slap the envelope on the porch banister.

"He wants to see you. But he can't, not with that restraining order you have against him." Her mouth twists. "A little much if you ask me."

"I didn't. I don't want the money."

She doesn't respond. Her chin juts forward, her eyes contemplative as they rest on me. "I told him you wouldn't take it."

"And he sent it anyway. Of course."

"It's a natural reaction."

"To throw money at everything?"

"To seek what he thinks is the most effective solution to a problem."

"I'm not a problem! At least not his problem. He can't pull my strings and manipulate me anymore. And how the hell did you two find me anyway?"

"I'm very resourceful. And let's face it, with Getty behind bars, you haven't tried very hard to hide your tracks. Or he wouldn't be sending you those texts within days of your buying a new phone."

"Maybe I should try harder then. Maybe I should take this money and use it to place a few continents between us, hide in a place where he can't find me."

"He will always find you, Elyse. There's nowhere on earth you can disappear to that I won't find you, if the boss wishes me to."

"I know who he is now, Fionnella. You don't need to keep calling him *the boss.*"

"He may no longer be your boss, but he's mine."

"What's your deal, Fionnella? Why are you here, fighting for him?"

She looks off into the rolling fields and paddock for a minute, before she meets my gaze. "He tried to help me with my son. Michael came home from Afghanistan with PTSD. He was Adriana Nathanson's patient. You've seen the footage. You know how she treats her young male patients. He was under her care for a year before he committed suicide."

My hand lifts to my mouth as the horror of it drenches me. "I'm sorry."

Grief blankets her face for a moment, but then her brisk manner returns. "Take the money, Elyse. If not for yourself, then for the sister you gave every dime of those eight hundred thousand dollars to. Think what this could do for Petra."

"Please don't say her name," I mutter, still caught in Fionnella's confession.

A dart of hurt crosses her face. "What did I do that was so bad, Lucky? Hmm? You signed up to do a job. I ensured you were taken care of so you could do it. Are you condemning me for that?"

"You knew what he was doing with me. With Elyse. Lucky knew what she signed up for. Elyse didn't deserve the mind-fucking that came with the deal. She didn't deserve to have her feelings fucked with."

"No, you're right. He never placed the ad with that Blackwood magazine until this last time. I knew it was a mistake."

I exhale in disbelief. "That's all you have to say?"

"It's not for me to apologize for him. But you wouldn't have met him otherwise, and you wouldn't feel this much pain if he means nothing to you. Also you wouldn't have had the means to buy yourself time from Clay. Think about that."

"So what, you want me to go have a cup of coffee and a conversation with him?"

"He can't have a goddamn coffee or conversation with you when you've got a restraining order out on him. And he certainly can't do that when he's hell-bent on killing himself!"

Icy chains shackle my heart. "What are you talking about?"

She sighs and it's a weary, hollow sound. "This was his plan all along, Lucky. Expose his father, stepmother, and shrink. Then find a way to end it all. Except you came along. You gave him hope! Probably even love. Am I right?"

I shudder in the face of the raw accusation.

"And now you're withholding it."

My eyes widen. "Please tell me you're not finding some way to blame me for all of this?"

She shrugs. "Love comes with responsibility. Whether you want to admit it or not, you're responsible for him. It's your name he toasts to every time he gulps down a mouthful of whiskey, and trust me, he does that very often. It's your name he screams out for in his sleep. You be the judge of what needs to be done. The jet will be at Vancouver International for the next twenty-four hours. I'll leave your name with the crew. If you're not there by midday tomorrow, it'll take off."

41

SYNC

QUINN

Maybe my cracks aren't so bad.
Maybe the chasm isn't as deep as I thought.
Maybe she'll take the leap with me.
Maybe with her, I'll survive the fall.
Maybe she'll even save me.
Maybe. Maybe.
Maybe… it's too late.

* * *

LUCKY

I step out of the limo and take a bracing breath. Above me soars the skyscraper that holds Quinn's home. Or so Fionnella tells me.

I've been in so many of his properties I've lost count. But this Upper East Side building is where he is right now.

Where fuck knows what will happen.

I'm still slightly stunned by my decision. The last-minute dash to the airport temporarily silenced the vicious butterflies demanding to know what the hell I was doing.

But here, now, staring at the glass façade, I hesitate. I shouldn't have come. Hell, I should have fled the other way. But will I ever forgive myself if, after all that's happened, I lend a hand in the downfall of a man who clearly needs help?

The Monday afternoon sidewalk traffic is light, or as light as can be without all the tabloid frenzy that dogged me a few months ago before I escaped to Vancouver. Everywhere I went I saw my face on the news. Pictures of Quinn and me outside XYNYC alongside a censored one of me and Q in bed seemed to be pictures of the year.

Although humiliation still burns from being publicly exposed by Quinn's film, I've made grudging peace with myself. Even before Fionnella pointed it out yesterday, I accepted that I walked into the Lucky/Q thing with my eyes wide open and therefore was accountable for my own actions.

It's the Elly part of my story that tore my heart in shreds. And that heart hasn't recovered.

Twenty-four hours. That's all I've promised to give him. I owe him that for the tracker he put in the cash that helped locate Clayton. I don't have the emotional stamina for any more. I'm still raw from the depth of his deception.

Pushing my shoulders back, I walk toward the revolving doors. I can't linger on the sidewalk. I'm already attracting curious glances.

The doorman holds it open for me and the concierge doesn't stop me as I head for the private elevator.

Fionnella provided me with the security code for the door. The possibility that Quinn won't be in a state to answer his own front door isn't something I'm prepared to deal with so I just open the slate double doors myself and walk right in.

The interior is gloomy. The air-conditioning is turned up high and the place is dark and cold and desolate.

I want to call out to him, but fear freezes my vocal cords.

What I can see of the minimalist decor looks bleak and clinical. The floor-to-ceiling glass wall is frosted, blocking out the blazing July sun.

I search the living room until I find the window remote. I'm about to click when I hear a sound behind me.

Quinn.

"Leave it," he croaks, his voice full of rocks.

He's a shadow in the darkened hallway, but I know it's him just by the ferocious awareness charging through my body. It freezes me in place as it rams its presence deep, punishing me for daring to attempt to live without it.

I need to say something. I open my mouth.

"I don't want you here, Nella. You mean well, I'm sure, but I just want to be left alone," he says. His voice is low and raw with naked anguish, but the demand is forceful.

I swallow and take a step forward. "It's not Fionnella. Quinn, it's me."

That fearsome deathly stillness shrouds him. For minutes we stay like that.

Then he stumbles forward. "Lights," he wheezes. Then more forcefully, when the room stays dark. "Lights!"

Soft light floods the room. Contrary to what I thought, there are warmer colors in here. Browns and soft grays blend with the sharper tones. But the decor isn't what interests me right now.

Quinn staggers forward again, his bare feet soundless on the polished hardwood floors. His black hair is overgrown and wildly unkempt, easily touching his shoulders. He's also sporting a full beard, which against the brilliance of his eyes makes his face even more hauntingly beautiful.

He's lost a lot of weight, his hollow cheeks not disguised by the facial hair. His body is leaner too, the T-shirt and jeans hanging off him. My gaze tracks downward.

And that's when I see it.

The whiskey bottle in his hand. It's half empty, the amber liquid sloshing around with his forward momentum.

"Elyse...you...no," He stops and shakes his head. Then he smashes his lids closed and takes a huge gulp of whiskey.

"Quinn."

He slams out his free hand, as if to push me away, and, eyes still shut, takes another drink.

"Not real," he slurs. "You're...not...real."

Another desperate, memory-wiping gulp and he chokes. He doubles over in a hacking fit. I drop the control and rush toward him. He rears up abruptly, his chest heaving as he stares me down.

One arm comes up and he swipes his mouth with the back of his hand.

Feverish eyes rake me from head to toe, and back again.

"Quinn. It's me. I'm here."

He takes a tentative step forward. And another.

He stands before me, tall, strong. Half the man he used to be. And my heart breaks. For the childhood he can never look back on without pain and sorrow. For the path he chose because he didn't manage to do the impossible and save his beloved mother.

For what he's doing to himself now.

His eyes are severely bloodshot, which makes the silver-blue stand out even more vividly.

I've missed his eyes...

"Elyse?"

I nod. My throat clogs as every emotion I've staunchly squashed these past few months attempts to break free.

The hand he lifts shakes uncontrollably. He bunches it into a fist but the shaking doesn't stop. "Please be real. God. Please."

"I'm real, Quinn."

He shudders at the sound of my voice. I walk backward into the living room; he follows, his gaze bolted on mine. Letting him touch me would probably convince him, but I'm not ready for that. Not by a long shot.

"I came...like you asked. But if you want to talk, you need to put the bottle down."

He shakes his head. "I can't."

"Yes, you can."

His grip tightens around the neck of the bottle. "No. It's all I have. It's the only thing that works. I can't...you can't take it away from me."

This was his plan all along...find a way to end it all.

His whiskey breath washes over me and my heart somersaults in my chest.

He's trying to drink himself to death.

"Give me the bottle, Quinn." Alarm hardens my voice, but he's equally resilient.

"I said no!"

"Okay. Do you want me to leave? Fine, I'm leaving."

It's a lie. I do a quick search and head for the kitchen. Sure enough, he races after me.

He skates to an unsteady stop opposite where I stand at the center island, hands propped on my hips. "How about we put your precious bottle right here, on the counter? It can stay here while I fix you something to eat. I'm hungry myself. You don't want me to starve, do you?"

The act of frowning makes him dizzy. He sways on his feet. "Of course not," he slurs. "You can eat. But I don't want anything."

I shake my head. "That's not going to work for me." I walk around and push a stool toward him. "Sit down. I'll fix us *both* something to eat. You wanted to see me, Quinn. I'm here, but I have a life to live. I'm not interested in talking to you unless you're sober. So what's it to be?"

He eyes me for several moments. Then he sits, the bottle still tight in his grip.

I take a deep breath, move around the massive kitchen, opening and closing drawers, fridges, and cupboards. I find enough to make two ham sandwiches and a bowl of mixed fruit. His eyes track me throughout, and when I sit down next to him, his whole body shudders.

"You're here," he murmurs.

My breath shakes out, and I hold my hand out for the bottle. "Yes, I'm here, Quinn."

He slowly releases his stranglehold on the whiskey. I set it down

out of arm's reach and push a plate in front of him. He barely acknowledges it. My throat feels too tight to contemplate chewing,
never mind swallowing. But I pick up the sandwich, take a bite.

He makes no attempt to copy my move. So I pluck a couple of
grapes off the stem and hold them against his mouth. He slowly
parts his lips and takes them. He chews without taking his eyes
off my face. Heady with the small triumph, I take turns eating and
feeding him.

He's halfway through his sandwich when his face contorts. Before
I can ask what's wrong, he erupts from the table and darts out of the
kitchen on surprisingly steady feet.

I chase after him. "Quinn!"

He doesn't respond, but I see him disappear into a room at the
far end of the hall. I go after him and enter the bedroom to hear the
sound of gut-rolling retching.

Shit.

I'm halfway to the bathroom when the image on his large TV
screen catches my eye. I stumble to a halt and stare at the shot of myself, asleep in the Hell's Kitchen loft. There's a time stamp on it and
the footage is frozen in place. I'm more shocked than disturbed by
the fact that Quinn is still in possession of images of me. That he's
watching me even after all this time.

Another bout of vomiting refocuses my attention. I enter the
bathroom to find him crouched over the toilet. His skin is sallow and
beaded with sweat and his whole body shakes as he expels whiskey-
drenched stomach contents.

I grab a washcloth and run it under cool water. He groans and
closes his eyes when I press it to his forehead. The heaving eventually
stops and he collapses against the vanity.

Sinking down next to him, I'm lost as to how to help him.

"Can I get you anything?"

His hand blindly searches for mine, pulls it onto his stomach, and
clamps tight. "Stay," he rasps.

He takes a deep breath, two, then he's surging toward the bowl
again.

The retching continues for the better part of an hour, by which time, I'm shaking with fear. The part of me that suspected Fionnella's concern was exaggerated to get me to come here shrivels and dies. Quinn is in serious trouble, and as much as I'm hurting over what he's done, I can't help but feel for him.

The second he quiets down, I race back to the living room for my phone.

Fionnella answers immediately.

"What's wrong?"

"He won't stop throwing up," I blurt.

"Shit, I was afraid of that."

"Afraid of what?" I demand.

"Possible alcohol poisoning."

"*Jesus*. Does he need to go the hospital?"

"No. Keep an eye on him. I'll call you back in five minutes."

"*What?*" I shriek, but she's hung up.

She calls back when he's in the middle of another vomiting bout. "His doctor is on his way. ETA twenty minutes."

"Are you sure he shouldn't be in the hospital?"

"Dr. Hanley will decide that. We don't want to give the press another scoop unless it's unavoidable. Elyse . . . are you okay?"

"No, I'm not," I snap, worry and fear making me cranky. "It's bad, Fionnella."

"I know. That's why you're there. You're my last hope," she says softly, before she hangs up.

Heart in my throat, I return to Quinn. He looks like he's passed out, but I realize he's fallen asleep. There's no way I'm going to get him into bed so I tug the covers and a couple of pillows off the bed and make him as comfortable as possible.

When the doctor arrives, I let him in, my breath held as he examines Quinn.

"He's severely dehydrated, but he hasn't quite slipped into poisoning territory."

Relief shudders through me, and stupid tears prickle my eyes.

"When he wakes, give him a couple of these, then repeat every four hours. They're rehydration pills." He hands me the vial. "And obviously, no more booze," the small, wiry man says with a wry smile. He extracts a card from his pocket and sets it on the vanity. "If anything untoward occurs, call me."

I nod and see him out.

Quinn is still sleeping when I return. I can't leave him, so I go in search of more blankets, and I make my own makeshift bed on the bathroom floor.

* * *

"Elyse."

I open my eyes. He's staring at me. His color is healthier, but faint gray lines fan his mouth.

"I'm sorry," he mutters.

I blink as the pain rushes back. I'm not ready to deal with my emotions, or even his, so I ask abruptly, "How do you feel?"

He closes his eyes for a second. "Like hell. But...I'm glad you're here. I'm sorry," he repeats.

My throat clogs all over again. I try to get up to fetch his pills. His hand jerks across the space between us and holds me still.

"Don't go," he pleads. "I need you to forgive me, Elyse. Please."

I shake my head. "I need to get up, Quinn. To get your pills."

He tenses. "What pills?"

"You wouldn't stop throwing up. The doctor came."

A tinge of embarrassment flushes across his face. "Shit."

"Yeah."

He releases me. I fill a glass with water and shake out a couple of pills. He sits up and swallows them without complaint. He sets the glass down and spears me with surprisingly piercing eyes. "Elyse, tell me what I need to do. I'll do anything."

"Can you stand up? I love the under-floor heating and everything, but it's going to play havoc on your bones and mine if we keep sleeping on the tiles."

He gives a short nod and staggers to his feet. In silence, we return to the bedroom and he slides into bed. I arrange the covers over him, but when I step away, he grabs my arm.

"Stay." The voice is Quinn's but I hear Q's power behind it. I can't help the shiver that runs through me. How the hell could I have missed the visceral connection? "Please, stay."

My gaze finds his. His blue eyes plead. My head moves in a nod. "I'll stay in the room, but I'm not getting into bed with you."

I'm strong enough and weak enough to know that's not a good idea. After a moment, he releases me. I retreat and settle in the wide armchair and matching footstool. Quinn turns sideways to face me and the intensity in his eyes grows.

"Can we talk?" he inquires solemnly. "I've missed you, Elly. God...so much." He stops and takes a deep breath. "I need to know how to make you forgive me. Show you how sorry I am for what I did."

"I'm not promising anything beyond saying we can talk when you're better. Sleep now. I'll fix us something to eat when you wake up and we'll take it from there, okay?"

His eyes gleam. "You're still obsessed with food."

"And you look like you've given up on it."

His expression turns mournful and dark, and he looks away. "Giving up is surprisingly easy when you have nothing left in life to look forward to."

Even though my heart weeps, I harden my voice. "Is that what I'm here for? To watch you give up?"

He doesn't respond. He heaves a sigh and reaches out his hand toward me. I force myself to remain still. When he falls asleep, I allow the tears to fall. I watch him breathe, dream. Knowing that the love I confessed three months ago outside the loft still burns as bright. But then, so does the hurt.

I must fall asleep too. I jerk awake to the sound of fresh vomiting. But this time, when I rush to his aid, he's not crumbled on the floor. He stays on his feet throughout. And the bout lasts only a few minutes. When he tugs his clothes off and staggers into the shower, I follow.

"Are you okay?"

He nods, but his whole body is caught in relentless shudders. His hand slips when he tries to turn on the spray.

Without a second thought, I strip down to my panties and top and join him in the shower. If he hears me, he doesn't make a move to acknowledge me. He just stands there with his forehead against the wall, his chest heaving.

I turn on the shower and wrap my arms around him. Hot water cascades over us, and after a few minutes, his shivering dies down enough for me to release him. I grab a washcloth and shower gel and bathe him from head to toe.

His cock stirs when I wash his groin and when his gaze catches mine, his mouth twitches.

I ruthlessly ignore the arousal that stabs me and finish rinsing him off.

When I'm done, he eyes my sodden top. "You're wet."

"Yep."

I catch the hem of the shirt and tug it over my head. Wild eyes immediately land on my chest. He makes a pained sound at the back of his throat, but he still makes no move to grab me. I don't know whether to be sad or impressed.

"No bra," he states gruffly.

I shake my head. "Was in a hurry to get to the airport."

He lifts one brow. I step out of my panties and rinse the trans-ferred suds off my body. When I'm done he follows me out. The towel I intend to pass him stays clutched in my fist as I look him over. His body is still drop-jaw magnificent, but it's suffered changes.

He catches me watching him, and a twinge of emotion passes over his face. "I couldn't...didn't want to live. Not without..." Wary eyes meet mine. "Elyse..."

"Here's what's going to happen. You're going to take the pills. You're going to eat. You're going to get better. Then we'll talk. No guarantees, but I agree to talk. Do you want that?"

His nostrils quiver as he takes in a huge breath. "More than I want my next heartbeat."

My lips purse. My eyes drop to his elbow, the almost invisible scars I noticed when I washed him. "Wanting your next heartbeat is kinda required for the talking, so maybe let's not take that off the table just yet?"

He frowns for a second. "Okay."

"What does that mean, *okay*?"

His eyes sizzle where they're riveted on my chest. "It means let's get the *fuck* out of this bathroom and get some clothes on before this hard-on kills me."

My eyes drop to the killer erection he's sporting and shocked laughter bursts out of me.

Okay, so Alpha Quinn isn't quite down and out.

I hand him the towel. His movements are a little slow, but he dries himself off just fine. He takes the pills I pass him and we head to his dressing room. He pulls on shorts and hands me one of his T-shirts.

We fall back into our bed arrangement, and he's asleep in minutes. I take the time he's sleeping to check messages and call Vancouver to let them know I've arrived safely and might be staying for longer than the planned twenty-four hours. In the kitchen, I find boxed-up ready meals in the fridge that I missed before in my agitation. I heat up pasta and sauce, grate Parmesan over it, and set out the meal on a tray.

Quinn is up, staring at the screen when I return to the bedroom. He turns it off when I walk in, but his gaze searches mine.

"What?" I ask as I set the tray on his lap.

He nods to the TV. "You saw what I was watching."

"Yeah."

"Are you mad?" he asks warily.

"That depends."

"On?"

"Why were you watching it?"

He catches hold of my wrist and rubs his thumb across my pulse. "I want to see you. All the time," he whispers fervidly. "You probably want me to get rid of it, but I . . . can't."

I swallow, allowing just a little hope to build. "Why?"

"Because it helps…it keeps me…here. Because without that connection, I don't think I can go on. I need it, Elyse. I *need* you."

"Okay."

"Okay?"

"That's all I have right now, Quinn."

A wave of pain breaks across his face, and the eyes that meet mine are oceans of desolation. "Don't ask me to destroy them. Please."

I shake my head. "You can keep them."

"I can?" His voice is rough with hope.

"Yes. For now. Eat, Quinn."

He polishes off the meal in record time. I return the tray to the kitchen. He takes another dose of his pills, and I grab a blanket and return to my lounger. We watch normal TV until we fall asleep.

The pattern continues for three days, then I move to the guest bedroom. Quinn doesn't put up a fight, but his eerie silence, the tapping finger against his thigh, and flashing eyes tells me he doesn't like the idea.

On Friday morning, I'm awakened by a knock on my door. I jerk upright, disoriented. I push my hair out of my face and croak, "Come in."

He enters, carrying a tray. And he's wearing jeans and a T-shirt, with a baseball cap tucked into his back pocket. Over the past couple of days, signs of the streamlined, athletic lover who captivated my every breath have reemerged. He may look a little gaunt, but Quinn Blackwood's presence in my bedroom still had the power to make my belly quiver.

"You've been out?" I ask to cover the rampant thoughts and emotions zinging through me. One of which is that, now that he's better, I needed to think about making plans to return to Vancouver.

He nods, and my gaze is drawn to his square jaw. He shaved off his beard yesterday, but his lower face is covered with a designer stubble that makes my thighs clench with the need to experience its roughness.

"Was in the mood for fresh bagels. I slathered yours with cream cheese, just the way you like it."

He waits until I sit up and sets the tray down before taking a seat opposite. I salivate at the smell of warm bread and he smirks as he passes me a bagel.

"Eat."

His dominant side has been creeping back in over the last forty-eight hours too.

I finish the bagel, coffee, and juice he sets before me. My breath catches when he leans forward and brushes the corner of my mouth.

"Cream cheese," he states, before he licks his thumb.

Heat spikes through me. I watch hunger grow in his own eyes, and I know our impasse is coming to an end. Once our meal is finished, he sets the tray to one side and pins me with those piercing silver eyes. I clear my throat and focus on what I need to say.

"We need to clear up a few things."

He nods. "Yes."

"The whole Q thing. It was a little more than just a film to you, wasn't it?"

Pain slashes across his eyes. "Yes."

"Why?"

"Maxwell and his friends were part of the group who bid for those types of films. I set the first one up as bait. Maxwell was the highest bidder of Q's first production and every one after that. It gave me a kick to take his money and donate it to charity, while I knew I'd humiliate him eventually with the irony of what he was paying for."

My heart aches but I nod. "Okay, I understand how things rolled with Q and Lucky. I'm not really upset about that."

He breathes out. "Okay, but I still want to make it up to you. Will you let me?"

"I'm thinking about it."

He nods again.

I clear my throat and continue. "You and Elyse…Sully offering me a job, me working at Blackwood Tower, did you—?"

"No. That was total coincidence. The ad I placed in the magazine was our only link. I didn't orchestrate anything else. You started working at Blackwood before you came to me…to Q."

The knot inside me eases a touch. "And getting evicted from the motel? Did you have something to do with that?"

His gaze drops and his jaw flexes once. "Yes. The moment you said yes to Q, I saw you as mine, in every way. I couldn't have you living there. I needed to remove you from that vile place."

"What if I hadn't come to you?"

"I would have found a way. I'm not going to apologize for wanting you safe, Elyse. I will apologize for the way I did things. For not coming clean later, when I realized I didn't want you to end up as collateral damage in the shit storm I created. What I did to you was wrong. So wrong. But…I was caught up in a decade-long, twisted game. Reason had long ceased to matter."

I catch a glimpse of the mental anguish still riding him, and I touch his hand, trace it to the lines on his forearm. "Was this part of the game? Cutting yourself?"

"For a while, yes. It got me the attention I needed. It got me into Adriana Nathanson's office."

"God, Quinn."

He grabs hold of my hand, and stares deep into my eyes.

"Forgive me, Elyse. I went into this with my eyes shut to everything else but getting my brand of justice for my mother. Even when I realized I wanted you to see me, maybe even save me, I still wasn't prepared to stop."

"But I did see you. I knew who you were. What you were. I tried to convince myself it didn't matter. But it did."

Bleakness flashes through his eyes. "It still matters, doesn't it?"

I hesitate. Then go with the truth. "Yes. You need help, Quinn. To help you get over losing your mother that way. But I want to be there for you while you get that help. Maybe I need help myself. I'm not without fault."

"No. God, you're perfect."

"I'm not. You know what I was…what I did in Getty Falls?" I enquire tentatively.

He nods. "I know everything. And you're still perfect to me. God, I love you, Elyse. I was too twisted to recognize until it was far too late, until you saw nothing but the monster. But I do, baby. I love you. Inside and out, no matter what you've done. *No matter what.*"

My heart shakes, threatens to fly, but I need to state more truths. "I hated you for being two people, but so was I. You signed up for Lucky, but I wanted you to like Elyse, maybe even love her. Having that opportunity taken away from me before it had a chance to grow into something hurt, and I lashed out at you."

His head jerks downward, and a lock of vibrant hair falls over his forehead. I brush it back as he links his fingers through mine and stares in fascination at our fused palms. "Sending me away when the FBI rescued you cut me to shreds. The restraining order killed me."

"I'm sorry. The shock was just too much, you know? I think I filed it because although I wanted to hate you, I couldn't stop thinking about you, or missing you. It was my way of stopping myself from craving you."

"And do you crave me?" he asks.

"I do," I murmur.

His eyes fire a blaze of silver-blue. "Fuck, you don't know what hearing that does to me."

"Good things, I hope."

"Seriously awesome things. I love you. I love you. Please forgive me. I'll spend the rest of my life making it up to you. Please give me the chance?"

"You talk a good game, Mr. Blackwood. Let me think on it for a minute."

We grin at each other for several heartbeats before he sobers. "I'm so glad Fionnella agreed to come find you for me."

"So am I. Is she…okay now that this is over?"

He nods. "I think we're both ready to put it behind us, however we can."

My heart turns over in anger and sorrow for the wrongs done to them.

"I can't stand the thought that they did that to you and your mother."

He looks at me solemnly for several beats. Then he nods. "Would you like me to have them killed?"

I gasp. "Quinn. Please don't joke about things like that."

He doesn't reply. I look deeper into his eyes. And shiver. "Please tell me you were just joking?"

He shrugs. "You're distressed. Forget what I said."

I shake my head. "That's...just on the off-chance you weren't joking, I don't want to have *anyone* killed."

"Okay."

"Okay?" I repeat incredulously.

He grabs me by the waist and pulls me beneath him. The breath is knocked out of me and when I take a deep breath, his gaze drops to my boobs. Then with monumental effort he drags it back up. "Okay."

He stares at me for a long while. "I love you. Fuck, I never thought I'd say those words. To anyone again besides Mama."

Tears fill my eyes. He brushes them away and drops a light kiss on my nose.

"Let's talk about us some more. I still have a lot of making up to do."

"Okay. I think you should know, I'm not accepting that five million."

He grimaces and rises off the bed. He paces agitatedly for a minute before he stares at me. "I really want you to take it, Elyse."

"Why?"

"I can't take back some of the things I did. But this would help. Give it to Petra, or give it to your favorite charity if you want. But take it."

"If it means that much to you—"

"It does."

"Then okay, it goes to Petra. What next?"

He eyes me from head to toe. "I'm obsessed with you. Have I told you that?"

"Not in so many words." I recall my images on his TV screen. "But I have a fair idea." I smile.

He smiles back. My insides melt. "I intend to fuel that obsession.

Night and day for a very long time. Do you have any objections to maybe considering making this thing between us permanent? Maybe after I get a proper therapist to sort out my..." he indicates his head.

My smile widens until I'm scared my face will burst. "Hmm, definitely maybe."

He exhales. "Okay, do you have any more objections I need to deal with?"

"Not an objection. More like a condition."

"Which is?"

"Am I allowed to be equally obsessed with you?"

His smile widens by a mile. "Fuck yes."

I laugh. My gaze tracks over his hard, beautiful body. "Quinn?"

"Hmm?"

I sit up, tug my T-shirt over my head, and lie back against the pillows. "I love you."

His breath explodes out of him, but his eyes don't stay on mine for long. They drop to my breasts and I almost see him salivate. "I love you, too," he croaks.

"Quinn?"

"Hmm?"

"Are you going to stay all the way over there all day?"

A ragged groan erupts from his throat as his wild eyes light brush fires all over my body.

"It's been three *months*, firecracker. I'm dying to fuck you. But I also want to prolong the agony, deserve you properly. So I'm going to just stay right here for the next hour, and fuck you with my eyes. Think you can handle that?"

No. I can't. And from the hard-on he's sporting I don't think he can either. "Are you sure that's wise?"

An arrogant brow arches. "Is that a dare?"

I cup my breasts and just smile. He groans, and starts moving toward me. At the last moment, he veers toward the door. "I have something for you."

"Oh?"

He dashes out and returns with a red velvet box, which he hands to me. I open it to see a delicate platinum chain, on which hangs a pink teardrop diamond.

"What's this?"

He grins. My heart lurches. I swear I'll never get used to a smiling Quinn Blackwood. "The diamond I promised your pussy."

I can't help it. I laugh. I pluck the chain off its bed, rise to my knees, and hold it out to him. "Do you want to do the honors?"

His gorgeous eyes light up. "You sure?"

I nod, because there's only one answer I can give. "Your body, your pussy."

His whole body shudders. "My heart?"

"Your heart."

He gets on the bed, crawls closer. "Say it all together. I want to hear it together, Elyse."

"Your body. Your pussy. Your heart. Your soul. Your love."

We don't last an hour. Of course we don't. We were insane to even attempt to try.

The moment he secures the chain around my waist and the pink diamond drops perfectly into place above my clit, he grabs my hips and drags me beneath his body. Our reunion kiss is the stuff of dreams. He kisses me until my lips are bruised and my heart screams with joy.

Then Quinn brings Q to the game. The two men I adore love me to within an inch of my life.

And as I'm thrust to the edge of the precipice, the most stunningly beautiful eyes in the world pierce mine.

"God, I love you, Elyse."

"I love you, too."

"Always?" My alpha demands.

"I belong to you, Quinn. Always."

His eyes gleam with unshed tears. "Thank you for taking a chance on me, my sweet firecracker. With everything that I am, everything I hope to be for you...for us...*thank you*."

Please see the next page
for a preview of

BLACK SHEEP

CHAPTER ONE

FUCK BYGONES

Childhood Sweethearts.

Even way back then, I despised the term. There was nothing childlike about what I felt for her. Even less was the implied sweetness of our connection. But we let them smile and label us as they pleased. All the while knowing and relishing our truth. She was pure sin, and I was the devil intent on gorging myself on her iniquities.

I lived for it. For her. The sexy, hint-of-sandpaper voice that could bring me to my knees. The limpid blue eyes that paralyzed me. The killer curves that made me want to kill every other boy or man who dared to look at her sixteen-year-old body.

At nineteen, I was fully cognizant of my obsession, was aware that it was a live grenade destined to blow me apart one day. But I was ready to die the first time I looked into her eyes. As long as I died in her arms.

I should have known my end would come the day she called me by her special name.

My Romeo.

She called me that the day I took her virginity beneath the stars on the beach of our families' joint Connecticut property.

My Romeo. As if she knew we were doomed. Perhaps she knew *I* was. Perhaps she'd known of the plan all along. Or she hatched it the day my father enrolled me at West Point.

The irony was that I was the only fool in the piece. I may have accepted my role as Romeo, but her name wasn't Juliet.

No, the devil's siren went by the name of Cleopatra McCarthy.

And when it came right down to it, Cleopatra McCarthy was only too happy to watch me burn in the flames of my obsession. Happy to watch me die.

Childhood sweethearts. Fuck that.

Whatever we felt for each other was as old as dirt, filthy as sin. What I feel for her now is...too fucked-up to name.

So now I watch her. She watches me.

Strangers. Enemies. Our hate sparks between us like forked lightning. Bitter, twisted. *Alive.*

There may be a wide dance floor between us and jazz funk blaring through the speakers inside the walls of XYNYC, my New York nightclub, but we may as well be cocooned in a little bubble of our own, merrily breathing in the fumes of our hate.

Eight years is a long time to drip-feed yourself poisonous might-have-beens. But I'm more than comfortable in my role of rabid obsessor.

I lean back, elbows on the bar, ignoring all around me except the woman tucked away in my roped-off VIP lounge. The elevated lounge means I can see her clearly without obstruction. The short black dress clings to her hips and upper thighs, the halter neckline and her caught-up hair leaving her lightly tanned shoulders, arms, and legs bare.

The glass of vintage Dom Pérignon champagne in her hand hasn't been touched. Not a single inch of her voluptuous body has moved in time to the music, even though music is...*was* a great love, once upon a time. Even after all these years, I feel residual resentment that

I had to share her with Axl Rose and David Grohl, watch her body twist in ecstasy that wasn't induced by me.

She shakes her head when a waiter offers her a platter of food. When the server turns away, she takes a step toward the black velvet rope that blocks the lounge. A beefy bouncer immediately steps in front of her.

She glares at him.

Without glancing my way, she reaches into her tiny purse and extracts her phone. She sets her glass down, and her fingers fly over the screen.

My own phone buzzes in my pocket. I take a beat before I pull it out and read the message. "I've been coming here almost every night for two weeks. You have to talk to me sometime."

I glance up, make her wait for a full minute before I reply. "Do I?"

Her nostrils flare lightly. "He wants an answer."

My mouth twists, and I swear the impossible happens, and I hate her even more than I did one second ago. "What are you now, his messenger?"

Her gaze flicks up to me before she shrugs, her bare, slender shoulder gleaming under the pulsing lights. "You've ignored all his e-mails and your brothers' calls."

"They're spineless assholes."

"Are you going to talk to me?"

"No."

"Then why keep me here?"

"I told you the terms of admittance. You come of your own free will; you don't get to leave until the club closes. That's in two hours."

"This is ridiculous, Axel."

My stomach knots just from seeing her type my name. "Then don't come again."

She looks up. Our eyes meet across the dance floor. Her hatred washes over me in filthy waves. I want to roll around in it. She holds my stare defiantly for a minute before she swallows and bends her head to her phone again.

"It's not that simple. Please hear me out."

Again my stomach clenches, but this time it's accompanied by a crude little jerk in my pants that grabs my attention. "Please? You begging now?"

Annoyance flickers across her features. I see her thumb hover over the screen for the longest time. Then my phone buzzes. "Yes."

I didn't expect that. The Cleo I knew never begged. My mind trips over why she would do so now. A few crazed seconds later, I decide it's safer for my sanity not to know, and I settle back into sublime hate. "Too bad the first time I hear you beg has to be via text. Answer's still no."

"Axel, this is important. Let bygones be bygones and hear me out. It won't be more than five minutes. Please."

I'm doubly pissed off that I can't hear her say that word. I've waited a long fucking time to hear it. I'm even more angry that I can't cross the distance between us to ask her to repeat it. I put everything into the two words I text to her. "Fuck bygones."

It may be a trick of the light, but I swear she feels my new level of rage. A tremble seizes her as she reads my reply.

She turns away and stalks to the private bar in the lounge. The waiter looks up and nods when she murmurs to him. He slides a shot glass across the counter and reaches for the premium tequila sitting on the shelf behind him. He pours, and she picks it up, turning and raising the glass to me before she downs it in one go.

I stride to the edge of the dance floor, my lips curled back in a sneer as I struggle not to think of the consequences of what she's doing. Breathing deep, I remind myself that it's been years since I witnessed Lightweight Cleo topple over after one shot of tequila.

All the same I watch her, narrow-eyed, as she downs another shot before heading for one of the velvet sofas. There is the tiniest little weave in her walk, and I have to clench every single muscle to stop myself from charging across the space between us.

The simple, undeniable truth is I can't.

Because of Cleopatra McCarthy, my life exploded in a billion little pieces. Pieces I didn't bother to put back together again because I knew the exercise would be futile.

So for eight years, I've lived with this new, permanently-altered-for-the-worse version of myself. A version I'm not in a hurry to reassess or remodel. A version that keeps me steeped in the obsidian fury that fuels my existence.

And I stay on my side of the divide because to come within touching distance of her is to succumb to the carnage raging inside me. After eight years, I should have enough of a hold on myself to smother the compulsion.

I don't.

But even worse than the control I sorely lack is the fact that I'm a glutton for punishment. Hell, it's the reason I run the highly successful and exclusive Punishment Club. In the eighteen months it's been open, I've made over twenty million dollars in membership fees alone. Who the fuck knew there were crazies out there like me seeking to be exposed to the very thing they hate the most?

I derive a little perverse satisfaction in the fact that I'm granting them an outlet, even while I'm unable to find one for myself. I accepted my fate a long time ago. What I have can only be cured one way—the moment I stop breathing.

"Macallan. Triple. Neat."

I reel back my thoughts and turn my head at the sound of the deep, raspy voice.

Quinn Blackwood.

He's not exactly a friend but there's mutual respect and acceptance of the otherworldliness inhabiting our blackened souls. It was why we gravitated toward each other when we found ourselves in the same group at West Point. Although Quinn never served, we kept in touch and ended up owning several nightclubs together, XYNYC being one of them.

Like me, he doesn't need the income. Like me this place is one of many outlets for the demons that haunt us. I make sure Cleo is still seated and retrace my steps back to the bar.

I watch Quinn knock back the large drink in one ruthless gulp.

"You know there's a better blend in your VIP room, right?" I say.

He slams the glass on the counter with barely suppressed violence. "Too far," he replies.

We're roughly the same height so, when he shoots me a glance, I'm well positioned to see the hounds of hell chasing through the icy landscapes of his eyes. I don't flinch. I welcome the horde like kindred spirits. Our souls have endured more than enough to last us several lifetimes, and we both know it. "That bad, huh?"

His jaw clenches as he takes a breath. "Worse."

"Need any help?"

A harrowing shadow moves over his face, and he shakes his head. "It's done. I have what I need."

I don't press him for more information. Ours is not that kind of friendship.

Besides, I have more than enough to deal with tonight. I catch movement from my lounge, and my gaze zeroes in on my nemesis. She's risen from the sofa and is leaning against the railing once more, the untouched glass of champagne again in one hand. The bodyguards are once more alert, and a few of my errant brain synapses attempt to be amused by the glare she sends their way. "If you need anything else, let me know," I say absently, unable to take my eyes off the woman whose presence looms as large as the Sphinx before me.

I sense Quinn following my gaze, then returning to me. "Looks like you have a situation of your own that needs taking care off."

"Yeah." My voice emerges in a rough rumble. "Fucking tell me about it."

He doesn't nod or smile. Quinn Blackwood rarely smiles. But then, neither do I. Another thing we have in common.

He asks questions that bounce off the edge of my consciousness.

I shrug. I nod. I respond. But throughout, my senses are attuned to the other side of the room.

I barely register him stalking away. I click my fingers, and Cici, one of my waitresses, sidles up to me with a smile. I relay instructions and refocus to see Cleo raising her nearly empty glass to her lips. My jaw clenches when I realize that somehow I've missed her drinking the champagne. Added to the two shots of tequila, I'm uncertain what the result will be. So I grant myself permission to open my senses wider, sharpen my focus with an even more vicious blade. Everything falls away as I saturate myself with her presence.

Every breath. Every blink.

I catch the moment her hips sway, ever so slightly, to the throbbing rock anthem.

The move resonates through me like the cuts of memory's blade. In an instant, I'm thrown back to my bedroom in the summer house I claimed for myself the day I turned eighteen. It was the single thing I requested when my mother asked me what I wanted for my birthday. The need to distance myself from my father had grown into a visceral, unbearable ache. My mother saw it. She granted my request, despite my father's firm refusal. It was most likely what earned her the black eye two days later.

I don't know because I didn't ask. It would've been useless to do so anyway. She would've lied. And I was too selfish, too thankful for the mercy of not having to live under the same roof as my father, to rock the boat.

So I claimed my tiny piece of heaven in hell. And it was there that Cleo danced for me for the first time. Where we celebrated a lot of *firsts*.

That particular memory flames through the charred pits of my mind. I don't fight it. Like the fleeting moments of pleasure and pain, it would be gone in an instant, devoured by the putrefying cancer that lives within me.

Sure enough, it's gone from one heartbeat to the next, and I'm left with rotting remnants of what once was.

"All taken care of, boss."

I snap my head to the side. Cici is standing next to me. Her gaze slides over me from head to toe before it settles on my face. She's wearing that special *do me* smile she's worn since she started working here six weeks ago. I made the mistake of fucking her as part of her interview process. I shouldn't have. I could pardon myself by basking in the excuse that her presence in my office that day coincided with the first call in three years from Ronan, my oldest brother.

Like one hundred percent of our interaction, that call hadn't gone well. So I needed an outlet. It was either a fist through a wall or my cock in a pussy. I chose pussy. I refuse to make excuses for that choice. Because what's the point of having a black soul, of making choices that leave your hands permanently soiled in evil, if you don't fucking own it? But I do admit to a modicum of regret. She's not the first employee I've fucked, but usually I'm a little more circumspect with my choices. My black rage prevented me from seeing that ill-disguised, *you-fuck-me-I-own-you light* in Cici's eyes until it was too late.

Now, irritatingly, ever since our one encounter, the ever-growing stench of possessiveness has clung to her every time she's in my presence.

She sidles closer now. "Is there anything else you need?" she says in a low, intimate voice. "I couldn't help but notice that both you and your friend are wound up tighter than a drum tonight. I...I can help relieve your stress...if you want?"

In the next minute, she'll find an excuse to touch me. I'm slammed with the smell of cheap perfume and shameless arousal. Because my senses are wide open and raw, I take a deeper hit than I normally would. Which makes me direct more anger at her than I know is warranted.

"Cici?"

"Yes, boss?" she responds with a breathy eagerness.

"Fuck off and do your job," I snarl.

She recoils from me and turns red-faced to face the bar.

"Jesus, twice in one night. I must be losing my touch," she mutters under her breath as she busies herself collecting a drinks order from the bartender.

I feel no remorse when she walks away in a huff. I don't give a shit what's got her ass in a vise or who else she's hit on tonight. Under normal circumstances, her feelings matter very little to me. Tonight, I care even less.

When she moves away, I exhale and glance at my watch. On Thursday nights, the club shuts at 3 a.m. It's almost one. Two more hours to go.

I brace myself before I raise my gaze.

It does absolutely nothing to buffer the potency of Cleo's stare or the effect of the evil little smile I see playing at her lips when our eyes hook into each other.

She's under my skin, where she's lived for fifteen years. And she knows it.

Fifth Harmony's "Work" blasts from the speakers. The hard beat and dirty lyrics produce a lusty, almost unconscious sway of her hips. The look in her eyes and the movement of her body are almost dichotomous. Her eyes tell me she hates me. Her body beckons me with the promise of transcendental lust.

I should retreat to my office, where I can watch her from the relative safety of security cameras. Or walk the other upper and lower floors. There are a few VIPs who would love a personal acknowledgement from me.

But fuck that.

I stay put and nod tersely at a few regulars who are brave enough to breach the no-fly-zone around me. When my bartender slides a glass of scotch to me, I pick it up and down it.

We play the staring game until she reaches for her phone once more. She toys with it for a beat before her slender fingers fly over it.

My blood thrums harder as I take my phone out and read her message.

"Stop this, Axel. Be a man. Come over here and talk to me."

My cheek twitches in a grotesque imitation of a smile. "You're not senile so you wouldn't have forgotten that I don't rise to dares. Or taunts."

"Dammit. What do I have to do?"

Those six little words send all the blood fleeing from my heart. It turns harder than stone, and my visions blinds for several seconds. I cannot believe her gall.

"You're eight years too late with that question, sweetheart."

Her head snaps up. She's breathing hard. She shakes her head. I'm not sure if it's denial or disbelief. It's probably neither. It wouldn't be the first time I've attributed sentiment to her actions where none existed.

The roaring in my head continues but I feel my phone buzz again. This time there's a single word on my screen.

"Axel."

A whispered caress. An entreaty. A demand.

It's a thousand other things. All wrapped in sugared poison. I push away from the bar, despising the knots in my stomach and the steel in my cock. I feel her gaze on my back as I stalk through the door next to the bar that leads to my office.

Shot after shot of adrenaline spikes through my bloodstream until dark, volatile sensation drenches me to my fingertips. My office door slams behind me, and I throw the bolt, as if locking myself in is the answer.

Already I want to tear the door off its hinges and rush back to the bar. I force my feet the other way and throw myself into my chair. Across my large office, the screens reflect the various areas of the club. My eyes zero in on where she is. I don't even fool myself into thinking that she's as lost as she looks. Her skin may look satin-smooth, but it's coated with steel armor.

Deliberately, I shut off the feed to that camera and activate my phone. As I type the words, I silently urge her to accept my words.

"You're free to leave. Don't come back. Take this seriously."

As I power down my phone, the reality of my weakness cannons through me.

I don't want her to come back, and I don't want to hear her out for one reason alone.

She's here because of my father.

She's here on behalf of the man I hate more than anything else in the world. The man who made sure that, at nineteen, redemption would never be an option for me.

He's used his sentries in the form of my brothers, and now he's pulling out the big guns. I give him kudos for sending her. With each visit, I've felt my edges crumbling away.

Despite everything I feel for her, I've tortured myself with the urge to give in. To hear that voice up close and personal. To smell her. To touch her.

Even when I know it would be the last straw once she speaks the words I know she's been sent to deliver.

Between the two of us, we turned armies of men against one another and changed the course of our destinies.

The Rutherfords and the McCarthys.

Two dynastic families with feet firmly entrenched in underground crime. Once friends turned the bitterest of enemies.

In the family of cold-hearted black sheep, I, Axel Rutherford, am the blackest. Abundantly despised by my three brothers, actively hated by my father.

She was the golden princess. Put on earth to test every single one of my hardened edges.

And I happily burned away every last one for her.

But my reward wasn't forever with her.

Instead she turned away from me. And crawled into my father's bed.

Acknowledgments

My thanks to the usual suspects who make this writing journey a heady ride: my Minx Sisters, you know who you are. To Kate, my friend and editor. Here we are again, another day, another story! To all the bloggers, reviewers, Goodreads readers, FB Groups, Tweeters, and Insta followers who selflessly share my stories, I love you all hard. Thank you for all you do.

Finally, to my husband and kids. Thank you from the bottom of my heart for every single moment of love and support you lavish my way, and for your enthusiasm for what I do. I couldn't do this without you.

Much love,

Zara

xo

About the Author

Zara Cox has been writing for almost twenty-five years but it wasn't until nine years ago that she decided to share her love of writing sexy, gritty stories with anyone outside her close family (the over-eighteens anyway!). This series is Zara's next step in her erotic romance-writing journey. She looks forward to bringing her readers even more sizzling-hot stories featuring panty-melting alpha heroes and the women who rock their world.

You can learn more:

ZaraCoxWriter.com

Twitter @ZCoxBooks

Facebook.com/Zara-Cox-Writer